ABRAHAM'S REDEMPTION

By Kevin Lawrence Williams

CHAPTER ONE

ABRAHAM SCHWARTZ: AGE 17

An ocean of shiny black buggies gave the typically green pasture a coal color. Chestnut-hued horses munched hay, seemingly oblivious to the action a bit farther in the field.

"Stee-rike!"

My bat flailed through the air like one of Mom's homemade noodles, the ball landing with a dull thud in the catcher's mitt, a puff of wheat dust billowing up.

"You swing more like a girl than Loretta!" one boy shouted from the sidelines.

My face reddened, and I fiddled with my suspenders. I glanced over and saw my younger sister Loretta watching the game. Her face furrowed with compassion and a blush of embarrassment. A couple of cars were pulled over on the shoulder of the road. Tourists were watching the game, some with clunky cameras around their necks, others with binoculars. We had all grown up with them watching our every move. I never did understand what the fascination was, but we tolerated them.

Amos Raber, tall and lanky-limbed like a scarecrow, reared upward and fired another pitch.

"Steee-rike," someone shouted as my bat cut through the air with the ease of a blowtorch on a stick of butter.

Our team was going to lose. We all knew it. I was always the bookish kid, the one usually picked last for teams, and as my bat poked at the air, it was evident why. Amos was still mowing batters down even after eight long innings under an unforgiving June sun. Finally, at game's end, he was beginning to show some strain. Two on our team had managed to get on base, one with a slap single to left and the other after Amos plunked him on the shoulder.

Our last reasonable hope, Roman Neuenschwander, had just whiffed, and now it was two strikes into my turn and Amos seemed reinvigorated. The Raber's Warriors vs. Graber's Giants baseball games were weekly affairs during the summer and fall: East Church District against West. The matches were a time of fun and fellowship, a moment to escape the confines of church rules a bit and just let loose. They were open to any unmarried boy over the age of 16. When I had turned 16 last summer, I sat out the games. I didn't want to embarrass myself, but my younger sister insisted that I join the games this year.

"You're never going to make friends or meet any of the girls sitting at home reading," Loretta admonished me. All last summer I had resisted her pressure. But this year had been different, Loretta had just turned 15, and was even more in tune with the approaching anxieties of adulthood than I was.

"If you don't play, you'll never marry and everyone's going to think you're a loser," she warned day after day.

"No, if I DO play they'll think I'm a loser, `Retta you know I'm not good at sports,"

"You don't even try!"

So I relented and a whole season of strike-outs had come down to this. Our team was down 2 – 0. Raber's Warriors had already begun gathering their equipment. Sunday morning church services would be here before we all knew it, so everyone was eager to head home to wash up and relax before turning in for the night.

The young ladies, all big smiles and bare feet, cheered on the boys, their white head-coverings shining in the sun like just-polished pearls. The girls all wore solid-colored dresses: turquoise, mustard, and rust gave the blankets and bleachers where they sat a colorful splash. The most eligible of these young ladies was Rachel Miller. She was about to turn 16, which meant she would be able to date and hang out with the other *youngie* in the church. It was pretty much a forgone conclusion that she would end up on the sinewy arm of Amos Raber. Amos was athletic, available, and ambitious, and the women swooned over him, watching his every pitch with jaw-dropping ooohs and ahhhs.

The gathering dusk meant the inky shadows of tall trees began to stretch across the dusty diamond. I had to squint to see the baseball as it left Amos's giant paw. Its seams twirled through the twilight, through sunshine and shadow, before piercing the plate. My bat had already begun its journey. One more slice through nothingness and we would all go home. But something different happened that evening. An ear-splitting crack muted the crowd and echoed over the surrounding fields. Enos Yoder put down his equipment bag and stared up. The snickering stopped and the baseball orbited in an arc of stunned silence skyward, over the split-rail home-run fence, over bales of hay in Mr. Raber's pasture, and just clearing the roof of a corn-crib before finally coming to an ignominious rest in a hog pen. Grunts and squeals could be heard in the distance as the curious porkers first scattered and then reassembled to examine the now mud-splattered orb.

The bases cleared and the girls cheered. I was greeted at the plate by a hail of high-fives, hugs, and heys. Even Rachel Miller joined the assemblage, casting a shy smile my way. At that, Amos Raber stood on the mound glaring, his eyes like ice.

That evening Mom put out a spread fit for a king: homemade rolls the size of softballs, a crock of homemade butter bright as the sun, pan-fried chicken, the tender morsels of meat clinging to the bone. Oh, and pie. Plenty of pie. Mom made her famous (well, at least in our church) raspberry pudding pie, mounds of fresh berries incased in a decadent vanilla pudding.

"This meal is for our budding Babe Ruth," Dad said, always a baseball fan.

Bashful, I swirled at my peas with my fork.

"Mmmm, I just got lucky," I muttered.

"Lucky? That ball left your bat like it had rockets attached to it," Loretta marveled. "I can tell you that some of the girls were really talking about you."

"Me?" I asked, incredulous.

"Rachel, Esther, and Mary Jane were all swooning over you as you raced around the bases," Loretta said with a broad smile, her white *kapp* covering her thick locks of blonde hair, with a few strands of flaxen hair peeking out, as always.

"Yeah...right," I said.

Amos and his buddies with their lanky looks and athletic prowess usually got the girls. None of them could quote Plato like I could, but most of the teenage girls would be more interested in who could run the fastest or hit the hardest, and not so much who read *The Republic.*

"Maybe your sister's right," Mom encouraged.

Outsiders always get lost in a maze of names when they encounter a large family like ours. So here's the run-down of my family when I was 17: there's my Mom, Salome my father, Marvin, me, my younger sister Loretta, then Daniel, sister Nancy, brother Benjamin, twin girls Velma and Verena, and Marvin, Jr., who was born a couple months before that summer ball game. Dad's mom, Grandma Ada, lived in the *dawdy haus*, a separate little cottage about 20 paces from the main house. Then there was the family business–a small furniture store--located in an outbuilding behind our house.

While most outsiders viewed our family as being very large, we were actually considered to be on the smaller side among the Amish. Many in our church had 10, 11, 12 or more children. One family had 17 and needed two large buggies to come to church each Sunday.

FOUR YEARS LATER: ABRAHAM, Age 21

Rachel was beautiful, with bright, wavy red hair, pinned beneath her *kapp* most days. The smell of homegrown lavender and lilies would fill my senses when I would pull her toward me. Despite all of our common interests, goals, and virtues, we were quite opposite in many ways. But in the beginning we made our differences work for us, not against us. Sometimes opposites *do* work. I'm not sure that there's anything more opposite than ketchup and ground beef, but put the two together and they're magic. And we were magic in the beginning.

Amos Raber had his sights set on Rachel long before I had. But Rachel liked an underdog, and I think that's what attracted her to me. Not long after I was the unlikely foil for Amos in the baseball game, I had summoned the nerve to ask Rachel to accompany me to the young people's Sunday evening singing. She had just turned 16 the week before and everyone was expecting Amos to make his move, which meant I had to t fast. Loretta practically begged me to do so.

"Ask her! She'll say yes!"

"What makes you think so?"

"I know so, just ask! You're so shy, you'll end up alone if you don't get out there a bit."

So I had mustered the courage to ask Rachel out and that began a long courtship that was, in the beginning, perfect in so many ways

I'd gather wildflowers from our back prairie and compile them into colorful bouquets, then drop them off to her at work where she did some part-time bookkeeping in her father's sawmill office. In return, Rachel would pack picnic suppers with all my weaknesses in a single basket: tender deer bologna sandwiches with thick slices of homemade bread that she baked herself, her own special macaroni salad, and soft, chunky chocolate chip cookies made from scratch. She would even pack some apple cider made on her family's own press. She'd playfully pour cider into two "wine glasses."

"Here's to forever," she'd say as we enjoyed a picnic by our back pond.

"Forever," I would reply back.

I'd talk about the books I was reading (back then she seemed genuinely interested), and she'd talk about finding a farm for us where we could raise 10 children and have a sprawling garden. Rachel craved order and I think she thought she could tame me over time, channel my energy into a canal of sorts and then use it. But the more she channeled, the more confined I felt.

We both had a love of the outdoors, of simplicity,and beauty. , We savored long buggy rides together deep into the country, far away from hideous Highway 27, which cut through our verdant land like an open-heart-surgery scar.

"Look at the land," Rachel would say, pointing to a random patch of rolling prairie and woods. I'd clasp her hand and she'd continue: "Oh, Abe, can't you imagine our house there…by that creek…we'd have an orchard over there, a garden behind it…perhaps the Yutzy crew could build the home…maybe even Daddy would co-sign…."

Sometimes it made me a little uncomfortable when she dreamed like that. What if all I could ever afford was a one-floor ranch like the Stutzmans lived in over by the highway? But I'd push such thoughts aside and simply use them as motivation to succeed.

And as Rachel and I continued our courtship, she and Loretta became like sisters themselves. They were about the same age and had a lot in common. They both had a deep reverence for rules, one that I didn't always share. At least not at the time. Some people thrive on order while others flourish only in a cacophony of chaos. Perhaps I was scared of order.

After a couple of years of romantic and fulfilling courtship, Rachel and I began drifting apart. It happened very slowly, almost imperceptibly at first.

Rachel could be so exacting, so precise, so demanding of her life and mine, that over time our union became more work than enjoyment. "You only live once so it's got to be done right," was Rachel's thinking, whereas I took the opposite, more existential, approach: you only live once so why be so uptight? Who's to say which route is right?

Despite all my struggles with rules and religion, I love the Amish life. But I saw it then and guess I still do, as a continual compromise. Maybe it's okay if we use a telephone sometimes? Perhaps a flashlight or a battery-powered alarm clock won't destroy our faith? Sometimes one needs room to wiggle. Shackle someone and they'll try to escape. Give them room to walk and they'll stay.

But the more Rachel read the Bible and spoke to the ministers, the farther from mine her faith grew. She became even more like my sister Loretta, uncompromising, wedded to rules. It became a battle of literal versus liberal, and it began to pull us apart.

One time when Rachel and I were sitting on the outdoor swing and shelling walnuts that had dropped from a nearby tree, a non-Amish friend of mine pulled into the driveway. He had his windows down on such a gorgeous day, and his car stereo was blaring the latest Top 40 tunes from a Fort Wayne radio station. When we had first met, if Rachel had heard such music she probably wouldn't have been bothered. She might even have danced a joking jig when she heard it. But things had changed.

"Tell him to turn that off!" Rachel snapped, her face turning a shade similar to the Cherokee purple tomatoes Mom used to grow.

"I…" I stammered.

"Well, aren't you going to back me up on this?" Rachel roared. I stood there, mute. I just couldn't find the fury. Life's too short to get one's suspenders in a bunch over that. And besides, it was my friend listening to the music and he wasn't Amish.

The music kept warbling out of the car.

Rachel stormed into the house.

At that moment, my head knew that our relationship was over, but my heart couldn't accept it. In retrospect, I probably should have ended it then and let life take its course. I still wanted more than anything to stay with her, but I think I was clinging to a Rachel who no longer existed.

I wanted so much to stay with her that I focused on all the wrong things: I bought a 12-acre farmette and a little fishing boat and added silver racing stripes to my buggy, all of those in a desperate attempt to keep us together. The 12-acre farmette was my maneuver at establishing some independence and the promise of a future life together. But nothing I did seemed to pull her back from the direction she was going. Perhaps had I poured the same resources into the emotional aspect of our relationship, our union might have survived. I know I overextended myself buying all of those things, but they were good deals and I had been hoarding my earnings ever since I started working in the shop. All of these actions seemed to be little more than staving off the inevitable. I could feel it and that's why, one day, I panicked.

Over time, our mail route became a carousel of letter-carriers. Inevitably, after a few months the postal worker assigned to our route would grow tired of dodging the rumbling semis, belching tour buses, and meandering buggies that made Highway 27 such an obstacle course. Rarely would a letter-carrier stay on our route more than a year. This resulted in almost weekly mail mix-ups, especially since our house number was only one digit off from Mr. Doty's across the highway.

At least once a week we'd get some mail that was meant for Mr. Doty. Mr. Doty was a kind but curmudgeonly codger with graying hair and usually a day or two of snow-sprinkled shadow on his chin and cheeks. Beginning when I was a teenager, taking Mr. Doty's mail to him became a weekly ritual that was assigned to me, although as I got older and , the mail volume decreased. Some weeks no mail at all would come for Mr. Doty.

For as long as I could remember Mom would keep a wicker breadbasket by the door and any mail that arrived for Mr. Doty would go in there. Once a week I'd trudge down our long brown sugar-colored dirt driveway to US 27, look for my opportunity to dart across the busy highway, and then walk down Mr. Doty's equally lengthy honeysuckle-lined driveway. Mom would usually wrap a piece of pie or some homemade bread to take along to him. He wasn't Amish, so I sometimes felt like I was entering another world once I arrived on his property. I did have plenty of interaction with non-Amish while working in our shop, but there the interaction there was perfunctory and all business. At Mr. Doty's I'd sometimes sit in one of his front-porch rockers and we'd talk about baseball and the weather. As I got older, the talk would drift to politics, crops, or other news of the world.

"Why'd you even bother to bring that stuff over? It's just junk. Burn it next time," Mr. Doty said of the assorted offers for credit cards, political mailers, or coupons that I would bring him.

Of course, Mom would never do that.

"It's his mail. Let him burn it if he wants," she told me when I passed along Mr. Doty's message.

One day during the autumn of my 20th year when my relationship with Rachel was beginning its slow unravel, I did something dreadful. I'll spend the rest of my life trying to reconcile the cascading torrent of bad behavior it unleashed with the good guy I saw in myself. As I grabbed the week's mail for Mr. Doty out of the breadbasket and walked into the warm June afternoon, something caught my eye. Oh, I had seen these plenty of times before. But this time the words seemed to leap off the envelope and shout to me.

"Congratulations! You've been pre-approved for a $10,000 PLATINUM CARD!"

I began to imagine the many ways having $10,000 might change my life. I know what I did next went against everything my church had taught and all the values my parents had instilled in me. But these pieces of mail would come from time to time, and Mr. Doty would usually grumble something like, "Banks, I'd as soon dance with the devil than get into bed with those evil institutions. My brother-in-law is president of a bank...it's like being the skipper of the devil's schooner." Then he would tear the mail to shreds.

Now, really, you might be thinking, you're Amish, why do you need the money? To which I would give a hearty laugh. If you think that, then you must have us mixed up with the Hutterites, who live communally. Amish are as capitalistic as they come. So, yes, the prospect of $10,000 to a 20-year-old still-insecure man was very seductive.

He'd never miss it, a dark voice inside me whispered. He can't miss what he doesn't have. *Use it.*

I slowed my walk as I shuffled the mail between my fingers.

$10,000.

I waited for a break in US 27's seemingly never-ending parade of school buses, semis, and sedans, and then darted safely across the road. I paused for a moment in the shade of a sprawling, unkempt hackberry bush at the end of Mr. Doty's driveway. The bush blocked my view from everyone but passing motorists. I folded the credit card offer, slid it snugly into my back pants pocket, and headed down Mr. Doty's driveway carrying the rest of his mail. It was a "safety net," that's all. I'd never use it, he'd never miss it.

That night, I stood at my bedroom window and looked across the surrounding fields. The kerosene lamp by my bedside hissed softly, bathing my bedroom in a halo of light. Somewhere in the distance a coyote bayed and a barred owl called. Haunting sounds of a country night. I shivered even though it was quite warm outside. Rachel and I had argued earlier in the day and I was feeling uneasy over our unspooling relationship. I felt the still neatly-folded envelope in my back pocket. It's only insurance, I told myself. I tucked the credit card offer into a small wooden box on my dresser. I'd keep it there. I'd never use it.

CHAPTER TWO

ABRAHAM

I never felt like I measured up to Rachel's father's exacting standards. One time when I was picking up Rachel to go to a young person's gathering, he was standing in his driveway polishing his buggy. I admit mine was looking past its prime, an observation Mr. Miller wasted no time in expressing.

"Beautiful day to clean out and wash the buggy," Mr. Miller said.

"Yes, it is. But I've had my nose in a book, *Fahrenheit 451*. It's quite a read. Makes a person appreciate books even more," I said.

"Books don't earn much interest," Mr. Miller chuckled.

"But they are interesting," I replied.

"You know, you'd do better to start parking that buggy in your barn. Looks like weather's been a bit rough on it. They hold up much better under shelter. The weather really wears them down over time," Mr. Miller said.

Now, I'm in no way blaming arguments with Rachel or my impressions or misimpressions of Mr. Miller for my misdeeds. They're mine and mine alone. One of the few things we truly own in life are our actions. Maybe he was genuinely looking out for me, just wanting the best for his oldest daughter, or was hoping to preserve the structural integrity of my buggy. But I took the conversation as a slight. Insecurity is a black light which turns all stains purple.

That night before bed I unfolded the platinum card offer in the shoebox. On the outside of the envelope, the bold lettering called my name:

"Just call our toll-free number! You've been pre-approved!"

I thought of a new buggy with LED lights, a carom board, maybe even a trip with Rachel to the Smoky Mountains. It was too intoxicating. If I used the card, I'd pay it back fast. I'd get some carpentry jobs on the side. Heck, if I paid it back fast I'd even be *helping* Mr. Doty, right? I tore open the envelope.

Hello, Mr. Doty:

Wouldn't you like the finer things in life? A new car? A boat? Or how about some extra cash just for improvements around the house? You <u>deserve</u> it, and we can help make your dream a reality. Just call our toll-free number and you can be the proud owner of our Platinum Card within 72 hours. What are you waiting for? Call now! Just two minutes of your time will give you everything you deserve.

What was I waiting for? Just one problem: I wasn't Mr. Doty. But maybe I could be for two minutes.

The next day I invented an excuse to go into the town nearest us. I took one of our buggies into Berne, went to the pay phone, and called the toll-free number. I answered a few easy questions from some person sitting in a cubicle in India. I gave the operator our address, hoping he wouldn't notice since it was only one digit from Mr. Doty's. And the operator didn't. His job was probably to corral in as many new accounts as he could, volume-based commission equaling a quick call.

"Congratulations, Mr. Doty, your card is now on its way!" the man said.

The card would arrive, but I told myself I'd never use it.

The whole scheme almost came crashing down before it ever began.

A few days later, the platinum card made a clumsy entrance into my life. Mail usually arrived while Dad and I were working in the shop. Mom would walk to the end of the driveway and grab it from the mailbox while she was outside hanging laundry or tending to the garden. She'd then take our mail inside, and anything that came for Mr. Doty would go into the wicker breadbasket. We had extra furniture orders that week, so Dad and I were really pinned down in the shop, but my plan was to take Mr. Doty his mail as usual after closing. Dad and I weren't the only ones busy, though. Apparently our hens had picked that week to lay a bonanza of eggs.

"Nothing for Mr. Doty this week?" I asked Mom, eyeing the empty breadbasket as I came into the house.

"I sent Loretta over there. I know how busy you are in the shop. Don't know what's gotten into the henhouse, but we have enough eggs this week to make omelets for everyone in west district, so I thought Mr. Doty would appreciate some, too," Mom said.

"Oh...well, I would have been happy to do that. It's baseball season and you know he's the only one I can talk sports with around here," I said, hoping my mother wouldn't notice the sweat beginning to bead on my brow.

"It was just junk. I'm sure there will be more for him next week," Mom said. "Where are you going?"

"Nowhere...just left something in the shop." I slipped out the door while Mom went back to getting supper on the table.

Where did Loretta go? Our dirt driveway formed an elongated loop behind our house. The shop was on one side of the loop, our house on the other. The long driveway then ran beside our house in a ruler-straight line to US 27. No one in the loop. I ran to where the driveway straightened, and looked out. I could see Loretta, her rust-colored dress a distant blot on the horizon. She had already crossed the highway and was halfway down Mr. Doty's long driveway.

I went back inside and before Mom could say a word, grabbed a small loaf of zucchini bread wrapped in foil on the counter and sprinted down the driveway.

"Loretta!!!" I bellowed. But she couldn't hear me over the thundering traffic on US 27.

I tucked the soft loaf under my arm and bolted towards US 27. My straw hat fluttered off my head and twirled like a Frisbee into our front yard as I ran. Had this been an Olympic time trial, I might have qualified. Lungs seizing and legs pumping, I cleared our driveway and found myself on the wide shoulder of the highway. The broader shoulders on each side of US 27 allowed for cars and buggies to share the road a bit more safely.

"'RETTA!!!!!" I shouted.

But she kept her brisk walk toward Mr. Doty's house, my shouts still muffled by the parade of late-day traffic. Loretta was only 20 yards from his front porch where he sat on a rocker, reading a newspaper.

Two grain trucks thundered past, followed by a tanker, buffeting me with a hot, fume-filled wind. After the tanker, there seemed to be enough of a gap in front of an approaching Cadillac, so I figured I could make it. Starting in a sprinter's crouch, I lunged across the highway in a blur of beige and denim. The deafening sound of the driver pressing on his horn filled the surrounding fields. I felt the breeze from the passing Cadillac against my back, and barely made it across without being turned into road kill. But the horn had accomplished what I hadn't: it got Loretta's attention. She spun around, gaping disbelief on her face, as I continued barreling toward her.

"What the...? Is everything OK?" she asked. Mr. Doty had folded his newspaper on his lap and was watching in silence from his porch.

Wheezing for breath I managed, "Yes...Mom...forgot...she...wanted you to take this zucchini bread," I blurted out.

"But I thought that was fo..."

"...for Mr. Doty..." I choked.

"But she specifically said that that was fo..."

"'Retta you heard wrong...I was just there...," I gasped. I was too busy catching my breath to worry about how my lie was appearing.

"Mr. Doty lives here alone and we're giving him this whole basket of eggs *and* a loaf of bread? Did we forget a side of beef? Whatever...you're here, you take it to him," an exasperated Loretta said, handing me the basket of eggs and the mail. She waved to Mr. Doty.

"Beautiful weather," she shouted and turned around for home.

Standing under Mr. Doty's distant gaze, I flipped through the mail and found the envelope I was searching for.

"Piece of mail for me accidentally got mixed in with yours," I lied, folding it tightly into my back pocket.

Lies are like feral pigs, they multiply furiously and are just as destructive.

My lungs were pumping like an accordion I had seen someone playing in town once, and my heart was beating like a rock band drum.

"We should all get one group P.O. box," Mr. Doty laughed. Disaster averted.

Credit cards were beginning to gain a foothold in our church. Levi Bontrager began accepting them at his bulk food store after much debate. Over half his customers were non-Amish and didn't carry cash much anymore, and checks were too risky. Dad talked about allowing them at our store, but quickly dismissed the idea. Accepting credit cards required adopting some expensive technology that he was morally, theologically, and financially opposed to. Bishop Hochstetler did permit business owners to adopt certain technologies so that they could compete. Still, once some got the taste of technology at work, they had difficultly giving it up. Elmer Eicher kept a laptop hidden under his bed for a year before deciding he needed more, and eventually left the church.

Throughout the winter I could feel my relationship with Rachel crumbling. Sometimes the smallest thing would set her off. One evening I absent-mindedly left a pen in my front shirt pocket without a cap. Rachel had made the shirt only a few months earlier as a Christmas gift and I really did like it. She noticed the ink oozing across the front shirt pocket and lost it.

"Do you know how long I spent making that shirt? Look at you, you don't even care!" Rachel seethed.

"But, I do care…I loved that shirt…" I pleaded.

"You didn't care enough to not put a pen in your pocket after I've warned you about just that type of thing." She was boiling, her face reddening to match her hair.

"I'm sorry…" I said.

"You sure are. I could have had *anyone*…Amos Raber wanted to date me but I chose you, and what a mistake that has turned out to be," Rachel roared.

The pen might as well have been a bullet, the ink blood.

"But…" I started to say, grasping some words to make it better, but Rachel would have none of it.

"Shut up! You're always getting in the way of how I want to live my life. A dream destroyer is what you are. My life isn't turning out the way I want it to and it's all because of *you!*"

Again, I stood there, mute.

And somehow our relationship plodded along. But Rachel became increasingly doctrinaire.

She even started corresponding with a pen-pal who was a member of the ultra-conservative Swarztentruber Amish church in Ethridge, Tennessee. Those Amish are among the most backward I've seen (Amish are allowed to call other Amish backward, but if the English did that, it'd be a wretched insult).

"In Ethridge, black is black and white is white…sounds Heavenly to me," Rachel would say.

I couldn't imagine LeRoy Miller was pleased with his daughter's interest in that church. I felt, perhaps without good reason, that maybe he blamed me for driving a wedge between Rachel and our church.

Meanwhile, Miller's sawmill prospered while Dad and I battled a persistent national recession. Customers trimmed back purchases. *Maybe we can do without a hand-crafted desk. Let's just go to the big box store instead and buy something cheaper*, people would reason. Conversely, Miller's seemed to benefit from the recession forcing people into more "do-it-yourself" projects, so his lumber business boomed. By the end of the winter the Millers had a fleet of brand new buggies for their still-growing family, roomy buggies with all the latest accessories. All the while I'd pick Rachel up in my battered buggy and feel Mr. Miller's eyes on me.

"Got your buggy painted?" Mr. Miller asked.

"No," I replied, puzzled.

"Yeah, you did, it's painted with dust," Mr. Miller chuckled.

My buggy *was* looking rather ragged, but it was comfortable and it was paid for. But my own insecurity couldn't allow me to make such an argument.

Tucked away in a rare bend in one of the ruler-straight roads in our county was Hershberger's Buggy Shop. For years the Hershbergers kept the Berne Amish settlement supplied with reliable transportation. They even had a line of used buggies for sale. A small sign out front said simply "BUGGY SHOP".

"The tourists like the simple signs," Atlee Hershberger would say when asked why he didn't have something flashier.

"This baby's a beauty," Milo Hershberger was often heard saying as he ran his hands over sleek steel wheels or tested out the horn. His father, Atlee, founded the business 40 years prior and still showed up for work each day even though he was well into his 80s.

"You're Marvin and Salome's boy, right?" Atlee asked. "What brings you out this way?"

"Well, same thing I'm sure brings a lot of people: my buggy's getting a bit beat-up. Had to repair an axle and a shaft this year. Getting to be where I'm spending more money on upkeep than enjoyment," I said.

"I've got some great buggies. Just got a great pre-owned one in yesterday that'd be a great fit for you. Belonged to a young Amish man who died in a farm accident in Holmes County...tragic...but, oh, don't worry, I've completely refurbished it," Atlee whispered. "And I'll throw in a one year warranty, yesirree," Atlee said.

"I'd rather not a used. Rather a new," I said.

Atlee's eyes narrowed.

It wasn't unheard of for someone my age--I was 21 by this time--to be buying a brand-new buggy, but I guess the economy's rough spot had made such purchases rarer.

"Been saving and..." I started to lie, but Atlee interrupted.

"Don't much care where you got it. Money's money, right? Guess as long as you didn't rob anyone, it's fine with me," Atlee chuckled.

I gulped.

"Let me show you some designs. You planning a family someday? You just want a single-man's buggy?"

And on and on Atlee went. A really well-crafted buggy could last 50 years, he explained. He was fond of repeating that there were still buggies on the roads near Berne that he'd built during his first year in business.

"My joints are weaker than theirs now," Atlee laughed. Flecks of dandruff dropped from his beard onto his dark blue shirt like baby powder, momentarily distracting me. I vowed right then and there that if I were fortunate to marry and grow a beard, I would wash it daily.

I finally settled on a sleek four-person rider with plush seats and all the latest upgrades and accessories.

"Total comes out to $5105.33. I'll need half up front and half on delivery," Atlee said.

The credit card company had included some paper checks in with my "Welcome Kit," so I was easily able to deposit a check for $2500 from "Mr. Doty" into my account. The checks were cash advances against the credit card. Of course, I had to forge a signature. The feral pigs kept multiplying.

"Okay, we'll get to work. Should be about four months, you'll be taking your special sweetie to summer picnics in your new buggy," Atlee said.

I endured a cold winter of Mr. Miller's slights and a heavy workload in the shop while Rachel and I went through the motions and machinations of a relationship. One day when the warmth of spring had arrived, I showed up at Rachel's in my brand new buggy to pick her up for a Sunday evening volleyball game. .

"Wow....where did you get this?" Rachel gushed. It was the most alive-looking I had seen her in years.

"It was a surprise. I put the order in at Hershberger's months ago," I said.

"Wow, still has that new buggy smell," Rachel marveled.

"Check these out," I said, showing her the hand-cranked windshield wipers. A tiny bottle under the dash could be squeezed to squirt windshield wiper fluid. Rachel climbed in, and for a moment she reminded me of the girl I first made eyes at: the carefree smile, the effervescent enjoyment, the appreciation. For a few moments, how I had obtained the buggy didn't matter to me. It had all been worthwhile.

And my parents seemed proud.

"We really taught him well about saving," Mom beamed to the ladies at church.

Loretta and her new boyfriend, Timothy, were also impressed. But inside I felt tortured. The buggy was tainted and so was I.

ABRAHAM: age 24

For the next three years, my life settled into a sort of numb auto-pilot. The credit card interest had ballooned to such a point that I was having trouble paying Mr. Doty's bill, so I would sometimes miss a couple of months. Often I'd just slap together the minimum payment. My farmette was sitting unused, and my relationship with

Rachel was only motions now. The loving luster from the brand-
new buggy had lasted a couple of months before we fell back into
the same brooding fights. We'd see each other on Sundays, special
occasions, family gatherings, but we rarely talked of marriage
anymore. Our family business somehow survived, but it was a
struggle. Meanwhile, the Miller's mill continued to prosper.

One bright spot during that time was my baptism. I had finally
decided to commit myself to God and the church for the rest of my
life. I love the Amish life, and while I knew I had perpetrated some
moral sins, I thought joining the church might offer me a road to
redemption.

While I tried to stay within the bounds of our church, my old
baseball nemesis Amos Raber decided to strike out on his own. A
lot of outsiders have the misconception that if one leaves the faith,
they are shunned. That's true if you leave after being baptized, but if
you just decide not t join, a shunning is not imposed. I think Amos
believed he could do more with his life outside of the Amish church,
and I don't begrudge him that. This life isn't for everyone. So he got
his GED, started taking classes at community college, and began to
get into high finance. All the people in the church just seemed to
adore him. Even Rachel still seemed smitten with him.

"But he didn't even join the church," I said, "and you get mad at ME
for breaking rules?"

"He didn't join the church. You can't break rules if you aren't bound by them, right?" she rationalized. That seemed to twist her usual rule reverence like a pretzel. So while my life stalled, Amos Raber's seemed to soar.

I was almost 24 now, and what started out as a singular, somewhat impulsive act had morphed into over three years of lies. I needed to put an end to it, and I had a plan. I was going to pay the $8000 on Mr. Doty's card by selling off an acre lot from the farmette. It was only an acre and it was sort of an odd-shaped piece of real estate, but it was centrally located so the bishop thought it would make a good spot for a new parochial school. The church was offering to pay me $7500 for the parcel. I was elated, but the excitement was fleeting.

"Abe, I've got bad news for you. I know you wanted to sell that plot, but old Mrs. Stoll has agreed to donate five acres. *Donate it!* I think she's kind of lonely since her husband passed away last year. She'll enjoy watching the children come and go with the school on her property," Bishop Hochstetler explained to me one evening.

There was only one thing to do: sell the whole farmette and use the proceeds to pay off Mr. Doty's card. That was the quickest way, and with my Rachel relationship going nowhere, it didn't look like I'd be needing the farmette anyway. The question was, would I get any buyers in the middle of a lingering recession? Banks were foreclosing on homes in the area like rats coming to a garbage dump. Even the Amish in our area weren't immune. With the plummeting real estate values, I'd still squeeze just enough out of the sale to pay the card off.

But as the months slogged by, my farmette remained unsold and every attempt to make inroads into the illicit credit card debt failed. In fact, making only minimum payments had assured that the debt kept ballooning. As I had matured, not only was the secret stress of my dilemma with Mr. Doty taking its toll, but I was having deep guilt about what I had done. I resolved that I was going to start selling produce that summer at the Farmer's Market in Berne. I had heard of some Amish making $10,000 a summer just from selling tomatoes, cantaloupe, and cucumbers to the tourists. As I lived in some sort of hazy purgatory, I watched more and more friends of mine marrying and settling into normal lives on their own. It was time to end this, and move on once and for all.

I had more responsibility at the shop and my brother Daniel was now a teenager, he was in charge of taking mail to Mr. Doty most of the time. It had become too difficult for me to have a relaxed conversation with him because the guilt of my darkness would surge through me as we talked. On one occasion, though, Daniel was choring so I took the mail to Mr. Doty. When I arrived with the few pieces of junk mail that had accumulated, he seemed agitated.

"You doing okay?" I asked.

"Not really," he grumbled, grabbing the mail from me.

"Are you feeling okay?" was all I could really think to ask.

"No, my health is fine...other than almost having a heart attack because I couldn't get my house approved for refinancing. Turns out someone somehow managed to open up a credit card in my name, was late with the payments, and now I'm paying the price. Who could do such a thing? I hope whoever did this gets the book thrown at them," he growled.

A slimy slick of sweat began to bead on my brow, and now it was I who was feeling ill.

"Wait'll I find out who did this," he said. "Now I may lose my house. I'd like to find whoever it is and grind them to hamburger with my bare hands...there's still a little fight left in this old man."

I thought of confessing right then. It probably would have been the right thing, even if it meant someone scraping my remains off Mr. Doty's porch.

"If I could get my hands on him now, I'd strangle him, you know what I mean?"

"Oh, well, now...no...no...I don't really don't know what you mean...we're pacifists," I stammered.

"Huh?"

"Never mind...I just mean...I thought you once said your brother-in-law was a banker. Can't he do something about your house?" I was grasping for any sort of solution. Sweat was beginning to pour off me.

"Won't talk to him...I'd rather lose my home than deal with him. My sister and I haven't spoken in 15 years...hey, what's gotten into you? You look like you've seen death...."

CHAPTER THREE

ABRAHAM

Of course, I had known this day might arrive from the moment I began taking that dark walk. But after all these years, and with the promise offered by the upcoming Farmer's Market season, I had begun to think I'd be able to pay it off and forget the whole thing had ever happened. A better life beckoned if I could finally bury this horrible chapter. But on the morning of February 16th, my world finally came crashing down.

We were eating a big breakfast of homemade biscuits and gravy. Mom was known for her thick, gooey gravy with chunks of fresh sausage swimming around in it. Ever since talking with Mr. Doty a few days earlier, I could sense the wagons circling. I felt my life imploding, so I was taking great comfort in the smaller things: homemade gravy, blooming spring flowers, fresh air, and even my conversations with Rachel. But those pleasures were a thin mask to the churn of anxiety just below the surface.

Thump. Thump. Thump.
It was an ominous knock on our kitchen door. To this day I recoil when I hear a similar noise.

"Doyle, what brings you out here?" I heard Mom say, a hint of concern in her voice.

Doyle Stutzman was a county sheriff's deputy assigned to our area. He was two or three generations removed from the Amish, but the last name was a comfort to many Amish people uncomfortable dealing with the law. Doyle had come to our house on occasions in a friendly way, like when a coyote was trapped in our hay mow, but this time he didn't look at all friendly.

"Is Abraham here?"

The thick gravy seemed to freeze in my throat.

Mom turned my way with a forlorn look. She didn't know, but in some ways I think a part of her might have known something was wrong.

"I need to take you down to the station for questioning."

I set down my fork and nodded.

"This must be a mistake," Loretta said, wiping her hands on a dish towel and running toward us.

"You know what this is about?" Doyle asked me with a hint of a tone that I couldn't quite place.

"I think so," I muttered.

"Then this is all a mistake, right?" Mom said, grasping for something that might make all of this unfolding drama go away.

Loretta stopped, looking crestfallen. The older brother she had looked up to and admired all those years vanished forever that morning.

"If we book him, he'll be allowed to call you. I'll make sure of that,"

Doyle said, softening his demeanor a bit. I was tossed into the back of the cruiser and watched as the familiar farmstead disappeared in a cloud of dust behind us.

We went to the police department where two detectives were waiting.

"We know what you did. We just don't know why," said a detective with a neatly trimmed handlebar mustache and a crisp, white button-down shirt and tie.

I shifted in the hard folding chair.

"Hi, I'm Detective Michael Michaels," a balding, rangy man said, holding out his hand.

I shook it, but I didn't say anything in response.

"Coffee?"

"No, thanks."

"Okay, is there anything you would like to tell us?" Detective Michaels asked.

My eyes darted to the folders of paperwork on the table. Was there really enough to fill a folder?

"I don't know...."

"You don't know?" Detective Michaels said. *"You don't know?"*

I shook my head.

"Is there anyone else involved? Is this part of a larger network or are you a lone wolf?" He stood up and began pacing, his expression intense, brow furrowing and eyes blazing.

I was quiet.

"If you're part of a group and you can help us bring in the whole lot of credit card scammers, then I can get you leniency."

"There's no one else..." I muttered.

"So, it's just you...you weren't put up or paid to do this?" This time the question came from Detective Stanley.

I shook my head.

"Ha, you hear this, Frank! We've got a live one. This guy was stupid enough to get this credit card using his neighbor's name, thinking he wouldn't get caught!" Detective Michaels shouted to someone in the next room.

Both detectives guffawed.

"But I don't think the judge or prosecutor will find anything funny about this. You're under arrest," Detective Michaels said.

The sheriff let me wear my own clothes for the time being, something about not being certain if I were exempt from those because of religious rights. Courts had been mixed in their verdicts on such things. But they took my shoes, pocket watch, and anything else of value for "safekeeping." There was a sickening click as the cell door closed behind me. My bare feet pressed against the cold concrete and my hands wrapped around the iron bars. I didn't belong here. I was alone in the cell, trapped like a wasp in one of those homemade bug traps Mom made. At least I thought I was alone.

"Hey, are you one of those Quakers?" a heavyset man asked, rising from a bottom bunk in the corner. He was wearing a fire-hydrant orange prison suit. He was about a foot taller than I, completely bald, and his biceps were as large as muskmelons. I was wishing now that I had opted for the orange jumpsuit.

"Well, actually, I'm...Mennonite," I lied. Best pass off the blame on those Mennonites. We've always had a love-hate relationship with one another.

"I knew it!" the man snarled. "You won't fight for your country; you HATE America. I've given everything I have for my country. What have you given? While I was in Iraq, what were YOU doing?"

"That's not true. What I hate, what we hate, is violence. Being a pacifist is something that America allows. You were fighting so I could be a pacifist."

It was a loop argument, and for an instant we both seemed confused.

"Like I asked, pal, what were YOU doing?"

"I was here making a country like for the USA possible."

My cell-mate moved toward me, glowering.

"Go easy on him, Butcher," a guard said with apparent nonchalance.

I gulped. *Butcher?*

"Easy on HIM? When he was over here milking cows and making cheese while I was dodging IEDS and missiles? And you want ME to go easy on HIM?"

I paced. What was I supposed to say? It wasn't like I had dodged a draft or invoked some conscientious objector status. I merely didn't volunteer. I can't say that I didn't feel a twinge of guilt. What made me so special as to be exempt from wars? But I didn't think of myself as being "special." It was our religion and we were trying to elevate the human experience to something above violence. Someone, someday, has to take the lead to rid the world of the scourge of war, and why not us? But I didn't look down upon those who did fight. They were doing a job they believed in, just as I was by staying home.

"I am not a pacifist and if I didn't think they'd add more time to my stay here, I'd show you just how violent I can be," Butcher said, edging toward me.

I backed into the corner, almost hoping he'd sock me and get it over with. But then he paused.

"Wait a minute...what are YOU doing here, anyway?" Butcher asked. "You steal someone's cow?"

I wasn't going to tell him. It wasn't any of his business. I might have done something awful, but I wasn't about to divulge my dark secret to him. My thoughts, however, were interrupted by a visitor, her soft hands clenched tightly around the bars. And for a moment all arguments and insecurity disappeared and I just wanted to be with her, the way it used to be: the picnics, the buggy rides, the fresh apple cider.

"Rachel..." I said, moving toward the bars, starting to place my hands on hers, but as soon as she felt my touch, she recoiled.

"I don't want to hear what you have to say. You've brought shame upon all of us," she hissed, crimson red hair and blue eyes seemingly extra out of place in the harsh confines of jail. "Your heart must be in a very dark place for you to do what you did."

"Rachel, I'm sorry...I don't know how to explain what I'd..." I said, tears beginning to dam up behind my eyeballs.

"You can't change and you won't change...ever," Rachel seethed.

"But I was just...Rachel, please just listen," I whispered, still conscious of Butcher's presence not far behind me in the cell.

"Listen? Listen to what? More lies? I wasted the best years of my life with you, years that I'll never get back. I believed in you and you turned out to be nothing but a soulless, deadbeat, lazy liar and thief. Daddy was right about you. I should have listened. That's the listening I should have done. Goodbye. I hope your life is happy in your web of lies."

Can't change. Her words clattered around in my head like a metal milking pail being dropped to the ground. Numb, I walked backward from the bars and sat on the bottom bunk, but no sooner had my rear touched the bed than I jolted upward.

"Dude, what the...?"

"Sorry, I didn't see you laying there, I wasn't thi...."

Butcher lunged toward me.

"I don't walk on that side of the street and if that's what you're after, I'll...."

But we were both interrupted by a gravely-voiced, grandfatherly-looking man standing outside the bars.

"Mr. Schwartz?"

"Sir?" I answered.

"Come with me." The man wore a rumpled tweed jacket and had a wild shock of gray hair.

I admit that everything that happened next seemed like a blur of conversation, scribbled notes on legal pads, and snap decisions. I was taken to a claustrophobic conference room. A half-full box of day-old doughnuts sat on a table. It made me miss Mom's homemade doughnuts: fried golden and crisp and then rolled in scratch-made maple glaze. Styrofoam cups with half-consumed black coffee littered the table in the center of the room.

"Name's Geoffrey Williams. I'm your attorney. Now let's get down to business."

"But I never asked for an...."

"Here's my card," he said, sliding it across the table at me. I looked at it.

GEOFFREY WILLIAMS – PUBLIC DEFENDER

"Mr. Williams, I never meant to...."

"Ah, ah, ah...I don't want to hear it, I don't want to know," he said. Let's just get this over with."

"But, I at least want you to know that I'm so s...."

"Ah, ah, ah...save it," Geoffrey said, putting a finger up to his lips. "I don't really care. Here's what we're dealing with. They've got everything they need to put you away for three years. This is a class D felony in Indiana," Geoffrey said, peering at his paperwork. "This is pretty serious stuff."

"But, I need you to know how sor...."

"Ah, ah, ah...not now. I'm pretty tight with the prosecutor's office and I've got good news. They've agreed to a deal."

"A deal?"

"You don't have many options, Mr. Schwartz. You need to plead guilty to the lesser charge of receiving stolen property, with the maximum sentence being 18 months. Good behavior could get you out in six. You'd have to pay restitution. If you don't plea and they get you for full identity theft, you could be put away for three years. You think about that tonight, Mr. Schwartz. We'll talk tomorrow."

With that, he whirled around and disappeared. The guard led me back to my cell for a long night with the Butcher.

I never asked for special rules, but lying in the cell in clothes different from the other prisoners, in a room with a man who fought in a war I considered myself exempt from, I felt uneasy. Maybe Loretta was right, maybe I did too often think the rules–whatever the rules were–didn't apply to me. I immersed myself in prayer.

"Heavenly Father, I'm an imperfect soul. If you get me out of here, I promise to never travel down that dark path again, that I'll always try to..." But a fist the weight and size of an Easter ham came crashing into my skull, and the prayer remained unfinished. At least in the blackness that followed, the Butcher's fist had freed me from the horror of being behind bars that night. Already, though, my church's own wheels of justice were beginning to turn.

*   *   *

Our bishop and two of our church's ministers had heard the news about my arrest, and gathered in an empty stockroom at the sawmill. One of the church's ministers happened to be Rachel Miller's father, LeRoy. This put him in an awkward position.

"I'm sorry, I just don't think we should help him. There are others in our church who are struggling through little fault of their own. Why should we step in here?" LeRoy muttered, pacing.

"In all due respect, LeRoy, I think you're too close to this to be making any decisions. I think it would be best if you let Jacob and me handle this," the bishop said.

LeRoy Miller left the room. He wondered how his daughter would handle the news.

*   *   *

I awoke the next morning in the county jail's dispensary with a bandage over a cut and bruise on my forehead.

"Looks like you got into a bit of a scrap," a nurse commented.

I nodded as she applied a salve to my head and re-bandaged it.

"Good news," she said. "Looks like you'll be okay. You can go back to lock-up."

 I realized at that moment just how far my life had fallen when going back to lock-up was considered "good news."

I was soon walked back into the main jail area, but this time to a private single celltt6. I asked any prison official I could find to not punish the Butcher.

"Oh, you mean Charlie?" the guard asked.

"Huh?"

"Charlie Butcher, the guy who was sharing the cell with you?"

Okay, I thought to myself. Charlie didn't sound nearly so menacing. Besides, I deserved the bash on the head for my behavior of the past few years. While I believe violence solves nothing, I also believe in equilibrium. I probably got what was coming. I had thought and prayed about the plea, and had come to the conclusion that the best thing to do would be to step up and admit it all. I wasn't comfortable with a "bargain." Why not just admit fully what I did and accept whatever fate awaited? That would be a thorough cleansing. I vowed to tell Geoffrey my decision when he arrived, which he did soon after I was locked back up.

"We're scheduled for a plea conference later today. I'll be back this afternoon with more information when I know the exact time and what they are offering." Geoffrey turned and started to walk away.

"I don't want to bargain, I want to plead guilty to all of it," I said.

Geoffrey froze and turned around. He looked pale. He lowered his voice to a whisper and put his mouth up to the bars.

"Are you out of your mind?"

"No, I'm just tired of dodging responsibility. I don't want some legal hocus-pocus to reduce the time for what I did."

"Legal hocus-pocus?" Geoffrey repeated.

"I mean no disrespect. You're just doing your job. But I never asked for an attorney to help me out of this, I jus..." I said, before Geoffrey interrupted.

"I'll be back and you'll sign the plea paperwork," Geoffrey said, disappearing down the corridor.

I was once again alone in my cell.

Confined to a closet-sized cinderblock cell, I found myself deeply missing the hints of home I had so long taken for granted: Mom's flaky buttermilk biscuits, the rose-colored sunrises in the eastern sky, the freedom of taking the buggy out for a ride on a pleasant afternoon with no particular destination in mind. Even the things that bothered me about my life began to look less harsh: the gaseous smell of our kerosene lamps, the seemingly endless grind of chores, and Loretta's love-affair with rules. While I had my doubts that this cell was a cure, it was a call, and I needed to answer it and listen. Geoffrey would just have to accept it. But first I would have to listen to other voices.

"Got another visitor...what are you, man, a rock star?" the guard said, leading another person to my cell.

It was Monroe Hochstetler.

Monroe Hochstetler was 80 years old, with the energy of someone decades younger. He ruled the church with the efficiency of a battleship commander. His long, thick white beard gave him an instant air of authority. I appreciated Monroe's reputation for even-handedness. Some churches get stuck with bishops who rule their churches like fiefdoms or who treat the church like their personal piggy-bank. Other bishops were so liberal, allowing their flock so many different technologies, that I couldn't see the point of even being Amish if as much time was spent trying to figure out ways to circumvent the rules as to live with them.

"Abraham, good to see you."

"Likewise, although I'd rather we be meeting over one of Fannie's suppers," I said, referring to his wife, whose cooking made dinner invitations from the Hochstetlers coveted in our church.

"Well, I'm sure. But let's get straight to the point. Did you do what they are accusing you of?"

I took a deep breath.

"Yes," I said. "But I'd like to exp..."

Bishop Hochstetler cut me off. No one was letting me finish a sentence, it seemed.

"It doesn't matter. We can deal with your explanation later."

He paced outside the cell door.

"Do you feel a desire to repent and repair? To admit to our Creator your sins, and live your life in a way that is humble and righteous from this day forward?"

A firm "yes" would have been the easy answer, but I wasn't so sure I could honestly provide such an answer. I was troubled by what within me pulled me down that path in the first place. I thought I needed to confront that first.

"Bishop Hochstetler...am I a bad person?"

He paused.

"I can't answer that. Only God can answer that. But life is a process, and processes are sometimes messy. You are a young man. One needs a whole life to look at someone's sins and see them in perspective. Take your work. If you make a bookshelf that falls apart when the first bound volume is placed on it, does that make you a poor woodworker?"

"I'd say yes."

"Ridiculous. If that's the only shelf you ever build, yes. But if the next 50 are priceless pieces that stand the test of time, then you can't say you are a lousy woodworker because one shelf didn't last."

I wasn't quite sure I could accept the analogy of a failed bookshelf with something as serious as swiping Mr. Doty's identity, but I understood what he was saying.

"Some people seem to have it so easy. Why does it have to be so difficult for me? LeRoy Miller, The Stutzmans, the Gingeriches...so many people in our church seem to h...."

Monroe Hochstetler interrupted, and for the first time he seemed genuinely perturbed. His cheeks reddened, contrasting with the whiteness of his beard.

"As clergy, I keep confidences so I'm not going to tell you anything I shouldn't, but if you only knew the problems some of these supposedly perfect people you talk about have. Be glad you don't know what I know, Abe. We only see of people what they want us to see."

I considered his words carefully. "In answer to your earlier question, yes, I want to begin to walk down that road. I want to be a better person, more humble and chastened."

"That's all I needed to hear," Monroe said. "We'll discuss the rest another time."

I could only imagine LeRoy Miller's participation in the church's response, I knew Rachel's Dad never thought I measured up and I confirmed his narrative. I tried not to think about it. Mom had wanted to call Monroe immediately after I was taken away, but Dad kept demurring, wishing that in some way this could be kept private.

CHAPTER FOUR

PAIGE ROBERTS, age 26

 Ask me what I knew about the Amish up to this point in my life, and I'd maybe be able to talk about some cute calendars that I used to see sold in mall kiosks. That was about the extent of it. I think I remember my Dad watching some documentary on PBS once, heard him mentioning something about many of them living near Uncle Ralph in Indiana. But that was it. So it was an instant education when I first laid eyes on Monroe Hochstetler.

Bishop Hochstetler and Jacob Eicher, another minister, had jumped into a waiting buggy and raced toward my Uncle Ralph's house. There was little time.

Despite his advanced age, Bishop Hochstetler bounded up the porch stairs to Uncle Ralph's front door two at a time. Jacob, some 40 years his junior, had to scramble to keep up. I watched from an upstairs window.

"We come in Christian love, Mr. Doty," Monroe Hochstetler said, removing his hat as Uncle Ralph answered the door.

"I don't want to hear it," Uncle Ralph growled. "That Schwartz boy almost sent me to an early grave."

"Which is why we wanted to give you this offering," Monroe said. "It should more than cover the credit card balance and a little extra for your pain and suffering."

Uncle Ralph's eyes rounded as he took the check, but otherwise his expression changed little.

"I know this can't all be wiped away with a check. I wish it could," Monroe admitted. "But we do ask with all humility if maybe we can begin walking down the path of healing together?"

Uncle Ralph stared at the passing traffic on 27, the visitors' black buggy in his driveway, and fingered the corners of the check.

"Forgiveness, it's what's for dinner!" Jacob piped up.

Monroe Hochstetler sighed. Jacob was sometimes tone-deaf about what to say and when.

Uncle Ralph sat, expressionless.

"Part of being human is making mistakes, but another part of being human is forgiveness. Humans have the power to sin, but they also have the power to forgive. Abraham needs to get right with God, to pick a path that is righteous and religious," Bishop Hochstetler implored, "and I'm not sure sitting in a cell accomplishes any of that. His sitting in a cell will not pay back what you've lost."

"You're right, it won't. No amount of money can restore my trust. That's gone forever."

"It doesn't have to be," Monroe said. "If a bone breaks and the doctor sets it right, that bone can grow back stronger than ever. And we want to set this right."

The conversation on the front porch seemed to be taking a long time.

I could hear most of it from inside. Since the reason I was there was to help Uncle Ralph navigate this, I figured now might be a good time to make my presence known. The church elders were probably surprised to see me stepping out onto the front porch with my hair pulled back into a ponytail and dressed in a college sweatshirt and blue jeans. At the office, my outfits were always crisp and professional. Otherwise I might be mistaken for one of the interns.

Monroe Hochstetler removed his hat. I found the gesture refreshing and charming.

"And you are?" Jacob Eicher asked.

"I'm Ralph's niece," I said. "I came to visit for a couple of days to help him sort some of this out. He doesn't have much family. And even though this isn't my specialty, I'm a lawyer, so I thought maybe I could help. It's a bit of a mess."

"Not quite as much of one now," Mr. Doty said, waving the check.

"Oh, that's wonderful...where did that come from?"

"It's an offering. We are humbly appealing to you to accept our apology, and offering with humility and prayer that we can all move forward together into forgiveness." Monroe Hochstetler lowered his head.

"Forgiveness, it's what's for di…" Jacob started to say. Monroe put up a hand.

"We would not like to see Abraham jailed. Yes, what he did was wrong and reprehensible. He was not raised that way. But we also believe that the best path forward for him isn't in a prison cell, but among church members who can nurture him and help him grow spiritually."

Uncle Ralph paused, appearing entranced in deep thought. His coffee-colored eyes stared straight ahead until he snapped back to attention.

"Nothing doing! He did the crime, he does the time. You can't hide behind your beards and buggies," Uncle Ralph coughed. "Now if you don't mind…"

"Uncle Ralph…"

I looked at Monroe Hochstetler.

"May we have a second alone?" I asked.

"Sure." Hochstetler and Jacob walked down the porch steps and stood near the buggy. They could see the animated conversation taking place on the porch. I found myself pacing up and down.

"Uncle Ralph…what do you think will be accomplished by having him locked up?" I asked.

"Accomplish? Punishment is the accomplishment, that is what! He needs to be punished or he'll do it again!" Ralph was roaring.

"I'm not sure in this case…seems to me that his church community will keep such a close eye on him that he'll barely be able to move. If he's in a cell for years, he'll emerge hardened, angry and alone, and then he probably will do it again. I'm just not sure that solves anything."

I didn't know the man who had violated Uncle Ralph, but perhaps I felt a kinship. I had been in trouble once myself.

"You remember when I first reached out to you? You remember what I was going through? Do you think being locked away would have been the right thing for me?"

Uncle Ralph was quiet, staring straight ahead.

"What he did was terrible, but from the research I've done, the interviews I've conducted, the transcripts from the detectives that I read, he seems to have suffered a great deal. Sometimes the punishment of letting down your loved ones, letting down yourself, is far greater than anything the criminal code can impose."

"Son-of-a-b…he violated me, and my house, my finances. What will I do?"

"Well, that's why you called me, right?" I reassured him. "We'll sort it out."

Finally, Uncle Ralph nodded. I leaned down and hugged him. He felt old, frailer than he used to. This ordeal had drained him, and I was happy it was over. I motioned Bishop Hochstetler to the porch.

"You can tell them to drop the charges," Uncle Ralph growled. "I don't care. But forgive? Not in this lifetime, nosirree."

"Forgiveness can be a long process," Monroe Hochstetler said. "But we hope that you can find forgiveness. God put a seed of forgiveness in every person's heart. Our job in life is to nurture that seed and watch the tree of forgiveness spread its branches over the darkest sins. Only through forgiveness can there be enlightenment and salvation. We know it's difficult, but we believe that's what we must do." He tipped his hat. "We thank you."

"Right now I feel like the tree's a cactus," Uncle Ralph muttered.

CHAPTER FIVE

ABRAHAM

For three days, I stayed in the cell while the prosecutor's office figured out how to proceed with their case without Mr. Doty's participation.

I was ready to plead guilty, so ready to repent. I knew prison would be tough, but I wanted to change. Thinking about the awkward, nerdy kid clumsily holding the baseball bat in that game against Raber's Warriors seemed like a lifetime ago. But I had risen to the moment then, and I'd do it now.

I never got the chance. Geoffrey Williams led me to an office where several people were sitting around a table. One was a pleasant-looking young woman who looked close to my age. Her face was not familiar. Geoffrey's assistant was also there, but a woman with horn-rimmed gold glasses and hair in a bun was in the center of the group. She slid her business card across the desk to me.

JESSICA JOHNSON – ASSISTANT PROSECUTOR

"I want to be clear, Mr. Schwartz. The only reason I am not locking you up is because the victim requested that the charges be withdrawn, and without his testimony we have no case," she explained.

I nodded. This woman was all business.

"But you WILL be on probation for the next 3 years," she continued. "Perhaps your church doesn't use computers, but the rest of society does...and I will enter your name into a database. If you get so much as a citation for littering, you'll be brought back in here, and I will put you behind bars. Are we clear?"

"Yes, ma'am," I murmured.

"I'm tired of the Amish thinking that the rules somehow don't apply," she huffed.

I nodded.

"Sign here, please," she said.

I scribbled my name, then said goodbye to curmudgeonly Geoffrey and a couple of the guards. As I collected my things, I was given my shoes and pocketwatch back.

"I'll drive you back home, sir," the young woman said.

"Abraham, please. And thank you," I could hear myself stammering.

PAIGE

When I first saw him, he seemed so...broken. I think that's the word I'm searching for. It was a mixture of embarrassment, anger, and perhaps a bit of frailty, as if–at least at that moment-he looked 40 instead of 24. I'm sure having that secret all those years, the public embarrassment, being in a jail cell, all of that combined to make him this broken. I couldn't help thinking when I first saw him: *that's* the man that wreaked so much havoc on Uncle Ralph? Of course, that is one of the first things one learns in law school...don't stereotype a client. The most gangsterish-looking thug can be a harmless Sunday school teacher, and the nerdy, harmless, accountant-looking guy can be a child-molester. So I try to go into any situation stereotype-blind. Still, he hardly seemed like the monster I was expecting.

"I'm Paige. Paige Roberts, Mr. Doty's niece," I said after the proceedings were over.

I could tell my introduction intimidated Abe.

He gave me a quizzical look. "Hello...but you mean I'm being spared prison simply so I can be taken back to Mr. Doty's and turned into human hamburger?"

I laughed at that. I know he probably didn't mean it to be funny, which is probably why I found it amusing.

"No, you get to live," I assured him. "I bet you're glad to be out of there. That woman wasn't Miss Congeniality, that's for sure."

Abe muttered agreement.

My plan was to take him home and then go back to Uncle Ralph's. I would say goodbye and get back to my life. I knew the ride would be a little awkward. After all, he had caused my Uncle Ralph a lot of harm, but I also wanted this to be over. People had given me second chances in life and I'm a firm believer in them, so I wanted to extend the courtesy. I began to hum some Top 40 tune along with the radio as we drove, while Abe seemed to retreat into a morose cocoon.

"You live right across the street from my Uncle Ralph, right?" I chirped.

"Yes ma'am."

"Oh, please...Paige. Call me Paige. I'm hardly older than you,"

He seemed to sink lower into his seat as I kept trying to put him at ease

"This whole ordeal gave me an excuse to come see Uncle Ralph. I hadn't been here in years," I said. "I know it took a lot of courage for him to call me,"

That only made Abe blush and grow even quieter. He looked as if he wanted to crawl under the passenger seat, or maybe jump out of the car.

"Meeting someone for the first time under these circumstances is almost more humiliating than the arrest itself," he said, sinking even lower

.

I worried that I might have to pull him off the floorboard if he sank any farther down.

"I know this is awkward," I went on, "but...I just want you to know that I don't...hold any ill will...show me a perfect person and I'll show you a purple giraffe."

That didn't seem to shake Abe's morose mood. He continued to stare out the window. My attention, though, was captured by something else.

"This doesn't look good," I suddenly said.

"I know...." Abe grumbled. "I'm sorry you had to get involved. I..."

"No...I mean the engine is overheating."

I motioned toward the temperature gauge and watched the temperature needle climb to the top of the dial. My father had taught me some basics about how cars worked, so I can change a flat or jump-start my car. But, I'll confess to being a bit of a girly girl. Not that I'm ashamed of that, but it doesn't help when a mechanical problem arises. Still, I knew enough to know that if the engine stayed too hot too long, it'd fry. My visible concern seemed to finally kindle some life in Abe.

"It's going to get a little warm in here," he warned, blasting the heat on high.

"What are you doing?" I asked, a little suspicious of an Amish man's mechanical acumen.

"This will blow the heat from the engine," Abe said. "Unfortunately, it'll blow onto us. But it'll allow us to get back to the house where I can take a look at it."

It did the trick. The temperature gauge slowly began to drop to more normal levels while we baked, although rolling down the windows helped. Soon we arrived at the Schwartz house, both beading in sweat despite the cold temperatures outside.

"Have I been gone only four days? It felt like so much longer." Abe was gazing at their two-story white clapboard farmhouse. There was a rusty windmill towering over it, which, to Abe, must have seemed like a welcoming beacon even on a frigid, overcast late February day like this one.

"Let the engine cool and I'll take a look," he suggested as I brought the car to a stop in the driveway.

"Well, your little trick did the trick. Thank you. You probably saved me $5000 on a new engine or a hefty towing bill," I said, grateful.

"No problem," he replied, with slightly more confidence. "It was a tip one of my non-Amish friends taught me once when we were out driving around. Of course, since I travel by horse and buggy, I didn't think I'd ever need to use it!"

A passel of brothers and sisters spilled out of the house in a pinwheel of colors, burying Abe in hugs and hellos. All except one, a young woman who also emerged from the house but stood back a bit, her expression flat.

"My name's Salome, and I am Abe's Mom. I want to thank you for what you did for us, and I'm sorry for what he did to you." The short, stout woman was dressed in a cornflower blue dress, white apron, and black bonnet. She sounded matter-of-fact.

"Really, it was nothing. I'm glad I could help. The best resolutions in life are when everyone comes out okay, and I think that happened here. Uncle Ralph will be fine," I assured her. I knew it couldn't be easy for the Mom to be confronting the sins of her son.

"It's too cold to stand out here. Won't you come in for a bit?" she offered.

The sun was now completely obscured by thick, cold clouds of gray. A stiff wind had begun to bite, making it feel much colder.

"Well, I really can't go anywhere at the moment," I said, with a nod to the car. "I was going to drive over to Uncle Ralph's, let my car cool a bit, and then figure out what to do. Engine's overheating so I can't go far."

"Go in and get warm, and I'll take a look at it," Abe said. "It's the least I can do for you." Abe was still surrounded by siblings who seemed awe-struck at his arrival.

"Sit down and make yourself at home." Salome set a steaming mug in front of me.

"Mmmm, what is this?" I asked.

"It's spearmint tea. We grew the spearmint in our garden last summer." She was beaming with pride.

"It's delicious." I clasped the warm mug with both hands and studied her face. She looked kind, but steely, as if she'd be your best friend unless you crossed her. Then watch out. Her hands were strong and muscular, probably from years of home-canning, sewing, and gardening.

"You'll need something to eat with that," she said, sliding a piece of pie on a plate toward me. A dollop of whipped cream–undoubtedly homemade–topped the thick, gooey slice.

"It's oatmeal pie," she explained.

I pictured a bowl of gruel-type oatmeal baked into a pie, but I soon discovered that it was a sweet, decadent confection belying its name.

"Mmmm, this is amazing. You say it's *oatmeal* pie?" I asked, shocked.

Salome nodded. "It's a specialty around here. Pecans are too expensive, but oatmeal pie tastes just like pecan. We've fooled people into thinking it's pecan before." She laughed.

"This whipped cream is heavenly," I said, remarking on its silkiness and fluffiness.

"Verena made it, just out of the milk-house this morning.' She smiled at one of the twins.

The kitchen was painted pale blue, perhaps a shade lighter than Salome's dress. A wooden table could comfortably sit six people, allowing for a cozy meal. One wall was covered floor to ceiling with cabinets Copper pots hung from hooks, and a wood stove in the center of the room coughed golden embers. A sealed Tupperware container crammed with cookies sat on one of the countertops, the Tupperware an anomaly in an otherwise undisturbed tableau of 19th-century simplicity. Running the length of one wall was a countertop, with cabinets beneath, just as in almost any kitchen. But there was no toaster, microwave, or any of the other electric amenities I was accustomed to seeing. There was also a stainless steel sink, but no faucets. Salome noticed the quizzical look on my face.

Loretta, the daughter who had hung back when Abe and I had arrived, also picked up on it. "Have you ever been in an Amish home before?" she asked.

I shook my head. "I'm from Chicago. I've heard about the Amish in northern Indiana, and I knew Uncle Ralph lived near some Amish people. I think we studied a few cases in school involving your community, but that's about all." I was still sipping the pungent tea.

"Cases?"

"Oh, I'm sorry. I should have introduced myself more formally. My name's Paige Roberts. I work as an attorney in Chicago." I slid a business card across the table toward Loretta.

"I see," Salome said, her words hesitant. "I knew you were Mr. Doty's niece, but that was about all I knew." Her eyes had narrowed as if the mention of my occupation made her suspicious.

"Don't worry, I have a law degree, not rabies," I said, trying to put her at ease.

She laughed.

That's the bad thing about telling people I'm a lawyer," I said, relieved at her response. "They either back away or they tell me, 'Oh, boy, have I got a case for you. I bit down on an olive pit that a restaurant accidentally left in my sandwich. Damaged my tooth something fierce, should be a slam-dunk settlement!'"

"My name's Loretta Schwartz, aspiring wife and mom," the girl said in a playful tone, producing a card from the folds of her dress and sliding it across the table toward me.

I laughed and picked up the card, rubbing my fingers around the edges, studying the colorful designs and the flowing letters that spelled out Loretta's name. The card was the same size as mine, the standard business card format that I had mindlessly pocketed at dozens of legal conferences. But there was no phone number, website listing, email contact, or even address on it. Just Loretta's full name written out in flowing letters surrounded by an intricate, colorful line-art drawing of sunflowers and daisies.

"This is gorgeous," I said, examining the card.

"Thank you. My cousin Alan designs these. He's an excellent artist," she said.

"I should have him design mine." I was only half joking.

"The young people exchange them with one another at Sunday evening singings or weddings, anyplace where the young ones meet," Loretta explained.

I thought I had remembered reading somewhere about the custom of "calling cards" in Victorian England, although in those days it was primarily men who left the cards. I assumed the Amish version was gender-equalized a bit for modern times.

Just then, Abe came back into the kitchen.

"It's getting dark. That may be about all I can do tonight, although I think I am getting close to figuring out what is wrong. I'm going to finish up some other chores. Looks like snow soon," Abe announced. I found it odd that he just seemed so nonchalant, only arriving home hours earlier. Salome must have read my thoughts.

"Getting back into a routine quickly was Bishop Hochstetler's prescription for putting the whole jail ordeal behind him," Salome said with a hint of embarrassment still. "I want to you to know that Abe's not a bad person and we're not a bad family, he wasn't raised that way, I'm sorry you had to meet us like this, I don't know wha..." she said.

"Please, don't say any more...it's okay...you are a wonderful family," I said.

"Well, thank you," Salome said. "This has just been difficult for all of us."

"Well, maybe I need to get back to Uncle Ralph's and hunker down there for the night. Do you have a restroom I could use before I go?" I asked.

Salome and Loretta looked at one another.

"You're probably not used to one that's outside…" Salome said.

"Oh, I think I'll be okay," I smiled. "A toilet's a toilet."

Salome and Loretta laughed.

"Here's a flashlight," Loretta said. "Just follow the stone walkway toward that fence and turn left. Go about fifty feet and you'll see it there."

"Or smell it!" Salome said with a laugh.

"Mom!" Loretta said.

Snowflakes were drifting down from the sky with greater intensity, whitening the ground with over an inch of wind-whipped powder. Each intricate flake illuminated like ivory in the narrow beam from the flashlight before resuming its fluffy fall to the earth. The outhouse sat adjacent to a barren field.

I shivered as I opened the outhouse door, half-smiling at the attempts to add a homey touch to what would otherwise be an ordinary outhouse. There were pretty lacy curtains over one of the windows, which let light into what would have been a very dark box. And this outhouse was a two-seater. I laughed at the thought of two people using the same stall at once. Not very romantic. But there were two toilet-sized holes on a raised wooden platform. I chose the left one and sat down. Traditional toilet seats, the soft, cushiony kind, were over the holes, which dropped about three feet below into a sewage-type septic system, which I presumed ran off into a nearby farm field. I could see a shaft or two of snowy moonlight shining onto the sludge below, but I tried not to look too long.

The toilet seat was glacier-cold, and occasional eddies of icy air swirled up from the putrid depths below. But the outhouse itself was remarkably clean. The privy shook as the wind began to roar outside. In the minutes since I had left the house, the storm seemed to have morphed into a monster. I reached to flush and then laughed at myself for the mindless action…of course: no plumbing, no flushing. So, as the outhouse trembled, I opened the door only to have the wind slam it back shut. The outhouse wobbled more violently, with snow as fine as talcum powder shooting in through tiny cracks in the wooden walls. I shoved the door open again, but the wind pushed back with greater fury. With more force, I finally heaved the outhouse door open wide enough to squeeze through into an unrecognizable world of overwhelming whiteness and wind.

The snow roared across the field in an eruption of pelting powder. I rubbed the snow from my eyes and shook it from my hair. I couldn't see the Schwartz's house, I could only hear a screaming storm and blinding whiteness. The flashlight was useless, the beam ricocheting off a billion flakes.

Suddenly I saw a dim glow inside a door so I grasped the handle and pulled it open. An elderly woman sat in a wooden rocking chair knitting some dark socks. Her pale visage and wrinkled, weathered face frightened me almost as much as my snow-covered apparition-like appearance shocked the elderly woman. We both screamed. I slammed the door shut and tottered on into the blinding snow.

Suddenly, though, I felt a firm hand on my shoulder reaching through the thick curtain of white, and I saw a bright, warm lantern. I grabbed the tail of the person's coat and followed in the deepening snow towards the house

"I was about to send out a search party for you!" Loretta said to me. I was snow-covered and shivering as I came into the house.

"I was just going out to latch the barn door and check on Grandma Ada. I thought it was you or Verena," Abe said. He held himself taller and more confidently than when he was slouched and humiliated in my car just hours earlier.

"Wow, that storm really blew up in the last few minutes…I've never seen snow like this…Abe, thanks," I called out. He grunted and then disappeared into the living room to stand by the stove.

Just then, Salome appeared in the kitchen.

"Well, you look like you've been making snow angels! Would you want some more tea?"

"No, I think too much tea is what almost got me into trouble in the first place," I said, motioning towards the outhouse.

Loretta giggled.

"Well, if it's too snowy even to walk to the outhouse, there's no way you're going to make it across the road to your uncle's house. We have an extra bed, so why don't you stay here?" Salome suggested.

"Oh, thank you...but I couldn't. Maybe the storm will settle down soon and I can walk to Uncle Ralph's," I said

"It's pretty bad outside. You barely made it back from the outhouse. There's no way you're walking across the highway," Loretta countered as she eyed the increasingly heavy snow.

"We've got plenty of room," Salome insisted.

"If you're sure...it's very kind of you," I said.

"Velma's getting your bed ready," Salome said matter-of-factly.

"Scott! I better call him or he'll be up all night worrying," I said, pulling out my phone and walking into another room.

Scott was a man I had been seeing for a while back in Chicago. He worked at the same firm as I did, and even though office romances were technically not permitted, we had been dating one another other on the sly.

"I'm staying with Uncle Ralph's neighbors, really nice people," I said, lowering my voice to a whisper. *"They're Amish."*

On the other end of the phone, Scott asked, "as in guys named Ezekiel and no electricity or cars?"

He spoke so loudly Loretta could hear him across the kitchen.

"Well, I don't think there is anyone named Ezekiel here, but, otherwise, yes," I rolled my eyes. "Anyway, love you...I'll call you tomorrow."

"Someone special?" Loretta asked.

"He's definitely special," I quipped with a hint of exasperation.

"I'll show you to your bed," Loretta said. "You're staying in my room tonight. Velma put fresh sheets on and added another blanket since it gets pretty cold up here."

"Oh, I don't want to kick you out of your bedroom," I protested.

"Really, it's okay. I'll be snug and warm with everyone else downstairs," Loretta said.

I followed Loretta up a dark flight of stairs. Most of the family, it appeared, was bunking down by a cozy wood stove in the living room. The floor around the stove transformed into a tangle of children, blankets, and pillows. I sort of wished I could just join them.

"So you don't have to go outside in the middle of the night when nature calls, Mom said to give you a bucket. I'll set it here." Loretta said, motioning towards the foot of the bed. "Need anything else?"

"No, I think I'm good," I said, staring at the tall yellow plastic paint bucket.

Snow swirled outside with increasing intensity. I looked around the bedroom, which was bare, not the typical teenager or young woman's lair. There were no posters of rock stars, smartphones plugged in, or pink and puffy pillows. There was a dresser with four drawers, and a tall grandfather clock loudly counting off the minutes in one corner of the room. Against a wall was a shelf with a collection of keychains on it, I guessed they were souvenirs picked up from travels. One keychain said "Rexford, Montana," another said "Pinecraft, Florida," another was emblazoned with "Charm, Ohio," and still another was embossed with a town from my home state, but I didn't recognize the name "Arthur, Illinois." In fact, none of the keychain names was familiar to me. A calendar with photos of horses was tacked to a far wall.

I slid into the queen-sized bed, pulling a hand-stitched quilt to my chin and listening to the wind rattle the eaves. I knew so little about these people. There were a couple of cases in law school involving the Amish that I could now recall studying. One was a landmark Supreme Court case, but I couldn't remember the specifics. Another involved buggies in Minnesota: *Hershberger versus*...? The exact case name escaped me, but I made a mental note to research it when I got home.

This all seemed surreal. Since I had wisely grabbed my overnight bag from the car, I had most of the essential overnight amenities: toothpaste, floss, deodorant, and sleeping clothes. Lingerie was one of my few indulgences. I liked the feel of soft, sexy, sheer Victoria's

Secret lace. The law firm I worked for was conservative, male-dominated, and the work was often dull, gray, and unglamorous. But it was a start. I'd move on to other more interesting work in the future. So sometimes during the grind of depositions, affidavits, and cases, it just made me feel more alive to know I had a bright burst of sexy color and a belly-button ring beneath the blanched, ashen world I worked in. I laughed at the irony of my racy, lacy underwear being covered by the quilt of one of one of the more conservative cultures. I put that thought aside and descended into a restful slumber while the winter storm beat its frozen fists on the Schwartz house.

CHAPTER SIX
PAIGE

I awoke the next morning, startled to see a landscape transformed by wind-whipped snow. US 27 was serene, buried in snow, and deserted. The Indiana Department of Transportation places diamond-shaped yellow signs emblazoned with a horse-and-buggy emblem to warn motorists that they are entering Amish country. Uncle Ralph said locals just ignore the signs, and out-of-towners usually regard them as nothing more than a charming curiosity. Anyway, a snowdrift along the highway reached the bottom of the sign.

"You're not going anywhere today," Salome said to me as I tentatively came downstairs from Loretta's room. I was wearing plaid pajama bottoms and a tight-fitting tee shirt. I hoped it wasn't too risqué for these people.

"I didn't pack enough," I said sheepishly, eyeing my pajamas while everyone else was wearing their usual daytime attire.

"Oh, don't worry about it. You make yourself at home."

Salome put out a breakfast of crisply fried bacon and a dish called "egg-in-nest." She said it was easy to make: just butter a skillet, put a slice of homemade bread in, cut a hole with an empty jelly jar, and then crack an egg into the hole. Flip the bread over, let the egg cook and the bread brown, and you've got egg-in-nest. Sounded like something even I could master, and I'm not great in the kitchen. Ham, sliced cheese, and homemade cinnamon rolls were also on the table.

The Schwartz children all seemed shy and they spoke among themselves in a dialect that I couldn't understand.

"*Nom ish Paige*," Salome said in response to one of the children's questions.

Benjamin said something in Swiss-German and everyone burst out laughing. Salome could tell I was puzzled.

"He just asked if your last name was Turner or Book…as in a 'page turner' or the page from a book," Salome explained.

ABRAHAM

I had Paige move her car into our barn before the storm hit, so it wouldn't be buried. Considering that it would have been days before a tow truck could come out, that turned out to be a smart move.

"I'll take a better look at your car today," I had told her.

"Thank you. I didn't plan to be marooned here and I need to hit the road soon," Paige replied.

"Sometimes our neighbors bring their cars here for Abe check. We sometimes joke he's the only 'Amish auto mechanic' on the planet," Mom laughed.

I just liked to work with anything mechanical. I wasn't necessarily great at it, but I liked seeing how things worked. I'm not one of those people who could disassemble a whole car engine and put it back together but I knew the basics, and if it was something simple, I could sniff it out.

PAIGE

I spent the morning across the highway visiting with Uncle Ralph. It was a long, cold trudge through snow that was sometimes waist-deep. Abe had made quite a mess out of my uncle's finances, but I was pretty confident that it was all fixable.

"You could have stayed here last night," Uncle Ralph growled. "You don't want to get too wrapped up with those people."

"The snowstorm came up so fast it kind of left me with no choice. But don't worry, the Schwartzes seem like lovely people," I reassured him.

"Well, they are, except for that young man," Ralph muttered.

I arrived back at the Schwartzes in the early afternoon while Salome and Loretta were rolling out pie dough. Velma and Verena, meanwhile, had their tiny hands in a pie plate patting down dough and attempting to flute the edges.

"That's how I start the girls on learning to make their own crusts,"

Salome said. "It's called pat-a-pan pie crust. No rolling, you just make it right in the pan. How do you make your crusts?" Salome asked, glancing over at me.

I was embarrassed and blushed slightly. My Mom had never taught me how to cook, so most of the time I just ordered take-out. Sometimes Scott would come over and grill steaks. He was skilled in the kitchen. I remember when he first saw my apartment, he was in awe–and not in a good way–of my empty cabinets and refrigerator.

"I open my freezer, remove from the packaging, and bake."

"Oh…" Salome paused, and then laughed.

"Let's just say we eat lots of take-out," I said.

"Oh, so you have a husband back home?"

"Well, not exactly…."

While Salome, Loretta, and the twins prepared crusts, I told them about my family and boyfriend back in Chicago. I talked about how I had attended law school and started working at a law firm as a page. "Paige the page" they called me. Salome and Loretta laughed.

ABRAHAM

While the ladies conversed, Dad and I attempted to open our shop for business. I doubted there would be any customers, but that didn't shake my father's firm belief that hard work was the asphalt on the road to Heaven. I think that's a big reason he was so disappointed in me after learning about what I had done with Mr. Doty's credit card. In his eyes, I had circumvented the hard work ethic he instilled in me for the lure of easy money. I knew working with him wouldn't be the same for a while. He and Loretta seemed to be taking my sins the hardest, and I knew I had relationship repair work to do with both.

Our store was open six days a week, 8 a.m. to 5:30 p.m., and unless there was a wedding or a funeral in the community, Dad didn't close the doors for any reason. And I'm not exaggerating.

Once a tornado could be seen swirling in the western sky headed straight for our farm. Mom gathered all of us into the cellar where her hundreds of colorful home-canned goods were stored. Seeing that Dad was still at the shop, I bolted from the cellar and ran outside to alert Dad.

"Tornado!" I shouted to Dad, who hadn't yet put down his saw.

"Tell it to come back at 5:30 after we're closed," Dad calmly said as he sanded down a rough spot on a china cabinet.

The cyclone chewed up our back field pretty badly and exploded our corn crib, but not 50 yards before it would have obliterated our shop, the tornado disappeared back into the sky, reclaimed by the clouds. The shop suffered nothing more than a little damage to the siding.

But storms weren't the only obstacle that wouldn't stop Dad. Another time, he was finishing an order when a gun-wielding bandit came to our door. Living on a main highway, we were an easy target for everyone. Evangelicals, tourists, beggars, peddlers, salespeople, and customers trying to find our shop would come knocking on the front door of our house. Of course, back when our 140 acres first came into the family, US 27 wasn't much more than a dirt horse path. I'm sure had they known then about the busy highway it would become, they might have reconsidered or at least gotten a lower price for the land. Dad eventually worried that farming wouldn't be able to support his family as it had for generations. So, like many Amish over the past 50 years, he had to find another way to earn a living. As a young man, he saw an opportunity in all those automobiles that were passing on the newly-widened US 27. Dad always had a knack for carpentry, so he started a business called Schwartz's Family Furniture, which is where I worked and hoped to take over someday. I started working in the shop with my father when I was barely old enough to walk. Anyway, back to the bandit. I was only about 13 years old when this happened, and what I'm about to describe terrified me, but it didn't seem to faze Dad.

Our shop was small by design. Dad never wanted a huge gallery and gobs of inventory to oversee, so there was a small showroom where we displayed a few hand-made hutches, sofas, china cabinets, and tables. That way if someone walked in, they could see our wares and maybe even buy one on impulse. But most of our business was "made-to-order" furniture. Customers came in and requested a piece made to their specifications. We built it for them and they picked it up later. Occasionally, Mom would run the register, a decrepit manual contraption. Most of the time she'd just get frustrated and say, "Heck with the register," and write receipts by hand. Sometimes if she had some extra loaves of homemade bread, cookies, or jellies, she'd put them out for sale.

It was late on a Wednesday afternoon when an unshaven, overweight man wearing a red baseball cap and gray sweatsuit strolled into the store. "Gimme all your money," the robber demanded, aiming an ancient Colt .45 revolver directly at Dad. Dad never even looked up.

"Can't you wait until I'm done cutting the end? If you stop mid-grain, it'll show and I'll have to do it over again.

Startled, the robber complied.

"Uh, sure. I'll wait."

While I stood petrified, Dad meticulously continued sanding, sawing, and measuring. There was an awkward silence. The robber grew impatient.

"Can you please grab the other end of this measuring tape?" Dad asked the bandit.

"Sure, where do you want it exactly?" the robber said. He relaxed his hold on the gun. Dad's sharp saw was gleaming inches away from the robber's face.

"Just hold it there for me while I measure…."

"Sure, that's a mighty fine looking…wait a minute! I'm robbing you, not auditioning for an apprenticeship! Can we do this now? All your money…empty the register!" the robber barked, getting impatient.

"I have to apply the varnish now, or it'll…"

"I can't believe this! I need money today, not tomorrow, not next week. Just forget it!" the man said, fleeing out the door and into his car, mission unaccomplished.

Dad never filed a report with the police or mentioned the incident after that day.

When my shaking stopped, I asked, "Dad…he could have blown our brains out, why didn't you just give him the money?"

Dad paused and started to say something before I blurted out, "Or better yet, rip his head off with that saw you were holding?"

That was one of the few times I saw my father forceful, far angrier with me than with the robber. He put down his tools and walked towards me. He put his hands on my shoulders and stooped to my level so that he was looking at me directly in the eye.

"Violence solves *nothing*! If it was our time, it was our time. We can't second guess the Lord."

"And the Lord wanted us to be robbed?" I asked, confused.

"Were we robbed? No. Maybe He was just testing us."

I must've not seemed convinced to Dad and, fact is, I wasn't. How could he have possibly known the robber would grow exasperated and flee? Couldn't the robber just as easily have pulled the trigger and killed us? Dad just had a way of reading people, and he could tell the robber was a lightweight.

"Why don't you at least let me run to the neighbor's and call the police?" I said, still rattled by the incident.

"Absolutely not. No one was hurt," Dad warned. "Vengeance is not our way."

"But he could hurt someone, and we have a chance to stop it, at least alert the police," I protested.

Dad sighed.

"Maybe...but that's the future and only God can see the future. Yes, good people do bad things, but it's not for us to judge. There is a Higher Power who is our only jury. Let Him judge. You just live to the best of your ability. But you remember, there is good in everyone...maybe it needs help getting out, but never judge a person by their worst moment."

I was 13, an age when I was just beginning to challenge my parents' wisdom, and I needed a lot of convincing.

"What if their worst moment is murdering someone? Or stealing? Or lying? What about that customer whose check bounced last month and you still haven't gotten the money?"

Dad put down his tools, fiddled with his suspenders, ran his hand through his long, thick still-black beard, and exhaled.

"We are not to judge. Let Him judge."

"So let everyone do as they wish, no matter how much it hurts people?" I pressed.

"Someday, you'll understand what I'm saying."

Would I want to be defined for the rest of my life by Mr. Doty's credit card? I thought of that often when I was pacing behind bars. I knew I didn't.

So, undeterred by tornado or bandit, Dad wasn't going to let a little thing like a blizzard stand in the way of opening our store. He and I attempted to open for the day while Paige lingered in the kitchen with the ladies. I'm not sure what they talked about, but I think Paige enjoyed their company. One of the joys of Amish life is that it assumes a sort of seasonal rhythm. Our life just sort of shifts with the seasons. Snow and cold mean fewer orders, so Dad and I were able to get caught up on inventory. Outdoor games became indoor games. Gardening became sewing. Nature can't be controlled, so you learn to work with it.

PAIGE

"What's that little cottage?" I asked, looking out the window of the Schwartz kitchen.

"Grossmutter's house," Verena said.

"Huh?" I said.

"Sorry, she sometimes doesn't realize that not everyone speaks Swiss. It's where Grandma Ada stays. We call it a *dawdy haus*," Loretta explained.

"Oh…" I said.

"She's 91…and quite spry," Loretta said. "Nancy is bringing her over now."

It was then that I recognized her as the same woman I had accidentally stumbled upon the night before, during the snowstorm.

"Oh, so who's this sparkling jewel?" Ada said, waving a cane at us, wisps of white hair visible from beneath her black *kapp.*

"Funny, I wonder where she gets these things. She's never worn a jewel in her life," Loretta whispered to me.

"Her name's Paige," Loretta shouted.

"Sage? Such a pretty name. Used to grow some in my garden."

Nancy and Loretta settled Grandma Ada into a big chair by the warmth of the fire. They figured she'd be more comfortable with us for the day rather than snowbound.

"This is a lot of snow. We don't usually get a ton here in Indiana, so it might be nice to get out and have some fun in it. Have you been on a sleigh ride before?" Loretta asked me.

"Well, my sister and I used to go sledding when we were kids, but I don't suppose that's the same as sleighing?" I replied, intrigued.

Loretta laughed. "Sledding is fun for a quick thrill, but 30 seconds down a hill and it's over. On a sleigh ride, you go where the horse chooses. It's great fun" Loretta said. "Velma, run over to the shop and see if Abe will get the sleigh ready?"

I was really enjoying Loretta's company. Despite our obvious differences, we had a lot in common.

Velma bundled up in a charcoal black coat, black mittens, and blue scarf, and scampered out the door.

"You always like to go with Timothy on the sleigh," her twin, Verena said.

Loretta blushed.

"Okay, well, it is also a very romantic way to see the snow," Loretta said.

"Who's Timothy?" I asked.

Loretta blushed again but didn't answer.

"It's a boy she's been seeing," answered Benjamin. At nine years old, Benjamin wasn't interested in dating, but he was very well tuned-in to the actions of his older siblings.

ABRAHAM

"All right, the sleigh is ready, who's going?" I asked, stomping snow off my boots and standing by the stove.

Velma, Verena, and Benjamin's hands shot up.

The 140 acres surrounding our house resembled a snow-covered quilt of farm fields. Pastures and forests looked like someone used a

butter knife to spread vanilla frosting over the earth. I had hitched
Cinnamon, one of our family's four trusty horses, to the sleigh.
Velma and Verena piled into the back. I sat on the driver's side,
with Loretta between Paige and me. Most of our land was fields that
a neighboring farmer rented, but 40 acres of it was unfarmed. We
called it the "Back 40," and it was a pristine area of brush, woods,
and ponds.

What looked like nothing more than drab, brown, frozen pasture 24
hours earlier had been transformed into a spectacular snowscape.
Drifts as fine and white as baby powder swirled around tree trunks
like riffles of a river that had been flash-frozen. Snow was two feet
deep in places, but the sleigh glided over the storm's spoils
effortlessly. The blizzard's winds had abated and been replaced by a
breezy snow with silver-dollar-sized flakes swirling like those in a
glass globes you hold and shake.

Paige pulled out her cellphone and started taking photos of some of
the beautiful snowscapes. She had no awareness of our cultural
customs prohibiting photos of people, so I figured if she captured
one of us in the frame, she could be forgiven. I thought I'd shed
some of my shyness and try to have a little fun, so I started hamming
it up for Paige's camera, mugging and making silly faces with the
snow drifts behind me. But then Loretta pulled me not-so-discreetly
aside.

"What are you doing???" she whispered incredulously.

"Oh, c'mon, Retta…she doesn't understand the rules…Bishop Hochstetler has no authority over her!" I said

"No, but what about you? Don't you think you need to be very, very careful from here on out about church rules? And besides, we don't know her that well…those photos could end up all over the internet," Loretta admonished.

" I know…I know…*Thou shalt not make unto thee any graven image, or any likeness of anything that is in heaven above, or that is in the earth beneath, or that is in the water under the earth,"* I said, uttering the verse from Exodus that has been ingrained in me since I was a child. It was the verse that many Amish used as their theological objection for not wanting to be photographed.

"I'm impressed. You do listen in church sometimes, after all," Loretta said.

Do I personally believe that I somehow will be barred from entrance into Heaven because I might smile for a snapshot? No, I can't say that I do. Does that somehow make me a bad Amish? That is for others to decide. But I know many Amish do believe that a graven image will steal one's soul and prevent their entrance into Heaven. Of course, there are plenty of others that have secret snapshots squirreled away in a bureau. This is one of the many areas of our faith that I struggle with.

Loretta was the sibling closest in age to me, so we interacted the most, but we were opposites in most ways. Loretta dutifully obeyed the rules of the church and the laws of life, while I questioned them, challenged them, and sometimes simply ignored them. Loretta could never understand how such grayness could bring happiness while I looked at her reverence of rules as very smothering. It's odd how two siblings raised by the same parents in the same household could hold such starkly different views. For her, a rule, whether it be the Bible's or a township ordinance, is an inviolable law. Loretta and I were always clashing over what rules to follow.

After her whispered warning about Paige's photography, I frowned and quit mugging for the camera. In this case, Loretta was probably right.

"Oh, I'm sorry, did I do something wrong?" Paige asked.

"No, it's just that our church doesn't allow photos of people," Loretta explained.

"Oh, I'm sorry, I didn't mean any…" Paige started to say.

Before Loretta could go into greater detail, we all were interrupted by a chestnut-colored horse bounding through the powdery snow about 100 yards away.

"Summer! Get back here!" Loretta yelled, her rosy-cheeked face showing an expression of alarm. But Summer kept barreling through the field, her pace slowed by the deep snow, but otherwise she was maniacally enjoying her unfettered freedom. "I better go after her. I'll meet you back at the house!" Loretta disappeared in a blur of bonnet, scarf and snow spray, scampering after Summer.

"Someone's going to be in trouble," Verena piped up from the back of the sleigh, glancing at her twin and at Benjamin.

"It wasn't me," Benjamin said, scrunching further down in his seat.

"Did one of you forget to close the paddock gate? If so, I'm sure Dad will want a word with you," I warned.

"They're adorable," Paige whispered to me about the twins and Benjamin.

We started our journey back to the horse barn. The blankets which had been draped over the three of us were now just over Paige and me. Benjamin and the twins were bundled up in back.

"This is so neat. Where does one go to get a sleigh like this?" Paige asked, admiring the polished wood and intricate carving.

"Here," I said, holding up my hands. "I made it."

"Wow! The craftsmanship on this is incredible…seems so sturdy, yet flexible enough to just slide over the snow. Do you make lots of things like this?"

"That's how I make my living. Dad and I make dressers, sofas, sleighs, about anything you'd want."

"That's so neat. Maybe I should buy my furniture from you," Paige said. "When I first moved into my apartment, I furnished the whole place with furniture from this big Swedish superstore. It's easy to assemble, but wow, it doesn't hold up well."

"We use only the best wood and I'd put my work up against anyone," I said, not wanting to boast, but I've always had pride in my craftsmanship and am not impressed by those cheap monster-sized store knock-offs.

Verena and Velma chattered and bickered with Benjamin as our sleigh glided effortlessly over frozen creeks and deep snow-smothered pastures. I build the sleigh runners to be flexible so that the ride will be smooth as possible. Some of my customers liked having their sleighs made with the runners attached to buggy wheel hubs so that they could be converted to horse-drawn carriages in the summer.

"It's gorgeous out here, but I definitely didn't bring warm enough clothes for a sleigh ride," Paige said.

She seemed surprised when I immediately offered my coat. It just seemed the gentlemanly thing to do. We're much more accustomed to the cold, the outdoors, the harsh reality of Indiana weather. She wasn't. I would have offered my coat to anyone else unprepared for the elements. Really. Okay, you may not believe that, but in my heart I think that's probably true.

"Thank you!" Paige said, pulling it around her and wrapping herself more tightly with the horse blanket.

"I think I may have your car fixed by tomorrow morning. Fortunately, it's just a coolant leak. At least I can get you on your way. We've got some things in the shop that I think I can fashion a makeshift seal with, but I just need to test it a time or two. It took me most of the morning just to isolate exactly where the leak was," I said.

"That's okay, I really appreciate it and, really, even if you had gotten it fixed today, I doubt I would have been going anywhere. Checked the news on my phone, and this county is under a Level 3 snow emergency with most roads closed," Paige said, looking at her phone, eying its rapidly dwindling battery.

"Watch you don't drop your phone. We wouldn't find it until the snow melts this spring. You really are attached to that aren't you?" I asked, perplexed how people could be so committed to an object.

"Probably too much so," Paige admitted.

"I wouldn't want one of those," I said.

But as we approached the barn, our conversation was cut short by an out-of-breath crimson-red Loretta leading Summer.

"Seems as if Summer likes winter," Paige commented.

"And it feels like summer to me after working up a sweat chasing her," Loretta countered, mopping her brow with her arm.

Paige laughed.

"I was able to catch her. I think she must have wanted to go sledding!" Loretta said, suddenly noticing Paige wearing my coat. "Looks like you fit right in," Loretta laughed. "Want to do the milking?"

"I don't think you'd want me doing the milking. I'm a city gal," Paige said.

Paige took off my coat and handed it back as I secured the horses and the sleigh in the relative warmth of the barn.

"Let's go inside. Maybe Mom will fix us some hot chocolate," Loretta said.

In the bright daylight, Paige was able to survey her surroundings. She was standing in back of our two-story farmhouse. A few outbuildings and a corn crib dotted the property. On the north side of the house, the side yard, were two laundry lines. While we were out on the sleigh, Mom and Nancy had trudged through the foot-high drifts to put some laundry out to dry, so Paige saw an assortment of coal-black pants, dark denim, and colorful shirts in hues of blue, rust, and green, flapping in the still-brisk breeze. A rusting bicycle wheel dangled from one of the lines, with clothespins attached. Providing a constant creaking hum in the background were the thick blades of the windmill rotating and groaning in the wind above. "We use it to hang socks, gloves and other small items. It's really handy," Loretta said, noticing Paige staring at the bicycle wheel. This really is a peaceful place," I overheard Paige say to no one in particular.

CHAPTER SEVEN
ABRAHAM

After supper, we could finally see orange flashing lights coming from Route 27, meaning that plows were on the prowl. But I could tell that while Paige seemed to be enjoying her stay, she was eager to leave.

"Looks like you may be able to get out by morning," Loretta said. "And Timothy may finally get to come visit."

"That's a name I've been hearing a lot," Paige said. "Someone special?"

Loretta blushed.

"I think he's my future brother-in-law," said Nancy, who was, at 13, a more precocious version of Loretta.

Loretta blushed again.

"He's just my friend," she said.

"Oh, do you kiss your *other* friends?" Nancy needled.

"I think it's time for you to start your chores," Loretta said. And with that, Nancy bolted upstairs.

"Would you like to hear a yodel?" Mom asked soon after we saw the snowplows pass.

Soon the room was filled with the tender and resplendent sound of Loretta, Nancy, and Mom yodeling. Velma and Verena added a note here and there as they were just learning the intricacies of the notes and harmonies. Benjamin and Daniel watched and listened politely while Marvin, Jr., tugged on Paige's arm as she listened. It was cute to watch and hear the twins learn yodeling, and to see Paige so captivated by it. I know she was expecting the harsh, insipid sound popularized in Hollywood films (yodel-lay-hee-hoo), but that's not what Amish yodeling is. The yodeling is an almost poignant sound, truly a balm for one's soul. And it's not just women who yodel, Dad often added his own yodel crescendo at the end. We don't use musical instruments. I don't know of any Amish church that allows them, I guess we've always believed the purity of the human voice is the most divine, and that a bunch of instruments simply distorts the vocals God gave us.

Paige seemed mesmerized by the yodeling. She would describe it to me later as an "amazing and haunting harmony."

"Who wants to play Aggravation?" Nancy shouted.

Aggravation was one of our favorite board games. It's a fast-paced affair that pits two-person teams against each other in a race to see who can get their marbles around the board first. It can be played with either four players or six. The living room quickly became a cozy competition of board games, books, and fabric. Loretta, Paige, Nancy and I played Aggravation, while Velma, Verena, and Mom sewed some shirts. Dad was reading. Loretta and Paige were on one Aggravation team while Nancy and I played against them. Before beginning, Loretta passed around strips of homemade deer jerky. Mom and Loretta had made a batch from the big buck that Daniel and Benjamin had brought down in the backwoods during the annual autumn hunt.

I always was good at board games and I think I brought out a competitive streak in Paige, who rolled the dice and moved the marbles with gusto. So much gusto that she and Loretta trounced Nancy and me in three straight games.

"Beginner's luck!" Nancy taunted.

"Well, if you're as competitive in court as you are in Aggravation, you probably win every case," Loretta joked. She was impressed with how fast Paige had picked up the game.

Soon the games ended and sleep began to claim its weary. The twins and Nancy were all bunked down on the floor in a tangle of blankets and pillows. Benjamin, Daniel, and Marvin, Jr., had retired to their shared room upstairs. Loretta had fallen asleep on a rocking chair with her nose in a book. Mom and Dad had gone to their first-floor bedroom.

Paige and I lingered by the stove a little longer, finishing our tea and starting some small talk. This wasn't intentional, really. We were just the last two standing at the end of a long night. Playing the board game in a group was one thing, but talking to Paige one-on-one was another. I was still smothered by a deep humiliation over what I had done and that this pretty, intelligent, and important woman knew about my misdeeds. First time she ever laid eyes on me, I was practically an inmate. How's that for a first impression?

"Delicious tea," Paige said.

I nodded silently in agreement.

"Your Mom grew it and brewed it?"

I nodded again, poking at the hot coals of the dying fire.

"You're a defense attorney's dream. You don't give up any secrets. So tell me your story, Mr. Blue-Eyed Sleigh-Builder…you're so quiet," Paige asked.

It's not that I didn't *want* to talk to her. It's just that even on a good day I probably would have felt mismatched and perhaps intellectually outwitted by this college-educated lawyer. A very attractive, unpretentious, and approachable one, for sure…but still, it's not like I thought we had a ton in common, at least on paper. Add to that my newly-minted rap sheet, and I just was too humiliated to talk to her, no matter her overtures. Why would she want to know about me? I fiddled with my suspenders and blushed slightly. At least she was noticing my blue eyes.

"Unfortunately, you know my story," I said, sipping my tea.

"Yes, but I doubt I know all of it…you've got a lovely family, a wonderful community here…there's more to you than what brought me here…there always is…" Paige said gently.

This is when I first found myself spellbound by Paige's beauty, her fair features, intellect, and empathy. There's a rich glow that natural light emits. Even the most unsightly troll's looks could be softened in the comforting halo of a stove's glow. And Paige was hardly a troll, so the fire-light simply enhanced her beauty. As Paige and I stood talking and sipping tea, I found myself increasingly attracted to her. There was a churning in my stomach, a sort of physical reaction to attraction. We spoke in a low voice so we wouldn't wake up the others.

"When I figure out my story, I'll tell you," I muttered. Fortunately, Paige didn't press the issue. I exhaled with relief at her moving onto another topic.

"Being here in Berne, the Amish life seems so full and rich, it makes me think maybe you have something the rest of us don't," Paige pondered. "So it just makes me wonder what makes you tick. Look, my phone has practically become a third limb," Paige said, waving it around for emphasis. "How do you survive without phones? I'm kidding…I know humankind did quite well without cellphones for millennia…but you all seem so happy, and you're doing it without all of this technology," Paige continued.

That's when I summoned the nerve to talk a bit more. She seemed genuinely interested, not like I was some curiosity in a Petri dish, and I found that endearing.

"A favorite naturalist of mine, Edwin Way Teale, once wrote something that I think summarizes the reasons I stay in our church: *Reduce the complexity of life by eliminating the needless wants of life, and the labors of life reduce themselves.* When I was sleepless in that cell bunk, I turned those words over and over in my head."

"Thought-provoking quote…" Paige said.

"I think there's a fullness in life lived with less," I said. "Maybe I forgot that...and that's why I came...unanchored from my moral moorings." My eyes moistened at the thought of what I had done and who I had disappointed. I turned away, but Paige could see I was pained.

"I know where you're coming from. I spent a year in India between my sophomore and junior year in college. I worked for a mission, helping to build homes and schools. I think my parents thought I was out of my mind, but, we weren't wanting for anything growing up...I needed to see first-hand what it was like to have less and, like you, I seemed richer for it...my childhood was great, it was my adulthood that was all...um...fudged up," Paige stammered, reddening at her almost word choice.

"We're Amish, not Puritans."

"Well, thanks...sometimes I need to watch my mouth, though, no matter who I'm around...anyway, I needed to see something different, to know life was more than manicured lawns, perfect cars, and picket fences."

There was an awkward silence. It seemed like there was more about her life she wanted to tell me, but I didn't press. So I replied simply, "That must have been quite an experience. I've got a bit of a travel bug myself, but India sounds exotic...."

"I don't mean to sound silly, but...don't you ever want..." Paige started to say. But I finished her sentence for her.

"Electricity, TV, a microwave, a car?" I asked.

Paige laughed. "You knew what I was going to ask...."

"You probably can't appreciate why unless you've been born into this..." I said, grasping for a way to explain.

The house had plunged into darkness, with nothing but the aura of light from the stove bathing us in an apricot glow. Snoring could be heard coming from my parent's room. A few of the children stirred in their sleep on the wood-plank floor.

"I understand...I could do without electricity or a car, but a hot shower? I think running water, having a nice, long, hot soapy shower would be what I miss most," Paige said, taking another sip of tea.

The combination of Mom's homemade spearmint tea, the crackling fire, the swirling snow outside, the conversation, and the visual of Paige taking a hot, soapy shower began to heighten my attraction to her. Sometimes I think outsiders see us in our plain clothing, bonnets, buggies, and beards, and lose sight of the fact that we aren't simple Bible-hugging, one-dimensional cardboard cut-outs, but complex humans with the same emotions and urges as everyone else. For Heaven's sake, of course we have passion and sensual desires. How does one suppose we end up with such large families in the first place? For a fleeting moment, I fantasized about pulling Paige close and holding her in my arms by the fire.

"Well...I'm curious. Do you ever want those things?" she asked, sipping her tea slowly.

"Oh," I said, snapping from my romantic reverie. "No...not really...a toaster or smartphone can't bring happiness. Not for me, anyway. I'd miss my family and this way of life. I'd miss the fellowship after services, the Christmas potluck, horses, the hard work...."

"I can see why," Paige said. "There seems to be such a fulfillment in the present here, in living for the moment. We could all learn a lot from you."

I kind of cringed when she said that. Her comment was typical of an outsider, putting the Amish on some sort of pedestal. But I let her observation pass, and appreciated it for the sincere sentiment.

She told me a little bit more about her life. Her father was a bank president, so she had grown up in an affluent and prominent household. She wanted to get a job with Legal Aid or as a defense attorney championing underdogs, but her father's banking connections had landed her a plum job with a law firm. Although she was never really comfortable there, her father had convinced her that she was doing noble work, protecting the banks, greasing the gears of capitalism. Deep inside, Paige felt otherwise. But she was young and jobs were difficult to come by, so she rationalized her way into her work and gradually fell into step at the firm. And it's not like Paige was taking peoples' homes personally. She was more of a paper pusher.

We spent the next hour standing by the fire, talking about everything from politics to baseball (Paige was a Cubs fan) to gardening. She had a broad range of interests as did I, so we were very conversationally compatible. She talked about the challenge of gardening in the city and I talked about the versatility of gardening in the country. Neither of us pressed too deeply into our pasts.

I was enjoying her company on that snowy evening. I used to have varied and deep discussions like these with the Stolls who attended our church, but slowly each one got married and moved away. I missed them. As our conversation concluded and we said our good nights, I knew I was attracted to Paige. But I also knew it was a dead-end crush, if that's even what it was. The next morning Paige would leave, and I doubted I'd see her ever again.

CHAPTER EIGHT
ABRAHAM

I was able to fashion a makeshift seal to stop the coolant leak in Paige's car, at least enough so that she was finally able to leave the next morning. She had been a pleasant distraction, but I knew that once she left, I'd have to start dealing with the consequences of what I had done. I wasn't behind bars, but I was still imprisoned by my actions. The next few weeks were spent getting used to life without the weight of a giant dark secret on my shoulders. The four days in jail had made me appreciate even life's smallest pleasures, and I felt a freedom I had never felt before. I worked in the shop, creating some of the best furniture pieces I'd ever done. I was becoming more artisan than craftsman, and despite Dad's initial skepticism, customers were responding and buying more. I was reconnecting with my family and church, and trying to figure out what to do with my life next. But the day I had been dreading arrived.

"It's time, this is the weekend," Mom abruptly said one morning, not even looking up from buttering her toast, the black strings of her *kapp* dangling.

At first I *was* puzzled at what Mom was talking about.

"I talked to Bishop Hochstetler...and he agrees...," Mom said, spooning some home-canned rhubarb jam onto her toast.

It occurred to me that she might be speaking about a confession.

"No...Mom...I can't..."

"You have to...," Mom said.

I stood up from the table and paced. I stared out the window. The first leaves of rhubarb were beginning to unfurl from the thawing earth, a sure sign of spring.

"I didn't mean to harm anyone...I didn't harm the church. This is between Mr. Doty and me, and I'll make it right...somehow," I whispered.

Mom put down her spoon, and her voice took on a bit of an edge. She wiped her hands on her white apron, which looked like a cloud against the blue-sky color of her hand-sewn dress.

"No, Abraham...that's where you're wrong. You didn't just harm Mr. Doty. Do you know how many nights I've spent crying myself to sleep over this? Do you know what a failure your father feels li..." her voice rising.

"But it wasn't your fault...I, and I alone, caused this," I said.

"It no longer matters whose fault it was, you have to confess and cleanseyourself of the sins," Mom said.

"This isn't the church's business."

"Oh, yes it is! How do you think that debt to Mr. Doty was paid? Listen to me. You harmed our family. Do you know how hard it was for your father to go to church the past couple of weeks? You've harmed us, you've harmed yourself, and, yes, you've harmed the church. We are supposed to be an example to outsiders, and you chose the path of greed and took us all down with you...Church is at the Hilty's this weekend. You will confess."

I was 24 years old, but I felt like I was 14. Up until now, there had been murmurs of my misdeeds and I'm sure that more people knew about it than I thought, but most of the church still remained oblivious, and most of me wanted to keep it that way. It's one thing to be in jail, separated from everyone, serving my time. It's another to have to see these people and stand in front of them.

I paced in the kitchen and muttered some words under my breath.

"Abe, you have to do this. If you want to stay in this church, you have to confess. This isn't just about you and Mr. Doty. You hurt each and every one of us, and now you must do the right thing,"

Mom said.

In our church, the sinner isn't the one who actually delivers the confession to the congregation. After confessing the sin to the bishop–which I had already done–he then delivers the news to the church, and the group as a whole decides what to do from there.

After the regular Sunday services had concluded, visitors were asked to leave while some church business was conducted. Bishop Hochstetler walked in front of the congregation, with Jacob Eicher and LeRoy Miller standing solemnly behind him. Bishop Hochstetler, wearing his perfectly pressed black-and-white Sunday best, cleared his throat and then began in a very business-like way.

"And now I need to announce to the congregation that one of our dear brothers has sinned, and we need to decide whether to bestow forgiveness upon him."

The congregation was silent. There hadn't been a confession in the church in about a year, when Mr. Yoder had to admit stealing some tools from a neighbor.

Bishop Hochstetler continued. "The evidence as I have it is that four years ago, Abraham Schwartz falsely applied for a credit card under Mr. Ralph Doty's name."

A collective gasp followed by some murmuring rippled through the congregation. Dad sat stoically on his bench looking straight ahead.

Monroe Hochstetler cleared his throat.

"We have spoken with Abraham at length and are satisfied that he has repented for his sins, feels genuine remorse, and has agreed to work with us to achieve a life in keeping with Christ's," Bishop Hochstetler said, pulling out a folded piece of paper from his inside jacket pocket.

"While I know this is a little unusual procedurally, Abraham really strongly wanted to express his remorse for his sin, so he asked me to read this to all of you."

Dear Church Family:

I want to apologize for my actions. I meant no shame upon the church. I succumbed to a darkness I didn't know was within me. We all have choices to make in our lives and I made some poor ones. I'm deeply sorry for my sins. I feel blessed to be part of such a loving and forgiving church family and I pray that you will embrace me as I try to build a more meaningful life. I walked in the path of darkness, but sometimes it takes dwelling in the darkest night to truly savor the morning light. Know that I am very happy to call this church home and wish to dedicate the rest of my life to building a stronger relationship with God and my church.

Humbly,

Abe Schwartz

I was asked to step outside while the church discussed my sins. I wasn't told until much later what went on inside, so I'm recollecting it here as much as I'm able.

"Is there anyone who doesn't think that Abraham should be forgiven?" Bishop Hochstetler asked.

"Let me just say that there are a lot of people in this church suffering financially. Our farms can't make it, home-based businesses aren't cutting it...for him to just go out on a credit-card-fueled joy-ride is very upsetting," said Pete Raber.

There were some whispers among the congregation.

Amos Raber, one of Pete's seven sons, shifted on his bench. He was dressed in a black vest, crisp white shirt, and black dress slacks. Even though he left the church, he still kept close ties to his family and friends. Still, his presence in church was unusual for an ex-member, even one on good terms. Part of the reason he was held in such high esteem is that while my life was just lurching along, word got out about Amos's increasing sophistication on money matters, something our church often sorely lacked. It all started when Lloyd Lambright sold some property and found himself flush with an extra $20,000.

"Hey, I hear you've been studying these here things called investments…is there anything you can do with my money to make it grow?" Lloyd had asked Amos.

Amos had eagerly accepted the challenge. And soon word started to spread that Amos could make money grow like rhubarb in May. Within six months, he had opened a business called "Plain Investments" with a tidy store-front office on a main street in Berne. The Amish and Mennonite moneyed were smitten with him and on the high yields investing with Amos could bring. His investment success occurring at the same time I was confessing to my sins only poured peroxide onto an open sore. He was likely enjoying my torment because he never had gotten over Rachel choosing me over him. It was a slight he would never put aside.

"I think this sort of financial fraud is inexcusable, it's an outrage, I vote expulsion," Amos suddenly said, springing from his seat to address the congregation.

Roman Neuenschwander whispered to one of his brothers. "Wait a minute, what is he doing in here…? He's not even a church member."

"He's so well respected, it doesn't much matter," the brother whispered back.

"But…" Roman whispered.

"Shhhh! Listen to what he has to say," the brother retorted.

"Well, we all know it's upsetting, but is it a forgivable sin? And does anyone know of anything else Abraham Schwartz has done that should prohibit us from allowing him to be forgiven?" Bishop Hochstetler asked.

Amos Raber stood up and continued.

"Just in observing his behavior, I'm not certain he's committed to church principles the way he should be. He just seems to flaunt the rules too much," Amos said.

Heads nodded.

Roman shook his head with disbelief and stood up.

"In all due to respect to my friend and former baseball adversary, shouldn't these decisions be made by people who are actually in the church? I'm not trying to be argumentative, but isn't that the way the rules work? If you want a say in the church, you have to stay in the church," Roman said.

There was some quiet conversation among people.

"You've been heard, Amos…I think Roman's point is well-taken… any other objections?" Monroe Hochstetler asked.

"He's young, he's got his whole life ahead of him. Yes, this was bad, but we've bestowed forgiveness on those who have done worse," someone said.

There were whispers throughout. Amos stood smugly watching. He'd attempt to accomplish here what he couldn't all those years on the ball-field: a strike-out of me.

In the end, I was called back in, though, and offered forgiveness, which I graciously accepted. I was greeted with hugs and handshakes by almost everyone except for Amos, who glared at me with the same frosty stare that he had on the ball diamond all those years ago. He had been publicly embarrassed again and that didn't sit well. I had a feeling this wouldn't be my last encounter with him.

We are a very forgiving church, and that is one of the traits that has always kept me coming back. I did want–as awkward as it would be–to speak to Rachel, to see if there were any way we could at least come to a place where we could be civil, friendly and forgiving. Perhaps even repair our relationship. But when I got to where the Millers were sitting, I was greeted by a stone-faced sister of Rachel's.

"She's gone, Abe."

"Gone?"

She handed me an envelope, which I folded and put into my pocket. I'd read it later.

I walked out of the Hilty's house and onto a lawn where the grass seemed greener, the sky bluer, and the breeze more soothing than at any time in four years. While I had dreaded the public confession at first, I now felt truly cleansed. Mom was right.

That evening I read the letter from Rachel.

Dear Abe,

We were two ships going in different directions. I'm not sure you'll ever understand, but I needed to feel closer to God. And in a life partner I need someone who I feel can protect and care for me. I want to be a mother, you know that. But I want to be a mother to a child, not a grown man. I pray this doesn't sound bitter, but I couldn't forgive you. Not now, maybe not ever. You were nothing but a big waste of my time. So I thought it best that I leave before church services on Sunday. I didn't want to sit in on the service agreeing to forgive you when I'm not sure I ever could. If I sat in church and publicly agreed to forgive you, I would be no better than you: a liar. Elizabeth has invited me to stay with her family in Ethridge, Tennessee. A new life awaits me there. I know Mom and Dad will not be pleased and I'll miss them terribly but I need to get back to Bible basics. I hope you find happiness someday, Abe. With deepest regret and Christian charity,

Rachel M. Miller

The note cut like a sliver of glass. My eyes grew wet with grief and humiliation. I'm not going to say that I didn't miss Rachel. I did. In fact, now that I was free from the secret I had been shouldering, I felt like maybe had we been able to reconnect, we might have been able to make things work. But for the time being my focus was on getting better, healthier, and mending fences with those I had harmed. I tried to make overtures to Mr. Doty, but he wouldn't see me. I even sent him a letter, but he never responded. I could only hope that time would bring healing. So I did the next best thing I knew, which was writing a letter to Paige, apologizing for what I had done to her Uncle Ralph, dragging her into the whole mess, and thanking her again for what she had done for me. A week later she wrote back.

126

Her first letter was brief. She humbly accepted my apology and had a question about pruning her window-box tomato plants. Everything has to be done on a smaller scale when dealing with city gardening, and I guess she couldn't find the answer she needed on the internet, so

I sent her a letter explaining how to make the most out of her limited garden space. And she wrote back.

Dear Abe:

"You may not believe this but I hardly ever write, at least not with a pen. I T-Y-P-E instead. So I don't know whether you can even decipher my penmanship! I wanted to thank you for sending me the instructions for pruning window-box tomato plants. I've read different things about whether pruning should be done in the morning or evenings. Could you tell me which is best? Before I start hacking away at these beautiful plants, I wanted to make certain!

Thanks! -- Paige

I often wonder whether anything would've happened were not for that one question about pruning. Despite the fact that we seemed to enjoy a connection, a chemistry, shared that evening by the stove, perhaps the correspondence would have ended right there. But I wrote back to her and, once again, she responded.

Dear Abe:

Thank you. I have been, as you advised, pruning in the early morning hours. Plants seem to be responding well. I admit, I had to do some research on your other questions, but, yes, they are planted in the proper soil mix.

Finding anything organic in the city is a challenge, so the idea of having these fresh vegetables within reach even in the winter seems too good to be true. I would love to learn more. Is this something you went to school to study?"

I chuckled. Paige hadn't a clue about the Amish. It made communicating with her all the more refreshing. We exchanged a couple of other letters that spring which I felt deepened our friendship.

Paige,

I hope you are doing well.

Your letter about studying made me laugh. We only go to school to the eighth-grade. I know that might seem crazy to someone as educated as yourself, but I think our Amish schools do a pretty good job. I've heard of cases where an Amish youth decided to leave the church and join the workforce or even go to college. Of course, no employer or university would accept someone without finishing high school, so these youth have taken GED tests and aced them because the Amish schools are so well-grounded in the basics of reading, writing, and math.

I don't think I would have been a good university student. I LOVE to learn, in fact, someone once told me I seem to love books more than people (not true...well, it depends on which people. Ha!). I just was never a good test-taker in school. My eyes would gaze out the window instead. And I'd be curious how things worked but I'd be more likely to learn if I set off to find out on my own instead of sitting in class. Hope that makes sense. I'm not putting down higher education, I admire your smarts. I can't imagine going to school for what, 20 years total? Wow!

I find that, for me, I'm a learning-by-doing kind of man. And I also don't know if...well, let me just say this, if you grew up Amish, you'd see very quickly that it would be quite difficult to have a "desk job." I love to move around, work with my hands, create beauty, and experience things in a way that I don't think would ever make me very happy behind a desk. Speaking of making things, I guess I had best get back to the woodshop. Hope you're winning some cases, Ms. Perry Mason. Ha!

Yours Truly,

Abe

While I was trying to cleanse my life of harmful secrets, I also wasn't too eager for my family to know I was continuing a correspondence with Paige. There wasn't anything wrong with writing to her, at least on the surface. But I didn't need Loretta asking me a bunch of questions, or second worst, Nancy needling me. When I suspected a letter from Paige might come, I went on higher alert as the mailman made his rounds. I could usually see from inside the shop the mailman's arrival, so I tactfully, subtly went outside for a stroll, glanced in the box, and if there was a letter from Paige I'd pluck it out and stuff it in my pocket for reading later. I admit I felt a little uncomfortable...after all, it was plucking mail that got me into trouble in the first place. But this was different, this was *my* mail I was plucking.

Dear Abe:

I feel like I'm on an episode of the Waltons, actually doing old-fashioned letter writing! Ha!

I hope you don't think I somehow think even one ounce less of you because you don't have a college degree or high school diploma. Yes, in the non-Amish world, these pieces of paper are helpful markers to determine a person's ability to hit a goal, but, in my opinion, that's really all they are. A diploma doesn't measure intelligence. I've rarely found that a scroll of paper determines someone's smarts. I work with plenty of people who have college degrees, but some of them don't seem any smarter than a loaf of bread. You seem to have a much keener intellect than most.

Fondly,

Paige

I wrote back to her.

Dear Paige,

Thank you for the kind words. I agree with you wholeheartedly about a diploma not being an accurate measure of intelligence. Among the Amish, education becomes very individualized. If a person chooses to exercise their intellect, they can through reading, study, observation, and experiments. I like to think I have a pretty well-rounded education based on a course of study of my own design. But I also know some Amish who aren't very intelligent. Sometimes, though, they are just intelligent in certain areas. Take Rosanna Keim's bakery down in Milroy. For the longest time the sign on her door said, "Fresh Kake and Bred Each Morning." No one had the heart to tell her that the sign was misspelled. I'm sure

*you'd agree with me that most people know how to spell "bread"
and "cake." Rosanna Keim didn't, but boy could she BAKE a cake.
And not just bake it, she could explain the science behind baking,
like yeast fermentation, bread leavening, and even altitude's effects
of baking (never knew how she knew since Milroy is on a sea-level
plain). But--and no disrespect meant--she was dumb as a bar of
soap when it came to any other topic. Nice a woman as you'll ever
meet, but conversing with her about something other than baking
was an exercise in intellectual futility, although I think she could
have taught a food science course at a great university, and I mean
that. Anyway, I am rambling. My point is that we all have special
gifts and talents, and I think the key to a happy life is to find what
you are good at and shine.*

*I bet you are good at what you do and I admire the hard work and
skill it must take to be a lawyer that interprets and analyzes the law.*

*Thanks again for taking the time to write. Mom and Loretta have
been baking feverishly these days. Got the annual parochial auction
and bake sale coming up, so that means our house is filled with the
scents of fresh kake (ha!), pies, and cookies. Yum! Feel free to stop
by if you get hungry.*

Yours truly,

Abe

But it was a letter I received in early May that set my mind and heart racing.

Dear Abe,

Sorry it's been a while since I've written. I've been busy with a grueling caseload. Tell your mother I miss her oatmeal pie. I've told some of my family and friends about it, and they say it sounds positively horrible, but I tell them they haven't tasted Salome Schwartz's!

I've got to go to Cincinnati the week of the 20th, so perhaps I could stop by? I want to check in on Uncle Ralph and I'd love to see your garden when it isn't covered in a foot of snow! ☺ And maybe I'll take you up on that piece of "kake!" ☺

Paige

I'll admit that the two weeks after I received her letter about visiting, time seemed to crawl. I did tell Mom that I had gotten a note in the mail from Paige about visiting, so her presence wouldn't come as a complete surprise. And when the day finally arrived, I was bounding around like an excited schoolboy. Trying to conceal my excitement from the rest of my family was difficult. One night I absent-mindedly left a horse stall open and Cinnamon, Apple, and Summer all spent the night roaming the pasture. Another time I vacuously spooned maple syrup instead of honey onto my peanut butter sandwich. The letters had kept us connected in a way that ignited infatuation within me. Maybe I was just filling the void left by Rachel's absence. I didn't really know.

Church services arrived the Sunday before she was to stop by, and the sermon seemed to creep by like a thick river of molasses.

Church services in our community aren't what some people might expect. At least, they weren't back then. We held them every other Sunday, with the services starting around 9 a.m. We would all arrive in our black and white Sunday best, crisply-pressed white shirts, black vests and trousers for the men, black dresses and white capes for the women. Most of the homes outside of Berne were surrounded by flat fields where we could park our buggies. Tourists sometimes would slowly cruise by on Sunday mornings just to gaze at a field full of black buggies. I can't say I blame the tourists because it would be quite a sight if you hadn't seen it before. Most of the time tourists are respectful, but one time a man and woman barged into services over at the Yutzys, demanding a front-row seat. The man was dressed in a garish red and white Hawaiian shirt and khaki shorts, and his wife was wearing what I think they call a moo-moo, and had a huge camera around her neck. They tried to pay $20 for the after-service meal. It was left to Monroe Hochstetler to tell the couple tactfully that this was a private church service, not a Convention and Visitors Bureau stop.

During services, people sometimes mill around while the bishop preaches. It's hard to sit for three hours on hard wooden benches. Homemade chocolate chip cookies are handed out for the children during church. Outsiders might think that much church would be pure drudgery, but it isn't. Our church is like one big family, and the fellowship and togetherness are what anchors us. But on that Sunday all I could think about was Paige's visit, and some people probably picked up on my distraction.

"Good morning, Abe, how's work at the shop coming?" asked Elmer Gingerich.

"Oh, she's wonderful," I said dreamily.

"Huh?" Elmer said.

"Um...oops, I mean, IT's wonderful. Work is wonderful, good, solid, lots of orders. Yes, plenty to keep us busy," I said, pulling my head from the clouds.

"Uh, glad to hear it," Elmer said as we headed into an outbuilding for services.

The Amish practice of home worship has long separated us from most other churches, and I love the custom. It's very unpretentious. Of course, all the furniture has to be cleared out of some rooms so we can set up the benches. Other times, if a person is lucky enough to have a roomy out-building, the services will be held in there, or even outdoors if the weather is nice enough.

Anyway, I tried to mix and mingle at services that Sunday as I would usually do. I, of course, also wore my best church clothes and eagerly indulged in the lunch of fried chicken, mashed potatoes and gravy, coleslaw, red beets, cheese, green bean casserole, and plenty of pie for dessert. But my mind was clearly not focused on the moment.

Elmo Gingerich, his plate piled high with fried chicken, peered at my plate.

"You always put gravy on your coleslaw?" he asked, puzzled.

I looked down at my plate, embarrassed.

"Um...well, it seemed a little dry," I replied sheepishly.

Elmo shook his head before digging into his own food.

May in Indiana is truly like being cradled in Heaven's bosom. Each spring the prairie behind our house became a carnival of colors: blue-eyed Marys, black-eyed Susans, pasture roses, and dozens of other flower varieties to sooth one's soul. I always imagined if that if anyone needed proof of the existence of Divinity, one only needed to look at the soft beauty of flowers. A spot farthest back on our property, not far from the banks of Loblolly Creek where a stunning patch of red trillium could soften even the most jaded of men.

So with our driveway lined by wild spring bouquets of phlox and blue-eyed Marys, and a toasty May sun warming the fields, it was a starkly different scene than when Paige was here during the blizzard.

Paige stepped out of her car, looking as stunning as the warm spring day. Her beautiful amber-colored hair pulled back into that ponytail again, tan slacks that accentuated her slim shape, and an azure short-sleeve blouse that harmonized with the brilliant blue of her eyes. Our letters had left me hungry, wanting more, wanting to connect. I imagined taking her on a walk back to the place in our woods and showing her the patch of red trillium as we talked and learned more about one another. But I couldn't appear over-eager, and had to make my move subtly and smoothly. I watched from the window and let Loretta do the welcoming. Paige was so gorgeous and mysterious and I wanted to know her more, but my yearning was quickly extinguished as I walked outside to greet her.

She had not come alone.

CHAPTER NINE

ABRAHAM

"Abe, so good to see you!" Paige said. "Scott, this is my friend Abe. Abe, this is Scott,"

Scott reached out to me with a firm handshake.

"This is the man who fixed my car," Paige said.

"Oh, it wasn't anything…just some seals that needed replacing," I said humbly.

"How much do I owe you?" Scott said matter-of-factly, pulling out a checkbook.

"Owe me?" I asked, startled.

"You fixed her car, kept her warm, dry, and fed, I want to pay you," Scott said.

Hmmmmm. I silently thought that one of those new solar-powered milkers would be nice, sure would save chore time. But I was vaguely insulted by the gesture, as if he were somehow trying to wipe away the entire episode with his big bank account, as if Paige's stay were just another business transaction.

"Tell you what: if my buggy ever breaks down in Chicago, you can fix it, take me in, and we'll just call it even," I said, the feeble attempt at humor seemingly satisfying him, I thought.

"Sure thing, but I'd make sure I locked up my credit cards first," Scott guffawed.

Everyone fell silent.

At that snide and cruel remark, a cocktail of rage and embarrassment swirled within me. Paige glared at Scott, a death look that could have brought down a wooly mammoth if they still walked the earth.

"Um…okay…hey, sport, what is that accent of yours…I seem to have heard it before, but I'm not sure where?" Scott asked. I wasn't sure if he was being patronizing again or genuinely trying to get the conversation back on track. I doubted the latter.

"It's Indiana hillbilly…what accent is yours?" I retorted.

"No, really, what is it?" Scott said. "I think I've heard it before."

"Oh, you've been to Switzerland?" I pressed.

"No, it's just that I...oh, wait a minute...I know, I've heard you all speak something called Pennsylvania Dutch...I think I saw that in a movie," Scott said.

I cut him off. "It's a dialect of Bernese Swiss German," I replied tersely. "What movie did you see that in?"

I could tell Paige was uncomfortable with the tension between Scott and me. Look, in reality, I knew that I didn't have a shot with Paige. But even with the very real sins I had committed, I still had some male pride to defend. And with his perfectly-tailored clothes and squeaky loafers that could signal a ship with their shine, he just rubbed me the wrong way. He seemed like a smart-enough guy but I doubted he could find his way out of a bread box.

"Can we see Summer and Cinnamon?" Paige interjected.

"Sure, we can see Summer. I think she missed you," I said.

We headed into the darkness of our barn. Beautiful chestnut-colored Summer was munching on hay in her stall.

"Last time I saw you it was a little colder," Paige said, reaching out to scratch Summer on the nose.

Summer snorted agreement and continued munching on hay.

"So, I take it for you Summer is sort of comparable to a car?" Scott inquired

I nodded, even though I really didn't totally find the analogy workable. If something breaks on a car, you just take it to a mechanic to get it fixed. If something happens to Summer and the vet can't fix her, we have to put her down. A buggy is more comparable to a car than a horse, but I stayed silent.

"Well, you sure do have high gas prices beat with that contraption!" Scott said, kicking the buggy spokes.

"Steel wheels," I replied, noticing a wince from Scott.

"Where did you go to school?" Scott asked

"West Branch Parochial. Where did you go?" I answered. West Branch was the name of the little Amish school I attended just down the road. It actually is more than one-room, but non-Amish people seem hell-bent on calling our schools "one-room." It connects them to that TV show "*Little House on the Prairie*" that I always heard so much about while growing up. But our schools usually consist of at least two rooms and a basement.

"Loyola University School of Law," Scott replied.

Paige interrupted, "Oh, can I show Scott the sleigh!?"

"Sure, she's all packed up for the season, but we can go into storage to see it," I offered.

We walked through the barn, straw crunching beneath our feet. The horse manure marinating in the spring warmth added a pungent smell to the air, and I had to stifle some chuckles as I watched Scott dodge droppings and then grimace when he was unsuccessful, soiling the soles of his prized loafers.

And there it was: my winter pride and joy sitting silently and solemnly awaiting the next snow.

"Abe made it himself," Paige said, beaming.

"All that is missing is Santa and some reindeer," Scott chuckled.

I was finding his attitude patronizing and condescending. Whether it was intentional or not, I'll not judge. But I decided to retreat to more familiar conversational turf.

"This really gave me some headaches to make, but I think she turned out well. When you do wood-working, do you prefer a left-tilt or a right-tilt table saw?" I asked Scott.

He stared blankly and stammered. "Well…"

"Hey, honey, why don't you show Abe your new iPhone," Paige countered, trying to extricate Scott from the conversation.

"Oh, yeah, it's pretty awesome…I can look up case files, the weather in Tokyo, and the best Sushi Bar in Wrigleyville, all simultaneously. And look at this, isn't this cool, it can even pair which wine works best with what meal. For instance, what are we having for supper tonight?

"Noodle casserole," I answered.

Scott fiddled with his iPhone. "Ah, a nice Sangiovese or Dolcetto."

"Why don't you just go with the wine you like best?" I asked.

Scott looked at me puzzled.

I wasn't trying to be a smart-aleck, but sometimes those machines really do keep a person from just doing what comes naturally.

"Supper!"

I thought Paige looked relieved at Mom's call to the table. The three of us headed into the kitchen. Scott made a dash for the sink to wash his hands, only to find himself searching vainly for a faucet. Scott whispered to Paige, "Um, don't these people have a bathroom?"

"You just passed it, honey," Paige said, motioning to the outhouse outside.

"You wash your hands in there?" Scott whispered.

"No, you wash your hands THERE," Paige said, motioning to a water-closet off the kitchen. Inside was a red-painted pump situated over a small basin. A quick pump up and down of the handle, and streams of cold well-water would squirt out. A bar of homemade lye soap sat on the basin's edge. Growing up with well-water, you could pump, soap, and rinse in almost one long, fluid motion. But a city boy like Scott awkwardly fumbled with the handle, splashing water onto his crisp, designer shirt. Some of the younger children stifled laughs as they saw Scott approaching the supper table with water splattered all over his shirt.

A long oak table, big enough to fit all eight of our family plus a few guests, was set with the plates reserved for company. Along with noodle casserole, Mom served her famous baked chicken, each piece rolled in homemade cereal to give every wing, thigh, breast, or drumstick a crispy coating. The twins and Benjamin always fought over who would get the drumsticks. We usually had chickens clucking around our property, and come butchering day they'd be cut up and stored for occasions just like this. Mom's cereal coating gave the chicken this combination of crunch and tenderness that I've never been able to find duplicated. A wicker basket filled with homemade rolls the size of softballs begged for butter, or at least Mom's homemade rhubarb jam and wild dandelion jelly. Both were on the table. A plate of sliced cheese, stuffed pork chops, and home-canned corn golden as doubloons gave the table additional color.

Salome Schwartz was often said to make the best pies this side of Chicago, and she didn't disappoint with an assortment of apple, peach, and oatmeal pies, not to mention some "double treat cookies" made by the twins. Double treat cookies were a local favorite packed with peanut butter and chocolate. Some people add butterscotch to make them "triple treat cookies."

There was plenty of chatter around the table, but as we all sat it quickly died down. Heads began to bow. But not Scott's.

"Well, look at this spread, if this is how you eat every day I..."

Paige elbowed Scott in the side, and he looked at her puzzled and pained.

"Shhhh, silent prayer time," Paige whispered exasperatedly.

So the room was soon quiet as we all reflected on our bounty. Scott sat sullenly.

But just as quickly the room came back to life, and the table hosted a clanking gathering of pouring pitchers, passing plates, and excited chatter.

"I didn't realize corn was in season," Scott said between bites, spitting out tiny flecks of food as he spoke. Had my father been sitting across from him at the time, I was certain that little bits of sprayed corn would have buried themselves in his beard.

"It's canned. Last season's harvest," Mom said, holding up a glass jar filled with corn.

"Looks like a jar," Scott said matter-of-factly as he buttered a hunk of homemade bread.

The twins exchanged glances.

"No, silly, it's home-canned corn. That way they can enjoy their garden year-round," Paige explained.

"Well, why don't they call it home-jarring if it's not stored in a tin can?"

Everyone fell silent.

"Work hard in the garden all summer and then you relax and enjoy it in the winter," Mom explained.

"Green beans in the summer means getting fresh in the winter," Dad said with a hearty laugh and a wink.

Mom blushed.

"Marvin!"

"Is canning difficult to learn?" Paige asked.

"It's just what we've always done. I've taught all my girls how to home can," Mom said.

"Maybe you could show me sometime?" Paige asked.

"And maybe how to make a pie crust" Mom chirped. "You still buying the frozen kind?"

"Sara Lee and I are very close friends, I'll just put it that way," Paige responded.

Scott never did seem comfortable at supper. I think he was accustomed to less earthy entrees.

"Oh, wow, these rolls are amazing and this jelly is superb," Scott said. What kind is it?"

"Dandelion," Loretta said.

Scott grimaced, managed a weak smile, and set down the rest of his roll.

The talk was stilted and awkward, but Loretta always had a talent for stirring up conversation. She asked Scott about his job. "You are an attorney also?" ~~Loretta asked.~~

"Sure am. My grandfather was a lawyer, and so was Dad. My Mom often joked that I was learning to take depositions before I was even potty-trained," Scott said.

"So are you like that fella that used to be in those TV law shows, what was his name? Perry Mason?" Dad asked.

Scott explained that his brand of lawyering wasn't the flashy, glamorous kind shown on TV. Scott and Paige both worked at the same firm, and it sounded to me like a pure drudgery of paperwork, long hours, cheap coffee, and dingy offices. Definitely not for me. Paige and Scott were attorneys with one of the largest mortgage mills in the Midwest. Actually, the firm frowned upon the term "mortgage mill", but that's what people called it. As I listened to them describe their jobs, it made me even more thankful that I had chosen to remain in the Amish faith.

"My job is to mitigate losses for the banks," Paige explained. Most often these cases don't go to trial, it's just a matter of protecting the bank's assets.

Scott nodded in agreement at Paige's explanation. My family politely listened, but I think we all agreed that these people worked in an unappealing profession.

"Let's not let the Neuenschwanders know they were here," Loretta whispered to Mom. Mom nodded vigorously and then changed the subject of the conversation.

CHAPTER TEN
ABRAHAM

I had been doing a lot of thinking, reading, and praying, trying to figure out what had led me down the wrong path in my life. I wanted to find ways to be true to myself and true to the church. It was all so difficult to sort out. Were Loretta and Rachel correct, that people can either choose a right road or a wrong one and there's no middle? Or can genuinely good people do horrible things but still be good people?

I wish I knew why, but I think I've come to the conclusion that humans are inherently resistant to change. It's like pushing a door, a door to change, and something is on the other side pushing back. But people *can* change. I've seen people change. But it's not overnight or easy, even with so much at stake. People seek the familiar, even if the familiar is ugly and uncomfortable.

Having gotten into trouble with the mail before you'd think I would have treated it with the utmost deference and respect. And if Paige hadn't been involved, maybe I would have. After Mr. Doty found out how his mail had been compromised, he opened a P.O. box in town and his mail quit coming to our house. On the rare occasion that a piece slipped through and arrived, Dad delivered it to him personally. On one particularly pleasant spring day, I went to get our mail, and among the junk was a letter addressed to Salome Schwartz from Paige.

What happened next was never intended. I was trying to be extra-careful, extra-scrupulous, but curiosity and infatuation got the best of me. I picked up the envelope and held it to the sunlight, hoping to be able to read a word or two, maybe. But the paper Paige had written on was too thick. So I held it up to one of our kerosene lanterns. Much to my horror, the edges of the envelope began to blacken. I cursed. I had held it too close to the lamp. So, it was either tell Mom I was trying to read her mail, or just pretend the letter never arrived. I chose the latter. I stuffed it into my back pocket, and read it upstairs. The righteous road was proving more difficult to follow than I had planned.

Dear Salome:

I was eating my lunch outside in a park on the shores of Lake Michigan, and it was so peaceful that I just thought I would write you a note. First of all, I apologize if my boyfriend Scott offended you or your family any. He can be a bit set in his ways, a bit inflexible. His behavior embarrassed me. I'm sort of taking a break from him right now. I need some breathing room. But you don't want to hear about all that! ☺ I just really wanted to apologize for his behavior and also to ask you if I might take you up on that offer to learn how to make a proper pie crust? I found out that I have to go to Columbus, Ohio, for work on the 15th. I'd love to surprise my parents with a homemade pie when they come for supper sometime! I'm not sure if this will reach you in time for you to write back to me

and I hate to just drop by. I'll be leaving on Monday of next week.
I'm sure Abe wants nothing to do with me after Scott's rude behavior
toward him, so maybe I can come in the morning when the men are
in the shop? Although, I'd like to pop over there and apologize to
him personally. What Abe did was wrong, but he didn't deserve
rudeness from a stranger.
Yours Truly,

Paige Roberts

My church's relationship with technology is much more nuanced and complicated than outsiders realize. Our church has set of unwritten rules that we call the *ordnung*, and those rules draw a deep distinction between *owning* certain technologies and *using* them. But that's for us to sort out and really shouldn't be the concern of non-church members. For some reason, however, outsiders love to cackle when they see us using a phone or a computer.

It wasn't terribly uncommon for an Amish person to use the library, and even occasionally the computers there. The Berne Public Library has a hitching post out back for us so we can safely secure our horses while we're inside. There used to be a librarian there who, like the tourists, seemed to regard herself as some sort of self-appointed guardian of the *ordnung*.

"I'd like to register for 15 minutes of computer time," I said.

"Oh…*really?*" the librarian said.

I fumed, but contained myself and quietly nodded.

I pulled my straw hat down over my eyes enough that I hoped it would disguise me from any potentially prying Amish eyes.

Your letter arrived so I thought I would surprise you. I know you needed an answer quickly and I was heading into Berne anyway, so I sneaked into the public library here. I bet you didn't think I could type! I even created my own account so you can email me back. I'll come back into town on Friday to check back. But, yes, Mom says you are welcome anytime to drop by." - Abe
AmishAbe@zapmail.com

Of course, Mom didn't say that. She never knew about the letter. I was upset with myself for lying, but this lie seemed harmless by comparison to what I had done. Still, the feral pigs were multiplying again.

Friday came and I hitched up Ruby for a quick run into town to check my email account. I was hoping I could slip out during the lunch hour without being noticed. Ruby was the family's fastest horse, a three-year-old chestnut-colored mare who could make an effortless sprint into Berne in about 10 minutes. But as I was hitching Ruby to my gig, Mom was standing at the door.

"This is your second trip into town this week." Mom noted.

"Yep. Need anything?" I said nonchalantly.

"Mmmm-hmmm," Mom said, standing in the doorway, hands on hips.

"Something's up." Mom whispered to Loretta.

I arrived at the library, eager to check my email. But not too eager. I pulled my hat down and tried to be inconspicuous.

"I'd like to register for a computer," I said, cursing to myself that it was the same stiff librarian with the hair in a bun.

"Sure. And, sir," she whispered, leaning over the desk. "You might want to make sure you log out of your email account next time. When I went to reset the timer after you used it last, you hadn't logged out."

Her loud whisper seemed to echo throughout the library like we were in a pharaoh's empty tomb.

"Okay, thanks," I said, reddening, wondering whether she had seen who I was emailing. Settling into the computer console I excitedly logged in.   My anticipation was rewarded with an email from Paige.

Dear Abe:

I can't tell you how surprised I was to get your email. I almost thought it was junk and deleted it. I can't believe you EMAILED me. Wow!! You brightened what was an otherwise dull morning at the office. I'm staring at a stack of cases. Kind of depressing. This isn't exactly what I had envisioned in law school. But, enough of my whining. I'll be excited to see everyone. Tell your Mom that I'm looking forward to making a pie crust with her! And tell Loretta I said "hello" also. See you Monday!

Paige

I probably should have thought through my response better, but I was too excited to write a carefully-crafted missive. I'm a realist at heart, and I didn't really think there was the possibility of anything, but Paige was attractive and interesting and that was enough for me.

"Go!" I yelled to Ruby, excitedly tearing out of the library parking lot and heading for home, the steel wheels of the buggy clattering as they rumbled onto the pavement. Ruby's hooves rhythmically clopped against the pavement in her speedy gallop. I had a lot to think about.

I arrived home just in time for supper. The table was full with plates of pan-fried perch that Daniel and Benjamin had caught in a nearby pond. Mom and Loretta had filleted and rolled them in a buttery mix of bread crumbs that magnified the crispy, flaky fish. Homemade bread, rhubarb jam, sliced cheese, broccoli salad, and cheesy carrot casserole rounded out the meal. As usual, we bowed our heads in silent prayer before digging in.

"So, anything new today?" Dad asked. After spending a day in the woodshop,
that's typically how he began the supper-table conversation. It was just a meaningless
ice-breaker, but it usually got the chatter flowing.

"Other than Abe running into town again?" Nancy chortled.

I glared at her.

She stuffed a fork-full of perch into her mouth and sat silently.

"How did Marvin, Jr., do at fishing?" Dad asked.

"Not bad, he helped me reel in one of the perch," Benjamin said. Marvin, Jr.'s eyes sparkled underneath his mop of curly brown hair as he imitated an adult casting a fishing line, moving his arms in an exaggerated motion. Everyone laughed.

"Oh, Lizzie Neuenschwander is having a quilting bee…she stopped by with some fresh beets earlier today. Ours have been slow, but hers are coming along well. Anyway, she invited me to the bee."

"See, Mom, they do like your quilting," Loretta said. "You're always so hard on yourself."

"They just want me for my Long John Rolls," Mom said, putting a big bite of broccoli salad in her mouth. The rolls were another Salome Schwartz specialty. They were frosted, deep-fried doughnuts in the shape of a stogie. Although some of the young adults would snicker at their vaguely phallic shape, they were one of Mom's most sought-after confections.

"Oh c'mon, Mom…you know you always have a good time at these things. You should go, get out of the house a little. What day is Lizzie's quilting bee?" I asked, sipping a glass of cool water.

"You're right, maybe I will go. It's Monday. Starts at 9 a.m. We'll be working our fingers to the bone all day!"

I almost spit out my drink.

"No!" I blurted out, dabbing a napkin to my mouth. "I mean,

no…don't you have…to sew Benjamin a new shirt for the Hilty wedding?"

Mom stared at me.

"For Heaven's sake, you were the one that just said I should get out a bit. The shirt won't go anywhere. Are you sure you're feeling okay, Abe? You just seem a little skittish lately. Maybe with all the stresses you've had you should make an appointment with Melvin Wainwright?"

Melvin Wainwright was the local Amish herbalist, who peddled all sorts of potions, vitamins, and chiropractor-type cures. Don't get me wrong, I think there's a place for holistic medicines. And I definitely believe in nature's ability to offer a cure, but I also believe in the merits of modern medicine, so sometimes Melvin's methods made me nervous.

"I'm fine, Mom. I just…I was just surprised the quilting bee is on a Monday. I know that's usually laundry day."

"Since when are you so in-tune with all the women's work?" Nancy asked.

I glared at her. Again, she fell silent and started shoveling pieces of perch into her mouth.

I'll admit that I was uneasy with the way things were unfolding. The lying, concocting cover stories, manipulating, those were all habits I had slipped into during over the past four years, and I was finding them maddeningly difficult to shake. I had vowed to change, and this behavior troubled me, but I figured I'd deal with it later. For now, I needed Loretta's help. Mom wasn't going to be around Monday and Paige was expecting to learn how to make a homemade pie crust. I can make a darn sturdy sleigh, but a pie crust?

The next morning, after breakfast, Mom had gone outside to do a little weeding.Loretta grabbed her gardening gloves and prepared to do the same. Nancy stayed in the kitchen to tackle the dishes. I pulled Loretta aside on her way to the garden. "Um...'Retta...can I ask you a favor?"

"I won't wash your buggy!" Loretta said.

"No, it's not that...something bigger," I said in a low whisper.

I explained the whole fiasco with the letter from Paige, the impulsive urge to peek at it that resulted in the near-charred envelope, the secret trips into Berne to use the computer at the library.

"Your pie crusts are just as good as Mom's, so could you please be here Monday to show Paige how to make one?"

"No. No, definitely not. Monday is Timothy's first weekday off from work in forever and he is planning on taking me fishing. "

"You don't even like to fish!" I protested.

Loretta blushed. "No, but in this case I like the fisherman."

"But you can see him anytime," I said, trying to plead my case rationally without resorting to begging.

"You've got to be kidding me. After all you've been through here, you are opening other peoples' mail, sending emails, using the internet...if Bishop Hochstetler found out..." Loretta said, her voice trailing off.

"Paige is pretty, she's nice, I like her...I know maybe I didn't handle this right...can you just help me this one time? I'll do the milking every morning next week if you'll do it."

"Every morning?" Loretta asked. "I don't know, I was really looking forward to spending the day with Timothy."

"I'll clean the horse stalls this weekend, so you can spend time with Timothy on Saturday instead. And I'll talk to Dad and see if we can finally start work on a new chest of drawers for you."

"Stalls cleaned and a bureau, finally? Deal. You do the milking, clean the stalls Saturday, and start work on my bureau. Wow, I wish Paige would have visited a long time ago," Loretta said with a cheerful grin, disappearing out the front door, her long rust-colored dress clashing with the green of the garden.

On Monday, I watched from the upstairs window as Paige arrived. I didn't want to appear over-eager. I ran my hands over my shirt to smooth out any wrinkles. Loretta had pressed my best shirt and denim pants last night for me. I really did appreciate Loretta's help, and I know that after all the lecturing she had done about staying true to church rules, playing co-conspirator was difficult for her. But I think she genuinely wanted to see me happy, and a little fun flirtation was all this was. She knew I was lonely after Rachel left, so I think she was just stretching the bounds of her own judgment to accommodate me. Meanwhile, I was elated at Paige's arrival that morning. She looked as beautiful as I remembered. And this time she was alone.

CHAPTER 11
ABRAHAM

On the day Paige arrived to learn the craft of crust, the temperature made the afternoon feel like the bottom of a frying pan. She was wearing cream-colored slacks that went down to about mid-calf on her tan, slender, smooth legs. People called them capris. I may know a lot about weather, constellations, how build a sturdy china cabinet, or even the fertility cycles of a sow, but please don't ask me about women's fashion. Whatever the pants were called, they looked pretty on Paige.

And she was wearing a yellow button-down blouse, loose-fitting, comfortable cotton for such a hot day. On her feet were a pair of yellow flip-flops that matched the color of her shirt. Going barefoot in the warm weather is as much a part of Amish identity as suspenders, straw hats, buggies, and bonnets. Some elitist snobs (that's what I call them) look down on this practice as dirty, uncultured, or a sign of being poor, but, really, to us, it's just an emblem of freedom and connectedness with the earth. Our feet, while not necessarily the prettiest things to look at, were never meant to be shackled and smothered in shoes. At least, that's my opinion. I'm no doctor or podiatrist, but I suspect that perhaps the reason feet aren't always pretty is that they are stuffed into shoes day in and day out. Paige's toes were painted with a pleasant shade of pink. Of course, an Amish woman in pursuit of perpetual plainness would never partake in such a vain cosmetic indulgence, and to this day I still prefer the natural color, but on Paige the polish looked pretty.

"It's wonderful to be here again," Paige said, inhaling deeply, her feet avoiding a couple of smelly gifts from the horses that had dropped onto our driveway and were serving as buffets for the flies.

Benjamin, Daniel, and Verena shared the every-other-day chore of cleaning up the "horse gifts" left on the driveway from the comings and goings of the horses. They'd put the manure in a compost pile where Mom would use it as a steady supply of first-rate fertilizer for our garden. Often when outsiders would stop by and ask Mom how she got such fat cucumbers, plump cardinal-colored tomatoes, and lettuce with leaves the size of sails, she would reply jokingly, "Get rid of your car."

Five runty apple trees grew in a cluster between our dirt driveway and our house. The weather had been unusually dry, so our driveway was dusty and rutted with buggy-wheel tracks. The apple trees were in bloom, the flowers fragrant, not unlike the fruit they'll become. A couple of two-liter 7UP bottles hung from the trees, which caught Paige's attention.

"What are those?" she asked.

"Bug traps. Mom makes them," Loretta said. "She puts a banana peel, one cup of sugar, one cup of apple cider vinegar, and fills the bottle 3 /4 full of water, shakes them, and then hangs them on the lowest tree branch."

"Neat, does it work?" Paige inquired.

"Takes a few days but, yes, they work. Once they fly in, they don't fly out," Loretta observed.

Mom had hung laundry that morning, so the lines were festive flags of rust-colored dresses, white aprons, and dark denim trousers. Mom and Loretta made almost all of our clothes.

"The colors of your clothes are beautiful," Paige observed.

"We don't make our own underwear. Those are Wal-Mart," Loretta whispered with a giggle.

Paige was greeted like family by Velma and Verena scampering out of the garden, each grabbing one of her arms so she was practically being dragged into the house. Any lingering awkwardness over how we all had met seemed to have disappeared.

Loretta poured a glass of iced spearmint tea, and put out a plate of cookies.

"Mmmm, thank you!" Nancy said, wriggling into a seat at the kitchen table.

"Hey, those are for Paige. You get your own!" Loretta said.

"So where is everyone else?" Paige asked.

"Well, Mom is at a quilting bee over at the Neuenschwanders. Dad is over in the shop with Daniel, which is where Abraham should be right now also," Loretta said, glaring at me.

I took the hint and headed over to the shop. As much as I wanted to be spending time with Paige, we did have some bookcases to finish, and Loretta and Paige had pie crusts to work on. I figured I'd have time to visit with Paige after they were done.

PAIGE

Loretta opened one of the cabinets, revealing stack after stack of shiny stainless steel bowls of all sizes.

"Those are some huge bowls," I uttered, awestruck.

"Imagine mixing slaw for 200 people. This dish almost isn't large enough!" Loretta said, pointing to a massive bowl that I thought looked like it could hold three soccer balls and still have room left over. "But we don't need that one." Loretta instead brought out a couple of smaller ones and set them on the kitchen table. Next she removed wooden spoons from a drawer and scooped out flour from a big ceramic canister on the counter.

"Mom buys flour in-50 pound bags and puts a little of it at a time in here. It's cheaper that way," she said, pulling a rolling pin out of a drawer. "This was great-great grandmother's rolling pin, so it's seen a few generations of crusts. My great-great grandfather made this himself out of beechwood."

"I guess I was just spoiled growing up. I never had to learn how to do some of these things, like making a pie crust."

"Spoiled because you didn't have to do it? Making a pie crust isn't a chore. Chores are milking or doing the dishes, but making a homemade pie crust is relaxing, at least to me," Loretta said soothingly. She explained to me that there are a couple of ways to make a crust. "One is called "pat-a-pan" and can be made right in the pan, no rolling. It's a great recipe for just starting out. If you want a little more advanced, you can roll your dough out."

"You're a superb teacher," I said, plunging my hands into some elastic-like dough.

"That looks perfect. You're a champion cruster. Roll it out just a little thinner and make it so it's the size of a dinner plate. You want some overhang on the edges of the pie pan. Then flute the edges," Loretta said, pinching some dough between two moist fingers. "I keep a small bowl of water on the table to dip my fingers in for fluting," she advised.

"But, ewwww, old Mrs. Yoder used to just put her fingers in her mouth to moisten the crust! I saw her do it…eeeeewww!" Nancy said.

"Okay, thanks, Nancy, but I think I can handle this lesson," Loretta said.

"Next class: making your own lattice top!" Nancy clapped.

"Oh, my gosh, I will be so glad when detasseling starts," Loretta whispered to me. "She really needs something to do."

A warm breeze blew in the kitchen window fluttering the white curtains and carrying the summery scents of freshly mowed grass, rhubarb, and clover.

"Detasseling?"

"I spent three summers detasseling. Worked my way up to crew leader," Loretta beamed.

"But what is detasseling?" I asked.

"Oh, you've never heard of detasseling? Certain varieties of corn require cross-pollination, a way to hybridize corn. For many of the children around here, that's their first job. It's long hours of hard work outdoors, but they make a lot of fast friends."

We both looked at the finished crust. I was proud of it. It looked a little rough, but all-in-all it was not a bad first effort. I vowed to try more baking of my own back home.

"Hmmmm, now what are we going to put it in?" Loretta asked. "We can't just eat a plain pie crust."

"I hadn't thought about that," I countered.

"Just fix a bread pie. Don't need all those fancy fruits!" a crackly voice chirped from afar.

Grandma Ada was coming into the room aided by her cane.

"Bread pie?" I said, "Sounds....interesting."

168

"It's not bad…Mom calls it 'poor man's pie,'" Loretta whispered.

"I don't remember a lot and my eyesight isn't great, but I can still hear plenty good. It's not a pie for the poor," Grandma Ada admonished.

"Her hearing really isn't that good," Loretta murmured.

"….You can fill it with day-old bread. Here's a loaf leftover from yesterday. Salome was going to put it out for the birds, but we can use it in the pie," Grandma Ada lectured, getting a bit more spring in her step at taking over the kitchen.

"Okay, I remember the rest. Crumble it up and fill the crust. Add some milk, cinnamon, sugar, and that's it. Bake at 350 and it's really not a bad pie," Loretta conceded.

"Of course it's not," Grandma Ada huffed, shaking her head. "Children are too spoiled today. Everything's so fancy!"

ABRAHAM

Grandma Ada Graber had lived all of her 91 years in the Berne area. At 5'3, she was a petite woman but she had a flinty streak that still showed itself even at her age. Strands of pearl-colored hair contrasted with her black *kapp*. Most days she would wear a dark turquoise dress. With each passing year, Mom would find herself having to make increasingly smaller dresses as Grandma slowly shrank, a concession to the ravages of age. Grandma Graber raised 12 children with her husband Abraham, after whom I am named. Abraham passed away when I was 12, and I find myself more and more sorrowful that I hadn't gotten to know him better, to probe my namesake for some insightful nuggets of wisdom that might have guided me through the dark of life, like my own North Star. Grandfather had a resourceful resolve that I admired. He made his own sugar solution to feed hummingbirds, taught me how to measure the pH level of garden soil, and was a voracious reader. I see much of myself in my Grandpa Abraham.

While the ladies crimped crusts in the kitchen, I continued to work in the shop. Dad and I were behind on orders and needed to catch up. But at some point I went out to the barn to give the horses some hay. It was a routine chore, but one I enjoyed. Sometimes I just need to clear my head or rest my hands. If the quality of a cabinet or a dresser was improved by me going out for a walk to clear my head, well, that was a compromise Dad was willing to make. As I was pitching some hay into Summer's stall, I saw Loretta and Paige strolling my way. The pies were finished and they had just deposited Grandma Ada back into the *dawdy haus*.

"She's a natural born crust queen!" Loretta chirped.

"I wouldn't go that far, but thanks," Paige countered.

"What kind did you end up making?" I asked.

"Grandma Ada was trying to persuade us to make a bread pie, but Mom has so many peaches left over from last year that we made a peach pie, so get some in the kitchen while it's still there…you know how Benjamin loves peach pie. We'll be lucky to have any left for dessert tonight," Loretta said.

"Sure thing. Maybe I can make some ice cream to go with it," I suggested.

"Abe makes great ice cream," Loretta said to Paige. "Never sure how he does it, but he adds some cinnamon and it comes out as this smooth, silky vanilla-cinnamon ice cream."

"Well, you'll have my heart with homemade ice cream," Paige said.

I made a mental note of that.

"Paige wanted to see the horses again," Loretta said to me as I finished filling their water troughs.

"Hi, sweetie," Paige said, stroking Summer's nose.

"Have you ever been on a buggy ride before?" Loretta asked Paige.

"Nope, not unless you count those white carriages that take tourists around in Chicago."

"What are those?"

"Oh, I was just joking. They're for the tourists. Horse-drawn buggies are supposed to be a more romantic way to see the city. A lot of young couples travel in them when they are dating, or tourists who just want a slower way to see Chicago. We took a carriage ride on prom night."

"What kind of horses do they use? Morgans? Arabians?" Loretta pressed.

"They're brown is all I really know," Paige laughed.

"What was prom like? Is it sort of like our young peoples' gatherings?" Loretta asked.

"Well…maybe…prom is sort of a rite of passage where I come from. It's supposed to be your first adult night out,'" Paige explained.

Loretta's eyebrows raised.

"Oh, no, not that kind…well, yes, I guess it is for some…but *that* isn't supposed to be what it's about," Paige said, slightly blushing. "The school holds a special dance with a theme. My senior prom was "Space on Earth." It's a pretty magical night. I think most prom-goers think they are the center of the universe on that evening. Looking back, though, it all seems silly."

"I think it sounds interesting. Was Scott your prom date?" Loretta asked.

"Oh, no…no, his name was Aaron…we dated my senior year of high school, but I haven't seen him since," Paige said.

I had been listening to the prom conversation quietly, wondering if Paige and I would ever get any time alone together. So far, her visit had been a bit of a letdown.

"How about now for your first buggy ride?" Loretta said, glancing at me.

"Sounds wonderful!"

The bookcases Dad and I were working on were finished, so maybe this was the opportunity I had been looking for to spend some time with Paige. We climbed aboard the buggy. I took the reins, Loretta sat in the middle, with Paige on the end.

"I noticed your buggies aren't enclosed," Paige observed.

"We like to go topless," Loretta dead-panned.

Paige seemed startled by the comment at first, but then laughed.

"It's just the way we've always done things here," Loretta sighed.

"Yes, even during winter's worst, we ride along in a carriage without a roof. Many Amish elsewhere sort of look down upon us, viewing us as wayward sheep who don't have enough to sense to come out of the rain," I said.

"It doesn't seem like it would be very comfortable," Paige noted.

But I beg to differ. "The other Amish are the ones missing out...on a gorgeous spring day when the wildflowers are in bloom and a gentle breeze signals the start of warmer days, no place I'd rather be."

We were just settling in for the ride when Loretta remembered something.

"Whoa, stop!" she commanded.

"Something wrong?"

"I forgot that one of Mom's egg customers is stopping by this afternoon. She needs five dozen…she said she'd stop by between 1 and 2 p.m., and we can use the money. Just go without me," Loretta said, hopping off the buggy.

I wasn't going to complain about taking a buggy ride alone with Paige. In fact, I was secretly ecstatic. And I'd thank Loretta later for concocting a cover story to allow her to leave us alone.

"Okay, all buckled up?" I asked.

Paige's hands reached onto the buggy seat, feeling around her waist, and then exploring down the side of the buggy in vain.

"Ha, I was just kidding."

Paige blushed slightly.

"Well, I didn't think so, but I didn't expect to see license plates on buggies, either!"

"Not something you see everywhere. Indiana is the only state that

requires the Amish to have them. Seems like just another gravy train
to fill state coffers, but whatever," I said, sounding a bit gruffer than
I wanted.

"If they require license plates, I'm surprised they don't require seat
belts," Paige noted.
"Occasionally some lawmakers demand that our buggies have seat
belts, usually after a rash of accidents have grabbed headlines. But
they don't understand the physics and mechanics of auto-buggy
collisions," I said.

"Are collisions common?"

"I wouldn't say common, but the dynamics of car-buggy collisions
are far different from cars in car crashes. If a car plows into a
buggy, you *want* to be thrown off. That is a passenger's best chance
for survival. The point of impact from the car is lower, since we sit
pretty high up on a buggy. The end result is often ejection,
hopefully into a row of soft shrubs. In a collision between a buggy
and a car, the car always wins."

"Comforting…" Paige said, eying busy Route 27.

So Paige and I began our ride, with my ever-wary eyes on alert for
careless auto drivers. Meanwhile, I couldn't help but admire Paige's
resplendent pony-tail. I found myself wondering what she would

look like with her hair not pulled back, if she just let her alluring brown locks tumble down around her shoulders. Outsiders know Amish women's hair only from being stuffed into a *kapp,* and while the head-covering conveys modesty, it does come off at night. Rachel Miller's red hair cascaded softly down past her bare shoulders and I would run my hands through it as I gently rubbed her back on warm summer nights. I wondered how holding and stroking Paige in the same way would feel.

"Okay, Summer. Show us your stuff," I exalted.

Steel buggy wheels began clattering down our dirt driveway towards its rendezvous with Route 27. Most Amish have the luxury of a quiet road to pull onto, but not us. Living on a busy highway required a special set of skills, and that's probably why Loretta usually wanted me to drive. She loved horses, but she didn't love thundering trucks and inconsiderate cars, and Route 27 was a haven for each. Making matters worse was that living south of town, we always had to make a left turn to go to Berne, which meant crossing the busy southbound lane of traffic before settling into the buggy lane on the opposite side. I rarely challenged a car, but would usually wait until both lanes were completely clear, which could be a while during a busy time of day.

Summer galloped across the southbound lane of US 27, and then banked left onto the shoulder of the northbound lane. Loretta's absence had put me in a bit of a bind. We were certain to be seen and people were going to talk. In one sense, I didn't really care. Amish took outsiders on buggy rides frequently, although it was admittedly a little unusual to see an Amish man and a young non-Amish woman alone. I could take Paige down rural County Road 850 and show her some beautiful Indiana countryside, but alone on a rural road with me on a buggy, Paige would stand out like a Holstein in a herd of Jerseys. Or we could go into busy Berne where we'd be lost among the crowds of tourists and townspeople. In actuality, though, it was a great time to go for a ride through the countryside. There was a wedding in West District and the quilting bee at the Neuenschwanders. Between the two events, most people would not be out at that time of day, so I decided on the more rural route.

"This really is a treat... the fresh air, the fields, the flowers…this is an incredible experience, Abe…thank you so much for taking the time to do this."

"Even though I do it almost every day, I still love a buggy ride myself, so I didn't have to be persuaded very hard."

Of course at a time like this when I was with Paige, a closed buggy would have been nice. There's no privacy in an open buggy. Hmmm, perhaps *that* is why we have open buggies in Berne? This area has always been a bit gossipy. An open buggy definitely allows people to see who is with whom.

As we talked, we passed Amish homes with chromatic laundry dangling on the lines, rusty windmills, bright red barns, and rolls of fresh yellow hay in the fields. I silently savored the scenery which, when I was behind bars, I'd feared I'd never see again.

"Hey, you really surprised me with the emails. That was so neat, I didn't think...well, I was just surprised that you..." Paige said, her voice trailing off.

"That I knew how to do it or that we're permitted to send email?"

"Well, both..."

I laughed. As was often the case with Paige, her reaction coming from someone else might have annoyed me, but from her it was somehow endearing.

"As far as being permitted...that's complicated, but let's just say that I don't think I was technically breaking any church rules. I don't own a computer, and the church draws a clear distinction between using some technologies and owning them."

We continued to converse and enjoy the placid spring scenery. Paige suddenly gasped..."What is that?"

"It's the Muensterberg Plaza and Clock Tower, looks small from out here, but if you go into Berne it's right in the middle of town, a token of friendship towards their Swiss brethren who have a similar tower in Switzerland," I explained.

Then it was my turn to spot something on the horizon.

"Crap" I muttered under my breath. I could see a buggy approaching far in the distance. If I could make it to the next crossroad before the other buggy arrived, I could perhaps discreetly turn and avoid inquisitive eyes.

"Summer, go!" I said, regretting now that I hadn't taken Ruby. Ruby can be a bit of a rough ride and I wanted Paige to enjoy herself, so I took Summer instead. But despite Summer's increasing speed, we wouldn't make the turn in time, so I decided calm and cool would be my approach. Loretta was skilled at deciphering who was driving a buggy even when it was just a smudge on the horizon, but was a talent I never mastered.

"Hey," I waved, managing a smile. Thankfully, it was a familiar face, probably my best friend in the church: Roman Neuenschwander. He had always stood up for me when we played baseball as teenagers and I was the uncoordinated, nerdy one. At least I was until that final game of the season against Amos Raber's Warriors. And when many in the church were contemplating imposing a shunning after my confession in church, Roman had stood up for me and urged them to welcome me back.

"Escaping the chatter," Roman said, thumbing towards the southwest, the general direction of his house. Roman was a few years younger than me, but a couple of inches taller. Young, wiry, with blonde hair and blue eyes, he never had trouble attracting the ladies. Roman's was a one-bench buggy with a storage bay in the back. The buggy was weighed down with boxes, plastic totes, tools, and the like.

"Thought I'd take this free time to move a few things. Who's your friend?"

"Paige Roberts, visiting from Chicago. Paige, this is my good friend Roman Neuenschwander."

"Oh, same place that's having the quilting bee today?"

I reddened slightly. I was trying to give as little information as possible. As far as Roman was concerned, Paige could have been a tourist.

"That's my Mom," Roman said, "They're quilting their fingers off now. Plenty of coffee, gossip, and Salome's Long John Rolls."

"Yes, I'm sure they're having a good time. Well, I best get a move on." I said.

"Hey, when moving day comes, will you be there?" Roman asked.

"Of course. I'll help any way I can." I said. And I meant it. The Neuenschwanders were a fine family, the best. Although I'd help anyone in our church who needed a hand, I'd do anything for the Neuenschwanders. As Roman was pulling away, he turned back.

"You want to come over for supper? Mom will have a lot of leftover food from the quilting bee. And why don't you bring your friend?"

"They're moving?" Paige asked as our buggy began rolling again.

"Yes, auction is in a few weeks."

"Where are they headed?"

"I think they're going to move in with Lizzie's sister outside of Geneva. Won't be easy, but they'll manage."

"Why are they moving?"

"Oh, I probably best keep it private,"

CHAPTER 12

PAIGE

"Salome, it's great to see you again," I said. I am a "huggy" sort of person by nature. I hug my girlfriends when we meet for lunch, or when I see family at our annual reunion. But I wasn't sure if the Amish hugged in that sort of way.

Salome picked up on my hesitation.

"I'm Amish, not the Queen of England," she said with a laugh.

I laughed and gave her a big hug.

"Looks like you've been out on the stone roads," Salome observed, looking at my dust-covered clothes.

"Yes, I was. I don't think dust is my color!" I laughed.

"So, I heard you were at a quilting bee. That sounds like fun!" I said. "We got seven quilts put into frame today," Mom said. "I don't think my fingers could shell a peanut tonight. I might have to have Loretta cook our supper."

"Or me, I can still cook," Grandma Ada, who had hobbled in from the *dawdy haus*, interjected.

Loretta and Salome looked at one another.

"She made a meatloaf last year but forgot what to do with it, and she ended up putting it in a frying pan on top of the stove instead of in the oven," Loretta whispered to me. "She's a little forgetful in her old age."

"You know, that actually wasn't half bad. I was going to have her submit a 'Fried Meatloaf' recipe for the next church cookbook," Nancy said, only partially jokingly.

"And last time Grandma Ada made cookies, I had to wear steel-toed boots because she baked them so long that they came out hard and heavy as clothing irons," Loretta continued. "If you dropped them, they'd break your toes."

"I can still hear!" Grandma Ada huffed, waving her cane. "That pretty little Sage is going to get the wrong idea about me. I'll have you know fried meatloaf was something new I was trying…"

"Okay, maybe that's enough activity for today for *Grossmutter*," Salome said. "Loretta, why don't you settle her in for the night and then take her some supper?"

Salome turned to me and Abraham.

ABRAHAM

"So, what would you like for supper?"

"Well, don't make anything special for us, we're going to the Neuenschwanders," I said.

"Lizzie stealing my supper guest?" Mom asked, still flexing her fingers.

"It's not Lizzie's fault. We ran into Roman and he invited us over for leftovers. Seems like they'd enjoy the company, with all that is going on," I explained.

"Roman just wants to make eyes at Paige," Nancy piped up, her eyes never leaving the book she was reading.

Paige blushed and I glared at Nancy.

"Don't you have some chores to be doing?"

"No, I did them all earli…"

"I am sure you can find some weeds to pull in the garden," I growled, cutting her off.

"Oh, all right," Nancy whined, grabbing some cleaner and rags, and bounding outside to soap up some windows.

I have to admit, going with Paige to the Neuenschwanders almost felt like a date. While Paige spent time with Mom, I ran upstairs to get myself cleaned up for the evening. A short time later, I came back downstairs dressed in a brown button-down shirt, dark denim pants, matching suspenders, and my best hat. I looked pretty spiffy, if I say so myself.

Loretta raised her eyebrows when I entered the kitchen, but said nothing. No such luck with Nancy.

"Just a regular supper at the Neuenschwanders? You're dressed like you're going to church!" Nancy cackled.

"Nancy, why don't you go help Loretta settle in *Grossmutter*?" I said.

Nancy rolled her eyes and headed out the door.

Paige and I climbed into the buggy. I stifled the urge to extend my hand. The step up is rather steep, and a hand would be a courtesy I'd offer almost anyone, but with Paige, I didn't want to be overstepping my bounds. So I let her clumsily ascend herself.

I had decided to give Summer a rest and have Ruby take us on the three-mile ride to the Neuenschwander's house. Ruby could cover the ground in about 25 minutes.

"So how long have you been interested in carpentry?" Paige asked as we began our journey.

"I grew up in the business. I'd go to the shop and help Dad when I was old enough to walk. I really like to work with my hands."

"I bet you'd give a great massage," Paige laughed.

"My last girlfriend thought I did," I said matter-of-factly.

"Ha!" Paige swatted playfully.

The steel wheels clattered down the pencil-straight dusty lane. Many roads around here are paved, but some aren't and the Neuenschwanders lived on one such road. On an open buggy you do have to sometimes contend with clouds of dust or pieces of gravel being kicked up. Perhaps the worst thing is when one of the horses sneezes, and if the wind catches it just right, you end up covered with horse snot. None of this seemed to bother Paige. She just kept commenting on how beautiful the passing fields and forests were. I wanted to comment on how beautiful she was, but I resisted.

"How long had you wanted to be a lawyer?" I asked.

"Well, I'm kind of like you. I'd been going into the office–which was in a bank–with my Dad since I was a little girl. And now I'm also working in the banking business, but on the legal end of things."

"And do you like the work?"

"It's a paycheck, but I don't want to be doing this forever."

The rhythmic staccato sound of horse hooves provided background music to any pauses in our conversation, making for a pleasant journey.

"Was your last girlfriend, the one who thought you gave such good massages, from around here?"

"Yes, she was. But she doesn't live here anymore, she moved to a more conservative settlement in Tennessee."

"Were you with her long?"

"A while," I replied. "We had planned to marry at one time…even reserved the wagon."

"The wagon?" Paige asked.

"Oh, I'm sorry…well, weddings are not small events around here, and 1,000 people could easily show up."

"Wow, that's considered a small city in some places."

"That's a lot of work for one family to put on, so they turn to wedding wagons, which is basically a giant rental kitchen on wheels, fully stocked with all the pots, pans, utensils, dishtowels, plates, cups, and anything else one might need for 1,000 of their closest friends," I explained.

Paige laughed.

"In our community there is Hilda Hilty's "Weddings on Wheels" and Anne Bontrager's "Mobile Memories." The kitchens are so popular that they have to be booked more than a year in advance, which presents somewhat of an awkward problem since most young Amish couples announce their weddings in church only a couple of weeks beforehand. When a wagon is booked, Hilda has to swear to secrecy. Anne is in a similar situation with her business, except her secrecy comes at a price. At least that is what I've always heard. I can't verify this for sure, but the rumor mill has it that she'll keep her mouth shut but only for an additional $100," I explained.

"Sounds like there are some entrepreneurial Amish out there!" Paige marveled. But then turning serious, she added, "I'm so sorry your wedding never occurred. That must have been heart-breaking for you…do you mind me asking what happened?"

"Well, I'm not sure our relationship would have survived anyway, but...my troubles…they were the final straw, and I understand why..." I said. Our arrival at the Neuenschwanders ended the conversation, and I was glad. Discussing Rachel's departure was still painful. I guided Summer into their driveway and we were soon surrounded by Neuenschwanders, the youngest being three and the oldest being Roman.

"You think OUR family is big?" I asked Paige playfully as Summer trotted down the Neuenschwander's dirt lane driveway.

The lawn was a hive of activity, boys wearing straw hats and suspenders, and barefoot girls with their *kapps* and turquoise dresses.

"Holy cow, is that all one family?"

"All 12 of them," I quipped.

"Please tell me I don't have to remember all their names," Paige asked.

"Yes, I'm going to quiz you afterward," I joked.

"What's THAT?" Paige said, pointing to what looked like a black semi-trailer parked in the Neuenschwander's yard.

"That's the bench wagon. The Neuenschwanders are holding church here this Sunday," I explained.

Lizzie Neuenschwander was a rotund woman with tan, leathery skin from hours spent outdoors in the garden raking, hoeing, and planting. She was wearing a black *kapp* and a sea-water blue dress. Lizzie had a round face and a missing front tooth on her top left side. Paige immediately took a liking to her.

"Roman said he invited you," Lizzie said, looking directly at me. "But he didn't tell me you were bringing a date."

Lizzie and a few of the girls that had gathered around laughed. The younger ones were checking Paige out: the odd capri pants, the flip-flops, the bright yellow blouse, all conveying the air of someone not from around Berne. Paige was startled by Lizzie's comment, but then laughed. Paige, like so many outsiders, initially had the mistaken impression that all Amish are these sour and serious people who don't like to have fun. If our family hadn't dispelled that impression for Paige, I was certain the Neuenschwanders would.

"Oh, we were just joking. Any friend of Abe's is a friend of ours,"

Lizzie said.

"*Danke schoen*," Paige said.

The Neuenschwanders laughed.

"Ohhh, you've taught her some of our language," Lizzie chuckled.

"That's about all you'll get from me," Paige said.

"Welcome to our home. Salome says you wanted to learn how to make a homemade pie crust? If you wanted to learn from the best, you should have come here!" Lizzie joked

"Mom!" said one of the girls. "Be nice!"

"Just kidding…Abe knows that…Salome's pie crusts are the talk of the church, so you won't go wrong with her, but she can't touch my cookies," Lizzie boasted with a competitive smile. And, indeed, Paige could smell the scent of cookies of some sort lifting from the ovens inside.

The Neuenschwander home resembled many of the other Amish farms sprinkled on the grid of rural roads outside of Berne. It was a tidy, two-story white clapboard homestead on a flapjack-flat piece of land. Unlike our property, which was a mixture of cropland, creek and prairie, the Neuenschwander home was surrounded almost entirely by soybean and corn crops, except for a lawn of green grass which spread out in all directions from the house until it met the farmland. A rickety windmill creaked high above the house and a few outbuildings on the property. A couple of picnic tables sat outside, perfect for outdoor meals. A neatly-tilled garden was on one side, filled with tomatoes, cucumbers, radishes, corn, marigolds, and sunflowers. Lizzie noticed Paige eyeing it.

"Would you like to see it?" Lizzie offered.

"That would be great!"

Paige, myself, and Lizzie strolled towards their ample garden.

"It's a gorgeous garden. When I was growing up, I thought cucumbers and beans just came from the grocery store," Paige remarked.

"We've never done it any other way. When you grow it yourself, you appreciate it more," Lizzie said.

"What are the little white balls scattered around the garden?" Paige asked.

"Mothballs. They help keep the deer away."

"The marigolds are so pretty," Paige said, surveying the rows and rows of orange flowers which circled the garden like the rings of Saturn.

"They keep out the rabbits," Lizzie said.

Just then a ball came flying overhead, and one of the Neuenschwander boys came galloping after, snagging it but crushing some of the potato plants underfoot.

"Now if I could just find a way to keep children out, my garden might actually be perfect," Lizzie said with a laugh. "But I guess as long as the children are in good health, we can't complain!"

The scene was one of controlled chaos. Some children played, others were getting supper ready, still others were taking wash off the line and putting dresses, aprons, and trousers into laundry baskets.

"Dinner's outside tonight if that is OK, but you're welcome to come in and see our place," Lizzie said.

"I'd love to," Paige said.

"It's nothing fancy, but it suits us fine," Lizzie said.

The Neuenschwanders' home was the classic Spartan Swiss motif. Floors were a rich, warm polished wood. A main living room had a wooden sofa with some cushions and a few rockers.

"Mose said he'd love to move to the next church district over because they allow recliners there," Lizzie whispered to Paige.

Like most Amish homes, the Neuenschwanders' didn't have much on their walls except for a couple of calendars and children's drawings from school. Two hand-made rocking chairs complemented the sofa. The rockers were made of wood, but a thick blue cushion was tied to each seat.

"Roman and Mose, Jr., made those. Try one out," Lizzie said to Paige.

"Comfortable," Paige agreed.

"Made of hickory," Lizzie said, clearly proud of her son's workmanship. The chairs were perfectly contoured, unlike stiff-backed Carolina rockers.

A flight of stairs ascended into darkness, where Paige correctly presumed the children's quarters were. The master bedroom was on the first floor, off the living room, typical of Amish homes in the area.

"I better get supper on the table. You can go outside with everyone else."

The Neuenschwanders were beginning to assemble by the picnic tables. The nearby outdoor grill which had been running at full capacity was empty now, its coals still smoking.

Lizzie and her daughters put out a sumptuous spread: platters piled high with pork chops, followed by heaping bowls of fluffy mashed potatoes, home-canned corn, homemade noodles--thick and buttery, sliced cheese, fresh bread, and several varieties of jam. The boys were already seated at the table waiting.

Paige whispered to me, "I thought Roman said they were serving leftovers!"

"I'm sure once Lizzie heard company was coming, she decided to pull out all the stops. I ought to bring you over here for supper more often. Last time I came, we just had leftover stew."

"Mose grilled the pork chops for us and made the marinade," Lizzie said, beaming at her husband. The Neuenschwanders pushed two enormous wooden picnic tables side-by-side so that everyone could sit together.

"We'd like to bow our heads in silent prayer," Mose murmured.

The silent prayer is a tradition in most Amish homes. I've always enjoyed the silent prayer. It acts as a "speed bump," to use a comparison to your world. Like so many of the things we do, the prayer causes a person to pause and appreciate God's gifts and one's blessings, whether it be a bountiful harvest from the garden, jars full of canned meat, or good health. There are, sadly, too many starving people in this world to not take a moment to reflect before feeding one's face. During the stillness of the blessing, the children's chatter silenced, and all that could be heard was the sound of crickets chirping in the gathering dusk, the persistent call of a killdeer, and the distant sound of buggy wheels clattering. The aroma of fresh pork chops and Mose's marinade added a sweet and savory scent to the air. The spread of mashed potatoes, barbecued hamburgers, warm homemade rolls, home-canned pickles, buttered corn, and seven-layer salad was enough to feed a village. If I ever needed a reminder of why I have always loved the Amish life, I needed to look no further than this table. There's a warmth, a wholesomeness to our life that's hard to find among your kind of people. Everyone sat silently, their heads bowed, each reflecting and praying in their own way. The Neuenschwander men and boys all sat on one side of the table, and women and girls on the other. Black kapp strings fluttered in the late-day breeze on their bowed heads.

Suddenly breaching the quiet, Mose, a big bear of a
man,exclaimed,"Well, what are we waiting for? Let's eat!"

Soon the table was a festive scene of bowls and baskets being
passed, belches being stifled, pitchers being poured, and chattering
conversation from crops to baseball.

"So, what is it you do?" Lizzie asked Paige between bites of her
dinner roll.

"Well, nothing exciting, I…"

Hmmm, this wouldn't be wise to discuss now, I thought, so I did my
best to distract.

"Hey, Mose, this marinade is AMAZING," I suddenly shouted.
"AMAZING! How do you make it? Practically makes the pork
jump right off the platter."

"What's gotten into him?" Lizzie whispered to no one in particular.

The Neuenschwander family was divided equally between boys and
girls, a fact Paige noted during supper.

"I always tell Lizzie I'm ready to try for the tie-breaker any time,"

Mose said, laughing heartily between bites of butter-soaked mashed potatoes.

"Oh, listen to him," Lizzie waved him off, blushing slightly.

"These are delicious mashed potatoes. Mmm, my gosh, I could eat just these for supper and be happy," Paige marveled, spooning more into her mouth.

"I add cream cheese to mine. It's a tip I learned from my mother...it helps the mashed potatoes hold up better if they are going to be sitting out for a while, such as they are sometimes for the after-church meal. But I find I like the taste of them that way, so even if they aren't going to be sitting out, I add cream cheese," Lizzie explained.

I have to admit I felt a bit of pride--something our church preaches against--at having this vivacious, attractive young lady accompanying me to supper at the Neuenwschwanders.

"So how long have younce known one another?" Lizzie asked.

"Oh...since last winter," I said between bites.

"Yes, since that January snowstorm. It really hasn't been all that long, but we really have become fast friends," Paige said, avoiding the topic of my sins against Mr. Doty. I was grateful for her tact. After a church confession, the congregation really is supposed to forgive and forget.

"Feel like I've known her a lot longer," I said.
"Back home I refer to him as my Amish brother," Paige laughed.

I felt as if my heart had just been thrown into a hay baler. I'm Amish; that doesn't mean I'm from another planet, I remember thinking. Paige and I had seemed to enjoy a compatibility and chemistry. Would she dismiss me as a romantic suitor if I were a Presbyterian driving a Volvo? Probably not, but an Amish man driving a buggy immediately eliminated me? It didn't seem fair. I suppose everyone else at the table thought I must have seemed suddenly sullen and sour. I think Lizzie picked up on my mood crash.

"Anyone ready for dessert?" Lizzie asked, trying to lighten the quiet that had fallen over my end of the table. A chorus of delighted children squealed "Yes!"

Several Neuenschwander girls, most blonde-haired and blue-eyed, matching their azure-colored dresses perfectly, materialized with a five-star selection of desserts.

"Okay, we've got banana sheet cake on this end, homemade honey bars in the middle, and whoopie pies on your end. And cookies, plenty of cookies! Help yourself!" Lizzie said.

"Thank you so much for this, Mrs. Neuensch…."

"Call me Lizzie!"

"Lizzie…thank you so much. I sure hope you didn't go through all of this on my account," Paige said. "But the food is truly incredible. I'm not even sure where to start."

"Looks like she could use some fattening up, Abe," Lizzie joked.

"Well, if I am going to fatten up, I might as well begin with a whoopie pie," Paige said.

One of the Neuenschwander girls passed the plate, and Paige indulged herself in a sandwich cookie confection that made her swoon. This was her first encounter with a whoopie pie. The whoopie pie comes in as many varieties as one's imagination can conjure from peanut butter cookies smooshed against a layer of peanut butter crème to blueberry-infused cookies and cream.

"Well, that was delicious. We'd probably best be heading for home," I said abruptly, no longer in the mood to socialize. *My Amish brother.* It stung. Here I was romantically thinking about her constantly, and she's calling me her "Amish brother."

"So, yeah, best be headed for home, I shouldn't put off the milking, "I said.

But Paige had barely finished her cake when a voice shouted, "Not so fast...water battle!!!"

Before you could say "shoofly pie," I was drenched, and the whole yard looked like a watery war zone with the whole Neuenschwander brood splashing one another with cups of water. Then out came the buckets. The six Neuenschwander boys had me surrounded in the peony patch, soaking me with bucket after bucket of water. There had obviously been some pre-planning involved. Six buckets full of water just don't appear out of nowhere on a farm without running water. I sensed "General Roman" was behind this ambush. I soon slipped out of the encirclement and ran for the relative dryness of the shade of a nearby apple tree. Meanwhile, the six Neuenschwander girls were soaking Paige with buckets of their own. Paige managed to slip free, and ran to the picnic table, grabbing the half-consumed pitcher of ice-water from supper and splashing its contents back at her "attackers." Soon all six Neuenschwander girls were shivering and soaked, but laughing.

Thirteen-year-old Levi decided to avenge his sisters. He came charging at Paige with another pitcher of ice water from the table, and returned the soaking. Shivering, Paige took refuge under the tree with me, shaking ice out of her blouse.

At almost the same instant, Paige and I noticed barrels of rainwater that were stored along the side of one of their outbuildings. We both looked at one another.

"Oh, we couldn't...." Paige said.

"Sure we could...they're moving soon. You think they're going to take the rainwater with them?'

While I ran for the rain barrels, Paige eyed the picnic table again. There were still a few half-finished glasses of ice water remaining from supper. Paige deftly picked one up and prepared to douse Levi, whose back was to Paige while talking to his father. But one of his sisters shouted a warning.

"Levi, she's coming!"

Levi jumped to the side just as Paige was tossing the ice water which came cascading down on Mose Neuenschwander's face and bushy beard. So far, Mose and Lizzie had been the only ones who had escaped the water battle. Mose looked stunned for a second and was silent and still. He shook ice chips from his beard. Paige started to apologize.

"Oh, Mr. Neuenschwander, I'm so, so sor..." but before Paige could finish, Mose's stone-faced broke into a grin.

"Lizzie, it's payback!" Mose shouted.

Paige whirled around just in time to receive a bucket of water over the head from Lizzie.

Then I came to Paige's rescue, tipping the barrel of rainwater over so that a river of water came rushing through the yard. And soon everyone was splashing, sloshing, and sliding in the fresh mud.

"THAT was the best water battle ever!" Roman said, his shirt soaked and sticking to his thin frame.

"Green's my favorite color, too" 18-year-old Mose Neuenschwander, Jr., said.

Laughter rippled among some of the Neuenschwander children.

"Oh, don't mind them. You come back any time. Well, not here, we'll be gone. But Abe will know where to find us," Lizzie said, surveying her yard in the twilight. There was a look of resignation on her face.

The darkness gathered, and I decided we had best head for home. The water fight had loosened my mood a bit, although I still felt like my heart had been run over by a steel wheel. Water was dripping from us as we climbed onto my buggy. Paige's clothing clung to her tan, athletic body, which stirred me inside in a way I had not been in a long time.

"Here, why don't you wear this," I said, pulling a dusty coat from my buggy box.

"Thank you, there is a little bit of a chill in the air," Paige replied.

"Yes, and I thought...well, the coat might save you the same jokes back home, at least until you dry off...believe me, Nancy and Daniel can be far worse than five or six of the Neuenschwander kids combined...not that green is a bad color on you," I said, my face flushing slightly. "In fact, I think green is now my favorite color, too."

"Huh?" Paige glanced down and caught on. "Oh, I'm so embarrassed. They must think I'm a total tramp."
"The boys didn't seem to mind," I laughed.

Paige wrapped it around her. Her lacy green bra, which had become quite visible under her soaked shirt, disappeared beneath my dusty coat.

"We all have our indulgences. This is mine," Paige said, clearly embarrassed.

"Well, those are probably more exciting than my boxers," I said.

Paige blushed but didn't say anything else until we had traveled about a mile. "What a wonderful family," she marveled. "But...ugh...I hope Ruby can handle the extra load. I feel like I ate 20 pounds of food."

"Oh, come on. I've carried sacks of flour heavier than you," I quipped.

Fact is, I didn't have a lot of social experience with non-Amish women. Occasionally a pretty young non-Amish woman might come into the shop, but that was a rarity. My relationship with Rachel was about the extent of my experience with women, although there were other Amish females who caught my eye. In fact, I often fantasized about Sarah Graber. She was gorgeous and sweet and shared my interests in nature and horses, but she never could escape the orbit of her oaf of a boyfriend, Enos. I was comfortable with Paige because she seemed earthy, educated, and non-judgmental. Truth be told, I usually find Amish women more attractive than non-Amish. The absence of make-up creates a believable beauty. I'm not attracted to women who apply makeup with a garden trowel. The few non-

Amish women I'd meet at the store and in town didn't connect with me the way Paige did.

"They're breath-taking," Paige marveled, staring skyward. I wasn't sure what she was suddenly transfixed by, so I brought Ruby to a halt.

"What?" thinking maybe she saw a Great Horned Owl. It didn't even occur to me that she might mean the stars. I was just so used to the nightly celestial show.

"The stars, they're gorgeous," Paige said.

"Oh, yeah....I guess they are...I suppose," I said.

I liked how Paige made me continually appreciate things I took for granted, whether it was the warm breeze on the buggy or a choir of spring peepers.

"The Big Dipper looks like it is about to scoop us up," Paige said.

We were quiet for a few minutes, scanning the stars, listening to the spring peepers singing from a nearby pond, and letting the breezes warm our faces and dry off our clothes from the water battle.

"Hey, follow my finger. There's one star that I swear looks like a tiny emerald among a million diamonds," Paige said, pointing to the southern sky. "What is that? Or are my eyes playing tricks on me?"

"I'll give you an even better look."

I turned around and rummaged through my little buggy box, which sort of served the same purpose as a glove compartment in a car. I used it to store an extra pair of gloves in winter, some birding guides, and my prized Swarovski binoculars that I bought from an Amish-owned optics store in Holmes County, Ohio. I took a cloth and wiped the lenses clean, and handed them to Paige.

"Take a look," I said. "You're not mistaken. It does look green. Its name is Zubeneschamali."

"I'll have to look that one up in my Amish dictionary," Paige replied playfully.

I smiled.

"No, no...it's actually Arabic, which I don't speak, so don't ask me any more words. But it means "northern claw" because it's the outstretched claws of the constellation Scorpius. Anyway, it's a star that has always fascinated me because it's the only one in the whole galaxy that appears to the naked eye to be green in color," I said. Scanning the skies had always been a hobby of mine, whether watching birds, clouds, other weather formations, or simply stars.

"Wow...it does appear green....why?"

"That's one of the great unsolved mysteries of space. I think most astronomers say it's a white star that just *appears* green. Some questions only our Creator has the answer to," I said.

Paige studied the stars with my binoculars. She put them down around her neck and continued to stare skyward but was quiet. It was a few minutes before she said anything.

"You're so certain of a Higher Power. I admire that," Paige declared.

"And you're not?" I asked.

"When I argue a case, I go with facts. I have to persuade a judge, a jury, or the opposing counsel about the facts of the case. There can be no room for doubt. But with God...sometimes I doubt the evidence, so I find solace in science. I know the meaning of everything...but then when I look at a sky like this...I feel small, insignificant, and I think there has to be a Higher Power of some sort."

"Well, if you're seeking a sermon, you'd need to see our bishop. I'd make a bad bishop."

"Why do you say that?"

"Well, I'm Amish, but that doesn't automatically mean I'm pious...I, well, you –unfortunately – know that I have my flaws. Outsiders have this view of the Amish that we all share the same mindset. I was born Amish. I couldn't choose that. You can't choose what you are born into, or who you are born to, but the rest is up to you," I said. "I don't blindly believe; I question it, I question my church."

A cool breeze cut through the unusually warm June air, and the shrill sound of a barred owl pierced the silence of the night.

"Wow, those owls creep me out. Anyway, you always come back to there being a Higher Power watching over everything." Paige asked. "How can you be so certain?"

"That's what I am trying to explain. I'm *not* certain. That's what faith is, accepting that maybe 2 + 2 does equal 5 even if all evidence points to it being 4. Faith is earned. To me, faith operates like a savings account. You collect enough pennies, nickels, and dimes of faith that eventually you have a healthy balance. During hard times, you draw on that balance. If you have enough to cover the crisis, you come out with your faith intact. Spiritual currency...that's the only money I should ever have been focused on. Unfortunately, I stumbled." I explained as I began to get our buggy moving again. I really didn't want to revisit the topic of the Mr. Doty mess . Fortunately, Paige let the issue pass.

"Interesting way to look at it. I suppose there have been many times when I've overdrawn my account and haven't known what to do afterward," Paige said.

"Well, then, that's when you need to start saving again. The way I see it, you can embrace science and die empty and alone in blackness, or you can take the leap of faith and spend forever in light and love. My question is, why would anyone *not* choose God? But that doesn't mean you don't question..." I said. "To not question is dangerous. One's faith deepens when you question it."

"You're a very fascinating man, Mr. Lincoln."

"Don't you start with that," I admonished. "Okay, onward, Ruby!"

We headed in the newly-minted night towards home where we were met by a welcoming party.

"Well, hi...the Neuenschwanders kept you out late!" Mom said. "Did you survive Roman and his brothers? They can be ornery!"

"I think Paige held her own," I said.

"Guess it's a good thing it was dark when you came home. Wouldn't want anyone asking too many questions," Mom said, eyeing Paige, who was still wearing my coat.

"Water battle. It got a little cool on the buggy ride back home. Glad I had the jacket with me."

"Hmmmm…looks like it got HOT to me," Nancy said.

I glared at her.

"Nancy! Velma's got your bed ready, Paige. You can turn in whenever you're ready," Mom said.

"Nancy, don't you think it's time for you to be headed for bed now?" I said sternly.

Nancy rolled her eyes.

"Oh, alllllright." She disappeared up the wooden staircase, her blue dress flowing behind her.

"Marvin has to get up early to finish the bedroom set for that couple from Fort Wayne, so he's already gone to bed, and I think I'll join him," Mom yawned.

*   *

*

I thought of Paige laying snugly in Velma's bed, milky shafts of moonlight coming through the windows bathing her slender body in an opaque light Occasionally coyotes yapped and yelped in the fields to the west of our house, or a loud truck rumbled by on US 27. Paige had been offered a bucket by Mom, but she had politely declined, preferring the pleasant walk outside into the summer night. When there wasn't a blizzard, it was actually not a bad walk. I don't think of a flush toilet as being essential to a rich and happy life. Getting up at 1 a.m., taking a refreshing walk outside, knowing I still had hours to sleep before milking time, I loved it.

Sometimes I would sleep without any clothing on or perhaps a pair of boxers. It felt natural and normal, and on a warm summer night downright sensible. Amish homes don't have air-conditioning, so sleeping with clothes on runs counter to logic. I kept a pair of trousers by the bed in case, God forbid, there were a fire or other emergency. Modesty is exaggerated by outsiders among the Amish. It's less a prudish thing and more about practicality. One of our culture's most endearing traits--to me anyway--is that we aren't supposed to stand out from one another. We are supposed to live as a separate people; wearing simple clothes, all solids and denims, head coverings and hats, is a way to enhance our solidarity with one another while reinforcing a sense of separateness from everyone else. But plenty of Amish men walk around shirtless in the privacy of their home on a hot summer evening, and I was no different. I certainly wasn't going to wear pajamas when I slept during a sticky, sweltering June night.

But I did pull on a pair of trousers on this night to head to the outhouse. Still, I wasn't expecting a traffic jam.
"Come here often?"

Paige let out a startled puppy-like yelp. "What the heck are you doing out here?"

"Probably the same thing as you. Too much tea at the Neuenschwanders," I laughed sleepily.

I'm sure she was just as surprised to see me as I was to see her. I probably would have thrown a shirt on if I had thought I would run into her, but I was so groggy. I felt a little self-conscious standing there in just a pair of sweatpants. She looked ravishing in the pale moonlight, her hair out of its usual ponytail, falling in wavy curves to her shoulders. She looked so young, not like some big-shot Chicago attorney.

"I just hope Ruby hasn't left any gifts here that I can't see," Paige said, tiptoeing tentatively into the grass.

"Well, I can give you a lift if you like," I said, playfully scooping her up. Her arms instinctively clung around my neck. She was light as a sugar cookie, and I could smell a pleasant perfumey scent around her neck. Paige was laughing and so was I. Until Loretta emerged from the outhouse.

I abruptly put Paige down, almost dropped her, and headed back to my bedroom. Nature's call could wait.

"Never realized the outhouse was such a popular spot at this hour," I muttered.

I could feel Loretta's eyes drilling into me as I headed back into the house.

CHAPTER 13
ABRAHAM
Paige rolled on top of me and we stared into one another other's eyes as our mouths met in a passionate, sensual kiss. Her lips tasted

sweet, like spring strawberries, her tongue soft and electric as it brushed mine. As our bodies pressed against one another, my hands explored her back and her delicate and smooth skin. She felt so light on top of me. I slid her tee shirt off, and tossed it behind her into the darkness of my room where it landed atop the kerosene lamp on my bureau. The glass globe of the lamp rattled. Her body felt warm and rhythmic on mine. She was everything I had dreamt about, fantasized about.

And then I woke up, the dream punctured by baying coyotes somewhere in the back field.

I had trouble sleeping the rest of that night. I lay in bed imagining I was spooning Paige, just like I used to with Rachel. Her scent lingered and excited me, but my room was empty. Just across the darkness of the hall she slept, but across the hall might as well have been the moon. I was relieved when the morning arrived and sunrise began to brush the dark face of night with a rosy blush. I put on my usual dark denim, tan button-down work shirt, and suspenders, and headed out to the barn to do the morning milking. But someone had beaten me to the chore.

"What do you think you are doing?" Loretta demanded, her eyes stern as she held a bucket full of fresh milk in one hand, some of it sloshing out onto her dress.

"What do you mean?" I asked nonchalantly.

"Oh, c'mon. I thought you were just having fun at first, that this was harmless flirting," Loretta hissed.

"You're an accomplice…you made up that story about the egg customer so Paige and I could be alone on the buggy!" I reminded her.

"No, we really *did* have an egg customer," Loretta responded icily.

"Oh…" I said, looking toward the ground.

"And besides, it was more than just a buggy ride. You spent the *whole evening* with Paige at the Neuenschwanders. And I don't even want to know what you two were doing outside last night!"

"We were just..."

"Shhh...I said I don't want to know. But I see the way you are looking at her. You've worked so hard to get back in good with the church. I just worry you're headed for trouble. Yes, she's nice, but she's not one of us. She can't be, she's an attorney of all things...it's not like you've met an English seamstress. How far are you planning to take this? How many times must you break rules before you learn that they are there for a reason?"

"I thought you said this was my business. Look, I know what I'm doing," I said tersely.

"I sure hope you do. You're on your own from here on out. I'm done. No more help from me," Loretta huffed.

Loretta's life path was always so much easier than mine. Loretta was in love with Timothy and she knew what she wanted: a big garden, a husband, and a houseful of children . She didn't seem to have nearly the restless streak that tortured my life.

"I think you're heading down a path that could get you in a lot of trouble," Loretta warned. "If Bishop Hochstetler gets wind of this…you could be in trouble, and I don't know how many chances he'll give you."

"How can you be so sure? Only God judges, I thought."

"Your turn to milk, I'm done with this conversation," Loretta hissed, tossing an empty milk pail at me. Loretta and I had always had a close relationship and arguments between us were rare, so this one had me rattled.

I muttered furiously under my breath and started milking. I'm sure the cows felt a bit more of a tug on their udders that morning.

PAIGE

I awoke to the distinctive sound of eggs cracking into a skillet. And then there was the smell of something else: fresh cinnamon rolls rising in the oven, the heat lifting thermals of cinnamony, buttery bliss throughout the house. They told me that a pan of Salome's cinnamon rolls once brought in $200 at a relief auction. Judging by the smell of them as I lay in bed, I could believe it.

This story is largely about truth and lies, so I won't lie to you here…there was a part of me that was feeling an attraction to Abe. Some of it, I'm not ashamed to admit, was physical. When he picked me up last night, I could feel his arms…they were like iron bars, and his body…tan, fit, and I think I could have grated a block of Romano cheese on his flat, rippling stomach. Abe is incredible and earthy and probably all the more seductive because of the contrast with the smartphone obsessed, flabby, office-type men I generally spend my days with. His curly brown hair and piercing blue eyes didn't hurt either. But it was more than just physical lust, there was a genuine connection that we seemed to have, and that was intriguing. Still, I knew this couldn't go anywhere and shouldn't go anywhere for many reasons, a big one being that Uncle Ralph would rightfully think of me as a total turncoat.

I decided I'd better go downstairs. I was wearing pajama pants and a short-sleeved t-shirt that said "SummerFest 5K Run."

"Smelled too good to keep sleeping," I declared.

"I made this casserole with 12 eggs, all laid this morning," Salome said. "Marvin, Jr., loves to help collect them from the henhouse."

My shirt caught Salome's eye.

"5K run?" Salome asked as she stirred a pan of sausage gravy.

"Running is my therapy," I replied. "You probably do more physical work before 8 a.m. than I usually do in a whole day , so I really have to run to stay in shape."

"Well, it's just the way we live. I'm not sure I could run like that, so I guess it's just the way different people do things."

"Sailing is my other exercise; it's a lot more physical than most people think," I explained.

Sailing for me was like breathing or eating. I had sailed since I was old enough to walk. My father's high-stress job at the bank required an escape, and sailing on the always unpredictable waters of Lake Michigan was the elixir. And while a lot of my father's high-end hobbies hadn't transferred to me, sailing was an exception. I loved the freedom the open water offered and the challenge of navigation, wind mastery, and current circumventing. Many men, for some reason, found my independent streak threatening. I never understood why. What was wrong with being a physically fit, successful career woman who also wanted the steady, loving arms of a man to be there for her? It was a combination that never seemed to come together.

"Really? Sailing? I've never even seen the sea," Salome marveled.

"I do most of my sailing on Lake Michigan, which, really, is practically like seeing the ocean."

"You have your own boat?"

"Yes. She's named "*Bank on It*," I said. "We name our boats kind of like you name your horses."

"I think Rainbow Lake over in the next county where Marvin likes to fish is about as much water as I have ever seen at once," Salome laughed.

"The breakfast smells so good, is there anything I can do to help?" I asked, feeling a little guilty about the hive of activity while I just sat.

"Just keep us from having leftovers, that'll be a help," Salome offered.

As everyone was eating breakfast, Loretta walked briskly into the house. She wasn't her usual sunny self. Everyone was eating in the midst of typical table chatter, which included the children peppering me with questions about sailing.

"I don't think I could live here, I'd gain too much weight," I said, spooning a second helping of breakfast casserole.

"Then maybe my brother wouldn't be able to lift you anymore," Loretta whispered into my ear as she walked into the kitchen and sat at the table in an empty chair next to Daniel.

Salome looked up quizzically, not quite hearing the exchange.

"Everything OK, Loretta?" Salome asked as she poured herself a glass of homemade rhubarb juice.

"I don't think you'd gain weight here. Mom would put you to work. I don't think I could work indoors like you do, I'd have to be able to go out to the garden, or feed the horses or pitch some hay. Our lives are *very* different," Loretta said, her voice carrying a bit of an edge to it.

"Believe me, I think I'd trade places with you in a heartbeat if I could," I said, peeking at my phone and then sliding it back into my pocket.

"Would you, really?" Loretta asked icily. "You might miss your phone."

The question took me a little off guard.

"I think there's definitely something very appealing about your life. I'm not sure if I could do it, but, I think I'd gladly trade the stack of paperwork back at my office for a rolling pin," I said.

"Wow, so you actually have an office of your own with a desk and everything?" Nancy asked, her eyes widening.

"Yes, I do. But, really, it's not all it's cracked up to be," I said, again checking my phone. "Excuse me," I had to answer a coworker's message about a case and started tapping a response, but Marvin, Jr., swiped the phone and ran outside. I went running after him.

"Marvin, I'll trade you…candy for my phone," I said.

"It's practically a third hand for you isn't it, that phone?" Salome asked, following me outside. "Marvin, give it back!"

"Unfortunately, it can be and I don't like it. Believe me, I think your church has the right idea. Yes, the phone's convenience is nice, but being constantly connected and on call is a bit draining," I explained, as Marvin finally relinquished the phone.. "It was my office needing some information. And speaking of offices, I probably do need to head back for Chicago. Ugh, I wish work didn't call. Hey, before I go, where's Abe?"

"Oh, you mean your *boyfriend*?" Nancy said, picking at the last of her casserole.

I was startled and embarrassed by Nancy's comment. She certainly was a precocious child. As soon as I was about to respond, Salome jumped to my rescue.

"Nancy!" Why don't you help Velma and Verena with the breakfast dishes?"

"I don't really feel li…" Nancy started to say, but saw Salome glaring. "Oh, okaaaay," Nancy said, getting up from the table and heading into the kitchen to help the twins.

I went upstairs to change clothes and pack my overnight bag, and came back downstairs.

"Abe's probably over in the shop with Dad…they have a big order to finish today," Loretta said.

"Okay, I'm not sure when I'll see you next, so I wanted to thank you again for your hospitality. Hopefully, I can make a great pie crust like yours," I said.

"You're welcome here anytime," Salome interjected

"Let me walk you to your car," Loretta said.

""Hey, about last night….we were ju…" I started to say.

"No…don't want to hear it…that's between you two and God," Loretta said. "I guess I chose the wrong time to go to the outhouse."

"But…"

"Nope…look, you've become such a good friend and I'd like to keep it that way…I don't want to get in the middle of anything between you and Abe."

"Oh, please, there's nothing between Abe and me, we were just having some fun. I think we both surprised one another at the outhouse."

"He's been through a lot with the church and he's just getting back into good standing. I don't want to see that change. You're such a nice person, but we do live very different lives..." Loretta protested.

"I know, and I'd never do anything to take away from that," I said. "Promise. I need to go now anyway, so I'll be out of your hair."

I reached for a hug and she, reluctantly at first, returned the embrace.

"I'm sorry, I didn't mean to cause any awkwardness and I didn't mean any harm. We'll stay in touch, okay?" I said.

Loretta nodded finally and smiled, "Remember, a pinch of salt in the crust,"

ABRAHAM

A bell alerted us when Paige opened the door to our shop. Seeing it was Paige, Dad did a U-turn.

"For you," Dad said gruffly, motioning towards the door.

It's not that Dad didn't like Paige. It's just that he was shy and uncomfortable around women other than Mom and his daughters, so he just didn't have much to say to her.

"I wanted to come over here and say goodbye. I'm not sure when I'll be back," Paige said.

Suddenly aware of my father's prowling eyes, I motioned Paige towards the door.

"Let's step outside," I suggested.

"Thanks for a wonderful evening at the Neuenschwanders. They really are a sweet family. I'm curious about something…why didn't you want them to know what I do for living? I don't mind, I'm just curious."

She was dressed in a white, linen sleeveless sundress, matching flip-flops, and her hair was pulled back into its usual ponytail.

"Well, you're an attorney…" I answered thoughtfully. "It' a very different life from what most of the women in our church are used to…you're such a nice person, I wanted them to focus on you and not your job."

"Thank you, I appreciate that. But, really, I think your Mom, Loretta, Lizzie Neuenschwander, all of them probably work harder in a day than I do in a week, and that is saying a lot because my weeks can be quite full."

"And it's not just you being an attorney...it's what *kind of* attorney you are..." I said, knowing I couldn't avoid this topic any longer.

"What do you mean about what kind of attorney I am?" Paige asked.

"Well, the Neuenschwanders are moving...."

"Yes, I kept meaning to ask them why and where, but I didn't want to pry," Paige said.

"Well, they aren't moving voluntarily, and this is a source of great embarrassment to them, but...they're being forced to move," I said, searching for the right words.

"What?"

"Yes," I continued, "The bank is taking their home."

"Oh, they're going through a foreclosure?" Paige asked, her eyes widening.

"Yes."

"Ugh. No one wins in a situation like that,, really., I work with those cases every day. Everyone loses."

"That's why I didn't want to talk about your job in front of them, I don't think they would think the bank is 'losing.' The bank is getting a house out of it."

Paige was quiet.

"I guess I didn't realize the Amish used banks," Paige said.

I turned to face her and stared directly into her resplendent blue eyes.

"Now you sound like one of the tourists," I said, immediately regretting the sarcastic tone. Paige looked pained. "We aren't cave people. We use banks. Go into town enough and you'll see a buggy pulling up to an ATM."

Paige laughed.

"But you're right, I'd say the majority of people in our church bought their homes in cash, saved up, parents gave them some seed money. Many of them got loans through the First Bank of Berne.But the Neuenschwanders, they..."

I paused. "The Neuenschwanders are fine, fine people...sometimes too good for their own good, too trusting."

"What do you mean?" Paige said. "Maybe I can help? There are programs that can help, social service agencies that can step in."

I waved those suggestions off.

"I'm not saying all Amish people are this way, because they aren't. But some of us--just like some of your people--are too trusting. Last year there was a "pigeon scheme" that swept through many of our churches. A slick huckster came around recruiting people, promising they could make thousands of dollars investing in pigeons. Mose Neuenschwander fell for it, lost $1800 dollars, and was stuck with a bunch of pigeons."

"But that couldn't have caused them to lose their home...what happened with the Neuenschwanders and their house?" Paige asked.

"They lost a lot of money and couldn't make their monthly mortgage payments, so now they are being foreclosed upon," I said hesitantly. "It was something else Mose got roped into..."

"What was it?" Paige asked.

"It's something our church is trying to deal with internally."

"There has to be something I can do to help."

"But don't you help banks? That's why I didn't want to talk about your job with them."

"I hope you don't think that's *all* I do," Paige said, sounding defensive. "I'm trying to help everyone,"

"How is someone losing their house helping anyone?"

"Sometimes…ugh, Abe, I don't want you thinking I'm out doing bidding for the bank…let me explain it like this: maybe someone has a crushed leg…the leg can't be repaired….so the best thing to do for everyone--the doctor and the patient--is to remove the leg. It's not something anyone is happy with, but it does the least damage. Some foreclosures are for the best," Paige explained.

"Yes, but in your analogy the doctor gets to keep the leg."

"Maybe you should have gone to law school…" Paige said, a little flustered. "Anyway, I don't know…maybe I can help?"

"No, ol' Mose is too proud and would never do something that involves the legal system. The Amish as a general rule don't sue, did you know that?"

"No, I didn't know that, but now it makes sense why they might be such easy targets for the likes of the pigeon people."

"Yes, I'm afraid so," I muttered.

"Well, at least give me their address. I have access to a lot of proprietary databases and foreclosure files. I want to at least take a look. By the way, these flowers are gorgeous...what are they?"

"They're purple coneflowers. They come up early every summer...one of the first flowers of the season," I said, picking a couple and handing them to her.

"Mmmm, smells almost like citrus. Your knowledge of everything out here amazes me," Paige said. We slowly strolled back to her car, enjoying the warm morning sun. What I said next still kind of surprises me because--especially back then--I was pretty bashful.

"I hope you don't mind me saying something to you before you go."

"Sure...."

"I...think you're very...pretty...as pretty as a purple coneflower," I stammered.

"That's sweet Abe...thank you," Paige said. "I always learn so much when I'm with you. Okay, goodbyes are difficult. Let me give you a hug," she said, embracing me. The embrace seemed to linger longer than a typical friend-type hug, so I savored the split second of extra closeness. I gently patted her back. And for a moment my mind was a hazy fog of sweet scent, Paige's soft skin, tender touch. Then it was over.

"Oh, and before you go…I can give you the Neuenschwanders' address, but I don't think they'd accept any help from you or anyone else. They've already started moving, and unless lightning strikes down the auctioneer, their house will be sold in a few weeks," I said.

"Okay, but it would help to know how they got into this mess," Paige practically pled.

It was only a hunch, not a grudge, but there seemed to be a lot of financial problems befalling people in the church lately and I had an idea who might be behind it.

"You might want to look up the name Amos Raber and Plain Investments. But you didn't hear that from me," I said. And with that, I turned and walked away.

CHAPTER 14
ABRAHAM

Outsiders always lump all Amish together as if we're one

personality or person, whether it be "we don't pay taxes" or "we are dirty" or "we aren't patriotic." Blanket statements like that against any other group would be absurd, but they are a daily occurrence if you're Amish. It always mystified me.

One incident of this bizarre lumping together stands out in my mind from years ago: Dad and I were in the shop putting the finishing touches on a dining room table. We had put hours into it and were pleased with how it had turned out. Our craftsmanship was especially exquisite, and Dad and I had sanded it down just perfectly. The bell clanged on the door, and a dishwater blonde woman with a mop of unruly hair came barging into the shop shouting something about "mills."

"You horrible, horrible people!!!" the woman shouted, flailing her arms.

"Huh?" Dad said.

"Arrrgggh, you're admitting it!!!! You HORRIBLE, HORRIBLE man!!!!" The almost hysterical woman shouted.

Dad remained calm.

"Ma'am, what are you talking about?"

"Labradoodles!!! Bichon Frise!!! Money! Money! The almighty dollar, you don't care, you don't care!!!"

"Dogs?" Dad asked.

"You admit it again!!!" The woman asked, spittle shooting from her mouth and landing on Dad's crisply-pressed green shirt. He began to get annoyed.

"Ma'am, look, I don't have...."

But she cut him off.

"I'd never buy from you, NEVER. You Amish and your puppy mills! How'd you like to be shoved into a crate with no food, water, or room to move?! You DISGUST me!"

Dad, Daniel, and I first thought she was just a harmless crackpot, but then she took her handbag and swung it at me. She missed and hit an open can of dark varnish that we had just used on another job, and it spilled its molasses-colored contents all over the light walnut dining room table. Daniel and I were about to intervene when she spun around, vanished out our door, and sped down the driveway in her gas-guzzling SUV. I think because we were Amish and on the main route we were easy, but misplaced, targets for her anger.

Dad was less upset with the woman and more at Daniel for leaving a can of varnish open. But, really, at that time none of us had a clue as to what she was even talking about. Dad wouldn't have known a puppy mill if he walked into one. We always had a dog on the farm growing up. Speck was a border collie that was great at keeping our horses in line. While we weren't brought up to treat dogs like family members as most of your kind of do do, I also have no interest in contributing to the suffering of an animal. Ruby and Summer always had the best of veterinary care, and Loretta treated them like they were members of the family.

Anyway, I don't want people thinking because ol' Mose Neuenschwander fell for such a gullible trap that somehow all Amish would. Yes, some did. But I wouldn't.

I remember the day Amos first showed up at the Neuenschwanders, hawking what he called his "investment club." It was shortly after the collapse of the pigeon scheme and I was helping them chuck hay up into their hay mow. We were in their barn when Amos's car came rumbling down the driveway, a cloud of drought dust trailing it. This was shortly after my confession to the congregation and the near-shunning. I was still bitter over Amos Raber's presence there and his seeming enthusiasm for getting me expelled.

Amos wasted no time in obsequiously ingratiating himself to ol' Mose.

"Nice place you've got here. I've always liked it," Amos said.

"Amos, good to see you again," Mose said. Like everyone–male or female–Mose seemed captivated and charmed by Amos's movie-star looks and winning persona.

"I was just at the Keim's and was telling them about our investment club, and they just went wild. Seven to nine percent interest annually. You can't get that parking your money in a bank!" Amos said, gesturing wildly, his teeth gleaming like white pieces of Chiclet gum.

"Lizzie, come over here for a minute, I want you to hear what Amos has to say!" Mose called to his wife.

Looking back at it, it was all so easy. The Neuenschwanders and Amos were talking in loud, animated tones and I could hear bits and pieces of the conversation.

"What do you think is going on over there?" Roman asked me.

"I'm not sure, but whatever it is it seems to have caught your Dad's interest."

"Last time something caught his interest, we got stuck with dozens of pigeons," Roman said dryly.

I listened more intently. Among the snippets of flattering fawning were more troubling pieces of pitch.

"All your problems will be over FOREVER. Such pretty fabric, Mrs. Neuenschwander. Great house you have here. Mmmmm, best cookies I've ever tasted. You'll never have to worry another day in your life."

I decided to see what was going on. I put my pitchfork aside, although if I had known then what I know now, I might have held on to it.

"I'm looking forward to speaking to your parents," Mose said to me. "This is a deal that is too good to pass up!"

"Whoa, there…" I said. "Amos, good to see you again," I lied. This was the first time I had seen Amos since the confession. Our animosity went back years. I didn't like him back in our baseball days and I didn't really like him now. The feeling, I'm sure, was mutual. He seemed to eye me with the same disdain as he heaped upon me on the diamond years ago.

"Hello, Abe…how is your little shop?" Amos sniffed.

I ignored the dig. "I mean no disrespect, but do you mind if I ask some questions?"

"What's there to ask? This sounds like the answer to our prayers," Mose interjected.

Amos carried a clipboard with a list of names. "These are all of the people in this area that I have signed up. I know you know most of these folks. They can all vouch for me!" Amos declared. "You'll get a much better rate of return with Plain Investments than with your money just sitting in the First Bank of Berne, that's for sure."

I looked at his list. There were plenty of people we knew on it.

"I'm not doubting you, your company, or your product. It sounds great. it would just make me feel more comfortable if I knew more before advising Mose to sign away his savings," I said.

Amos glared.

"Did he ask for your advice?"

I conceded his point. "No."

Lizzie had been silent through most of this. While Amish society is very much structured by gender, Amish marriages can be very egalitarian institutions, but Mose and Lizzie were old-fashioned. Mose took care of all the financial transactions and big decisions, while Lizzie kept the home fires burning, doing laundry, cooking, gardening, and mending.

"Lizzie, what do you think about all of this?" I asked, hoping to pry free the opinion of the person who really ran the Neuenschwander household. But if Lizzie disagreed with her husband's actions, she never told me.

"Sounds like something worth looking into," Lizzie concurred.

Exasperated, I had a conversation with Mose in heated Swiss that he ought to think about this a bit longer before jumping into it.

"He's one of us, Abe. You grew up with him. He's a good man. And I know his family. My cousin's wife's sister is related to Amos's uncle who lives in Greentown, Ohio. He's family. I wouldn't write a check to just anyone, but he's the real deal," Mose said.

"Wait a minute, if he's one of us, why isn't he still Amish?" I pointed out.

Mose paused.

"Well…he left before he was baptized. He's helping all of us in ways he couldn't had he stayed."

Amos watched our conversation with concern, but his fears eased when Mose spoke next.

"Who do I make the check out to?" Mose asked Amos.

CHAPTER 15

PAIGE

Being back in the city was unsettling. There was something soothing and comforting about the Amish community around Uncle Ralph's. It made Chicago seem jarring and unforgiving, noisy and crowded. I had trouble focusing on work. I had always appreciated the city's excitement: the roar of the L trains, the hot dog vendors, exhilarating runs along Lakeshore Drive. It was such an opposite environment from the quiet outside Berne that I found myself tugged in two directions.

I lived in a cozy brownstone apartment in the neighborhood of Wrigleyville, an enclave on Chicago's north side with quaint boutiques, ethnic eateries, and, of course, the Cubs. My parents, who lived in the suburbs, would often stop by on the way to or from the theater or other opulent outings in "the City," as they called it from their suburban redoubt.

"Amazing pie, Paige..." Mom said. "Pecan is my favorite."

"It's not pecan pie, Mom," I said, trying hard to stifle a giggle.

"You're kidding me. What else could it be? This is a delicious pecan pie," Mom uttered.

"Oh, and I made the crust myself."

"It's just divine. Where did you learn to make this?"

"Well, first of all, it's oatmeal pie."

Mom put her fork down and started chewing a little more slowly.

"But, it tastes just like pecan…," she said, her fork dicing through the pie, poking for pecans. She found none.

"Anyway, back to your question of where I learned to make this. Remember the Amish family I told you about, the one that fixed my car?"

"Never should have gotten that car. Piece of junk. If you had taken your father's advice…is that also the same Amish family that stole Ralph's identity? Bunch of thieves..." Mom huffed.

"Now, Rita, don't interrupt her. Yes, I remember you telling us about them," Dad said.

"Mom, you're not being fair..." I interjected, growing impatient. Mom and I just never saw eye to eye on anything. It's no surprise that I'd rebelled as soon as I was old enough.

"Fair? I'm not being fair...sounds like those people almost gave Ralph a heart attack, and I'm not being fair?"

"You don't even talk to one another anymore, so why should you care, anyway?" I retorted, but Mom just waved me off.

"They're a wonderful family. Everyone does things they aren't proud of," I said.

"Well, you would know..." Mom shot back. I was boiling inside, but I just ignored her and looked straight at my Dad.

"I visited them last week and one of the women showed me how to make a homemade pie crust. It's really simple," I explained. "You make it right in the pan."

Mom seemed unimpressed.

"It seems so...quaint...families that still live like *Little House on the Prairie*. It must be quite... entertaining to see," Mom said with a slight chuckle.

"I don't go there to be entertained. I actually learn a lot whenever I visit."

"I'm sure you do. Are they going to teach you to churn butter next?" Mom said dismissively. "Oh no, I'm wrong...they're going to teach you how to steal someone's identity."

My fork clattered onto my plate, and I glared at Mom.

"Now, tell us, are there any new men in your life? Don't see why you quit seeing Scott, seems like you two were so well suited for one another." Mom sniffed.

"Ugh, don't go there," I said.

"Wait a minute, Rita, I'd like to hear a little bit more about Paige's Amish friends," Dad said between forkfuls of pie. "Anyone that teaches you to bake like this is probably worth learning more about."

"Oh, Richard..." Mom waved him off with an eye roll.

"Thanks, Dad...the Schwartzes really are incredible. It's not so much like you're stepping back into the 19th century. I think that's sort of the version the tourism bureaus sell. In so many ways they're just like us, they just....how do I explain?" I said, grasping for words. "There's an appreciation of life stripped to its essence: family, food, faith...you spend a weekend there and see how much fun and fulfillment they get out of life with a fraction of the material goods we have, and I can guarantee that you'll start to reprioritize your life a bit."

ABRAHAM

While Paige was in Chicago, I was spending my days sweating, sanding, and sawing. We had a big furniture order and that was a good thing. I needed something to take my mind off Paige. Meanwhile, Loretta was doing everything she could to keep me occupied.

The Sunday after Paige departed, church services were at Joseph and Laura Yutzy's house. The Yutzys' after-church lunch was an assortment of fried chicken, mashed potatoes, pickled beets, lettuce salad, pudding, and four different kinds of pies. Oh, and "church peanut butter spread" -- no after-service meal is complete without that. Amish church spread consists of one part peanut butter, one part marshmallow crème, and one part corn syrup. Most people just spread it on a slice of bread. After the meal was over, many of us gathered on the Yutzys' lawn under the shade of some walnut trees. The Yutzy daughters handed out cups of lemonade to those who lingered.

"I think she likes you," Loretta whispered to me.

"Who?"

"Dorcas Petersheim."

"Oh, come on, you've got to be kidding…she's 17 years older than me."

Dorcas was making the rounds, laughing and trading gossip. She was wearing a roomy rust-colored dress and black *kapp*.

"Well, it seems you like older women," Nancy chortled, a subtle reference to Paige's age.

"Very funny," I said. "Shouldn't you be heading for home with Mom and Dad?"

"No, I'd rather ride with you, Loretta, and Timothy." Nancy shot back. I sighed.

Dorcas Petersheim was a sweet woman, but she was built like a linebacker for the Cleveland Browns and was a little loud for my taste. I tend to be more cerebral and subdued, while Dorcas was out there backslapping, roaring with laughter, and hugging anything that didn't move.

"What about Verena Lehman?" Loretta asked.

"What about her?" I asked.

"She always seems to me making eyes at you…" Loretta said.

"She makes eyes at anyone with a pulse," I countered.

"You're impossible. You've got to try to get out there and mix a bit, or you'll never meet anyone. Come with Timothy and me to the young persons' gathering tonight."

"Mmm, I don't know…I thought I might just sit in the back prairie and sketch or write in my journal."

"Dude, you need to get out some, you're never going to meet anyone sitting out in the back prairie unless you want to marry a wild turkey or a bobcat," Timothy said. "Come with us."

"All right," I said, knowing that Loretta would make the rest of my weekend miserable if I didn't. "But I'm only going in order to make you two quit bugging me. I'm not in the mood to hang out with anyone."

"Except for Paige," Nancy snickered.

"Okay, that's it. Out of here, go home with Mom and Dad," I ordered. And Nancy scampered off to find them.

Many Amish go home on Sunday afternoons for a few hours of rest and relaxation before heading back out in the evening for supper, often at the place where church was held.

I enjoyed a relaxing afternoon before Timothy arrived to take us to the singing. Loretta and Timothy had been dating for a little less than a year now after meeting at one of these Sunday evening singings. He was 22 years old, and in many ways Loretta and Timothy made the ideal couple, although admittedly I didn't know him that well. I clambered into their buggy but quickly realized I'd have company in the back.

"Abe, this is Katie Burkholder, my cousin from Middlebury. Didn't we tell you she was coming?" Timothy asked.

"Um…no…Hi…how are you, Katie?"

"Good, yourself?" she chirped.

"Fine…excuse me just a second," I said, climbing back out of the buggy

"What did you do, kidnap a kid from the parochial school? She looks like she's about 12!"

I noticed Katie frowning in the back of the buggy, so maybe she could hear our conversation. I hoped not, because she seemed nice enough.

"Oh, relax, she's 18," Loretta assured me. "And she's a very sweet girl."

"And what could we *possibly* have in common?" I growled.

"Oh, just have fun. You're too serious for your own good. Katie's a blast."

We soon arrived at the Hiltys' and found a festive youth gathering.

A volleyball net was set up in the front yard where a few youth were playing. On a picnic table, young women were putting out plenty of food. I perked up when I saw the haystack supper and homemade ice cream, two of my favorites. A haystack is a layered meal like a taco without the shell, with hamburger on one layer, lettuce on another, tomato on another, and so on. Sometimes spaghetti is added, and then it's all topped with cheese so the dish looks like a giant haystack. After admiring the meal on the table, I soon recognized the hulking figure of Dorcas Petersheim making the rounds, giving bear hugs, and loudly laughing. Soon it was my turn. I needed something to make myself look unavailable.

"Mr. Lincoln!!! So good to see you!!" Dorcas laughed.

"Uh, nice to see you too, Dorcas. This is my date, Katie," I said, putting my arm around her waist.

Katie blurted: "But I thought I overheard you sayi…"

"Thought you overheard me saying what a sweet girl you are?" I said. Just then, everyone got quiet, and whispers rippled across the makeshift volleyball court. A car was slowly moving down the quiet lane in front of the Hiltys'.

"Tourists," someone whispered. One of the girls grabbed a pair of binoculars and stared at the car, only to find someone staring right back at her with binoculars.

Some of the young people began to run towards the tourists' car, which spooked them enough that the driver hit the gas and peeled away. Meanwhile, Katie seemed smitten with me, but I found that the more I tried to disinterest her, the clingier she became. She'd hover around me like a bee, asking questions, wanting to know everything about me.

*   *

*

One evening I found myself missing Paige's company and companionship so much that I hitched up Ruby and headed for the Berne Public Library to send her an email.

"Back again?" the librarian asked crisply.

"Uh-huh," I muttered, trying to seem inconspicuous.

I sat at the station next to a blonde teenage girl who was watching something on the screen that I think had to do with vampires. She nodded at me as I sat down.

I typed Paige a quick email and sent it, but within a few seconds the computer made a "pinging" sound and I received the following message:

<<<<<<<<<<<<<< Email account full. This email is being held in queue until the recipient creates more room in their box.>>>>>>>>>>>>>>>>>>

When I logged into my Zapmail account, I noticed a little green dot by Paige's name with the words "Online – click here to chat." My heart was galloping faster than Ruby. I typed.

"Hi."

I waited.

No response. Minutes passed. I tried again.

"Anyone home?"

"Abe? I didn't know you knew how to chat!"

"I didn't know I knew how to either! But you sort of forced my hand" I typed.

"How so?" Paige asked.

"Your email box is apparently full."

"Ugh, sorry about that. For reasons unknown this new service I switched to has a very limited storage capacity. And I'm on some legal listserv that floods my box with innumerable meaningless messages. Anyway, so glad to talk to you in real-time! How are you?"

"Fine. How was the pie crust?"

"Mom loved it....seems, though, unless it's caviar or couscous she doesn't have much use!"

"I bet it was good. I've never tried caviar, but fish eggs don't sound very appealing, and couscous...?"

"Couscous isn't bad. It's a steamed wheat and vegetable dish, it's Middle Eastern. Maybe I can fix some for you sometime (although I'd have to learn to fix it for myself first lol!)"

"Couscous, doesn't sound like something that'd be served at the after-church gatherings." I typed.

"LOL, probably not." Paige responded.

"I'm sure anything you fix would be delicious! By the way, what is LOL? "

This was beyond my hopes, actually getting to "converse" with Paige in real time!

"I tried to yodel a verse or two for some co-workers, but they thought I was crazy. Need to get some of the Schwartzes yodeling for my iPod. Oh, LOL is laugh out loud. Talking online is a whole different language sometimes."

I laughed aloud at the thought of Paige yodeling at work.

The owlish librarian peered at me over her horn-rimmed glasses, and a few other non-Amish library patrons looked at me quizzically. I slouched in my seat and pulled the brim of my hat down a bit. Typing was not a natural skill for me. I'd much rather engage in the broad strokes of sanding, or just pick up a good heavy hammer and pound in some nails.

"How is everyone?" Paige asked.

"Fine...Daniel and Nancy are excited about detasseling beginning...still probably a couple of weeks away from starting. Corn's slow this season," I typed. "How are you?"

"Doing well, busy at my office, and doing extra running to work off all that food I ate at your place."

"I told you, you are plenty pretty as is," I replied. I was finding that bashfulness is easier to overcome online than in person.

"You have me blushing now, but I doubt I'm in nearly as good shape as you, all that work you do on the farm. You are all muscle."

"I do have a lot of muscle, that's why you are as light as a feather to pick up." I typed. I couldn't believe how much bolder I felt saying things when I just had to say them to a screen. It was kind of scary, actually.

"Yes, you seemed to have no trouble lifting me--told ya you're all muscle."

"Told you, I've lifted sacks of flour lighter than you!"

"Do you run?"

"Only if something is chasing me! Just kidding...I'd like to ride a bicycle, but they don't allow them in our church. But I do enjoy running. I've done it before, gone running in our back prairie. Do you run far?"

"I've done 15 miles before, would love to do the Chicago Marathon sometime."

"You could outdistance me, that is for sure," I replied.

"Would an Amish person be able to run a marathon?" Paige asked.

"If the Amish person were in good enough shape!"

"LOL, witty!"

"No, our church rules aren't like that. There's no stone tablet someplace that lists everything we can and can't do, we're just expected to know the rules. We aren't supposed to call attention to ourselves, we're a conformist culture, but running in a marathon? I don't see why not. Running is simply physical activity which the church doesn't discourage. Now if I were to run it and win and accept a trophy and go around and give speeches about running, that might be a problem on several levels. Does that make sense?" Whew, that was a lot to type.

"Yes, I think…"

"A Hutterite boy participated in the Olympic torch relay when it was in Canada."

"Hutterite?"

"Discussion for another day, they are a religion closely related to ours, Google it."

"Ha! You're so knowledgeable about almost everything, you sure you don't have a college degree hidden away in a drawer someplace?"

"My degree is just from The University of Life."

"Sounds like a good school!"

"Maybe we could run together sometime, we'll call it the Berne and Back 5K." Paige typed."

"I'd like that, and if you got too tired I could carry you."

"LOL, I think we already got in trouble once with you picking me up."

"I think I could run and carry you at the same time. My legs are strong."

"I bet you have muscular legs," Paige typed.

"Perhaps I can show you sometime. And I might have strong legs, but you have a beautiful body, at least what I've been able to see, I'd love to see more," I couldn't believe I just typed those words. Oh wow, I'd never in a gazillion years say anything like that in person.

There was a long pause.

"Well, I bet yours is amazing also."

I exhaled with relief.

"Oh, she's pretty," the librarian commented.

Holy crap, I thought to myself. Paige had a little photo of herself in the chat box, which simply made me long for her even more, but also made it very visible to whom I was talking.

"Do you mind?" I asked politely.

"No, I don't mind if you chat with her, but how about another time? The library closed half an hour ago."

"Oh…" I said, noticing the clock. That was something I found quite unexpected and troubling about the internet, how it seemed time shifted into some kind of high-speed warp when I was online. No wonder my church was so against it. The internet would eviscerate family life if we allowed computers in the home. I decided I agreed with my bishops. The computer is best kept in the confines of a library. And, frankly, it was scary to be so bold online. That wasn't me in person.

"I hate to leave on this note, but I need to go," I typed.

"Ha, worried I am going to seduce you online?" Paige typed back.

" No, I'd probably LIKE that," I wrote back. "Not leaving because I want to. The library is closing…er, it IS closed actually. The librarian is giving me the evil eye."

"Oh, well, in that case…it was great talking to you Abe, always is. I haven't had a chance yet to look up anything about the Neuenschwander's loan, but tomorrow I will do that. I know the auction is coming up, so there's not much time."

"Don't go through too much work, I told you old Mose is probably not going to be receptive," I replied.

"I'll keep that in mind. Bye, Abe."

It was kind of jarring going from such a seductive conversation to talking about the Neuenschwander's loan. But my heart was still fluttering as I hitched Ruby up and headed for home through the darkness. I was quickly jolted back to reality, though.

"Look who came to see you," Loretta said upon my arrival. "She's in town for a cousin's wedding."

"Well, hi, handsome," Katie Burkholder giggled.

CHAPTER 16

PAIGE

I'll admit to being excited by the Instant Message exchange with Abe. When it ended, I felt giddy, excited, like I did back in high school when I was crushing on a boy. But I talked myself back to reality by telling myself that this was just a flirtation and I shouldn't be encouraging it. What was I going to do, trade in my car for a buggy and live happily ever after? It was ridiculous. But I did want to help the Neuenschwanders and maybe make amends for all the faceless foreclosures I had so rotely processed paperwork for. So the next day I did a little research at work on Amos Raber and Plain Investments. Abe had given me very little to go on. I wasn't even sure I was spelling Raber right.

A search for anything about "Plain Investments" was coming up mostly empty. Plain Investments was an LLC registered in Berne, Indiana. But for an investment firm there wasn't the typical paper-trail required by the SEC. Amos Raber was listed as the President, with some other names I didn't recognize listed as officers. Something seemed off because I just couldn't find much about them. Not even a telephone number. But then I had a hunch.

I knew someone who might be able to help: Ashleigh Burton. She and I had gone to law school together and were running buddies. I pounded out a quick email:

"Hey, Ash, hope all is well. And I hope everything worked out with the Great Lakes Bank case. I was happy to help. We ought to do lunch sometime. Would you mind checking into something for me?"

ABRAHAM

As Paige and I continued our email exchanges, I began to run out of libraries. Yes, Amish on occasion will use the computer in a library. But frequent forays into these temples of books and learning would certainly cause gossip, and may, if overdone, run afoul of church rules. Looking up something on a computer is probably not a violation of the *ordnung*. Carrying on hours of instant message conversations and emails with an outsider, well, that probably would be an issue. The odd thing is that the more I used the computer, the more I disliked it. While I awaited messages from Paige with giddy anticipation, I didn't like being tethered to the computer, and I didn't like how time just seemed to evaporate when online. So in a strange sort of way--I don't think I'm rationalizing here--using the computer helped reinforce the church's teachings.

For me, the issue was logistical. There were only so many libraries near me. The Geneva Public Library was only 15 minutes away by buggy, the Berne Library 10 minutes. I didn't want to go to any one repeatedly. Really, this was much more about emotion than technology. That's how I justified, in my mind, using the computer so much. The Amish church has no prohibition on emotion, so I was using technology to nurse a crush, not to indulge in 21st century frivolity. When I was on the library computers, I never watched any movies or went to any other websites, just talked to Paige. And my church allowed the *use* of phones, so, I reasoned, this really was no different, it was just a phone by typing.

But one difficult lesson I learned is that for those who make mistakes in life or commit crimes, subsequent standards become higher. In other words, if this email communication I was carrying on with Paige had been the only questionable behavior I had participated in my life, no one would have probably ever said a word. It was this behavior coupled with my past that made me feel like the church was holding me at times to an abnormally high standard.

One late June afternoon, I managed to slip away from the shop for a couple of hours. It had been about five days since I'd used the Berne library's computers, so I thought I'd head there in hopes of catching Paige online.

I secured Ruby to the hitching post behind the library.

"Abe, *wie bist du?*"

I stiffened. A shadow spread across the sidewalk, the outline of a wide-brimmed hat visible. The voice was familiar. And to this day I'm not sure where he was, or how he knew I was there, because I had done some reconnaissance before hitching just to make sure there wasn't anyone around. The voice and shadow belonged to Monroe Hochstetler, our bishop.

"Abe, *wie bist du?*" Bishop Hochstetler asked again

"*Gut, gut.*"

We exchanged pleasantries under the shade of the stately elms outside of the library. Bishop Hochstetler was a hog farmer who owned 200 acres west of Berne, a large amount of land by Amish standards. One of his sons had taken over the day-to-day operations, but a fit Monroe was still active. Monroe and his wife Fannie had 11 children.

I was surprised to see Bishop Hochstetler in town on a weekday afternoon.

"What brings you into town?" Monroe asked. He was dressed immaculately--as he always seemed to be--wearing a hunter-green button-down shirt with a black vest, black trousers, and a black felt hat.

"Just some errands," I demurred.

"It is such a gorgeous day...I'll join you."

I was in a bind. I couldn't stomach the idea of lying to Bishop Hochstetler. Even if I didn't always agree with every position of our church, I respected the office of bishop. Lying to my bishop was out of the question, so I played it cool.

"I was just going to go into the library for a bit."

Bishop Hochstetler raised his eyebrows.

"Oh?"

I figured if I told him I was going into the library, I didn't need to tell him why. "I was going to...look up some information…"

"I haven't been into the library in a number of years, not since they remodeled. Be interesting to see," Monroe offered.

I hesitated. "Yeah, you know, I actually agree with you…this is such a gorgeous day, why spend it indoors? I think I'll skip the library today, run some of my other errands."

"Okay, I'd be happy to join you. My buggy is just around the side of the building," Monroe said. "I can leave it there."

"You know, Bishop Hochstetler, I actually probably got too caught up in this nice weather. Look at the time!" I said, glancing at my pocket watch. "I really should get back to the shop to finish some orders. You want to come along with me? I'm sure Mom and Dad would be happy to see you," I said, hoping that would shake him off. And for a moment, it appeared to work.

"Maybe you're right. I've got work to get to, also. I should go home too. Abe, why don't you stop by for supper this evening?"

That really wasn't an invitation. When the bishop invites you to supper, you don't check your calendar to see if you're free. You go.

CHAPTER 17

PAIGE

For most of my two years working at the firm, I hadn't been able to put a human face on the foreclosure crisis. My job was to mitigate losses for the banks, protect their investments, and help clear the clogged court dockets.

Usually, I arrived at 8 a.m. and worked long days until it was time to head home at 5 p.m. to my brownstone. It wasn't glamorous work, but I figured I'd accept the job, work for a year, sock away some money, ride out the recession, and then decide what I really wanted to do with my life. At this time, there was a glut of lawyers and a scarcity of jobs. A few of my law-school friends had found themselves working as hotel front-desk clerks, fast-food restaurant managers, or daycare supervisors, all honorable jobs but not exactly the wanted return on a $150,000 three-year educational investment. So the law firm where I worked was meant to be a port to ride out the storm of the recession before exploring areas that really interested me. But one year blurred into the next, and soon I found myself feeling as though I were on a treadmill to nowhere. I had a small circle of friends I'd go out with on weekends, an occasional boyfriend, but otherwise my life had settled into a sort of dull inertia.

For a long time, I completed tasks with efficiency and even felt, naively, that I was doing noble work, contributing to the free flow of a capitalistic economy. I was mainly a paper pusher. I had never argued a case in front of a jury. One time a foreclosure case of mine had come tantalizingly close to a trial, but the parties settled at the last minute.

My thoughts drifted to that wonderful evening at the Neuenschwanders, the supper, the dessert, the yodeling, the water battle. These were good, hard-working people who were snookered by a greedy snake-oil salesman and were now going to lose everything because of it. It wasn't fair.

ABRAHAM

I went back to the shop and helped Dad sand some china cabinets, something we did with utmost care before applying the varnish. I worked quietly, in a morose mood, not sure what Bishop Hochstetler wanted. My brother Daniel, who just turned 16, had been spending more and more time with us in the shop, which was welcome. Being almost nine years apart in age, we hadn't been very close through the years. As he was becoming a young man, though, we were finding more and more common interests, so it was enjoyable getting to really know him, and Dad and I could use the extra help.

Once while we were both busy measuring and sawing wood for a table and chair set, Daniel -- out of earshot of Dad -- whispered to me, "She sure is hot."

"Katie?"

"No, Paige."

I laughed and shook my head. I wish I could pawn Katie off on Daniel, but she didn't seem interested in a younger man.

After the work day was over, I headed for the wash-house. I wanted to get cleaned up before going to Bishop Hochstetler's. In our church district, we didn't have indoor plumbing. I know many outsiders are amazed by this and wonder how we could possibly be clean and, believe me, I've overheard more than a few snarky comments from your kind of people in town. I always tell them there's this neat invention called "soap," which works perfectly well in a sponge bath same as in a modern shower. We had an old wash tub next to a kerosene stove. Mom kept some big stainless steel stockpots by the stove, and when one of us needed a bath, she would just heat a kettle of water. She'd also keep a ready supply of fresh towels and soap nearby.

Mom made our soap out of a combination of lye and lard. I'd often tease her that her full-time job seemed to be finding ways to make more work.

"Hey, you can buy bar soap at the Berne Community Market," I'd say.

"You don't really know what's in that soap," Mom would protest.

Anyway, back to my bath. I heated my own water. At my age, I didn't think I needed to have Mom draw my bath, although I will say that Mom always seemed to be able to heat it to the perfect temperature. Somehow she just knew. I always seemed to overheat the water so that it would be scalding, and then I'd have to stand there shivering naked in the tub for several minutes until the water cooled enough to use. Most of the time we all knew when someone was in the wash-house, so we didn't make a habit of locking the door.

Each November, Schwartz's Home Furnishings had an annual "buggy load" sale. It's sort of a tongue-in-cheek parody of some other stores owned by non-Amish that have "truck load" sales. Mom would make homemade doughnuts and press fresh apple cider to serve to customers, and we'd have an assortment of furniture for sale at deep discounts.

Once, a couple of ladies searching for our big sale somehow missed all the signs pointing to the shop. First of all, our store opened up at

8 a.m., so they shouldn't have been prowling around at 7 a.m., but they were, and I happened to be in the wash-house taking a bath. The door creaked open and I found myself eye to eye with two middle-aged ladies. It was usually fairly dark in the wash-house even in the middle of the day so maybe they couldn't see a lot, but they must have seen enough. One lady screamed. I grabbed a towel and they slammed the door.

"Oooh, I wish I could take him home with me!" I heard one of the ladies say as they headed for one of our other outbuildings in search of our shop. I have to admit that stroked my ego a bit.

I found the warm tub baths relaxing, thoughtful, not rushed like a shower. I rather liked them. With warm water and plenty of soap, I could get just as clean, perhaps even more so than in a shower because, like the buggy rides and so many other things we do, the tub baths force one to slow down and be more deliberate and thoughtful about the bathing process rather than just jumping into a shower for a couple minutes and saying you're clean.

I put on one of my better outfits, an azure button-down shirt, black vest, and matching black trousers. As I came out of the wash-house, I ran into Loretta, who was crossing paths with me on her way to do the milking.

"Well, look at you all dressed up…you going out tonight?" Loretta said slyly. "Have you and Katie been writing to one another, after all?"

"Please, she's six years younger than me. I'd adopt her before I'd date her!"

"Well, then, why the nice clothes? If you're going to skip out on supper, you picked a bad evening. Mom is serving pork chops and corn chowder, but looks like you're seeing someone special tonight instead."

"Oh, it's someone special all right."

Loretta put down the milk pail she was holding.

"Oh, please tell me!" she shrieked with delight. "I'm so happy! Of course, I wished it would have worked out with Katie, but…"

Annoyed, I cut her off. "It's Bishop Hochstetler."

Loretta's expression grew serious.

"You're going there? On a Tuesday night? Why? Oh no, don't tell me. I know. See, I told you that Paige would bring nothing but grief."

"Now, wait a minute. I don't know what it's about. For all I know, he could be offering me a job on his hog farm. I hear he's hiring," I said, trying to explore some rational, plausible reasons he might want to see me.

"Maybe he'd want to hire Daniel, but why would he want to hire you? He knows you're in line to take over the store," Loretta reasoned. "What did he say? How did this come about? You must have *some* idea."

"No, no, I really don't," I said. He could want to talk about Paige, but, really, it could also be something else. I'd been very discreet, or at least tried to be, in my library visits and online conversations, although I'll admit Bishop Hochstetler had seemed to appear out of nowhere outside the library. If he'd done that there, could he have been hiding in the shadows elsewhere? I suddenly found myself apprehensive.

"Bishop Hochstetler doesn't usually invite people over just to shoot the breeze," Loretta clucked.

"Not so fast. Didn't he have Timothy over for dinner once just to 'shoot the breeze?'"

"Well, yes, but that was different. He invited him over with three weeks' notice. It was right before he was being baptized. You know how Monroe…er, Bishop Hochstetler is about young people in the church. He does like to counsel them before baptism. But you're already baptized and this was very sudden…how did he contact you?" Loretta said.

I didn't really want to answer the question.

"In town…I ran into him in town," I said, hoping that would be enough to satisfy Loretta, but she pressed on.

"Where? When were you in town?"

"Earlier today…"

"Where?"

"At the library…."

Loretta frowned.

"What were you…?"

"Look, 'Retta, that's enough. This really doesn't concern you. You need to focus on your own life and not mine. I'll deal with this," I said tersely.

"You've been a real grump lately, is all I'll say. If you get booted from the church, at least I'll have a clean conscience knowing I did everything I could to prevent it. I'll pray for you."

"I'm not going to get booted. Your heart is in the right place, but you're not helping."

Dad was still in the shop, so I nonchalantly opened the door and shouted to him, "Hey, I'm headed out for a bit. I won't be around for supper. Bye!"

It was awkward being 24 and living at home. I wasn't telling them I wouldn't be home for supper because I felt they had to know, but it was just a courtesy because I lived there and Mom would want to know how many plates to put out.

I hitched up Summer for the ride to Bishop Hochstetler's house. Ruby would have made for a quicker trip, but I was in the mood for solitude, and there's no greater tonic for a tortured soul than an open buggy ride on a pleasant summer evening in Indiana.

Monroe and Fannie Hochstetler lived in a classic two-story white clapboard home set back from a gravel road. He had been elected bishop at the relatively young age of 39, and 41 years later he still ran the church with efficiency, fairly flawlessly navigating it through decades of societal and congregational upheaval. I considered ourselves relatively lucky. While Bishop Hochstetler had a definite stern streak, he was always seeking the best for the church. Some bishops in other churches would just cave in and allow anything because they were more interested in being liked than keeping the church intact, so when digital music players became popular, a few bishops allowed them. Same for cell phones. Not Bishop Hochstetler. Don't get me wrong, I think there needs to be room for a church to breathe and grow, but if I wanted a television or a car, I might as well be a Methodist or a Mormon.

Monroe and Fannie Hochstetler had been married almost 20 years longer than he had been bishop. They had raised 11 children together, and their farmstead was always abuzz with grandchildren and great-grandchildren. Monroe had long ago turned the day-to-day operations of his hog farm over to one of his boys, but he still was active in the business.

"Come on in, Abe," Fannie said, always warm and welcoming

"Thank you."

"Would you like a glass of lemonade? It'd go good on a hot evening like this!"

"Sure, I'll take one. Thanks for inviting me over for supper. This is a real treat," I said.

And I was sincere. An invitation to supper at Fannie's was a ticket to culinary comfort. She was known throughout the church for preparing the best casseroles. Not that Mom's weren't good, but Fannie's were melt-in-your-mouth amazing, the chunks of meat and vegetables and sauce would be proportioned just so that you felt as if you were having a four-course meal in each bite.

After supper, the women tackled the dishes and the Hochstetler sons and grandchildren headed out to the hog barns to complete the day's work. This left Monroe and me alone together. We stepped out onto the front porch, a long wrap-around veranda with a few rockers spaced out along the length.

"Have a chair, enjoy the breeze a bit."

"Oh no, that's okay, I shouldn't stay. I am sure you have work to do," I said, hoping that maybe this was just a friendly supper invitation after all.

"Abraham, I guess I should get to the point. I didn't invite you over tonight just for conversation …I've invited you over because I've been hearing some things…."

"About what?" I asked, trying to seem nonchalant. "About the highway?"

There had been rumors for a long time that US 27 was going to be widened from two lanes to four. The expansion would force the state to grab land by eminent domain, and there would be new traffic and growth. Many Amish in the area said that if this highway project were ever completed, they would move before living with the disruptions it would cause.

"No, have you heard more about the highway?" Bishop Hochstetler asked intently.

"Well, I did hear that the state is preparing to start making offers to buy land," I said.

"Really? That is…no, wait a minute," Bishop Hochstetler said, seeming momentarily flustered at veering off topic. "No, not the highway…the talk has been about *you*," Bishop Hochstetler said, running his hand through his thick white beard.

"Me?"

I set down my glass of lemonade.

"I've been hearing about an English girl you've been apparently been spending so much time with."

"Oh…I…she's just a friend."

Monroe Hochstetler looked thoughtful as he sunk his hand deeper into his beard.

"You could have such a bright future in this church, Abraham..."

"I appreciate the love and forgiveness everyone has shown me since...my confession."

"You keep wanting me to bend the rules for you. I stuck my neck out for you...when no one else wanted to give you a chance, I spoke up..." Bishop Hochstetler said, sipping his lemonade slowly. "If it had been left up to some of the other ministers, you'd still be behind bars."

"And I appreciate that," I said carefully. I thought of LeRoy Miller.

"I'm getting too old for this, Abe."

"For what?" I asked.

"For these games of yours. Fannie says I need to step down, enjoy my health and what time we have left together...being a bishop is a lot of responsibility."

I nodded, still not quite sure where this conversation was going.

"Is your friend a Christian?" Bishop Hochstetler asked.

I wasn't even 100 percent certain where Paige stood on the spectrum of religion. I know she had doubts about a Higher Power, but she also didn't dismiss the notion. I didn't know yet, so I decided I'd cover for her until I found out for sure.

"She's a good person with deep Christian values," I said.

I'm not sure the answer satisfied Bishop Hochstetler.

"I'd like to meet her," Bishop Hochstetler said, unaware that he already had. "But I do believe the company you keep is important. That's why I think all the factory work we've accepted over the past 20 years has hurt us: the coarse language, the conveniences, the snack machines, even tobacco use…being around bad habits is sort of like being around someone who uses tobacco…even though you don't use cigarettes yourself, you still come away with the stain and smell of smoke. So…this is how it may be with your friend…spend too much time around her and you may find her influencing you in ways that could be harmful. Am I making sense?"

He was. And, oh, how I wanted to say that I would love for some of Paige's sweet scent to linger on me in the same way tobacco smoke lingers. But I kept quiet and respectful. "Yes, you are….but, really, she's just a friend…and I have no intention of doing anything to reflect poorly on the church, to undermine God's will, or be disrespectful of your authority…I truly love the Amish life and way of worship."

Bishop Hochstetler looked thoughtful and not completely convinced.

"Are you reading the Bible?" Bishop Hochstetler asked.

"I've been a little…lazy…about that," I admitted.

"You are quite a bookworm, and in the same way one needs to watch the company they keep, one also needs to be careful of the words they read. You must read with an open mind," Bishop Hochstetler said. "I have my own library and I hear you do, too, but mine's…respectful of the Lord."

Most of Bishop Hochstetler's books came from Amish-owned Pathway Publishing based in Aylmer, Ontario.

"Pathway really publishes all the literature one needs to live a whole, Godly life," Bishop Hochstetler said.

Now it was my turn to appear unconvinced.

"But I think a variety of voices makes for a more intellectually empathetic person, which is, I understand, a Godly virtue?" I said.

A warm breeze kicked up a cyclone of dust in the Hochstetler's dry driveway. I think we both felt that we were jousting with no one really getting the upper hand.

"You know, I don't know that I've ever told anyone this before…but back when I was a couple of years younger than you, I was detasseling corn one summer and there was a Mennonite girl on the crew…her name was Amanda…we got to know one another quite well during the …"

Just then, Fannie came out of the house with a plate of cookies. Monroe stopped mid-sentence.

"Cookie?"

"Sure, thanks," I said grabbing one. Molasses cookies, mmm, they were one of my favorites. Fannie disappeared into the house.

"Point is, she was going to go away to Goshen College the following year," Bishop Hochstetler said.

Goshen College is one of the oldest Mennonite-run colleges in the USA. The Mennonites, unlike the Amish, do not have the same objections to higher education.

"Okay, and…?" I asked.

"…She was going to go study, learn, explore, and with it all the modern technological temptations….She asked me to come with her."

I obviously knew the story's ending. I was sitting here talking with an Old Order Amish bishop, after all.

"The point is, if you are going to be in the Amish church, you have to be in the Amish church. You have to follow the rules with not just your head but with your heart. I believe that this church offers the most direct way to Salvation, the best way to glorify Him, and in a world full of violence, on a planet being overrun by technology that I fear one day will control us and not the other way around, this church offers the best safe haven," Monroe Hochstetler said, sipping from a glass of lemonade that Fannie had put out for him.

I considered his words, letting them sink in as we watched some of his grandchildren playing on the front lawn.

"You give me good food for thought," I said, taking another swig of lemonade.

"Let me be a bit clearer: consider this your last warning. If you break

the rules of the church again, you will never be welcome here. Ever.
Okay?"

CHAPTER 18
ABRAHAM

It was July 4th and the air was stifling in the thick of an Indiana
sauna summer.

Our shop was closed for the holiday. Some people are under the
mistaken notion that the Amish aren't patriotic. It's not that, we just
are a pacifist people and don't glorify or celebrate war. We're
grateful for Independence Day, but it's not something we spend a lot
of time dwelling on. We do enjoy the day off, though. Loretta and
Timothy had gone fishing. Nancy, Velma, and Verena along with
Mom and Dad had taken the buggy to a local park for a picnic.
Mom's macaroni salad was the prize of any picnic and that would
usually be enough to make me go, but I stayed behind at home.
Bishop Hochstetler's words were still weighing on me, and
sometimes days like the Fourth of July were the best times to get
caught up on work. The shop was closed so we didn't have
customers coming in, and I had a bed frame to finish. It was around
3 p.m., Loretta and Timothy wouldn't be back until late, and the

rest of my family would hang out at the lake until fireworks were set off. Even Grandma Ada was away, staying with one of Dad's sisters for a few weeks, so the *dawdy haus* sat empty. Having our entire 140-acre farmstead completely to myself was a rarity, so I was going to savor it.

"Suit yourself, stick-in-the-mud," Loretta had said to me before leaving.

"Sure you don't want to join us? The twins made monster cookies," Mom said.

"Dorcas Petersheim will probably be there if you want to come," Nancy said gleefully.

But I waved away all the good-natured taunts and headed into our shop to work on the unfinished bed frame. I didn't have the farm to myself for very long, though, before a car appeared unannounced and seemingly out of nowhere.

It was Paige.

"Wow…what are you doing here?" I asked. I wasn't sure whether I was excited at seeing her, or embarrassed that I hadn't put on my best shirt and slacks and combed my hair better.

"Well, it's not like I could call before coming," Paige joked.

"True," I chuckled.

"I came because of the Neuenschwanders. I haven't figured out exactly what is going on yet. In fact, I can't find anything about Plain Investments, and that in itself is a red flag, which is why I came…I want to talk to them, to encourage them to fight the foreclosure and give me some more information."

"Now hang on a second, Paige, this is all very noble of you, but, first, they don't have an attorney and, second…it's too late. We don't sue people. Pacifism extends to the courtroom as well as the battlefield, and I have to agree with the church on that…nothing good ever really comes from conflict, physical or judicial."

"Hold on. This is a wrong being done against THEM, so you mean they wouldn't fight back against that?" Paige asked incredulously.

"That's just not our way. It's hard for outsiders to understand," I explained.

"Try me," Paige said.

"I don't agree with our church on everything, but I do agree with the principle of pacifism. Violence, force solve nothing…litigation solves nothing."

"Ha. You've basically just trashed my whole profession. And solves *nothing? Really?*"

I nodded affirmatively.

"I've done some research….the litigation that you say solves nothing produced the right for the Amish to educate their children only through the eighth grade in *Yoder vs. Wisconsin.* And there have been other cases: *Pennsylvania vs. Petersheim.* What about that? And the case that won Amish construction workers the right to be excluded from wearing the bright yellow hard hats?"

"Fair enough, you've been doing your homework; it's just that our religion teaches that God is the ultimate judge, not the courts…but you make fair points. Those are instances where the courts have protected our religion, and I think most intelligent-minded Amish realize this….You know one of the things I actually like about our church is that it *is* dynamic. A lot of outsiders are probably under the impression that it's the most rigid religion there is, but it really isn't. There is room for compromise, discussion, and broadening of rules."

"If there's room for compromise, then we can save the

Neuenschwanders' home," Paige cheered.

"Okay, you've convinced *me,* but Mose Neuenschwander is the toughest juror you may ever have to face. He'll view fighting the bank not only as undermining God's laws but also as a breach of our church's pacifist teachings. He's very old-school as far as the Amish go."

Paige paced. "So does pacifism even extend to self-defense?"

"I've said before, I'm not a theology expert, but according to the strictest interpretation of our church's rules, yes."

"Well, what if someone broke into your home and held a gun to your child's head and you had a chance to shoot the person...would you?" Paige asked.

"Some, like Mose, would say no, implying they'd stand there twiddling their thumbs as their family was slaughtered. Fact is, I'm not sure any of us know what we would do in a given situation until we are in it. But I really personally believe that violence is a poison best not swallowed."

"My instinct is to say that's all just incredibly naïve, but it's admirable. The fact is that the world has become a violent place, and I think the Amish offer a needed refuge."

"So, the Neuenschwanders lose their home--they'll find a new place to live. That's the attitude they and many in the church have," I explained.

"But this can be stopped!" Paige practically pleaded, slamming her legal pad down on our table.

"I can tell you now, if it means filing a motion, going to court, they won't do it. They won't. To old Mose, that is the same as picking up a gun and firing it. Many Amish believe that way."

"Do you?" Paige asked.

I stopped in my tracks. Outsiders rarely understood.

"Do you agree with every rule of the law firm where you work?"

"Oh, please…no eating at our desks, no open-toed shoes, no dating co-workers. I could go on and on."

"And do you follow every rule?"

"Most, yes. I'd get fired if I didn't. But every rule? No…" Paige conceded.

"Well, yes, being afraid to get fired is one reason to follow rules...but another reason to follow rules is because you agree with the broader mission and principles. Pacifism and rejecting litigation is one of the rules. Someone bounced a $1500 check for a hand-made china cabinet from our store...we didn't prosecute. God will judge them in the end, not us...and that's why we generally abstain from the courts, because it undermines the authority of the ultimate Judge."

"But the Neuenschwanders don't have to lose their home," Paige countered.

I have to admit that I *was* troubled by the Neuenschwanders' situation. And the irony wasn't lost on me that I was playing the role of rule defender now after defiling so many myself. I had committed my own sins against others, but perhaps helping Paige save the Neuenschwanders' home would be my chance at redemption. Would I ever be able to erase the shadow of sin from my life? I had to try. For a moment, I thought of Rachel Miller. I hadn't thought about her in a long time. And while I was captivated with Paige, part of me found myself missing Rachel. I felt like none of this would be happening if I had just followed the rules.

"Fine, I'm not going to speak for the Neuenschwanders. I'm just warning you that Mose is very old-school. You know, I think times are changing. Many younger Amish, if given the evidence you have presented, would consider fighting back against the bank, but I doubt old Mose will."

"Well, I at least have to try," Paige said.

"Okay, fine. I think it's a waste of time, but let's go...by the way, what is in that folder? What did you find out about the Neuenschwanders?" I asked, heading for the horse stables.

"I didn't find out anything about the Neuenschwanders, but I did find out something about Plain Investments and Amos Raber. I'll tell you all when we get to their house," Paige said, waving the file.

"Climb aboard," I said, instinctively taking Paige's hand to help her up. "We'll have to take Ruby. Mom and Dad have Summer," I warned.

"This is always a treat. I've just spent the past three hours in my car. I think I'd prefer the buggy any time."

I had just washed my buggy earlier in the day. With a good scrubbing and soapy water bath, it seems to sparkle and shimmer in the sun, like a just-polished black wingtip shoe.

"Beautiful buggy," Paige said, admiring the polish.

"Did you know not all Amish buggies are black?"

Paige shook her head.

"In some settlements in Pennsylvania, the buggy tops are gray and, in one place, even yellow. In a couple of places the buggy tops are actually a chocolate brown," I said

We arrived at the Neuenschwanders' farmstead. More boxes had been packed, and it definitely had the look of a family on the move. Many families from our church had pitched in to help. The Neuenschwanders were going to temporarily stay in an abandoned house on Lizzie's sister's property. The house was pretty run-down and there was virtually no land, but it'd have to do. It was seven miles away by buggy, so the task of moving was time-consuming.

Children playing in the yard came to a standstill as our buggy arrived. While the mood at the Neuenschwanders was somewhat subdued, Lizzie came bounding out of the house when she saw us arriving, a smile on her face.

"Hi, Abe. You've brought your friend again. I didn't think she'd ever want to come back after the soaking she experienced last time," Lizzie laughed.

"It's okay. I dried out quickly, and the delicious dinner more than outweighed the near-drowning."

"So what brings you out this way again? Coming to lend us a hand with packing? Or maybe you'd like some tea?" Lizzie offered.

"That would be wonderful, thank you. I mean, *danke schoen*," Paige smiled.

Lizzie laughed and put a pot of water on the kerosene stove. She set out some homemade summer sausage, crackers, and cheese.

"I have something I want to talk to you about. Is Mr. Neuensch…er, Mose around?" Paige asked.

"He's in the barn. Is everything okay?" Lizzie asked. "Aaron, go get your father." One of the boys, barefoot and suspender-clad, ran out to fetch his father. I stood solemnly by, as this was Paige's fight, not mine.

Mose came in. Dust from the hay mow had collected on the black brim of his hat. He stomped his work boots by the door .

"Hi. Gorgeous day here today," Paige said, invoking small talk's most go-to topic: the weather.

"Do you remember Paige?" Lizzie asked her husband.

"The water battle. Yes, how do you do?" Mose said softly.

"Fine, fine, thanks."

"Paige has something she wants to talk to us about," Lizzie said to her husband. If she sensed what was coming next, she didn't give any outward sign.

The children seemed a little spooked outside suddenly as a car slowly moved down the gravel lane in front of the house.

"Tourists," Lizzie said, swatting.

"Abraham told me about what is happening with your house," Paige said gently.

"Oh…Abe…I," Lizzie Neuenschwander's eyes welled up. Mose just sat solemnly, staring straight ahead.

"No, it's okay. I…I'm an attorney. In fact, some might say I work for the enemy. I actually work for a firm that specializes in foreclosures, so I'm usually on the side of the bank. But not this time. I can file an appeal. I can save your home."

"Absolutely not. I'm not getting involved in these here courts,"

Mose said, his expression serious, his eyes narrowing.

"You wouldn't have to do a thing, maybe sign some paperwork. I can prepare everything. We'd stand a real chance of winning. But I need more information about what happened..."

"Nothing doing," Mose said, wagging his finger "this is God's will."

Paige looked incredulous.

"It's God's will that you be cheated out your home?"

Mose was quiet.

"Look, there's nothing to be embarrassed about," Paige said, reaching across the table and putting her hand on Lizzie's. Lizzie had been looking downward at the table, the tea kettle whistling on the stove. She nodded toward a daughter lingering in the next room out of earshot. The daughter took care of the kettle, poured everyone some tea, and then quickly disappeared.

"There's nothing to be embarrassed about," Paige repeated. "Millions of Americans are finding themselves in foreclosure, and there's been some really shady stuff to make it happen. I think that was the case with you."

"But we believe in God's laws, and turning to the courts would mean that we accept human laws over God's. Do you have a way of doing this without using the courts?"

Paige sensed an opening.

"In all due respect, Mose, you're permitted to live the way you do precisely BECAUSE of the courts." Paige continued to lay out her case as if she was trying to persuade a jury. She had come dressed in navy slacks and a white blouse and carried a leather bound briefcase, making her the picture of professionalism. But none of this seemed to sway Mose Neuenschwander.

Mose shifted in his seat.

"*Yoder vs. Wisconsin.* If it weren't for that case, your children would be in public school learning about computers and evolution," Paige said. Lizzie looked startled, but Mose was unmoved.

"That may have been okay for them back then, but we believe in God's law, not the courts," Mose said.

"So you WANT to lose your home?" Paige said.

Mose was quiet.

"Look, if you had simply fallen behind on your mortgage and lost your home, then so be it…that's just life and sometimes bad things happen to good people, but something is fishy here," Paige said.

Mose continued to sit stone-faced, so Paige reached for the one question she hoped would get a reaction.

"Who is Amos Raber?"

Mose cast a fleeting glance at me and but remained quiet.

I finally decided to speak.

"You've worked too hard for this, 20 years of your life in the soil, the land, your children's memories. I don't know that I would turn a cheek on this."

"And I truly don't believe it was God's will to make some crook rich at the expense of hard-working Mose Neuenschwander. Could you please tell me who Amos Raber is? Something doesn't seem right, but I need more information," Paige said.

"You shouldn't question God's will. He will decide our fate," Mose said. "I need to finish my milking." With that, Mose disappeared out the door.

*   *

*

"Who do you think those two are?" Amos Raber said, passing the binoculars to one of his cohorts. Their car was parked on the shoulder of the road partially obscured by some corn stalks.

"I'm not sure, but she's hot," said Melvin Beachy.

"Let's stay with the program here," Amos said. Paige was carrying a satchel with folders and the bright yellow of some legal pads were visible. This visitor struck Amos as unusual.

"Get her car's license plate number," Amos said.

"Uh, she came in a buggy," Melvin replied.

"Well, then, get THAT license plate number. And who did she come with?" Amos demanded, growing impatient, although he wasn't sure whether the state plate databases he could access contained Amish plate numbers.

Amos was apprehensive, which was why he was staking out the Neuenschwanders. He had received a disturbing phone call earlier in the day.

*   *   *

"You tried, that's all you can do," I said as I guided Ruby out of the Neuenschwanders' driveway.

"We'll see about that," she muttered under her breath. "All your talk of pacifism is truly admirable, but sometimes if you spot a wrong and you can do something about it, you have a duty to right it, right?"

"Do you mind if I tell you something?" I asked, my heart galloping as fast as Ruby.

"Sure, what?"

"I know I said it online, but I want…to tell…you…in person. I think you are very pretty, very nice…and I…would love to get to know you better."

"That's sweet. I'd like to get to know you better also. Life's too short. One can never have too many people in their life," Paige said, sounding pensive, never taking her eyes from the clear Indiana sky. While I silently stewed, Ruby picked up her pace, and the rhythmic sound of hooves hitting the pavement began to echo through the air.

Paige held onto the side of the buggy, steadying herself against the rush of the breeze in our faces.

Really? I thought to myself, do I have to spell it out? I was very much attracted to her. I was being led by a combination of lust and intellectual infatuation. I wasn't thinking about leaving the church or what *ordnung* rule I might be violating--I just knew I was happy with her and that I wanted to spend time with her. The rest, I figured, we'd sort out later.

On the surface, Paige and I were a laughable mismatch. I wasn't stupid; I realized how it looked to an outsider. My straw hat, button-down workshirt, suspenders, and denim fed into the cookie-cutter caricatures and often-incorrect conclusions people draw about the Amish. But I felt sure Paige and I had more in common than some of the shallow suits she met in the city.

Other than the sound of Ruby's hooves, Paige and I fell into silence. I knew she was upset by Mose's reception to her, but I had warned her ahead of time. I tried to explain that while Mose's behavior might seem to non-Amish as though he were being a doormat, in his own eyes he was being strong. And Mose was not alone. In the eyes of many Amish, to fight would be a sign of weakness. Resistance caters to our basest desires, and it's only by avoiding violence that we elevates the human experience to something better than the rest of nature. Mose may not have been thinking of it in such articulate and philosophical terms, but that's how he felt at his core, and nothing Paige could say would change it. But I still detected the deep disappointment she felt, as if somehow winning this one battle could right the wrongs of the whole banking industry. And there had been many wrongs.

I decided to lighten the mood. I also decided I had to act. It was now or never, cast aside the cloak of shyness which had bedeviled me my whole life, or lose an opportunity for something special.

"You did your best. I could see the gears turning in old Mose's head. You actually had him thinking. You got farther than I thought you would. Let's salvage what's left of this evening. How about I take you on an Amish date tonight?"

"That sounds sweet, and I don't have any place I have to be. I obviously failed in my mission at the Neuenschwanders. So what is an Amish date?"

"I'll tell you in a second. But, first, will you promise me something? Quit saying that you failed! I warned you that Mose would be a tough customer. I'm not saying I agree. I'm troubled by this too, but I guess I can see, and admire, where he is coming from. As far as the date goes, well…we won't be going anywhere in a car, and we'll be keeping it simple."

Paige and I arrived back at the homestead, the fragrant scent of ripening apples drifting across the driveway. I led Ruby into her stall. It was only 7 p.m. and the rest of the family wouldn't be back for hours.

"Well, if we're going on a date, I'd like to get myself ready," Paige chirped.

"You do that, and I'll start to prepare our date," I said.

"I don't have everything I'd have back home, but I think I can make do with what I brought," Paige laughed. She then disappeared into the wash-house.

Meanwhile, I found one of Mom's picnic baskets high up in a kitchen cupboard. I knew my way around the kitchen a bit, although typically among the Amish a kitchen is the woman's domain. Still, Dad on occasion would help Mom stir cookie batter or flip pancakes. And I had watched Loretta and Mom prepare picnics enough that I knew what to do.

Mom had left a little of her macaroni salad behind. Mom's macaroni salad was a rock star at the after-church meals. It was slightly sweet with a hint of crunch in it from the celery bits she added. So I grabbed that. Mom had made a couple loaves of homemade bread earlier in the day, so I carved off some thick slices.

Then found some deer sausage for sandwiches. I also sliced some of the Colby cheese which Mom buys by the horn from the local bulk food store, added some lettuce from the garden, and some of her homemade sandwich spread. The sandwich spread was a flavorful concoction of tomatoes, peppers, onions, and mustard. I'd far rather eat that any time than store-bought mayonnaise. If it were possible to seduce someone with a sandwich, I'd try it on Paige.

I have to admit, I was a little out of my element here. I was much more comfortable running a lathe or sawing wood, but I had to seize the moment and improvise. I didn't think my sandwiches looked bad. I quickly wrapped them in butcher paper and put them into the basket. I also have to confess that the thought of Paige in the outbuilding taking a sponge bath while I was preparing our supper was almost too intense for me to take. I tried to push aside such feelings and finish the task. I packed a couple of glasses and put a thermos on the counter. Using a dipper, I scooped several swallows of a special treat: homemade dandelion wine.

I wrapped a few homemade honey bars and put them into the basket. If I couldn't charm Paige into my arms, seduce her with my sandwiches, or ply her with wine, honey bars might do the trick.

Paige emerged from the washroom. I was temporarily rendered like lard when I saw her. She had taken her hair out of the tight bun it was in, and gone were the dark conservative courtroom clothes she had worn to the Neuenschwanders. Her beautiful brown hair cascaded down to her shoulders. She smelled of fresh lye soap. She was wearing a bright yellow sundress and flip flops.

"You look stunning…like one of Mrs. Hilty's cinnamon rolls."

Paige laughed.

"I've never been told I look like a cinnamon roll, but thanks."

"I'm sorry, I just don't know what to say. I keep saying the wrong thing. You look…how about…simply incredible?"

"Thank you, Mr. Lincoln," Paige said playfully.

"Well, you aren't going to be the only one going on this date all cleaned up. I need to change, too. Wait here, and I'll be back in a few. And no peeking in the picnic basket."

"Anything I can do to help?" Paige asked.

"No, I asked you on the date, so I'll take care of everything. You just make yourself at home in the meantime."

So Paige sat in a rocker and picked up a copy of *The Budget*, losing herself in the tales of simplicity from Amish scribes scattered across the USA.

*   *

*

Back at the office of Plain Investments, Amos Raber entered the buggy plate number in a database but nothing came up.

"So he had a woman with him, so what?" one of Amos's associates asked.

"It's just a hunch," Amos said as the search engines combed through thousands of records.

The associate had a puzzled expression.

"The universe is a predictable place. Humans thrive on order. People eat lunch at the same time, go to sleep at the same time. People are creatures of habit. A young woman that looks and dresses like that does not typically accompany someone in a buggy. Maybe it's nothing, but then again maybe it's something. And if it's something, I want to know what it is!"

"Here it is…M. Schwartz, Lot A-3939 US 27," the colleague said.

"Melvin Schwartz…she was with Abraham…that criminal, what was he doing with her? And what were they doing there?" Amos asked icily.

*   *

*

While Paige read *The Budget,* I started about cleaning myself up. I went into the wash-house, put a pot of water on to boil, stripped down, and began to bathe, the anticipation of an evening with Paige almost too much to bear. I wore a freshly-pressed dark blue shirt, a brand new pair of denims, and matching suspenders. I had chosen my black felt hat for the occasion. I was hoping to look dashing or debonair. Last, I dabbed on a little cologne, just something I had picked up at the drugstore in Berne. I looked in the mirror and generally liked what I saw. Some outsiders have the mistaken impression that the Amish don't use mirrors. I'm not sure where that misconception originated, but I suspect it has something to do with our church rules eschewing photography. But the graven image command has never applied to mirrors. It's true, sitting in front of a mirror primping and preening would not be viewed kindly, but simply glancing in a mirror on the way out the door or using one to look up the chimney to make sure there's not a fire, well, that's just a matter of course.

"Look at you, you look as handsome as a Buick."

I looked at her, puzzled.

"That was payback," Paige laughed. " So where are we going on our date?"

"Not far. Hope that's okay?"

I hitched Mosey to our cart. Among the Amish, ponies are sometimes like tricycles are to non-Amish youngsters. Mosey was a trusty, dependable pony. I, Loretta, Daniel, and Nancy learned to drive with this dependable gray mare. Driving a pony is good practice for the more rigorous work of learning how to steer a horse and buggy. Mosey gave us a slow journey to the back part of our 140 acres where there was a small patch of prairie next to a peaceful pond. It's where I went to get away from the world to sketch, to write, or to watch birds. I wanted to share my favorite spot with Paige.

We followed the pony path along the winding creek, the trail providing a makeshift rutty road between the soybean field and the creek. The path then opened up into a flower-filled clearing. Butterfly milkweed, false sunflowers, scarlet-colored royal catchfly, and Queen Anne's lace made for a brilliant chorus of colors. A small pond ringed by reeds and cattails was in the far corner of the glade. A few startled frogs splashed into the water when they heard our arrival. A thick mixed forest of sycamore, birch, cedar, and sugar maple surrounded the clearing on three sides, with the fourth opening up to the soybean field and pony path.

"It's gorgeous back here!"

"This is where I come to get away from it all."

"I didn't think someone Amish would have a need to escape."

"You know, outsiders romanticize our life, and there are some wonderful things about it that I wouldn't trade with your world for anything, but it doesn't mean there aren't stresses…they're just different."

Paige nodded.

"Maybe instead of cases or bossy bosses or heavy traffic, my stress is getting our furniture finished, or whether I'm being true to our church rules."

I spread a large, thick blanket out on the grass and tied Mosey to a nearby tree. Paige scratched the pony's head lovingly and Mosey nodded in approval.

"She's a sweetheart," Paige cooed.

"She's a dependable pony. She was the first 'car' for all of my brothers and sisters. Okay, I hope you're hungry," I said to Paige.

Paige slid her flip flops off and sat on the blanket, her smooth tan legs stretched out. I handed her a sandwich wrapped in butcher paper.

"Mmmm, this tasty, what is it?"

"Deer sausage sandwich," I replied, taking a bite out of mine.

"Daniel bagged the buck last winter. We're taught not to waste anything. We've used every morsel of the meat. And the herd needs thinning around here. Mom and Dad taught us how to carve up the meat, where the best steaks are, how to grind it down into hamburger, and how to make deer jerky."

"I think a lot of the children that I went to school with just thought meat came from the deli at the local supermarket," Paige observed wryly.

The sky began to blush purple as the sun started its descent over the western horizon. Mid-summer cicadas began their chorus, and the occasional belch of a bullfrog could be heard coming from the pond. The cattails that surrounded the water bristled in the breeze.

"What was your school like?" I asked, eating the last of my sandwich.

"High school?"

"Yes, I'm curious since I just went through the eighth-grade."

"High school…I don't know….not much to say…I went to a Catholic high school, I was on the school newspaper, cheerleader, cross-country, just a typical teenager. What was your school like?"

"Oh, probably a LOT different from yours," I laughed, handing Paige a spoon and a small container of Mom's macaroni salad.

*   *

*

Amos Raber and Melvin Beachy pulled into the Schwartzes' driveway. Melvin was one of several young Amish men and women that were on the payroll of Plain Investments.

"Looks like they've got some company here," Amos noticed, spying Paige's cranberry-colored Dodge Avenger parked under the sprawling shade of an elm near the end of the circle driveway.

"Yeah, maybe the car belongs to the hottie," Melvin suggested.

"Well, let's find out," Amos said. "Let me do the talking. We're just seeking some information. She could be some relative, an ex-Amish visiting on a holiday…probably the most likely."

Amos pounded on the door.

No one answered. The rusty rotors of the windmill turning creaked in the breeze. A few hens pecked around in the dirt, wandering aimlessly.

The house seemed deserted, no one in the outbuildings. Amos pounded on the door to the shop and tried the doorknob. Nothing.

"Okay, I guess no one is here. Let's take down that license plate number…something seems fishy to me, but it's just a feeling…I don't know…just take it down and we'll see who it belongs to," Amos said.

"This place kinda creeps me out, all deserted…let's go," Melvin suggested.

*   *

*

"I attended the local parochial school, called West Branch. Started at 9 a.m. and the day was done by 3 p.m. But believe me, I started work long before 9 a.m. I was always out choring, milking, and feeding the horses by 6 a.m.," I said.

"So did you attend the same school building for all grades?" Paige asked.

"Yes. Same teacher, too, Mr. Yoder. And he was strict, strict but soft. A lot of outsiders are surprised to hear of a male schoolteacher, but it's pretty common in Amish schools. Many Amish around here attend the public school in Berne. The tuition at the Amish schools can be pretty pricey, but the education, I thought, was adequate."

"Whoa, I don't mean to interrupt you, but this macaroni salad is the best I have ever tasted."

"It's usually the first dish to disappear at our after-church meals."

"So were you always interested in the law?" I asked, still savoring the irony that I was having a romantic picnic dinner with an attorney. The Amish don't totally eschew lawyers; we do use them on occasion when it comes to wills or land transactions. But generally we prefer God's laws, not a paid person to interpret the country's.

"Well, it's kind of a long story. My father is president of a very old, prestigious bank in the Chicago suburbs. You've got to keep in mind that I grew up in a carefully-choreographed family. My father--the respected banker, my--Mom, the doting socialite wife...Dad's two daughters were expected to follow him into the family business. My Mom about had a coronary when my sister decided to study dance in college," Paige said, pausing. She took another bite of Mom's macaroni salad and then turned more serious.

"Abe, may I ask you a question?"

I set down my drink.

"No such thing as a bad question...so go..."

"Well...this is a little awkward...but you're such an intelligent, well-rounded, caring man...your family is the best...none of this squares with...um...how we met. Why did you get into trouble? Well, I know how...but, why? It just doesn't...seem like you."

I stood up and paced. I picked up a flat stone from the bank of the pond and skipped it across.

I exhaled and turned back towards Paige.

"I'm not sure. And I know that's a horrible answer, but it's an honest answer."

"Is it?" Paige pressed. "And I'm not being judgmental...I just wonder if somewhere you do know, maybe you don't even know that you know, but you know..."

I was uncomfortable with the conversation, but I also didn't blame her for bringing it up.

"Abe, do you know why I persuaded Uncle Ralph to drop the charges against you?" Paige asked.

"I've wondered...."

"I've battled my own issues. You and I seem kindred spirits in so many ways. And I guess I just want you to know that there is life after arrest...people will try to define you by your worst mistakes, but only you can define you. Don't let others."

"I appreciate that. I think at the time I was placing value on the wrong things in life. I've got big plans for Schwartzes Home

Furnishings now, but even if they don't work out, I'm happy for my health and just for the gift of life. At the time I think I just wasn't sure in my head about a lot of things...I'm working through them now. I'm more confident, and I've come a long way. I think if you ask me in five years why I did it, I might be able to tell you. But lack of confidence can definitely translate into lack of judgment."

"I understand..."

"I think human goodness is cultivated and created, not pre-programmed into us...I know that now. Loretta is always trying to box people into either 'good' or 'bad,' but I think the reality is that most people are a bit of both. Few winners can claim 100 percent. A baseball team has a great season if they are 60 percent victorious, and a politician that squeaks by with 55 percent of the vote, a bare majority, is called a victor."

Paige nodded.

"Why have you been so forgiving?"

"I guess, as I said, I feel a bit of a bond with where you've been. Growing up, we never wanted for anything, and while some people would thrive in that environment, I just sort of went along with it. When one day I found a chance to rebel against it, I did. It wasn't the right way to handle my emotions. But I was feeling smothered and programmed."

"What wasn't the right way to handle it?" I asked.

"I ended up lashing out at everything I was raised to believe," Paige said haltingly.

"Really?" I asked, intrigued. "Explain..."

Now it was Paige's turn to pace. It seemed impossible that such a young-looking, well-spoken, intelligent woman could do anything that would upset. But she continued with her story.

"It was after my freshman year at Mercyhurst College that I met a boy who decided I needed a little bit of...fun..."

"So, what happened?"

"His name was Wayne...he was an older charming, seductive guy who...well, let's just say I was like a pile of dry brush and that man happened to be the match that came along. I can't blame it all on him...I went willingly."

"So you think you would have gotten into some sort of trouble eventually, that this guy just sort of brought it out?"

Paige nodded

"I horrified my parents. I started riding around with him on his motorcycle, and while I was like a prairie fire waiting to happen, Wayne actually did set fires. We drank, partied, smoked. I moved in with him. He smoked weed like a kid would scarf Halloween candy. One night he got the bright idea to set a warehouse that he owned on fire to collect the insurance money. I was with him the night he did it. Wayne was caught and convicted, and I was charged with being an accomplice to arson. One of the firefighters that evening got seriously hurt battling the blaze. There could have been people killed, and I live with that burden. I made some very, very poor choices that summer."

"It sounds like it was your own very severe *rumspringa*," I said, thinking to myself that this was actually a case where the word was applicable, not like a lot of the media silliness that portrays *rumspringa* as some required rite of passage among the Amish.

Paige laughed sardonically.

"If I had known the term then, maybe the judge would have gone easier on me."

"So what happened?" I asked, reaching into the picnic basket for dessert.

"Well, to make a long story short…Daddy brought in the best attorneys…not sure if he did it to save me, to save his reputation, or both, but the lawyers persuaded the prosecutor to just charge me with misdemeanor aggravated trespassing. And they agreed, but they warned me if the firefighter ever died of his injuries they could refile accessory-to-murder charges. Naturally, Daddy gave the firefighter the best treatment possible, the best nurses, around-the-clock care for a couple of years. Happy to say, he's almost fully recovered today."

"And what happened to the boyfriend?"

"He's still in prison, last I heard…"

"Mercyhurst expelled me for violation of the Student Code of Conduct, and that's when I just needed to get away and clear my head…I went on a mission trip to India, spent almost a year there helping to build homes and bring clean water to a village. I slept on a dirt floor. I lived without electricity or plumbing."

"I do that every day. Well, everything except for sleeping on a dirt floor."

Paige laughed. "Yes, if I would have known what I know now, maybe I would have just come here."

"You would have been welcome."

"I don't think you would have liked me back then...I was confused...after I came back from India, I enrolled in college, sped through, went to law school. So, after hearing all of that about me, you probably want to hitch Mosey back up, go back to the house, and not speak to me again."

I was quiet for a minute. She *could* have cost someone their life, easily. It sounded as though she had gotten into some serious trouble. But I admired her ability to regroup and grow. It was something I was struggling with myself.

"I believe in forgiveness, and Lord knows I have no room to say anything. I'd be inhabiting the biggest glass house on the planet...I don't think it's our job to judge. To judge undermines God's ultimate authority," I said.

"I really do admire your faith," Paige said. "I do believe in Martin Luther King, Jr.,'s belief that the arc of the moral universe is long but it bends towards justice."

"Me, too, but who do you think bends that arc?"

"Fair enough. I've tried to take to heart what you said, about faith being like a savings account. I'm trying to build my account back up."

"And if that doesn't work for you, think of faith like a muscle…the more you use it, the stronger it gets. I've discovered that muscle is a metaphor. Muscles aren't just found in physiology, they're found in philosophy. Goodness is a muscle, but so is evil. And sometimes people choose the wrong muscle, because the more you flex a trait, the more you lift the weights of evil or the heaviness of happiness, the stronger the characteristic gets. Unfortunately, for a while, I was choosing the wrong muscles to exercise. I believe that's the essence of humanity, that what gets used gets strengthened, and what doesn't, withers away. I choose to use my faith even when I doubt the most."

"And you once told me you wouldn't make a good bishop…"

"Ha! Here, hold your glass, I have something special for you ," I said, filling Paige's glass from the thermos.

"Mmmm, I could become Amish on the food alone," Paige joked. "What are these?"

"Wish I could say I made them but `Retta and Mom made them yesterday. They're called honey bars." The bars were moist and cakey with a hint of a glaze on top.

"They are very, very good. Don't tell me, you harvest the honey yourself?"

"I didn't, but Dad and Daniel did. I'll have to show you our hives sometime," I said. "Now, try the drink."

Paige sipped.

"Mmmmm, this is superb. You really do know how to plan a date." What kind of wine is this?"

"Dandelion."

Paige paused and looked down at her glass.

"You mean this is made from the weeds that everyone in the suburbs declares chemical warfare on each spring?"

"That's it. While you all make war on the plants, we love them. We use dandelion greens in salads and use the flowers for wine. Grandma Ada always made dandelion jelly. You haven't lived until you've had a peanut butter and dandelion jelly sandwich."

"It's light, smooth, better than some of the supposedly best California vineyard wines," Paige admired.

"But this isn't just any dandelion wine. This is reserved for special occasions and special people. This is from the last batch of dandelion wine that my Grandpa Abraham ever made. He passed away when I was 12, so this is supremely aged."

"Don't take this the wrong way, but I'm just surprised that...you have wine," Paige said.

I sighed at the typical outsider image of the Amish as stone-sober, Bible-clutching teetotalers.

"Our church isn't like that about alcohol. Remember most Amish are German...the land of beer, brats, and sauerkraut. Everything in moderation."

"Well, I think this dandelion wine is heavenly," Paige said, sipping and seeming more relaxed. "How do you make it?"

So I described to Paige how one needs several quarts of dandelion blossoms. We'd make a game of it, all of us brothers and sisters hitting the fields and drainage ditches with pails and those plastic gallon ice cream containers, and start picking the blossoms early in the day because that's when the flowers are freshest. All the stems and leaves have to be removed to get the sweetest wine.

"I'd heard of dandelion wine, but never tasted it. I've read the book
Dandelion Wine by
Ray Bradbury. He's one of my favorite authors."

"Mine, too," I said, suddenly enthralled. "I've read *Fahrenheit 451*
and *Dandelion Wine*. The Berne Public Library has a used book sale
every autumn and I usually come back with a whole buggy full of
books."

Paige laughed.

"*Fahrenheit 451* makes a person appreciate even more the value of
books and literature, so I'd say that Bradbury probably did more to
sell books than anyone except maybe Oprah."

"Never watched her," I said.

"It's strange how you and I can have so much in common yet live so,
so differently. I didn't know there was anyone alive who hadn't
watched Oprah."

"I've heard of her, but that's about it," I shrugged.

"Being from Illinois, watching Oprah is almost required, and
Dandelion Wine I found to be a compelling read, connecting me with
simplicity in a way few other books have."

"Yes, he really was a great writer. So you get to go from reading *Dandelion Wine* to now drinking it."

"The book really made me aware of our own mortality. I think that was one of the themes Bradbury was trying to convey: that we truly do need to appreciate every minute we have here and embrace the simpler things in life, you know what I mean?"

"Uh, yeah, I think I can relate," I smiled.

"Okay, now THAT was kind of dumb, asking an Amish person if they understand simplicity," Paige laughed.

I stretched out on the blanket, still sort of trying to take my cue from Paige about what she wanted out of this. We definitely had a lot in common: our imperfect pasts, our mutual love for books, nature, and travel. But I couldn't tell whether she was attracted to me or just intrigued. Fortunately, she made the first move.

"Is this how you are on dates? Sit next to me, I don't bite," she said, her back propped up against a tree. I was wondering if the wine was getting to her.

I gingerly moved to sit beside her. I was captivated by her scent, the pleasant summer evening, and the dandelion wine. I felt a surge of courage.

"Do you kiss on your dates?" I asked.

"Well, if I'm attracted to my date…" Paige said softly.

"Are you attracted to me?"

The answer came not in a word, but in a tender touch of lips. Our mouths met, tentatively at first, our lips touching softly in a sensual but gentle kiss. Even though I'm Amish and I don't have a lot of experience with electricity, I felt a current coursing between the two of us.

"You do realize this is crazy?" Paige said softly, tenderly resting her head on my shoulder.

"Why? What's so crazy about this? The same way a buggy pulling up to an ATM is crazy?"

Paige laughed.

And we kissed again as the symphonic sounds of summer surrounded us. Our hands explored one another, the last of my shyness evaporating in the sensuality of the moment. We lay on the blanket together, watching the sky and the stars.

"I'd love to take you sailing sometime," Paige said suddenly. "I think you'd like it. Just us, the open water, birds like you've never seen before."

"You have your own boat?"

"Yes, Dad was an avid sailor and that's just something I grew up doing. I go out on the water when I want to clear my head."

"Where do you go?"

"Lake Michigan, usually. It's not like the ocean in that if you blow off course you could end up adrift for days...I love Lake Michigan because it gives you the adventure of the ocean without some of the dangers. Don't get me wrong, if you don't know what you're doing, it's still dangerous, but it's a contained danger."

"Is that something a lot of women do?" I asked. And I wasn't trying to be sexist by asking, I was just curious.

"No...no...not a lot. Many times I am the only woman out there, at least sailing solo. But I think you'd love it, and maybe we could go sometime."

"Sounds fun," I said. And it did. There certainly wasn't anything in the *ordnung* that would prohibit enjoyment of the ocean and the water. Although, I admittedly was probably twisting the *ordnung* like a pretzel. But bodies of water are natural wonders, and the church never discouraged us from partaking in God's gifts. That's why Amish families travel so much. Vanloads will go to the Grand Canyon or Glacier National Park. Maybe I was rationalizing a bit, stretching the limits of the *ordnung*, but I was living in the moment. I figured I'd deal with any consequences tomorrow.

CHAPTER 19
ABRAHAM

We could see the fireworks from Berne as a spectacular summer show in the sky which capped an amazing evening. Now Paige lay in my arms as we let the night breeze dry us off after our playful moonlit midnight dip in the pond. I spooned her, just like I used to Rachel, and we listened to the chorus of crickets and the plaintive wail of a barred owl. In the distance, coyotes could be heard eerily baying and yelping. The blanket I had spread beneath us felt soft and cozy.

"I'm not sure I've ever been held by arms so muscular," Paige whispered.

"Is that a good thing?" I asked.

"Yes, it's a good thing," Paige said, resting back in my arms, as our mouths met sensually again.

Paige turned over on her stomach, laying stretched on the blanket, propping her head in her hands and looking up at me. The milky moonlight bathed her soft skin in an opaque light.

"You know, at the risk of overthinking this moment, I just think so many non-Amish have gotten used to our cushiony lives. We don't really have to do anything anymore. Everything is done at the press of a button, from rolling up a car window to cleaning the floor. No one walks anywhere. No wonder I don't meet men like you in the city," Paige pondered.

"I *like* hard work, I wouldn't want it any other way. There's no satisfaction whenever a task is done for you. You know the ice you had in your tea at the house? I cut that myself in big blocks from a pond in the dead of January. I'm not saying that to be boastful, but it makes you appreciate that ice just a little bit more when your sweat goes into it," I said. "Well, don't worry, there's no sweat *in* the ice, but you know what I mean."

Paige smiled. "I wish we could stay out here all night and just sleep under the stars."

"We can. No one needs to know you are even here!"

"That's a not a bad plan, except for one thing," Paige said, sitting up.

"What?"

"My car is in your driveway," Paige said.

"Crap," I muttered. "I forgot about that."

Paige's visit was unexpected, so the family would arrive home and see her car. In fact, they were probably home already and were puzzled by her car and not finding anyone home. When Daniel went out to do the chores, he'd see Mosey and the cart missing and would probably assume…assume what?

"Arrgh," I muttered.

"Well…" Paige said.

"We're adults. No one needs to know what we were doing, just visiting and watching the fireworks, which is true," I said, gathering Paige in my arms and kissing her softly on her neck and shoulders.

"We better both go back, I don't want your family worrying," Paige said.

We climbed onto the cart, the ride back being spent in a snuggle. Mosey pulled us through the darkness, the soft moonlight providing enough light to see the pony path as it wound between the fields on our left and the tree-lined creek bed to our right. I could see the dark outline of our barn and soon our house. The narrow lane of the pony path merged with our driveway up ahead, but a dark object blocked the way.

"What is it?" Paige asked.

"Not sure," I said. I was concerned. The path should be clear, and from our distance I couldn't tell what it was. I brought Mosey to a stop.

"Wait here," I cautioned Paige.

I walked quietly in the darkness, not wanting to alert whatever it was that was blocking the path. As I got closer, I realized what it was: a buggy.

"Looks like a late night for everyone," I observed.

"You about scared the butter out of me!" Loretta said, adjusting her *kapp*.

"Dude, what are you doing back here??" Timothy asked, less startled than Loretta and more annoyed at having their make-out session interrupted. He adjusted his hat and suspenders.

Just then, the sound of Mosey shuffling behind their buggy could be heard.

"Sorry, I didn't know how to keep her from moving," Paige yelped.

"*Paige*? What are *you* doing here?" Loretta huffed.

"Well, I..." Paige started to say.

"Paige, what are you doing here?" Mom said, peeking her head out of the kitchen door.

I led Mosey to her stall for the night.

"Well, I..." Paige started to say.

"What is Paige doing here?" Velma and Verena both said in unison as they joined the growing crowd in the driveway.

'We were just enjoying the fireworks," I interjected, figuring as little information as possible was best.

"Fireworks…*I bet*," Nancy said. She eyed Paige. Paige's hair was a little disheveled. And in my haste to get home, I left my suspenders back in the clearing. I nervously hoped no one would notice.

"Shouldn't you be in bed right now?" I asked, glaring.

"Hey, where are your suspenders?" Nancy observed. She was almost 14, but precocious as they come.

Mom eyed me curiously. I was an intense jumble of emotions, from the lingering taste of Paige's lips to the more sobering realization that we had both probably unleashed something that would now be very difficult to contain.

"Well…so what brings you to town? This is unexpected," Mom said evenly. "Let's all go into the house, too buggy out here," she continued, swatting at a cloud of gnats.

Of course, no one knew about the intense "email courtship" that Paige and I had been engaging in the past couple of weeks, although there was gossip in church about my frequent visits to libraries.

Finally, Paige spoke.

"I thought I could help the Neuenschwanders. That's why I came."

I started to stare at her in bewilderment and a little anger, but she waved me away.

"Oh, you heard about what is happening to them?" Mom asked.

"Yes, and I think it can be stopped. But my appeal tonight fell on deaf ears."

Both my parents looked at one another but were silent.

"Would you stand idly by and let someone take your house unjustly?" Paige asked Mom and Dad.

"I'd likely take a frying pan to someone who tri…" Mom started to say. But Dad cleared his throat.

"Well, okay, not really. If losing one's house is God's will, so be it." Mom finished.

"Mose tried to get us to sign our savings over to Plain Investments, but I didn't go for it. If it sounds too good to be true, it usually is. Dad said. Mose is a good man, but he is always trying to find the easy way out. I guess this time he's learned his lesson in the most painful of ways."

Paige looked at mê for backup, but I was quiet. I had said all I could that evening.

"It's well after midnight. I think we all ought to go to bed," Mom said, yawning. "Paige, you can have Velma and Verena's room tonight."

CHAPTER 20
PAIGE

I awoke to the smell of cinnamon rolls baking downstairs. These were Salome's big puffy pastries drenched with butter, smothered with cinnamon, and pasted with thick icing. The scent summoned me from sleep with more vigor than any alarm clock. I stretched and looked out the window at the gentle mist hanging over the dew-covered pasture behind the barn. And then last night came rushing back, and I felt a little sick. I mean, it was wonderful. It was indescribably wonderful. But also indescribably stupid. I told myself it was the wine, the warmth, Abe's earthy body, anything but emotional reality. This was beyond crazy, it was also a little cruel and selfish of me. This was Abe's world and I shouldn't be jeopardizing his place in it.

My thoughts were interrupted by Marvin Jr. racing into the bedroom.

"Get up! Get up!" he yelled.

"Marvin! Come back down here," Salome shouted. Marvin, who looked like a miniature version of Abe, scooted down the stairs in obedience.

"It's okay, I'm up!" I said.

"He's not used to people sleeping that late. He thought maybe you were sick," Salome laughed from downstairs.

It was 9 a.m., late even by my Saturday morning standards.

"I guess I must have needed the rest," I yawned.

"I'm sure you did," Nancy chortled. She was at the sink washing the last of the breakfast dishes.

"Nancy!" Salome hissed.

"I've kept a plate warm in the oven. You ready to eat now?" Salome asked.

"You didn't have to do that," I said appreciatively "But, sure."

An omelet, cinnamon rolls, cooked apples, and a glass of cold rhubarb juice was set out on the table.

"We call the omelet Egg Dutch, a Swiss specialty among the Amish in Berne. It's really just a thick omelet, with some flour and milk added to bulk it up," Salome explained.

"Nancy collected these eggs this morning, so it's about as fresh you'll find," she continued. "You make yourself at home and enjoy. I'm going to go out and help with the laundry."

Salome and Nancy headed out to the laundry lines with Velma and Verena. She jokingly called her hand washer the "Armstrong" brand because it really built up her muscles pumping it once a week.

"So…" Loretta said, not turning away from the dishes she was washing.

I paused, sensing what was coming, and tried to head it off. "These cinnamon rolls are wonderful, as always. Did you make them?" I asked casually.

"No, Mom made them." Loretta answered crisply.

"Maybe someday you can show me how to make those," I said.

"Look, we're friends. Let's be honest with one another. It happened, didn't it?" Loretta said, turning around to face me. Her eyes blazed as she started at me intently. She dried her wet hands on a dish towel and then wiped them on her apron.

I set down my fork and took a sip from the rhubarb juice but was otherwise silent.

"I saw the way you both looked last night and the way you were looking at one another."

"Like you and Timothy looked when you got out of the buggy last night?" I playfully replied.

Loretta wasn't amused.

"That's different, we are dating, we both are going to be baptized, and we might..." Loretta paused.

"Marry?"

Loretta blushed.

"Well, he seems like a great boy and I wish you both the best. You know that, if that is what you decide to do."

"You changed the subject…" Loretta said, pulling out a chair and sitting at the kitchen table. "I know I said last time that this was between you two and God, but….he's my brother and I *know* something happened between you two last night…Paige, what are you thinking? Do you realize that if this got out, my brother could be shunned by the church? Does that matter to you? I think if you were really our friend, you would realize this and leave Abe alone. He's got too much to lose."

I was quiet, poking at what was left of my omelet. Loretta was right.

"I…didn't mean for anything to happen."

Loretta watched and listened intently, lowering her voice to a whisper.

"But something *did* happen, right?"

"Your brother is a wonderful man but…"

"So what are you going to do?" Loretta interrupted.

I took my plate to the counter.

"I don't know. I know that I need to go. I need to get back to work, to clear my head, to think. And I still want to help the

Neuenschwanders."

"Paige, I like you, you know that. This isn't about you," Loretta said, walking over and embracing me. "It's about our church. As you know, Abe's been in trouble...and we appreciate all you've done for him...but he can't get in trouble again. To be an upstanding member of the church, one has to follow the rules. I'm sure it's the same in your faith or in your work: you have to follow rules. And our church doesn't allow…well, I just don't see how this could work out, is what I am saying," Loretta said, releasing me from the hug.

"I understand," I replied.

"I wish it could work, believe me I do. But it can't work…you know that, I know that."

"I need to go now."

Loretta nodded.

"I think it's for the best. I think you need to go and not come back. This can lead nowhere good. Our family needs to be whole and you would destroy that. I do wish you the best in everything you do and God's blessings to you."

"If that's really how you feel, I don't want to be a home-wrecker or a church-wrecker. Thanks for your hospitality and friendship. I'll never forget it."

I walked across the dirt driveway towards the shop. I needed to say goodbye to Abe and put this behind me.

ABRAHAM

The bell on the shop door announced Paige's arrival, but there were some customers browsing. I was waiting on them, answering questions about what kind of wood various items were made from and the price of each. I motioned to her to wait.

"Give us a minute to talk about it," said a heavy-set woman with copper-colored hair, walking next to her balding husband who, I thgought, looked a little like a rat, with a pointy face and thin mustache.

"This here Aim-ish furniture is the best. You could drop one of these magazine racks from a 10-story building and they'd probably hold up," whispered the woman.

"How much is this rocker?" The rat man called over to me.

"Two fifty," I replied, "made of a poplar hickory blend and

contoured for the most ergonomically comfortable feel."

"Two fifty, you call that ergonomical?" the man replied. "Can't you go any lower?"

"Huh?" I said. I could see Paige stifling a giggle. I turned to her and away from the couple for a second and rolled my eyes.

"Well, I can bump it down to 225, but that really is as low as I can go."

I was annoyed, actually, by customers who thought the Amish lived by a barter system. One wouldn't walk into a chain furniture store and start haggling. Well, I guess some people would and do, but put a beard, suspenders, and a hat on a proprietor, and most tourists think they're automatically entitled to bargain.

"I don't know," the woman hesitantly said to rat man husband.

"Maybe we need to think about it," rat man said. "Does your store have a website we can order from?"

"No. But we partner with the Berne Chamber of Commerce. They have our prices on their website and you can email them if you need to contact us," I said. These types of customers weren't uncommon, so I usually calmly dealt with them. Even stupid people carried cash, and a sale was a sale whether it was from an annoying person or a Rhodes Scholar.

"What? No website to order from, what an inconvenience!" the woman objected.

I kept my cool, but Paige looked incredulous. I started to say something, but Paige interjected.

"Now, just how do you suppose they'd have a website with no electricity anywhere?" she asked tersely, motioning up at the skylights.

"Well, I…don't they have a computer or something tucked away back there somewhere?" the woman whispered to Paige. "Come on, I've seen Amish people on the phone. They're putting on a little bit of a show."

The woman turned back to me.

"Well, if you can't lower the price more and there's no website, I think we'll just head on to the flea market in Fort Wayne," the woman said.

Paige looked disgusted, while I stood there calmly. I always tried to maintain a professional exterior even if the customer was a clod. Dad always taught me that the customer was in charge and we worked for them.

"Hey, we are on vacation…will you take our picture next to the bearded man back there?" she asked, pointing towards Dad, who was in the workshop area. The woman fished a cell phone camera from her purse. Dad looked annoyed--a rarity for him--and walked back into the stockroom.

"They don't permit photos," Paige said crisply.

"You really are a wet blanket," the woman said tartly. "We never asked you for your opinion."

"How about I take a picture of you leaving right now?" Paige suggested.

"Well, this is not the way I expected to be treated here. Aren't you going to do something?" the woman asked me.

Paige had been a drama student standout in high school, so she relied on her old acting chops to put on a marvelous performance to startle the shoppers.

"Oh, I don't think he'll do much, he's my boyfriend," Paige purred, walking up to me, embracing me and giving me a deep, passionate stage kiss on the lips.

"Well, this is…most unexpected. I've never seen an AIM-ish like HER before," the copper-haired lady said, eying Paige and her sundress, flip flops, and ponytailed *unkapped* hair.

"Come on, Ruth, we won't be coming back here again!" rat man said, storming out of the store with his wife in tow.

After the door closed, I laughed.

"Wow. I'm sorry, I hope that was okay. I couldn't help myself. Is that typical tourist behavior?" Paige asked incredulously.

"Not everyone," I said. "Really, we get some wonderful customers, and some of them even become friends. But, yes, we do get some like that. I'm sure they won't be coming back, though."

Paige looked alluring.

"So, now I'm your boyfriend?"

Paige smiled.

"Let's go outside," she suggested.

"Be back in a few minutes," I yelled to my father.

Paige and I held hands as we walked down the pony path Soon Paige turned toward me, my hands in hers, and stared directly into my eyes. The bright July sun made her squint.

"Abe…"

I was quiet, savoring the feel of her soft hands in mine, the scent of her hair, her beauty…I knew it was probably going to end, so I wanted to freeze us in that moment, to let it linger. I got the same feeling now that I had just before Rachel left me.

"You're an incredible man, but I can‘t stay. I have a job, rent, clients. And I don't think you need me here."

"So…well…I think I should be able to decide what it is I need," I uttered nonsensically.

"You know this is crazy…we both know it, this couldn't work," Paige replied.

I was quiet. Inside I knew she was right. It couldn't work. Could it?

"Abe, I need to go. I think I'd cause problems if I stuck around here, for you, for your family. I've learned so much from you. You've raised the bar for anyone I may want to spend my life with…"

"So, that's it? That's what I am to you, some sort of 'pace horse' in the love laps of life?"

"Please…"

I released her hands and headed for the shop. I didn't want her to see me cry. Paige disappeared down the driveway, a cloud of dust swallowing her car. I doubted I'd ever see her again.

CHAPTER 21

LeRoy Miller knocked crisply on the door of Monroe Hochstetler's house. It was nearing midnight. Monroe's bones creaked as he climbed out of bed. This couldn't be good news. He had been bishop long enough to know that if someone came calling in the middle of the night, the news was almost always bad. Monroe opened the door to find his two ministers, LeRoy Miller and Jacob Eicher, standing grimly.

"We've got some bad news," LeRoy said, his normally youthful features appearing drawn.

"Has Annie Keim's health taken a turn?" Monroe asked.

"No, no it's not that," LeRoy said.

"It's Plain Investments…" Jacob said.

Monroe Hochstetler ran his hand through his thick white beard.

"I don't understand…" Monroe said.

"It's plain that it's Plain," Jacob continued before LeRoy waved him off. Once again, Jacob's penchant for misplaced humor made him seem tone-deaf.

"Is there someplace more private we can go to talk?" LeRoy said grimly.

"This can't wait until morning?" Monroe asked groggily.

"I don't think so…" LeRoy said.

"Well, let's go into my workshop," Monroe said.

ABRAHAM

In the days and weeks after Paige left, I poured myself into work. I'd go out and check the bee hives before breakfast and do the milking of cows. Always the milking. There was something oddly calming about pulling on cow udders when one was in a foul mood. I generally stayed away from the back 40, usually my haven during times of turmoil. It was just too painful to return. So I made my morning rounds, feeding the chickens, helping Daniel with his chores, going into town to buy supplies, and just generally keeping myself busy.

There was something jarring that occurred one morning shortly after Paige left. I went to get the mail, something I tried to avoid doing. Just too much baggage with that minor endeavor. Mr. Doty's mail no longer came, but there was a letter addressed to me. It was from Rachel. "What could she possibly want to say to me after all this time?" My heart skipped beats. I almost opened it. Maybe I should have. What I did next I know was childish, but I was trying to move on. Maybe reading it and contemplating the contents could have been therapeutic. But then I thought of her final words to me:

"I hope your life is happy in your web of lies."

I tossed the letter into a pile of burning brush outside, and its words went up into the sky in a trail of smoke.

Besides that event, life had settled into full work mode.
I had created a dining room suite, three sofas, and bookshelves. I
think I had done more work in the week after Paige left than I
usually did in four months. If it wasn't the silence during supper or
the time in my room with the door closed, it was my constant work
that gradually caught the attention of my family.

*   *   *

"Light is on in the shop," Dad whispered to Mom.   "I'm telling you,
he's been working almost nonstop. It's after 2 a.m."

Dad pulled back the curtain and spied the glow of kerosene lamps
coming from the workshop area. Dad paced their bedroom floor,
occasionally stepping on a creaking wooden floor board.

"He's going to use up all our kerosene," Dad said.

"Something's up," Mom whispered. "Hasn't been himself since
Paige left. We can talk about it in the morning."

"He needs to move out on his own," Dad said.

"Oh, I'm sure he knows that. But his help around here has been
nice, just think of it that way. Get back into bed and go to sleep.
We'll talk about it later," Mom said, snuggling against Dad and

pulling one of her hand-made quilts up to their chins.

The next day after a hearty breakfast of egg-in-nest, bacon, ham, fried potatoes, orange juice, and toast with rhubarb jam, Dad headed out to the shop to begin another workday. And possibly to have a few words with me. I, however, was already there. I don't think I had gotten any sleep that night.

*   *   *

"Huh…you're here early," Dad muttered as he came in for the day. "So, today we can finish the order for the Floyds…" he suggested. Usually each morning we conferred over which order we should fill and which could wait.

"I finished that," I said.

"Okay," Dad said, moving down the list, crossing off the Floyds.

"Well, good, then we can begin the Williams' bedroom set," Dad said. "Get the measureme…"

"Done. I finished the order. It's in the stockroom, ready for them to pick up."

Dad seemed unfazed.

"Okay, well, you've been busy, but that's good. Then let's start on the Murphys' china cabi…"

"Done," I said. "In the stockroom."

Dad showed a flash of anger. He hooked his fingers into his blue suspenders and stared at me.

"Okay, I don't know what's gotten into you, but if your personal problems are affecting the quality of our customer's work in any way…there's no way that china cabinet is up to the Schwartzstandards and you know it," Dad huffed, marching back into the stockroom and motioning for me to come along.

"Yes, see, this is exactly what I was worried about. The quality is…well, wait a second…let's turn it around here. I bet you that you missed…" Dad paused…

"The work is perfect," he declared, whirling around to face me. He then stomped over to the desk where we kept the work orders.

"*Done…all done???*" Dad said, incredulously, looking at the stack of completed jobs.

He stared at me for a long time.

"Is there something you want to talk about?"

I was quiet. My father would never win an award for warmth. I remember him more as a slow, steady presence in my life, a provider and rock for the family. But he was rarely someone you had a deep discussion with about emotions and feelings. I could tell he was having difficulty broaching the subject, but he eventually sputtered it out.

"Is it…because of….her?"

I answered with a question of my own. "Have you ever just wanted something so badly that you didn't care about the consequences?"

Dad ran his fingers through his long, graying beard and was quiet for a minute. He picked up a scrap of wood from the counter, wrapped his palm around it, and then released it. "Isn't that what got you into trouble in the first place?" he answered back.

"This is different…it's not the same," I countered.

"Of course, I've wanted something. But wanting something and acting on it are different. The *ordnung* exists for a reason. A religion without rules, a society without consequences is like a china cabinet without proper support. It'll collapse when the first dish is placed in it."

This was a more pensive tone than I was used to hearing from my father. I often thought I got most of my philosophical hunger from his father, but I began to hear it in Dad now, too.

"But shouldn't rules be flexible? Our customers special order shelving sometimes and we make it for them. And we do it because one size doesn't fit all. Each customer has different needs and we cater to them. But the one rule that doesn't waver is that we give them quality and craftsmanship that is first-rate," I pondered.

"But religion isn't a bookshelf. I believe in a loving, forgiving God, but I also believe that one has to commit himself to the Bible and the Lord."

"Oh, come on, how does who I am attracted to get dictated by the Bible? I read the Bible, I go to church…" I said.

Dad was annoyed. "It's not good enough to just read the Bible. You have to follow it, live it, know it…and if you had been doing that all along, you probably wouldn't be where you are today."

"That to me just seems like a dodge. You can't hear what you don't like and just bury it in the Bible. That's a smokescreen," I said.

Dad paced. His brow was furrowed, but his lips were pursed in a patient, steadfast manner.

"You don't understand. And you won't until you live as long as I have. Our rules exist for a reason. Our religion is more than our clothing and buggies. Living plainly means you reduce life to its essence, and then it's the sweetest. You know in the spring when it's syrup-tapping time? You boil the sap, and what's left is the sweetest syrup you could ever taste, right? That's how living plain is. You are boiling out the excesses of life, and what you are left with is simple and sweet."

I nodded.

"And, remember, you chose this. You were baptized into the church, and when you did that, you signed a contract with God, your family, your church."

"I believe in living plainly, and I did get baptized, you're right, but…" I said, now not even certain what it was we were discussing.

I missed Paige and I think I loved her.

"But don't you think if you love someone or something, you have a duty to express it, to tell them your feelings?" I asked Dad.

"Love can be a very, very messy emotion," Dad cautioned.

"Was it messy with Mom?" I asked. I had heard the story of how they met too many times to count, but it was almost always from Mom's perspective, not Dad's. So I was curious.

"Oh, you better believe it was messy. The minute your grandparents found out I was seeing a Swiss Amish girl they nearly disowned me."
"But your family is Swiss Amish," I countered.
"Yes, but they wanted me to branch out," Dad replied.

"How old were you again, when you first met Mom?"

"She was 17, I was 21...you remember Moses Coblentz's old place? Well, it was there...at a Sunday evening singing. Your Mom had caught my eye for some time and I finally got up the nerve to talk to her."

"And...?"

"Well, we talked for a long time and then we slipped away under the moonlit sky into the pine grove and..."

I was rapt, hanging on every word.

"Wait a minute!" Dad said, suddenly embarrassed. He never did finish the story.

"Anyone can be non-Amish, Abe. Anyone. The world is a sin-soaked place, full of suffering and hate. But our faith is different. I'm not going to say better, that's for God to judge. The internet comes along and rules the world. The cell phone comes along and practically becomes an appendage. But in our faith we can choose what to let into our lives, and there is something very empowering about that. Do you realize how many people secretly would love to live the way we live every day?"

Dad paced. I wasn't used to hearing him talk so much, but he wasn't used to having every work order completed along with excess inventory.

"If you go after her, the door shuts, and there may be no coming back," Dad warned.

"Why? I don't understand shunning. Really, I don't. So I leave, why is the door not open for me to return? Why do the Amish have to be so punitive in that way?"

"That's where you're mistaken. Shunning is not an act of punishment, but an act of love…it protects the purity and integrity of the church. You can't just come and go…either you're in or you're out, and it seems you are having trouble deciding."

"Okay, well…there's not much more to say right now other than that I need to think," I said.

"You know you can come to me anytime, I may not be the best talker, but I am a pretty a good listener," Dad offered.

"Thank you," I replied and gave him a hug. He seemed a bit startled but returned the embrace.

Later that evening I was starting the milking in the barn when I ran into Loretta, who was collecting eggs from the hens. We seemed to be getting a surplus of eggs around then, which Mom, Loretta, and Nancy had been putting into homemade noodles and lots of egg salad. I knew I had not been the easiest person in the world to live with over the past few weeks. Loretta had been doing everything possible to make me feel better even though I hadn't shown my appreciation, so I thought it was time I told her.

"Hey, 'Retta…I know I've been a little difficult to be around the past few weeks…but I just wanted to thank you."

"Oh…" Loretta replied, seemingly surprised. "Well, I'm glad you feel that way. I thought you were mad at me."

"Mad at you? Why would I be mad at you?"

"Well, I know how…intense…it probably was for you, but you're on the right path now."

"Huh?"

"No, you," Loretta said.

"Are what? I was thanking you for picking up the slack in the milkhouse and the other chores lately. It's been a big help. What are you talking about??" I asked, suddenly suspicious.

"Oh…she didn't tel…I mean, I thought you were thanking me for…oh, Heavens, I need to clean out the chicken coop," Loretta said hastily. "Here, you finish the milking."

"Whoa, not so fast. Who is 'she?' What are you talking about?" I said.

"It was for the best," Loretta said.

"What was for the best?" I asked.

"'Retta, wait a minute," I said, putting down a full bucket of milk, some of it sloshing over the rim and dripping down the sides.

"What was for the best?" I repeated.

Loretta turned around.

"Paige..."

I moved closer to her.

"I talked to her before she left...I thought you knew," Loretta said, her round face reddening.

"What...did...you...talk to her about?" I stammered, a habit of mine when I got angry.

"Oh, nothing, just...you know, you two are very different."

"What did you say to her?" I demanded.

Loretta sighed.

"I told her you'd both be better off if she left and didn't come back."

My face turned as red as one of Lizzie Neuenschwander's ripe cherry tomatoes. Trying to control my fury, I spoke to Loretta evenly. "You know, maybe you're right. Maybe you're not. But either way, don't you think that was something for *me* to decide?" I seethed. "Maybe I'll just go behind your back and talk to Timothy and tell him he should break up with you."

Loretta glared at me angrily. "Timothy is a good man, unlike you. I don't blame Rachel for leaving you. You'll never change. Once a liar, always a liar."

"Really? Is that so?"

"And when people lie about something big like you have, then they're going to lie about smaller things too. What else are you hiding?"

"You sound like a real expert on lying. Makes me wonder what you have been up to," I countered.

"People can't change," Loretta said her voice rising. "You are what you are, and poor Rachel wasted five years of her life ignoring something she should have seen all along."

"How dare you bring Rachel into this? You have no idea what our relationship was like. And I think God decides what people can become, not you," I said, boiling, my voice rising to match hers.

"That sounds good, but the reality is that you'll never change.

You're a liar," Loretta said. "And because of you, I lost someone who was like a sister to me."

"So this is what this is all about? You think I chased Rachel out of town?" I asked, my anger reaching fever pitch. "Maybe if I had more encouragement from people here at home, changing would be easier. What separates humans from giraffes, zebras, or bacteria is the very fact that we *can* change. You deciding who can change and who can't change is a direct affront to God," I challenged.

Loretta was silent and brooding.

"It's easier to spout a shelf-worn platitude – 'once a liar, always a liar' – than to embrace the complexities of human nature. Change isn't easy, but people can and do change!" I shouted.

"Then why haven't *you*?" Loretta shot back.

Roaring with hurt and anger, I hurled the metal milking pail onto the concrete ground, and it went clattering into a cow stall, ricocheting like a pinball.

*   *   *

LeRoy Miller, Jacob Eicher, and Monroe Hochstetler gathered around an oak table. It was 2 a.m.

"I can't believe this," Monroe said, after being filled in by the elders.

"I didn't want to believe it, but it appears to be true. Even I misjudged him," LeRoy said.

"And you really think it could be a million dollars?" Monroe asked.

"I think it could be, could be more…he's been doing this for years, hundreds of investors…we all trusted him, or most of us did," LeRoy said. "I think we should call the authorities and let them handle it."

Monroe paced. The Abraham Schwartz matter earlier in the year paled in comparison to this, and that had been difficult enough.

"We should handle this ourselves," Monroe said.

"That is exactly what he is counting on," LeRoy countered.

Jacob Eicher nodded affirmatively.

"I've talked to an intermediary and he wants to confess…but he's unstable…he'll do anything, anything at all to keep from going to jail or getting the SEC involved, and that makes him dangerous," LeRoy said.

Monroe continued to pace, but he looked ashen.

"I've worked my whole life to protect God's laws. I cherish this country that allows us to worship as we wish, but law after law after law is passed, and soon one doesn't know what's right, wrong, or simply a law to keep lawmakers busy. This is a grave, grave crime and if what you are saying is true…"

"It is true…some people in our church have lost everything--they lost all their money, then fell behind on house payments, so some are also losing their homes…they were too embarrassed to speak up…but I did some investigating. It's not just the Neuenschwanders…this is why the Keims, Stutzmans, and Coblentzes are losing their homes, too," LeRoy said.

Monroe exhaled.

"If what you are saying is true," Monroe continued, "then we must show the world that we can handle this ourselves,"

"In all due respect, sir, I don't think we can. We need the law," LeRoy said.

CHAPTER 22

PAIGE

When I needed a break, I'd get together with a few of my friends –
fellow alumni from Loyola Law School - namely Ashleigh Burton
and Jamee Collins. We all worked fairly close in downtown
Chicago, so occasionally we'd all grab lunch together.

"I'm not even sure I understand what happened here, so if I can't
untangle this and this is what I do for a living, how in the world
would the Neuenschwanders have understood what they were
signing? I'd really like more information. Were you able to get the
folder?" I asked Ashleigh as we met for lunch one afternoon.

"You know, I'm just burned out. I think this type of thing is more
common than you might think," Ashleigh sighed, waving a thick
cream-colored folder.

"What do you mean?" I pressed.

"It's not just this, it's everything…definitely not what I envisioned
myself doing when we were at Loyola. I feel like I'm on an
assembly line…being told what the final product is, but I never see
it…I do what I'm told, putting the pieces in place, but for all I know,
I could be making a nuclear bomb when I think I'm making

microwave ovens. It's a maddening place to work," Ashleigh said.

I picked at my turkey sandwich.

"You know, there's a place where these turkeys roam freely…"

"Uh-oh, you aren't starting to go on a vegan kick again, are you?" Ashleigh asked.

"No, I just mean that…I've been doing a lot of thinking lately…it's been a crazy year. Do you know much about the Amish?" I asked, realizing that it was probably a silly question. They probably knew about as much as I did before I met the Schwartzes.

"You mean as in buggies, butter churns, and Bible-clutching, bonnet-wearing people?" Ashleigh asked.

"You know, that is what I thought…I didn't know much about them other than what I saw in books or on some of the stupid TV shows, but their life really isn't as it appears," I countered.

A waiter refilled our sodas, the sounds of a busy lunchtime crowd filling the air with an indistinguishable din.

"I know you talked about them after you got marooned there, but I don't know much about the Amish. Not exactly horse-and-buggy country here," Ashleigh said, gesturing to the packed city street outside.

"I know…they're just like us in the sense that there are some Amish whom I'm sure I wouldn't want to so much as spend two minutes talking to, but then there are others who are just amazing and…charming," I gushed.

"Charming? Makes it sound like you found an Amish prince," Ashleigh said, sipping her drink.

I thought of our evening by the pond and shivered with excitement for a second. I did miss Abe.

"Well, some of the Amish men are really cute," I said in barely a whisper.

"Farmboys gotta beat what we have here in the city, that's for sure," Ashleigh said. Ashleigh was from a small town outside of Peoria, downstate.

"Oh, the city boys aren't so bad. You both are looking in the wrong places," Jamee said.

"Oh, really? Where would you suggest?" Ashleigh huffed.

"Well, FindAMatch.com is a great site. I'm seeing an investment banker I met there," Jamee purred.

"For your portfolio or…" Ashleigh started, but Paige interrupted.

"So, what about you? Any of your dates turn out well lately?"

"Don't even go there. My view of men right now is making me want to become a nun or a something," Ashleigh said.

Jamee was doing the more glamorous work that most of us had dreamt of back in law school. She worked for the prosecutor's office, and while the pay of a public servant certainly couldn't match top private sector jobs, it was meaningful work. It was an ironic juxtaposition because Jamee wanted to go to law school to be a more corporate-type lawyer, while Ashleigh and I wanted to go into public service.

"Okay, gotta go put some more bad guys away!" Jamee said, slurping the last of her soda, grabbing her burgundy-colored bag, and heading out the door.

"I didn't want to say this in front of Jamee because she would have just…well, she wouldn't have understood. She's not happy unless a man's net worth is at least $200,000, his car is a Jag-E, and he has a wine cellar…" I said. "Believe me, I've done that, and it's not all as advertised."

"Well, I haven't done it before so I'd at least like to do the research!" Ashleigh laughed.

I also laughed. I knew Ashleigh was joking, or at least mostly. We had been friends in law school but had grown closer since graduation as our once-close corps of law school buddies had spread out to different cities and different jobs.

"You know, I have met a good guy…" I whispered.

"Oh?"

"Well, it's…it's complicated," I said, sipping the last of my sweet tea. "Definitely complicated."

"Aren't they all? So, give me the details!"

I blushed, suddenly feeling silly for even starting to bring Abe up in conversation. I imagined broaching the topic of falling for a suspender-clad, straw-hat-wearing, often barefoot guy with no college degree, let alone a high school diploma … it probably wouldn't go over really well with any of my friends, including Ashleigh.

"Um, why don't you give me the details of what you found first. I'm not sure how long a lunch we can take."

"Oh, no worries…we're caught up, pretty much. And besides, my boss is out of the office today," Ashleigh said with a wink. "So, tell me!"

"Well, I'd still like to talk about Plain Investments first."

"Okay. Wow, you owe me big time, big time. You don't want to know what I had to do to get this folder for you," Ashleigh muttered.

"I am sorry. I didn't want you to do anything too subversive," I said, not knowing how far Ashleigh would go to help. She's definitely got a silly and fun, crazy streak.

"If anyone found out, I could lose my job…although considering how much my job sucks, that might not be a horrible thing."

"Thank you, but I didn't want you to put your job on the line for me…."

Ashleigh waved me off.

Ashleigh was an attractive woman with dark mocha-colored skin, jet black hair, and a body rewarded by a running regimen more punishing than mine. She was never short of offers for dates

"Well, I'm still sorry if you had to do anything too…never mind. What did you find out?" I asked.

"Plenty…they aren't registered with the SEC, but one of the SEC investigators out in the field apparently has them on his radar. They know of one or two families that have lost a lot of money, but there could be many more. It appears this might be a Ponzi scheme."

"Hmmmm," was all I could think of to say. Some things were beginning to make sense. But some weren't.

"Well, what are they waiting for? Why hasn't the SEC shut them down?" I asked, knowing that in the post-Bernie Madoff era, the SEC usually pounced on Ponzis immediately.

"You know those Amish people you keep talking about? Seems like most of the victims are Amish and they want to handle this…what would you say, internally?" Ashleigh said.

"Interesting…"

"Here, I'm not supposed to have this file and I need it back, but these are the SEC field investigator's notes detailing everything," Ashleigh said, sliding a thick folder across the table.

The waiter came and topped off yet another glass of sweet tea.

"Now, tell me about this new man of yours…"

*   *

*

CHAPTER 23

ABRAHAM

Months had passed since Paige left, and I hadn't heard anything from her. Of course, she hadn't heard from me, either. I could have gone to the library and sent her an email anytime, I suppose. But I was trying to give her some space. And, meanwhile, I was attempting to pour my sadness and emptiness into constructive outlets. I was also making an effort to rededicate myself to the church, help with the garden, and just let the healing balm of time do its work. An old Amish saying is "a task takes as long as it takes." And I let that guide me for the moment. I wasn't operating on any timetable but just figured things would work themselves out.

One event happened that brought some brightness to my life. After being on the market for a couple of years, my farmette finally sold. Even though the debt to Mr. Doty had been paid by the church, I still didn't feel right holding on to the property. There were too many memories there. It was supposed to have been where Rachel and I were going to start a family and live our lives. Instead, it felt empty and tainted. I actually pocketed a cool $50,000 on the sale because two couples happened to want the property at the same time. The farmette did have charm, and they eventually drove the price way up. It was a happy day for me when I got that check. I promptly paid back the church what they had paid Mr. Doty. Selling the farmette helped me try to emerge from the sarcophagus of my morose mood.

I had slowed down on the feverish furniture-making and returned to a less manic pace. Things were returning to some semblance of normal. Except with Loretta. I hadn't forgiven her, and at the time I wasn't sure I ever could, despite all of our church's teachings about such things.

And my feelings were also still hurt by Paige's last words to me. Didn't our evening by the pond mean *anything* to her? I didn't feel as though I had a reason to contact her. At least, that was the case until supper one night.

Mom had fixed her usual sumptuous spread. We all sat around the table, bowed our heads in prayer, and then passed around dishes full of food. Mom had prepared a potato casserole and Dad had grilled some chicken. We also had a salad of Mesclun lettuces which Loretta had picked from our garden. Sliced Cheddar cheese, a loaf of homemade multigrain bread, and Mom's cottage cheese were also on the table. Velma and Verena sat across from one another in their lavender-colored dresses and white *kapps*, fighting over the last of the dinner rolls. Benjamin and Daniel talked about what they wanted to catch at the fishing lake this weekend. Loretta-- I tried to tune her out-- talked about the shirts she had sewn, and Mom tried to get Dad to talk about anything. Meanwhile, Grandma Ada sat silently poking at the fresh peas on her plate.

"The Stutzmans are having a frolic this weekend," Mom said to Dad. "I think it would be nice for you to go."

Dad mumbled something unintelligible.

"Oh, come on, they've been nothing but kind and helpful since they moved here from Milroy. This is a chance to repay them," Mom said, buttering the last bite of her dinner roll. When Dad's shoulder was dislocated, Eli Stutzman and his four boys helped get our hay in and tilled the garden for us, among other things. The Stutzmans, like the Neuenschwanders and, I hoped, us, are what made being in the Amish church so fulfilling. So many neighbors among your kind of people don't know one another and there's just this general disconnectedness.

A frolic is a scaled-down version of the better-known barn-raisings. Barn-raisings are relatively rare in these parts, as many of the farmsteads are older and well-established. Don't think there's been a barn-raising around here in over 10 years, when the Coblentz barn was struck by lightning and burned to the ground. Whereas a barn-raising might draw 200 men with hammers and jacks, a frolic is usually about a dozen men all armed and ready to hammer, saw, and nail a smaller job to quick completion.

"Well, I'll be happy to go. What time?" I asked.

"Usual, 7 a.m. Sarah is going to serve breakfast, so save room," Mom said.

I hadn't really talked to her much about anything that was going on with me. I was sort of smothered in my gloom, and I think Mom felt that she could probably best help me by staying out of my way.

Marvin, Jr., was dumping the last of his peas on the table.

"Marvin!" Loretta said.

"Tee-hee!" Grandma Ada chuckled.

"Mother, it's not really funny. Marvin, Jr., needs to learn some table manners," Mom said sternly.

"Tee-hee!" Grandma Ada chuckled again, swirling the corn on her plate around slowly with a spoon.

"Well, it seems like you're in a good mood today. You've been snickering up a storm over there this whole supper," Mom clucked.

"I played a trick," Grandma giggled, now playing with the last of her dinner roll with her gnarled fingers. There was a hint of a sparkle in her eye.

"You're an ornery one! What did you do?" Mom said.

Grandma Ada liked to sometimes loosen the handles on the irons so that when one picked up the iron to begin to press a shirt they were left just holding the handle. Other times Grandma was known to replace the salt in the shaker with baking soda. I thought it was her way of getting some attention in a world that seemed to be increasingly slipping away from her.

"Well, I didn't like him!" Grandma said. "He just looked too...slick, and I like our sweet little Sage."

Mom and Loretta looked at one another, and I couldn't figure out what Grandma Ada was talking about.

"Sweet Little S....oh, you mean PAIGE," Mom concluded.

Loretta and I looked at one another.

Grandma Ada nodded. "Sage Paige, that's it," she cackled, a smile brightening her face.

"Grandma, please. What are you talking about?" I suddenly asked. Any conversation involving Paige naturally caught my attention.

"Oh, let's see…lemme remember," Grandma Ada said, although part of me thought she might have been dragging everything out for dramatic effect, that she might have enjoyed suddenly being the center of attention. "He came this afternoon, came a knocking hard on my door. That was after I, uh, seen him pounding on the house door. He said he'd been here a couple of times and no one is ever home and that he needed to know who our Sage Roberts was," she recounted. "I asked him if she was in some kind of trouble. He said, maybe, but he needed to know where she was and needed to know now," Grandma recalled. "I swear I thought I, uh, seen this man before, but I couldn't place him. He got all shaky and his forehead was sweating like a hog before Easter dinner. Well, now, no one's gonna pull anything over on Grandma Ada. I may be old, but I still got my wits about me. I didn't trust him…"

"So what happened?" Mom asked.

"Then he a-tried to sweet talk me, said he works in banking, gave me names of all these people he knows that we know... he said can take care of everything, that there's probably just a misunderstanding...but he needed to see our Sage," Grandma Ada continued.

Loretta and I looked at one another again. The shop had been closed for about an hour earlier in the day while Dad and I went into town to pick up some lumber. We didn't usually close for that, but this was a special order and both of us were needed to haul it in the buggy. We tried to never leave Grandma Ada unattended, but occasionally it did happen. She was still pretty able to take care of herself, so it wasn't considered a major crisis if she had to spend an hour alone here and there.

"Where were you earlier, and Mom, and Daniel?" I asked

"You know, I think I know when this must have happened. Daniel took Marvin, Jr., to go fishing in the pond, and Mom, the twins, Nancy, and I went to see the Yoder's new baby, but, heck, we couldn't have been gone more than an hour," Loretta mused.

"What does it matter? I got rid of him, didn't want him to bother sweet Sage."

"It's PAIGE!!!" Loretta and I both yelled at Grandma in unison so loud that the glass globes on the kerosene lamps sitting in the center of the supper table rattled. First time we had agreed on anything in over a month.

"Let's go easy on her," my father said, who had been watching this unfold.

"He was probably coming to make eyes at Paige, just like YOU were doing," Nancy said, looking over at me.

I glared at her with enough heat to melt my homemade ice cream.

"Dad's right, doesn't matter what Grandma calls her, just tell us what happened. What did you tell him. Who was this man?" I asked gently.

"Told him Sage was in *rumspringa*.....and that she was just up here visiting from Hudson, Kentucky. I never did like the Amish down there," Grandma said beaming. "Threw him off her trail. Tee-hee."

None of this was really making sense to me. I started to say something.

"But he read me this address…in…Chicago, said he had that address for her, so he asked why would she be from Hudson, Kentucky. Told him she had moved to Chicago on *rumspringa*, and…"

"Grandma, did he tell you anything about where he was from, what he was doing here???"

Grandma poked at her corn. "I don't remember."

I was concerned, but without more information, I didn't know what was going on.

"But he left me this…" Grandma Ada fished a card out from somewhere in the folds of her dress and slid it across the table.

My heart accelerated. I turned the card over.

"Plain Investments -- Amos Raber"

CHAPTER 24
ABRAHAM

I sprang out of my chair and started to run outside, but then stopped. I turned around and gave Grandma Ada a hug and a kiss on the cheek.

"Thank you, Grandma."

She beamed.

"Grandma Ada did good?"

"Yes, you did," I said. "Very good."

Then I ran outside. My mind was a blur. I had to think fast. Grandma had bought me some time if Amos was dumb enough to fall for such a flimsy story. I had my doubts. Loretta followed me outside. The sky was a hazy, summery blue. Insects buzzed around the homemade traps in the apple trees and Speck snoozed in the shade under one of our buggies which was parked outside the shop. It was one of those heat-infused summer days where everything seemed to move in sticky slow motion. At least it had seemed to until Grandma Ada's revelation.

"Abe, what's going on? Is Paige in trouble?" asked Loretta, drying her just-washed hands on the white apron she was wearing over her rust-colored dress.

I was quiet for a second.

"Yes. Yes, I think she is."

"How? What's going on?" Loretta asked.

"I don't know for certain. But you know the Neuenschwanders are losing their home, don't you?"

"Yes, Mom told me. What does this have to do with Paige?"

"'Retta, I'm not sure now. I just know that Amos Raber was here talking to Grandma Ada…"

"Oh, you are worried about HIM?" Loretta asked.

"Yes, I think he's dangerous and…" I said before Loretta cut me off and glared at me angrily.

"You've always been jealous of him and his success, but if you only had an ounce of the character that he has, you'd maybe have a chance to be a decent human being. You need to get right with God before it's too…"

This time I cut her off, my face turning almost purple. I had had enough. I put my hands on her shoulders. "Shut up! Just shut up, you don't know what you are talking about!" I roared. I turned to Mom, who seemed shaken.

"I can't imagine why he would want to see Paige. How would he even know that I took her to the Neuenschwanders?" I mused.

"You mean when she was here for the pie crusts?" Daniel interjected.

"No...no, remember on July Fourth, the holiday, when....well, when Paige and I were ...last...together? We went to the Neuenschwanders' that afternoon. She tried to talk ol' Mose into fighting the foreclosure. She said she had found some things out about Plain Investments..." I said, trying to calm down.

"But how would have he known? How would have he made the connection between you, Paige, and the Neuenschwanders? None of this makes sense, Abe...you're delusional," Loretta huffed.

"I know. I know it doesn't...but something's not right. I have to warn her."

I paced for a second in the driveway. "I'm going to take Ruby into town now and call her to warn her," I said.

"I'll get the buggy ready," Daniel offered. At least he hadn't abandoned me.

"Thanks!" I shouted and began to tear down the driveway when I came to a sudden stop.

"Whoa....I just remembered something."

Daniel ran over to my buggy and looked up at me.

"What?"

"I don't have her phone number," I said sheepishly.

 But then I remembered Paige's first visit during the snowstorm.

"Her business card! 'Retta, she gave you her business card when she first came here back in February. Where is it???"

She looked solemn, staring down at her bare feet now covered in driveway dust.

"What?"

"Burned it in a brush fire…well…I…I almost kept it…but, oh, Abe, you needed to make a clean break."

"Your clean break may have cost me the best chance I had of warning her!" I snarled back at her. I turned to Daniel. "Sit with Grandma Ada and see if there is anything else she can remember that will be helpful. I'm going to ride into town, visit the library, and send her an email. I do have her email address. I'll be back home in an hour, hour and a half."

Loretta probably wondered how I had Paige's email address, but everything was happening so fast she didn't have time to ask.

Ruby tore down the driveway, leaving a cloud of dust in her wake, going as fast as her three-year-old legs would carry us. I tried to think of all the possible scenarios of why Amos Raber would have been searching for Paige. And the way Grandma Ada described it, he was searching for her with urgency. None of it made sense. Even if Paige had been turning over some rocks back in Chicago and somehow he connected her to the Neuenschwanders, how would he know to come to see us?

"Mr. Doty!" I just thought of him. He would have Paige's number. I hadn't spoken to him since that afternoon on his porch when he had found out about the credit card. I had tried to seek his forgiveness, but my overtures always went unanswered. But this was potentially a matter of life or death. I overcame my fear and tore down his driveway, my buggy leaving behind a whirlwind of gravel and dust.

"What do you want?" Mr. Doty snarled as he answered the door.

"I know you and I don't have the best history, and I pray that you'll one day forgive me, but this is about Paige. She's in trouble."

"Oh, and you expect me to believe you about anything?"

"I know this sounds crazy, but can you just call her?"

"And tell her what, that a lovesick Amish boy misses her?"

I cringed. Did he know?

"Mr. Doty, don't do it for me, do it for Paige. I only need for you to call her and warn her…."

"Okay, I will call and warn her about you. I'll call her and tell her to stay as far away from you as the moon!"

The door slammed in my face. Time was running out and this was going nowhere. I had to try to fix this myself.

As the eclectic mix of Swiss-motif storefronts, purely American dollar stores, and internet cafes of downtown Berne replaced the rural farm fields, I could sense some stares on me, but I ignored them. I secured Ruby to a hitching post and sprinted into the library. I stifled a groan when I saw that it was the same librarian who had often manned (more like policed) the internet desk in the past.

"I'd like to use a computer."

"Hmmm, it's been awhile…thought maybe you two had broken up," said the owlish-looking librarian.

I glared but was otherwise silent.

"Just sign here, but it'll be a while. All the computers are taken. Next one won't be available for 30 more minutes."

"But this is important!"

"I'm sure," the librarian said icily.

"Isn't there a computer in an office available that I could use for just a few minutes? I'll gladly pay," I whispered.

"Wait your turn. I'm sure your sweet muffin will still be there in 30 minutes," the librarian whispered back.

I felt my face flush with a combination of anger and embarrassment. I paced. I wasn't sure I had 30 minutes. I walked up to a woman sitting at a computer. She was heavyset, wearing a pink-lemonade-colored cardigan, black tights, and running sneakers.

"Ma'am…would you mind if I…"

She turned around and scowled at me.

"Um, I'll just hang out back here," I said to no one in particular. There were five computers sitting side by side that were available for public use, and all were occupied. The magazine rack was nearby, so I picked up a copy of *Popular Mechanics* and then feigned a severe, fluid-filled coughing fit.

"Ugh, sorry, just got back from Belize…I might have picked up something tropical," I muttered again to no one in particular.

I coughed and retched violently again. A couple of people grabbed their belongings and headed for the exits. The pink-lemonade-colored-cardigan woman glared at me as she grabbed her notebook and purse, and left the library.

The librarian glowered at me.

"Looks like a few people checked out early. May I?"

I logged into my Zapmail account and typed Paige a quick note.

Dear Paige,

I hope you are doing well. I've missed seeing you, but I also want to respect your request for space…I wouldn't be writing today if I didn't think this was very important. I just found out that Amos Raber (he and I have a long history, little of it good☹) from Plain Investments stopped by our house. I wasn't home when he stopped by. No one was except for Grandma Ada. Seemed like he kind of scared her, but she's a flinty one and held her own. He had an address for you in Chicago. He apparently was trying really, really hard to find you. Grandma Ada had a bad feeling and tried to throw him off your trail by spinning a story about you being from Kentucky. It was sweet and wily of her, but I'm not sure how effective it was. You know how much trouble that man has caused so I just couldn't imagine him looking for you could be anything good. But maybe I am wrong. I hope I am not being intrusive, but I am worried for you so I wanted to warn you that he has your address and he's looking for you. Maybe you already know. You can always come here. You are always welcome.

Yours,

Abe

A wave of relief swept over me. At least I had done *something*. I don't know if I could have slept at night knowing that I hadn't done everything I could to warn her. I exhaled mightily and started to get up and head for home when I heard a "ping" coming from the computer. It was the sound I usually heard when an email arrived.

Had she responded that fast?

<<<<<<<<<<<<<<<Email account full. This email is being held in queue until the recipient creates more room in their box.>>>>>>>>>>>>>>>>>

A feeling of trepidation grabbed me. This was the only contact I had for Paige. I was back to where I was an hour ago, which was nowhere.

"Damn," I said a little bit too loudly. The librarian stared at me over the top of her spectacles.

"Problem?"

I wasn't sure what to do next. I wasn't well-versed with the internet, but I knew my way around a little. I started typing things in search engines, but mostly got dead-ends. I found a Paige Roberts, porn star, website.

"Whoa…that's definitely not MY Paige," I said to myself, eyeing the scantily clad woman on the screen in front of me.

I knew how to do basic internet stuff and I was sure I could figure it out eventually, but time was critical here. Paige the porn star kept coming up. I gulped. She was very…eye-catching. I waved to the librarian.

"Could you show me how to search for something online?"

"Don't want to get near you if you have something tropical," she said sarcastically.

I glared back her. The librarian rolled her eyes and came to help me but recoiled when she saw my screen.

"Sir! We do not allow adult material in public viewing areas, you'll ne…"

I cut her off.

"I am not looking for her," I said, pointing at the screen.

"Yeah, looks like you are looking AT her," the librarian said.

I closed the window of the buxom Paige Roberts, and the librarian gave me a quick, grudging tutorial on search terms and engines.

The searches yielded a bunch of Paige Robertses. I found a photo of her from college and it made me feel sad. I missed her. But whatever my feelings were for her right now, they didn't really matter. She was potentially in danger and I needed to warn her. I was stupefied that with all the technology available enabling everything about everyone to be found instantly online, I still couldn't find a phone number for Paige. The librarian explained that technology in some ways has made it *more* difficult to find people, at least in the most basic ways. Used to be, she said, almost everyone was listed in the public phone book, but as cell phones took over, phone books never caught up. Someone like Paige who only had a cell was virtually impossible to find. Had I remembered the name of the law firm where she worked, I would have just called her there, but I couldn't, and nothing online came up. It actually can be easier to find an Amish person the old-fashioned way, I thought. We had a community directory of Amish. It was organized alphabetically just like an old phone book used to be, except our directories had no phone numbers.

I left the library, empty-handed and apprehensive. Telephones everywhere and no way to reach her. It really left me with no other options. I found Ruby, much to my relief, still tied to the hitching post. I stroked her on the nose and prepared to mount when a voice from behind startled me.

I spun around.

"Would you mind if we take your picture?" asked a silver-haired man wearing cheap sunglasses, a bolo tie, khaki shorts, loafers, and black socks. "Here, I'll give you a ten dollar bill."

"I'm really in a hurry," I said politely.

"Now, Jim, I don't think the Amish allow photos," said the man's wife.

"Listen to your wife. She's a wise woman," I agreed.

"Oh, but it's just for us. It's our anniversary. We won't show it to anyone but ourselves. Come on, let us take your picture. We just want a picture of a real, live Amish," the man whispered, and chuckled, "We won't tell a soul."

"But you'll steal mine!" I shouted as I climbed into the buggy.

CHAPTER 25

I headed to the First Bank of Berne. I wasn't thinking clearly, and I didn't know how much I needed, or what I even needed it for. But I withdrew $15,000 in cash and stuffed it into my pockets. I still had plenty left over from the sale of my farmette.

*   *   *

Part of how Amos was able to succeed with his Ponzi scheme was in part by motivating a small corps of loyal lieutenants who were eager for a piece of the action. Most of them were wayward young men who were wavering on whether to join the church or not, and thought they had found a future in Plain Investments. But once Amos found out the SEC was investigating him and that I was a part of that, he decided to finish me off once and for all. Amos knew that if I got into trouble with the law again that I would be put behind bars. And that's exactly where he wanted me.

"Officer, you might want to keep an eye on that man," Melvin Beachy said to two policemen who were sitting in a cruiser writing tickets.

"Come again?" the officer said, not looking up from his citation book.

"Look, I sell produce here in town on weekends and we make fine cabinets back at the house...if tourists start seeing drug-dealing Amish, that's gonna be horrible for business...and that man there, I just saw him buying drugs off someone, saw it myself with my own eyes...bad for tourism, yes, sir," Melvin said.

I reached under my seat to grab my sunglasses, something Melvin knew I'd do, because, it turned out, he had been watching me from his buggy. I felt a bulky, padded envelope and pulled it out. Mystified, I looked inside at the envelope's contents. The aroma was overpowering, and I recognized it at once as something I had smelled before at a *rumspringa* party or two. It was weed. I had never tried marijuana or any other drug. Life was difficult enough with a clear mind, and I couldn't imagine trying to function under the influence of something. Trying to pay attention to Ruby, to traffic, and the rising panic inside of me at having this in my possession made it difficult to control the buggy. I passed the imposing Muensterberg Plaza and Clock Tower looming over Berne and banked South onto US 27 towards more the more familiar turf of the countryside. I know I swerved a couple of times as I was trying to stuff the stuff back under the buggy seat. I calmed down. No one had seen me with this. I'd discreetly dispose of it at home, and find out how it got there later. But I was wrong. I had been seen.

"See the way he's swerving? He's probably high as an orbiting satellite," Sergeant Alcorn said.

"You're going to go after a buggy?" the rookie officer asked incredulously.

"It appears the eyewitness was correct...son, just because they're Amish doesn't mean they don't break the law. I've arrested Amish for almost anything I've arrested anyone else for-- drugs, alcohol, domestics. Now don't go mouthing off to anyone about that, though. We've got a good relationship with the tourism folks, and the misdeeds of the area Amish aren't something we really like to get out there," Sergeant Alcorn told the rookie.

"Surprises me. I thought they'd give you the least trouble," the rookie said.

"Don't get me wrong. They pretty much keep to themselves, but you'd be surprised how much trouble they can cause, and you won't read about that in the tourism brochures," Sergeant Alcorn stated.

I noticed the police car pull behind me after I had passed, and cursed at myself for not keeping Ruby under better control. Hopefully, the officer was just on his way somewhere else. I needed to remain calm and not call attention to myself.

"He seems to be keeping the buggy under control now," the rookie observed.

"Probably knows he's being followed. We've got probable cause," Sergeant Alcorn said.

"Shouldn't have we interviewed the witness more and maybe taken his name and address?" the rookie asked.

"No need. You're on the beat as long as me, you just get a feel for this sort of stuff," Sergeant Alcorn said.

I was now convinced the police car was following me. There was nowhere for me to go. I briefly considered tossing the envelope into the drainage ditch beside the highway, but there was no way I could do that undetected. Still, if I were caught with this weed, I'd surely be put into jail. The thought of being behind bars, helpless to help Paige, was too much to bear. I desperately didn't want to go back to jail. But I was trapped. In a few seconds the officer would flip on his lights and that would be the end.

In one of those instants when everything suddenly becomes clear, I noticed a congregation of buggies in a field off to my right.

"The Yutzy auction!"

"Ruby, run!" I barked. Ruby sped to a thoroughbred's speed. I then banked her a hard right onto the approaching cross street.

*   *   *

"He's going faster and turning," the rookie observed.

Genius, Sergeant Alcorn thought to himself. I don't need a play-by-play.

My buggy disappeared from view in a cloud of dust as thick and fine as brown flour. The unpaved roads outside of Berne often produced a fog of particles, but the extra-dry summer had made it worse than usual.

"Whoa, can't see a thing..." Sergeant Alcorn said, slamming on his brakes.

"We're losing him," the rookie said.

"Seriously?" Sergeant Alcorn said coughing, as some of the dust made its way into the cruiser. He stared at his young charge incredulously. "We'll just hang back a bit outside of the dust and follow him, for Pete's sake."

"Okay...but don't you think we sh..."

"Should what? Call in the SWAT team?? You have to be kidding. He's in a buggy going 10 miles per hour. We've got him trapped like a bug in a bottle," Sergeant Alcorn said, exasperated the rookie. "See, he's turning. He's trapped, we've got him."

*　　　　　　*　　　　　　*

Junior Yutzy was standing at the end of the driveway helping with traffic control, clearly visible in his straw hats, suspenders, and denim-colored clothes. He was looking the other direction, talking to the driver of an arriving van, as I slipped in and guided Ruby into the mass of approximately 300 buggies parked in the field. I secured Ruby, leapt off the buggy, and vanished into the milling crowd.

"Is there a problem, officer?" asked Junior, who had walked back to his post.

"No, we just wanted to ask someone a few questions," Sergeant Alcorn said.

"Help yourself," Junior said, motioning towards the field.

Sergeant Alcorn turned to see a field filled with buggies all virtually indistinguishable from one another.

"Did you see where he went?" he asked.

"See where who went?" Junior asked.

"The man we were following," Sergeant Alcorn asked impatiently.

"I'm trying to watch traffic coming and going from three different directions, and you want me to pick out one buggy? Take your pick!" Junior was exasperated, gesturing towards the field of buggies. Sergeant Alcorn surveyed a panorama of dozens upon dozens of buggies all appearing nearly identical.

"We can't search them all," the rookie officer said.

Sergeant Alcorn barked, "Let's go, and I never want to speak of this again!"

*   *   *

You're going *where?*" Mom asked me.

"I have to warn her. I think she's in danger," I answered.

Mom never seemed like much of an ideologue concerning the church, but my plans to head to Chicago seemed to stir something within her. It was anger, something I rarely saw from my mother.

"I thought you had changed. But here you are again going off on some flight of fancy for something you just THINK is true?" Mom said. "You're an adult, you can do what you want. But you were BAPTIZED into the church. You have to think long and hard about what and who you want to be in this life because you can't be both. You can't be Amish and English…it's one or the other."

"This isn't about the church. This is about who I want to be…this is a chance for me to do something right."

"Can't you just call the police? You may not have her phone number, but you have her address. Isn't there some way you can get a message to her without going there?" Mom challenged.

"Oh, you think the police are going to believe this story when I call them?" I asked her.

Mom was silent for a minute before she finally spoke. "How are you getting there?"

"I'm taking a cab to the train station."

"This is crazy."

"Daniel, you need to keep an eye on things. If my suppositions are correct, it wouldn't surprise me if, once they realize Grandma Ada duped them, someone might come back for revenge."

I was suspicious. Someone was out to get me. How else would pot end up in my buggy? Someone wanted me arrested and knew the consequences if I were. The police had half-heartedly searched the premises of the Yutzy auction before surrendering in a huff-filled retreat. I'd disposed of the pot in a nearby creek and taken the back way home.

PAIGE

Sterling Bank was a small player in the Chicago market, but they were stable, solvent and friendly, which was more than could be said for a lot of banks. Daddy's spacious office had a lime-colored sofa against one wall, and behind his desk was a large plate glass window that overlooked the leafy green Chicago suburb that it called home. Framed awards, photos, and certificates blanketed another wall. A black phone with a cord sat on a corner of his desk, corded phones being increasingly anachronistic but somehow appropriate for a bank that seemed like an old-time throwback. Daddy was a third-generation banker in his family, but he increasingly was feeling uncomfortable with the business. It used to be a gentleman's game where people were as important as profits.

He despised the way many banks made their money these days. He never did embrace features like overdraft fees and sneaky reordering of customers' checks so that the largest one would clear first, allowing the bank to collect $36 for a $1.39-doughnut-and-coffee overdraft. Daddy was rich, but he always prided himself on doing it the old-fashioned way, with satisfactory customer service, superb products, and extensive community stewardship. Daddy preferred Sterling to make money the way banks used to, by making loans. Overdraft fees were only $10 at Sterling, the bank cleared transactions in order of smallest to largest, and their website interface had won six awards over the years. Richard at first had no interest in websites, preferring to bank the way it had been done for most of the last 100 years: in-person. But he soon realized which direction the tide was turning, and hired a masterful young whiz kid from Northwestern University to be in charge of Sterling's website, and sterling it became. Daddy--unlike my more aloof mother-- prided himself on being approachable and open-minded. There had been more than one occasion throughout the years that a bank customer came sobbing into his office because they had overdrawn their account or needed a loan. Daddy and his staff knew most of their customers by name, and if someone needed a loan, they usually found a way to give it to them. Daddy despised the computer programs that most other banks used to score someone's creditworthiness.

"Why does a bank need a loan officer if they aren't going to do anything but follow whatever a computer tells them to do?" he often groused.

Sterling's loan officers were sent to special seminars to be able to truly assess a borrower's ability to repay. At Sterling, profiling was an art, and most of the time the loan officers were correct in their assessments.

Daddy often chuckled when he read about all the foreclosures. Historically, banks had tried at all costs to avoid foreclosures. Banks made plenty of profit-making good loans. But as the housing market had ballooned and more and more pigs came to the trough, some banks found a way to make money foreclosing through fat fees and greed.

"You know how many foreclosures Sterling has had in the past 20 years?" Daddy liked to ask. "Five...just five." It was a statistic he was very proud of. And if it weren't for privacy reasons, he could give you the names of the people himself. Losing a home wasn't a matter Daddy took lightly. The bank took a huge loss, and a family's life was uprooted forever.

The phone rang on the corner of his desk.

"It's Paige," the receptionist said.

"Great, send her in."

"Hi, Daddy," I said, planting a kiss on his cheek.

"So, what brings you here today? Everything OK?"

"I need some advice. It's about a company called Plain Investments."

He looked quizzically at me.

"Why are you interested in this?"

"Because a wonderful family without the resources to fight back is about to lose their home, and I just don't think it's fair. And if there's something I can do about it, I'd like to be a part of keeping someone in their home for a change, instead of taking it."

Dad exhaled and bristled at my words. Despite his own personal aversion to it, foreclosure was a fair tool for a bank to use, he believed. And when he first recommended the job to me, my firm was less of a foreclosure mill and more of a "mediator mill."

"Will you at least just take a look?" I asked, handing the file to him.

He thumbed through the pages. Occasionally he'd arch his eyebrows, mutter something to himself, and then after reading one document, he whipped out a pad and scribbled some notes.

"Crooked...," he muttered.

"And most of the people want to handle it themselves, but I think they are in over their heads...people will lose their homes, their life savings, and this guy is going to get off. I think there's been a Ponzi scheme," I said.

"Okay, I'll call my contacts at SEC and see if they can get moving now. But I can't make any promises, and these government agencies are notoriously slow," Daddy said. "But I'll do what I can."

"Thank you, Daddy," I said, getting up to hug him.

"But, let me ask one thing...why don't you just file an appeal? Gum this thing up in the courts a bit to give the Feds more time to investigate?"

Now it was my turn to sigh.

"They're Amish...."

"So? I don't care if they're Buddhist monks. If you think it's wrong, it's wrong. File the Amish appeal and be done with it."

"That's not the way they think. Believe me Dad, I tried."

"Well…let me see what I can do. I'll call you," He said. Daddy shared a personality characteristic with Loretta. Right was right and wrong was wrong, and if he believed something was wrong, he'd do anything to right it.

"Thank you, Daddy," I said gathering my purse.

"Oh, and sweetie…" he said.

I turned back.

"Be careful. This type of people can be nasty."

"Don't worry, Daddy, they don't even know I'm involved."

CHAPTER 26

ABRAHAM

My departure for Chicago, despite my best attempt at secrecy, was red meat for the Amish gossip machine.

"Thought I saw Abe at the Yutzy auction earlier. That was kind of strange."

"Saw Abe in the bank earlier. He didn't seem to see me at all. Seemed odd because he's usually so friendly."

"Oh, I bet this has to do with that woman he brought to the Neuenschwanders."

"No, no, he's prepared to turn English and enroll in university, THAT'S what this is about!"

"Young Abe's going to turn Mennonite."

A dozen black-*kapp*-clad, caped Amish women in blue dresses all clucked with the latest gossip at a community quilting bee. My sudden departure was the talk of the church. I was sure Bishop Hochstetler would soon be asking questions, also.

As the gossip, most of it wildly incorrect, began to germinate and spread, it took on a life of its own. Some people began to show up at our farmstead, others at the Neuenschwanders, some to genuinely console and comfort Mom, while others were just nosy. Casseroles began to pile up on Mom's table.

"People, please, no one has died…he's just gone….away for a bit….thinks one of his friends needed some help, that's ALL," Mom and Loretta would both take turns saying to people who showed up at the door.

"That's not what I heard," the *kapp*-clad and bearded visitors would whisper, each conveying their inaccurate information.

Mom would direct most of the visitors to the Neuenschwanders.

"They're the ones that need our help. They have to be out of their house in a few days."

*   *

*

PAIGE

"Good, glad you got my note. Wasn't sure if you had your cell with you, " I said to Ashleigh.

"Yep, got it. Okay, you ready to tell me about this new guy?" asked Ashleigh as we prepared for our run along Chicago's lakefront.

" I…look, it's crazy…and I…he's not exac…oh, you are going to think I need to be committed," I admitted, propping my right foot on a planter outside her apartment and stretching.

"Ready?" Ashleigh asked. She and I were both dressed in tight-fitting running shorts, t-shirts, and sneakers. We did make a fit pretty pair, and always elicited our fair share of catcalls from passing men. It was boorish behavior, but almost a little flattering.

We ran out of Wrigleyville's brownstone miasma and began running the well-lit paved path along Lakeshore Drive. Chicago's broad-shouldered buildings were framed by a hazy summer sky. An east wind purred off the lake, providing us with a refreshing spray-soaked blue breeze. A tapestry of soothing green parkland offered a pleasant buffer between concrete city and the choppy waters of the lake.

Once we settled into a peaceful running rhythm on the path, Ashleigh tried again.

"Oh, c'mon, just spit it out…he can't be any worse than some of the other losers you and I have dated over the years."

We kept a brisk pace, but we were both able to converse as we ran. I stared ahead, ponytail swinging. She looked over at me.

"Okay…so he's Amish," I finally blurted out between breaths.

Ashleigh was unfazed.

"Oh, well, that's not a big deal…I've known people like that…refuse to get cell phone, internet…" Ashleigh offered.

We continued our sprint past a tableau of peaceful parks, gulls perched on rocky breakwaters, benches with homeless people stretched out on them. The occasional fisherman tried his luck on the stony shore of Lake Michigan.

"No, not just an urban Amish…I mean, Amish-Amish," I pressed.

Ashleigh stopped.

"You mean like in the movie *Witness*, beards, buggies, and Bibles?"

I waved Ashleigh on to continue the run, and we started up again.

"Yes…that kind…but, oh no, don't get me wrong…I'm not ready to give up my iPhone just yet. I'd probably be a lousy Amish…but…he's a very…his name is Abe and he's just a very appealing, sexy guy."

"Somehow sexy and Amish aren't two words that I'd think of putting together," Ashleigh said skeptically.

"Oh, you'd be surprised. Most Amish men work hard, or at least Abe does…baling hay, chopping wood, making cabinets, breaking in horses…" I said, my voice trailing.

"Abe??? Um…okay…and…this means what? You're going to pack up and jump in a buggy and live happily ever after?"

"I don't know…I don't know…I just think I need some time…" I said, still keeping up a pretty good pace as we talked.

"Time for what?" Time to get your butter churn in order?"

"I just need some time to think. Sheesh, you aren't exactly being the most supportive of this!"

"Not trying to be hard on you, but if you think my questions are tough, trying explaining this to your mother."

"I know…you know me, though. For years I've sort of been trying to figure out my footing, and when I met the Schwartzes and the Neuenschwanders, it's as if they injected some clarity in my life that had been missing. And Abe, he's such a special guy that I sort of don't even see him as a 'special Amish guy.' He's just a remarkable man…I miss him…but I know I can't be with him…"

"So what are you going to do? I can't imagine you in a bonnet."

"Well, they actually aren't called bonnets, they are call *kapps*…and in answer to your question….I don't know…I don't know what I'm thinking."

Ashleigh rolled her eyes.

"You barely know how to toast bread, let alone make it," Ashleigh commented.

"I know...I'm not saying...I...I'm just saying I need some time."

"Isn't being Amish like stepping back into pioneer times or something?"

"It's not like that. That's what everyone thinks...I mean in some ways-- some good ways--it is. What if I'm deeply attracted to Abe, and I like the values and the simplicity, but I'm not necessarily wedded to the mechanics of the religion? Although, truly from what I've seen, they are less 'out there' in their beliefs than some other supposedly more mainstream religious groups are," I explained, a sheen of sweat beginning to form on my forehead from the brisk run and intense conversation.

We looped around a fountain in one of the greenways along the lake, and began circling back to Wrigleyville. The wind seemed to have shifted so that we were running directly into it.

"So, I'm attracted to him...but what do I do about it?" I asked.

"Tough question. I don't know if I'm the one you should be asking...I know some couples that are Jewish and Catholic or...heck, I think one of my parent's friends is an atheist, and her husband goes to church. I don't know if it can work in cases like that...how could it be much different this way?"

I laughed. Ashleigh was always great at bringing an argument back to its essence, which is why I always thought she would have made a great defense attorney or even a prosecutor. She definitely didn't belong in some back room processing foreclosure paperwork.

"Hey, you want to come over for some pizza? I can tell you more about my Amish friends."

"Would love to, but I've got a pile of work that needs to be done before I go into the office. Sucks, but I know if I don't get to it tonight, it'll just snowball. I'll take you up on that soon. I'd like to hear more about these hot Amish men. Heck, maybe you'll start something here."

I laughed.

"Maybe. One of his friends is pretty cute, too, and I think he's single. Anyway, that's okay about the pizza. It'll just be myself and a warm bubble bath."

"Bet you'd miss that if you were Amish!" Ashleigh laughed.

"You'd be surprised. The Schwartzes have a big porcelain tub. I don't think bubble baths are against their beliefs," I shouted back.

I always carried a cell phone with me on my runs, partly for a clock and partly for safety's sake. But it was also handy for mundane tasks like ordering a pizza, which I promptly did after pausing from my run. Sicilian Express was my favorite delivery pizza. I'd miss that if I became Amish, I laughed to myself.

Ashleigh and I ran our separate ways as evening enveloped Chicago. I needed to think, needed to reflect. My feelings for Abe were surprisingly intense even as I tried to shut him out, but I also knew that it couldn't work. As I walked into my apartment, I thought of the running water that I had and that Abe didn't, cars versus buggies, and computers versus handwritten notes. I closed the door behind me and started to strip off my sweaty clothes. I had another 45 minutes to shower and cool off before my pizza arrived, but my plans were abruptly upended when I heard a voice.

"If you wanted to know more about my company, you could have just asked," said a handsome man with tumbling blonde locks and ice-blue eyes. He was sitting comfortably in one of my chairs.

CHAPTER 27

ABRAHAM

By now quite a crowd had gathered at the Neuenschwanders. Melvin Beachy slipped into the gathering, trying to glean as much information as possible.

"Just heard about things and thought I'd see if there was anything I could do to help. You know, one of us in trouble, we're all in trouble," Melvin explained with a pleasant smile .

Melvin was frustrated because no one seemed to know much of anything, just that something was going on, but he couldn't find out what. For all he could figure, this Amish assembly had nothing to do with the Neuenschwanders and their foreclosure.

He spied my Mom and Dad on the Neuenschwander's porch, talking with Lizzie and ol' Mose. Had Melvin been able to get that far, he would have at least been able to find out that I was headed for Chicago. He could have warned Amos. But he never made it to the porch.

"Why's Melvin Beachy here?" Roman Neuenschwander asked a friend.

"Works for Plain Investments, probably just trying to help," the friend said.

I had stopped at Roman's on the way out of town to fill him in on what was going on. I just thought I needed someone I could trust on my team, and that proved to be a wise move.

"Don't let him know anything that is happening. Abe's in trouble," Roman ordered his friend.

Dorcas Petersheim, who had been making her usual raucous rounds, overheard their conversation.

"Abe's in trouble? That's enough for me. I'll handle this," said Dorcas, whose ample figure had been lurking nearby.

Her chocolate-colored dress and white apron disappeared in a brown blur.

"Yoo-hoo, you ARE a cutie," Dorcas said as she made a beeline for Melvin Beachy.

Melvin's eyes rounded.

"Um…uh, thanks…but do you mind?" Melvin said, trying to make his way to the porch.

"Oh, I thought you'd never ask. I've been watching you from afar," Dorcas said, grabbing Melvin's arm. "Let's you and I have some fun!"

Melvin ran for the Neuenschwanders' now nearly-empty hay mow, where Dorcas kept him cornered most of the night.

ABRAHAM

The train journey across northern Indiana to Chicago only took a couple of hours, although it seemed like the tracks to eternity. I settled into one of the bus-style seats and watched the verdant farm fields pass by in a blur. Occasionally I'd spot a horse-drawn buggy clattering down a quiet lane, and I'd find myself wishing I weren't on this train, that Ruby and I were just exploring the rural roads around Berne, the warm wind blowing through my hair.

"He's Amish," a Mom whispered to her soccer-uniform-attired son as they walked down the aisle of the train.

Tried as I might to blend in, I hadn't really been successful. I didn't really want to. I wasn't ashamed of being Amish, but I just didn't want to stand out too much in the city, so I wore a pair of dark denims and a nice brown button-down workshirt. You know, by the way, it's not true that no Amish have buttons on their shirts. That's another media misconception circulating out there. Now it is true that *some* don't. Wow, those Swartzentruber Amish women are like living pin-cushions with their dresses fastened together with straight pins, and they walk around looking like thimbles. But many Old Order churches, mine included, allow buttons or silver snaps. I don't think Bishop Hochstetler would permit big gold buttons or anything fancy, but a functional button is allowed.

So, anyway, I tried to be inconspicuous. I did take my hat along, but I didn't wear it on the train. I set it on the seat next to me, but somehow people knew.

"He's a cutie," I heard a young woman wearing a college sweatshirt whisper to her friend.

"Sure is, but he's one of those Hare Krishnas," the other girl said.

I stifled a laugh. I had been mistaken for everything from a Mormon to an Orthodox Jew before, but never a Hare Krishna.

When the train finally pulled into Chicago's Union Station, the afternoon was winding to a close. I bounded off the train and navigated a labyrinth of turnstiles, ticket takers, panhandlers, escalators, and snack bars before finally being belched out onto the people-filled streets of Chicago. It was a bit disorienting. Up until they built the massive Swiss clock tower in Berne, the largest structure I was accustomed to seeing was our barn. But here, buildings reached for the sky, monuments to man's technological and engineering acumen.

I had read enough books that I knew to flag down a yellow-colored checkered cab.

"Fifty-five Hawthorne Terrace, please," I said.

The olive-skinned cab driver looked at me quizzically for a split-second as if he wasn't used to seeing Amish men get into his cab every day.

"Get in," he said in a thick accent.

"Is it far?"

"It's just straight up Halstead. About 15 minutes," he said, gunning the engine and launching the cab into a crazed lurch. The driver haphazardly weaved between dump trucks and cyclists, limos and Lincolns. I dug my hands into the car door and seat, holding my breath, awaiting an impact that never arrived.

I watched the checkerboard of Chicago skyscrapers pass, the masses of people, hot dog hawkers, and pizzerias. I had traveled plenty, but never to such a sprawling city with so many people living in close proximity to one another. After five minutes in Chicago, I decided that this wasn't for me. While clearly humankind has made amazing strides in creating such cities and great universities which serve as incubators for all sorts of advances in medicine, engineering, and physics, I found myself ever prouder of the Amish ability to act as a counterweight to an otherwise unchecked runaway from our roots.

The cab had slowed to a creep before finally stopping altogether, hemmed in by fenders on all sides.

"Allah, I can't believe this!" the driver shouted.

"What's going on?"

"Not sure, but we're not moving," he said, picking up some sort of radio device and shouting something unintelligible into it. One of my eyes was on the clock, the other on the meter sitting on the dash. Sheesh, I thought to myself, I hope the Amish cabs in Indiana never see those--that would give them some ideas!

"You've got be kidding. Isn't there anything you can do?"

"I could cut over to Lake Shore Drive if I could get there, but we're locked in now, I'm trying to find out more."

I began to boil impatiently in the back seat.

"President is in town, they've closed off a bunch of roads. Halstead is open, but the roads leading out from it are closed…I think we are going to be sitting here for a while. You might be better off walking…" the cab driver considered.

He was right. Pedestrians were passing our parked car. If I walked briskly, I could cover the remaining ground in 45 minutes, maybe less. Walking, I always thought, was underrated and I often laughed at those non-Amish who'd take a car to the corner.

As my cab sat stalled, penned in by traffic, I stared out the window and stewed. But then something caught my eye.

A couple of carriages were parked on the shoulder of the road. The carriages were open, just like we had back in Berne. But these buggies were bright red, like fire engines, right down to the wheel spokes. And unlike our gray steel wheels in Berne, these wheels looked like they were fully rubberized. The front seat, like some of our buggies, was a single long bench for the driver. The bench sat above the passenger wagon. I had never seen a design quite like that one. Big, beefy chestnut-colored horses stood bored-looking, waiting for their next passengers.

"Yes, yes", I said to myself. "I think that just might do."

I handed the cabbie $20 and sprinted for the carriage stand. One of the drivers animatedly attempted to sell me a ride.

"Thirty minutes is $40, 45-minute tour $60, or an hour for $80. Skyline ride at dusk with dinner is $200, and I think we can get a look at the Pres..."

I cut him off.

"I need a couple of hours. I need to borrow this. I'll return it...promise," I said, stuffing 20 $100-bills into his hand.

I settled into the bench. I have to admit that after almost 10 hours of traveling by car, train, and taxi, it felt great to be back to the familiarity of a horse. I reached over to stroke the horse's head. There was even a buggy lane where the carriages took the tourists.

"Thank God no one from church can see me on this," I thought to myself, a little embarrassed to be seen driving this blazing red carriage by anyone.

I was sitting high up on the seat, with a goofy-looking crimson carriage behind me that could sit six. I felt as if I had stepped into a Cinderella storybook. But the horse was faster than traveling on foot, and as silly as it looked, I was more comfortable and in more control here than in the cab. A Chicago police officer smiled and waved me through one intersection. I supposed with my plain, old-fashioned clothes, I looked as though I were in costume.

"Hey, where you headed and how much?" one young, well-dressed couple shouted to me.

"Carriage is closed for maintenance," I gruffly replied.

Part of me thought maybe I'd be less conspicuous if I picked up passengers. But that might be risky. Perhaps one needed some sort of certificate or license to transport passengers, so I abandoned the idea. I might have found the whole episode amusing if I weren't so worried about Paige. I hoped I wasn't too late.

*   *

*

PAIGE

"I hear you've been mouthing off to the SEC and that you might have a file of interest to me," Amos said. "That's what I came for…although seeing how hot you are, maybe there are other reasons for this visit. Perhaps you can be my Rachel Miller. You realize he stole her from me? Now I can return the favor."

Confused by the comment and clad only in my sweaty sports bra and running shorts, I started to back away to turn toward the door and run. I'd sort this all out later. But as I turned, I heard a click as the door shut behind me, and a massive mountain of a man materialized seemingly out of nowhere.

"You were right, she IS smokin' hot. I'd like some of her, snarled the goon.

"You may get your wish, Jonas…but only after I'm done with her. Of course, if she cooperates, maybe we can just let her go."

Another man appeared from my kitchen and he was holding my iPad. I realized I had seen him before.

"Timothy?"

"I understand you two have met. Timothy here is my 'tech guy'…loves his gadgets…you've had an interesting life. I guess that's one thing my Amish brethren got right: it's not smart to keep your whole life cataloged on a computer--for many reasons," Amos sneered.

I was confused.

"Timothy, what are you doing here? Where's Loretta?" I asked with growing concern. I had once taken a self-defense class that my firm offered all of the female employees. I thought I might have been able to take on the Amos character myself, but three against one, no way. Timothy stared at me blankly as if we'd never met.

"Does she know?" I asked. But he didn't respond.

All of these men *looked* Amish, although on closer inspection maybe not 100 percent. This bizarre posse that had appeared out of nowhere in my living room were dressed like the Schwartzes and Neuenschwanders, yet there were differences. They wore black shirts, black suspenders, and dark denim, but their straw hats had a foreboding black band around them. In another time and place I might have even found them amusing, and my friends and I might have joked about they're being some sort of "Amish Gothic." But there appeared to be little to laugh about…they seemed tense. I thought I detected a whiff of alcohol on the breath of one.

"This is so cool," Timothy said menacingly about my iPad. "Wonder how much I could get for it?"

"I'll give it to you if you leave," I said, and then regretted it. That sounded weak. People like them prey on the weak.

"So, are you going to cooperate?" Amos asked.

"I don't know what you are talking about. I don't have anything of yours. I don't even know who you are. I think you've got the wrong person, the wrong place. Why don't you just leave, and I won't call the police?"

"I heard how you got that file. Pretty clever. Now give it to me," Amos ordered.

"I don't have it. And how did you get in here?"

"Doesn't much matter now, does it? I'm here. So, I'm just going to make myself at home until you cooperate. Okay?" Amos said, going to the refrigerator. "No wonder there's not much meat on your bones. There's not much in here. How about a beer? Ah, Halstead Ale, looks good. Care for some?"

"You release any claim you have on the Neuenschwanders' home, and I'll see to it that you get your file."

"Oooh, so, suddenly you know who I am and are able to get it to me. Interesting," Amos chuckled, taking a sip. "But it may be too late. See, you've turned the Feds on to me, in which case, I don't have very much to lose, do I? Someday you'll learn that you never pick a fight with a person who has nothing to lose. Right?" He placed his cold, clammy hand on my thigh.

"If you let me go and you let the Neuenschwanders keep their house, then I'll make sure you and your…" I glanced over at Timothy…"friends…are left alone. I have some very powerful connections that can stop any action against you," I continued.

"Funny thing is, when I first learned where you worked, I thought you were one of us. Your firm helps guys like me. People don't pay their mortgage, they deserve to lose their home, right? Sounds pretty clear cut to me."

He was trying to bait me and he succeeded.

"You know that's not what's happening! You tricked kind, vulnerable people who trusted you with their savings, leaving them unable to pay their mortgages and support their families," I said evenly.

Timothy and massive Jonas seemed oblivious to the verbal jousting.

They just continued to open files and explore my digital life.

"I'm keeping the MP3 player," Timothy said. "You've got some good music taste."

"Timothy, you should be ashamed of yourself. Loretta will be heartbroken when she finds out," I said.

"How do you know she doesn't know?" Timothy shot back.

I felt sick. She couldn't know. Could she? He was just playing mind games with me.

Amos turned to Timothy.

"We're not trying to make this look like a crime scene. Don't take everything," Amos said before turning his attention back to me. "Ha. You're doing what so many people do, you're falling for the Amish as some romantic throwback to a different time like it's some world of peace, prosperity, and simplicity."

"I never said that, but I think maybe YOU are the one who is..."

Amos slammed down his ale bottle so hard that some of the drink sloshed out onto the table and carpet. "Let me tell you something, something you don't see in the tourist books and on the postcards and calendars…the Amish….they're NOT who you think they are!"

"I think they're…human. They're imperfect…just like you're proving now. I'm not sure I ever heard Ab…" I started to say Abe's name but then stopped myself. I still wasn't sure how much Amos knew. "I have never heard an Amish person claim to be perfect. That sounds like something you are doing."

"You've got yourself an Amish lover. Well, you can civilize him, you can teach him the world's ways."

"I think you're the one that needs civilizing--cheating people out of their life savings all because they trusted you…they thought you were one of them. Well, you're the farthest thing from one of them," I said evenly, trying not to lose my temper, which is what he wanted.

Amos looked as though he were about to fly into an uncontrollable rage, but he seemed to steady himself, putting his ale down gently this time and hissing, "the file, please?"

"Bite me!"

"I'd love to," Amos said, running his hands gently on my neck, and I could feel his fingertips slowly moving across me. I felt revoltingly violated, and contemplated kicking him in a place where he'd really feel it, but I saw Jonas and Timothy behind me out of the corner of my eye.

Jonas looked at me with a maniacal, lusty look.

"How about we go someplace more private?" Amos cooed, tenderly brushing back a lock of my hair. "I always liked Abe's taste in women, and I bet you taste great."

"Yes, that's brilliant. Harm me, and when they find you, in addition to bank fraud you'll be up for assault. That's just genius," I said sarcastically.

"Oh, you must be thinking of a murder charge. I'm surprised you don't know the law better, being an attorney. But that won't happen because we're going to make it look like an accident. Timothy told us how much you love that boat of yours. You've got more pictures of that boat than your boyfriends. Sometimes accidents happen even to the most experienced sailors, right?" Amos said. "You see, maybe this will teach you to be more careful about who you choose as a lover, who you mess with, and who you pick to romanticize. I'm sorry it had to end this way."

I started to scream, scream for the heavens, but then I felt Jonas's heavy hand sealing my mouth. Jonas's other meaty palm shoved a sheet over my head and wrapped it around me as if I were a mummy. What happened after that was a blur.

ABRAHAM

My carriage was making slow but steady progress down Halstead. An average horse should be able to cover the distance in 20 minutes, Ruby could probably cover it in 10, but this horse acted like a mule on siesta. Used to just ambling tourists along, I supposed. I reached under the seat and found a name card and a whip. I used the whip, but it was like a bullet bouncing off the hull of a warship. Did nothing. His name was "Spooky," but nothing seemed to spook him. Commands, commands, a lot of horses respond to commands. "Go!" The horse just meandered forward without a care in the world. "Hurry!" Nothing. "Run!" That did the trick--the carriage horse began galloping along at a better speed. Spooky wouldn't be confused with Secretariat, but it was a better pace. I was also nervous on this ride, apprehensive at the thought of seeing Paige again and not knowing how I'd be received. But I really needed to warn her. I figured I'd warn her and then go home. I confess that part of me, somewhere, was kind of hoping she'd invite me to stay a day or two to see the city, but my motives were mainly noble.

I finally found the surprisingly quiet, tree-lined street that Paige lived on. Seemed odd to see such a placid place in the middle of the city. My heart raced at the thought of seeing her again. Would she even be home? I could at least leave her a note or something. I admit in my mind as I looked for a place to park that I was beginning to think this was a crazy stunt on my part.

Paige's street was jammed with parallel parked cars on either side. I was lucky to find a broad square around a planted tree on the edge of the street. I wished I had a little hay to put down on the ground. That's what I always did with my horses if I were going to leave them tied up for a spell. There was a large rain puddle and some brush and grass--an urban horse-feeding station crammed into a 5 X 5 patch. It would be enough to sustain Spooky.

"Taking your work home with you, bud?" one man said, obviously convinced I was one of the carriage drivers who take tourists around.

"Awwww, she's so cute, can I pet him?" asked a passing teenage girl.

"Not now, he's on duty," I said sternly.

I looked at the numbers on the brown-colored buildings, which were about five stories tall and stacked shoulder to shoulder on each side of the street. I couldn't imagine living like this, all on top of one another.

"No thanks," I muttered.

I rapped on Paige's door. Silence. The sound of constant cars on nearby Lake Shore Drive and Halstead churned the otherwise quiet of the street. No one answered. I wasn't sure which emotion was stronger, sadness at missing Paige or worry for her safety. I began to think more and more that I had created some implausible scenario out of my desire to see what I wanted to see. And in this case I wanted to see Paige. Grandma Ada could have been exaggerating Amos's urgency. Still, though, how and why would have he come to their house asking for Paige? I kept coming back to that question.

Anyway, I thought I could at least leave a note. I had brought a pen, and I found a flyer for a Thai restaurant posted to a bulletin board in the hallway. That'd have to do. I took down the flyer and started to write on the back.

"My Dear Paige,

I hope you are well and I'd be lying if I said I haven't missed you over the past months. But I'm not coming here to indulge in my own soul-soothing. I truly came because I'm concerned for your well-being.

I know that seeing a note from me is probably startling for you, but I felt that I needed to warn you about something. I tried to email you, but it bounced back. And since time was critical, I decided to come myself. I think

I was interrupted by a voice.

"You order?"

"Huh?"

"Sicilian Express...mushroom and onion, piping hot, that'll be $19.99," the voice said.

"Oh, no, that's not for me, I didn't order a pizza...and $19.99 for a pizza, are you kidding me?"

"Excuse me, then, I just need to knock on this door and I'll be out of your way," said a portly man with an untamed mop of brown hair, carrying a square red-and-white pizza box.

"Not home. I just tried."

The delivery man looked mildly annoyed. He checked his slip.

"Yeah, this is the address. Damn college kids," the pizza driver grumbled, his belly jiggling as he shook his head.

"Wait a second, when was this called in?"

"About 45 minutes ago…must have gotten the wrong address somehow. What idiot punk kids don't realize is that it comes out of my paycheck."

"Do you know WHO called it in?"

The driver shrugged.

"Look, dude, all I do is deliver…but the name on the order is Paige Roberts."

Why call in a pizza order and then not answer the door? I thought that was odd.

"Did you try the door?" the pizza deliveryman asked.

"No…guess I could…"

I turned the knob and, surprisingly, it opened.

"So, should I leave the pizza here?"

"Will you forget about the pizza for a second? I'm trying to figure something out."

At first glance, the apartment seemed undisturbed. There was the fresh scent of something in the air, but I couldn't place what it was. Tobacco?

I wanted to check the other rooms, but not by myself. I motioned to the pizza guy.

"Follow me."

"If you're here to rob me, you're making a big mis…"

"Shhhh, follow me!" I said, stuffing a $100 bill into his hand.

"Whoa…okay, where do you want me to go?"

I liked to think I was good at reading and interpreting landscape. I was just looking for something askew. "Just follow me!"

At first glance, Paige's small apartment appeared tidy. There was an alcove kitchen with turquoise tile floors, not that much different in color from the dresses Mom, Nancy, Loretta, and the twins wore. She had a microwave, coffeemaker, and toaster. A handwritten recipe for "Salome's Oatmeal Pie" was affixed to her refrigerator with a magnet. It gave me a homesick feeling, seeing that. Paige had a dining room table with a few files that were stacked neatly next to a sleek, silver-colored laptop computer that was still plugged in charging. Nothing looked out of place or indicated that I needed to be alarmed. There was a handwritten note on the table that said *"Ash, I'm on LSD."* Strange. I didn't know much about drugs, but I was vaguely aware that LSD was powerful.

I reflected on the uniformity and order of Paige's apartment and all seemed okay at first glance, although the note about LSD was alarming. But a pizza order had come from Paige and no one was here to receive it, and that alone was enough to strike me as odd. Still, perhaps she placed the order, ran out to get some Cokes, and got caught in a long line at the store. I didn't see anything else immediately amiss. I then noticed an open beer bottle. I felt it. It was still cool and only half-consumed. The scene in the living room did seem aberrant, as if someone had left in a hurry. Some of the beer was spilled onto the end table. Did Paige order a pizza, sit down for a cold beer, and was then startled by someone?

"Are you auditioning for 'CSI?'" the pizza guy asked with a chuckle.

I looked at him quizzically.

"CSI?"

"You know, popular crime show…who are you, anyway? What's with the weird duds? Is that your carriage out front? You drive tourists?"

"Not exactly…"

I couldn't decide whether I should try to explain to him what I was doing or not. He didn't exactly seem like the brightest cow in the herd, but harmless and possibly helpful.

"Let's go outside for a second,"

"Dude…"

I gave him another $100.

"Outside it is…"

Training a pizza man was easier than breaking a horse, I thought to myself, but definitely more expensive.

We surveyed the street scene. Spooky was contentedly munching grass in the gathering twilight. The street was otherwise remarkably quiet, a tidy urban oasis. But there was no sign of Paige. A white, windowless cargo van that was idling across the street and diagonal from Paige's apartment pulled out and started to slowly drive away. It was just a hunch, but…

"Can you please give me a ride?"

"Look, dude, I appreciate your generous tips, but I have a car full of pizzas here, so why don't you just call the police and…"

"I'm in a strange city, I know no one, and I need help. I'm sure if I call the police and say 'hey, my friend who just ordered a pizza may suddenly be missing,' yeah, I'm sure they'll come running right over to help," I said sarcastically. "Please, help me."

"Dude, pizzas! Ten of them, I have t…"

"Here's $1000."

"Get in, buckle up. Where do you want me to go?"

"Don't follow too closely. It's only a hunch."

I had picked up the crumpled note about the LSD. Was it a clue? "I just…it just seems…so…unlike her," I said, more to myself than to the pizza driver.

"'Ash, I'm on LSD,'" I said out loud, trying to figure out what it might mean.

"She usually stays away from there?" the pizza driver asked.

"Well, I thought…I guess you never know how well you know someone, but, yes, it's surprising…do you know much about LSD?"

"Uh…well, yeah, I deliver there all the time…I mean, it's gorgeous…and people living there usually give great tips."

"Huh?"

"Lake Shore Drive…myself I like it, but if you're…"

My face flushed. This didn't exactly inspire confidence in my hunches, LSD was just an abbreviation for Lake Shore Drive

I realized this whole thing could still be a foolish figment of my imagination, a manifestation of misplaced lust, or some misfired attempt at redemption. Not to mention that if this was a misadventure, it was turning into a very costly one. Maybe Amos meant no harm to Paige at all. Maybe she had simply ordered a pizza from somewhere and hadn't arrived home yet. But still, questions nagged. Why was her door unlocked? The universe didn't add up to order in this case and that troubled me. But in a weird way, I was happy it did trouble me. I thought back to that lost young man that swiped Mr. Doty's identity, a young man that thrived on chaos and disorder. I feel as though I *had* come a long way.

"By the way, name's Tony," he said, holding out his hand to shake mine as he drove.

"Abe…Abe Schwartz."

We drove silently, threading through Chicago traffic, the bright "Sicilian Express" sign on top of our car not exactly making us inconspicuous. On the other hand, in a city known for its pizza, it probably, in retrospect, was a great disguise.

"So, is your job fun? I've often seen those carriages around town and wondered what it would be like to dri…" Tony started to say.

"I'm not from around here," I interrupted him.

"Makes giving tours of the city all the more impressive," Tony said.

I needed to tell him who I was and why I was here. Maybe then he'd quit asking such stupid questions.

"I'm a woodworker, I'm Amish, and I'm from Indiana."

Tony paused and looked reflective.

"Never seen Amish buggies like that one before. Did you come a long way in it?"

I rolled my eyes. I couldn't believe this guy.

"I know a lot about the Amish. I've seen *Witness* before."

Witness was a blockbuster movie released in the mid-1980, and often the most exposure to the Amish that people got. One viewing of that movie, and suddenly anyone who watched was christening themselves an "Amish expert."

I didn't think the occupants of the van had any idea they were being followed. And for all of Tony's apparent intellectual shortcomings, I was pleased that out of all the people I could have had as my guide that night, it was a pizza delivery guy. This was only a hunch, but the longer we drove, the more suspicious I became. Occasionally the van's driving was erratic, lurching one direction and then quickly overcorrecting. But most of the time it was driving slowly, steadily. The glittering buildings of Chicago's skyline were visible in our rearview mirror. Darkness had now settled, which gave us better cover, except for the bright pizza sign on our roof.

"Is there any way you can turn that thing off?"

"Oh, sure thing."

The Sicilian Express light went dark. Our car now was totally shrouded in the city's ample night,

and I guessed that the van was still oblivious to us. It pulled up to a store-and-lock facility

in a seedy industrial area of Chicago.

"Park around the corner. I'll approach on foot." My thoughts were racing faster than my actions. On a whim, I opened the glove compartment but abruptly pulled back when I saw a shiny black revolver. I looked at Tony.

"I'm a pizza delivery driver. Being armed is practically a requirement of the job."

I stared at it for what seemed perpetuity.

"Hey, bud, I wouldn't…"

"Stay here!" I instructed Tony, and bounded out of the car. I tucked the gun into my waistband and slid stealthily along one of the store-and-lock walls, invisible in the shadows.

The door to the van slid open. It was a sound I was thoroughly familiar with since many of the "Amish taxis" back in Indiana were vans to accommodate large families. I came around the back to confront the captors. I was going to surprise them and hopefully never need the weapon.

"Where's Paige?" I asked quietly and crisply, feeling the gun's cold presence in my waistband.

"What the…Jesus, who are you??" asked a graying, balding man accompanied by a frumpy-looking lady wearing a blue velour track suit.

"Brenda, do you know this person?"

"Uh…mistaken identity, wrong person, wrong place. Didn't mean any disrespect, ma'am," I said sheepishly.

"Well, while you are here, can you help us move this dresser? We could use some young muscle," the man said.

"Um…sure," I said, quietly cursing the time-wasting disaster this was quickly becoming.

So I spent the next 10 minutes helping the Kropskys move their daughter's belongings into a store-and-lock. Seems their daughter was moving soon and the parents had agreed to stow some of her stuff.

'Dude, the pizzas…" Tony said to me as I got back into his car.

"Will you forget the pizzas!"

"No, I mean, I can't deliver them at this point, hate to see them go to waste," Tony said, wiping off a string of cheese from his chin. "Chicken Ranch Pizza, we're famous for it. You want a slice?"

I really wasn't in the mood to eat and I felt that we had just wasted an invaluable hour traipsing across Chicago, but I was getting hungry.

"Sure. Now, can you head back to where we started? Maybe she's home by now."

"Oh, I hope that wasn't her pizza we've been eating," Tony said, cramming another piece into his mouth as we drove.

Spooky was still lazily munching on grass in the courtyard. I was relieved at that. There was still no one inside her apartment.

"How do I find her cell phone number?" I asked Tony.

"Well, do you know either of her parent's numbers? Does she have any brothers? Sisters? Friends?" Tony suggested.

"Good idea…look for their phone numbers…where would they be?"

"Dude, how good of a friend is this if you don't even have her digits? And, really, most people keep their numbers in their phones. Their phone is their phone book."

I was dumbfounded how in a world so wired, so interconnected with high-speed everything, that there wouldn't be a trace of a phone number anywhere.

"Look for an address book, a scrap of paper, anything with a phone number."

So, Tony started rooting around the living room while I searched in the kitchen. While I was pulling open drawers and a few files, I heard Tony say from the other room, "Oh, man, she's a beauty…"

I was seething inside that we obviously had a very serious situation here and he was fawning, but then I thought that seeing Paige and knowing that he was rescuing a beautiful woman would motivate him all the more.

"Wow, what a stern,"

"Huh?" I asked, annoyed.

"Yeah, had to sell mine when the market tanked, but, oh, what I wouldn't give to have it back…maybe someday."

"Tony…can you stay on task here? What on earth are you talking about?"

"This…"

Tony pointed to a small framed photo on top of Paige's television. In fact, it was a gorgeous work of art: *"Bank on It."* Paige had called the sailboat her "home away from home" back on that beautiful Fourth of July night.

I paced and prayed, not knowing what to do next. I felt that the answer should be right here in her apartment. I've said that I may not be the most pious or theologically well-versed man, but I am guided by faith. I don't think you could be Amish and not be. So, yes, I did pray that evening.

"Dude, why don't you just call the police?"

"Okay, fine. Can I borrow your phone?"

"What? No way. I don't want to get involved in this!"

Tony was making me understand the limits of pacifism, but I restrained myself.

"One of us needs to look in her computer, one of us needs to search the apartment. Look for anything, anywhere. She's not here, she hasn't been here. Something is wrong, I'm convinced of it. Please…a phone number of someone we can call, somewhere we can go," I said.

"Okay, fine…you look in her computer, and I'll…"

I glared at him.

"Oh, yeah, right…I'll look at the computer."

I could find my way around a computer. I did at the library. But this had to be fast, and we had just wasted an hour honeycombing meaninglessly through the streets of Chicago's north side. I figured Tony-- anyone, really-- could find their way around a computer faster than I.

I went into her bedroom. Her bed was vast and smothered in lacy pillows and soft-looking comforters. I think I would prefer one of Grandma Ada's quilts any day. I considered going out to the street to find a pay phone, or throwing more cash at Tony to wrest his phone from him. But whom would I call? I was more convinced than ever that something was definitely wrong, but what would I tell the police? "Hello, I think my friend has been kidnapped because she wasn't here when her pizza was supposed to be delivered two hours ago?" Perhaps it was worth a try…but if I were totally 100-percent convinced that Paige was in danger, why did I feel a little guilty, embarrassed, and invasive by rooting through her bedroom? At the moment, I thought I could handle everything just as well as the police, so I continued the search. Wow…Paige wasn't kidding about racy underwear being her indulgence…I blushed. But I didn't find phone numbers, address books, anything helpful. Do people store everything on their phones, I wondered?

"Wow, she IS a smoking hot beauty!" I heard Tony gasp from the other room.

"Okay, you've told me and I agreed…great stern. Can we please stick to finding something meaningful?"

"No, this time I meant the girl. Is this your girlfriend?"

I paced to the dining room table where Tony was munching on some chips and looking through Paige's computer.

"Found this photo-sharing file of hers."

"The dude's no prize, not that I can judge guys very well, but this woman is a cat on a hot tin roof."

I'm not sure I understood what he meant by that. I'm not sure he knew what he meant by that. But I looked at the screen. It was Paige, standing on her sailboat wearing a skimpy hunter-green bikini, standing next to a shirtless Scott. Tony was right; he definitely wasn't a great catch physically, but Paige was mesmerizing. I didn't even know they made clothing that sparse. I tore my aroused eyes away and looked at the caption.

"Is this really helpful?" I said, exasperated. It felt as if we were just on a fruitless fishing expedition, and if it turned out I was wrong, then Paige would be rightfully furious at me and some pizza guy rummaging through her most personal space.

"Just looking through recently-opened files, hoping to find something, maybe a phone number…it's a bit of a stretch, but maybe?"

"That file was opened recently? How recently?" I asked, a little surprised, maybe a twinge jealous, that Paige would be looking at photos of herself and Scott.

"File was actually accessed not that long ago, not long before we both arrived…6:23 p.m. was the log-out," Tony said, pointing to some electronic signature that I didn't really understand.

"I always wanted to go into I.T., but never did," Tony explained.

"I'd imagine there'd be more money in that than pizza delivery," I mused.

"Dude, maybe she has the hots for that guy in the picture," Tony pondered.

"No, no...I doubt it....but why access that file at 6:23, order a pizza, disappear??...nothing makes sense here. Click through the rest of that file."

"Lots of photos of her boat," Tony observed.

"How do I find it?" I asked, suddenly gravitating towards another hunch.

"Oh, well, you just go to the lakefront and there she be. Look, dude, there are a million boats in this city on 40 miles of lakefront. How the heck would I know that?" Tony said, shoveling more chips into his mouth.

His sarcasm was getting to me, but he was my only hope.

"Are there more photos in the file?" I asked, pointing towards an icon of a folder.

"This one?" Tony said.

"Yes, titled 'Fun Times at Slippy's,'" I said.

Tony and I both looked at one another.

"Where is it? Where's Slippy's?" I suddenly shouted.

"What do I look like, 411? All I know is it's a marina."

"Her boat!" I shouted. "Type in 'Slippy's!'"

Tony quickly typed in the name.

"South Forest."

"Let's go."

*   *

*

"What's going on?" I asked Tony as we sat parked in traffic.

"President's in town. This always happens when he comes back home. Not much you can do other than roll with it."

"How long do they usually shut down the streets, and is there an alternate route?"

"It shouldn't be much longer…don't really want the Secret Service stopping me…"

"Maybe it's me that ought to be worried. Is there something that makes you not want to be found? You won't let me use your phone, you don't want the Secret Service seeing you?"

"Long story. Just sometimes it's best to not make waves. Do your job, pay your bills, follow the rules, and you won't get hurt."

"You sound like Rachel and Loretta," I muttered.

"What's that?"

"Nothing. Anyway, is there a quicker way?"

"Just might be. Seem to remember an alternate alley that might take us around some of this." Tony flipped on his Sicily Express light and banked a sharp left into an alley, a dark, bumpy underbelly of

Chicago.

"Why did you do that?"

"Oh, the light? Feds love pizza. They'll leave me alone with that on," Tony said.

Great, I thought to myself. If the terrorists found out that the Secret Service would ignore them if they worked for Pizza Hut, we'd all be in a world of trouble.

"Ah, okay," I said.

"Must be nice being you," Tony said.

"Huh?"

"Must be nice not paying taxes," Tony said.

Geez, I couldn't believe this. Paige's life might be in the balance, and I'm having to bat down typical tourist trash talk.

"Oh, come on, where did you get that garbage?"

"I told you, I know a bit about the Amish."

"Was there something in *Witness* about the Amish not paying taxes?"

"Well, maybe I read it on the internet or something."

"Well, for your information, I do pay my taxes. We all do. We go to H&R Block like anyone else."

"Yeah, I guess you couldn't e-file," Tony said, and then burst out guffawing. "Uh…okay, drive, Tony, drive."

I rolled my eyes.

We were heading to Slippy's on a hunch. I realized my hunches hadn't served me well so far, and if this didn't work I wasn't sure what I'd do.

"Well, if that babe is really yours, then I'll look at you in a whole new light," Tony said. "How long have you two known one another?"

"She's a relatively recent friend."

"I can tell you really like her…I was in love once."

"Really? What happened?"

"She moved away and quit ordering pizzas."

"That is your love story?" I asked incredulously.

"Well, I used to know what she wanted when she called in her order. And I could tell her mood by what she ordered…mushroom and onion meant mellow, pepperoni meant she had had a bad day at work, thick crust mea…well, you don't want to know what that meant. But she was a sparkling beauty."

"Did you ever tell her how you felt?" I asked.

"Nope, she just one day quit ordering pizzas, and…"

"Wait! There it is: Slippy's."

There was an electronic gate that opened and closed to let people into the marina. It must have required a special card or combination, of which we had neither.

"Just park here," I said, pointing to a spot on the street. "I'll walk in." It was just as well because it would preserve the all-important element of surprise. I opened the glove compartment.

"Hey, dude, I wouldn't do that."

"I'll return it," I promised. "Just stay put." For all his flaws, Tony had been very helpful.

There was a marina office, and dozens and dozens, probably hundreds, of boats, their sails silhouetted and bobbing against the inky blackness of the lake. It was disorienting. I slipped into the shadows, and almost into the water a time or two. I learned back at the farmstead when hiking in our woods that sometimes if you lose your way, the best thing to do is to close your eyes and listen. We've become such a sensory society geared towards the eyes that it's easy to forget the ears. There would be occasions when I was younger and the woods were smothered in snow when I would become disoriented in direction, so I learned to close my eyes and let my ears lead the way. If I kept my eyes shut long enough I might pick up the distant rumble of a truck on Route 27, or maybe the sound of the Miller's sawmill, and I would be able to orient myself. The masts of sailboats were like trees in the forest. All I had to do was close my eyes and orient myself with sounds. So I closed them, and there it was. An idling sound, some shuffles, footsteps. Slinking in the shadows, I followed the sound, and when I finally opened my eyes, I saw what I had come for. There was a small van parked near one of the boat launches. A couple of dark figures milled around the pier. I clasped the revolver. The gun felt cold, powerful.

"It's been a while," I said, aiming the revolver directly at Amos.

Amos was momentarily startled, and Jonas, whose massive arms clasped Paige around the waist, seemed terrified. I was incensed to see his huge paws all over her.

"Oh, don't get mad at him, he's just holding her for me," Amos said.

Jonas started to loosen his grip when he saw the gun. But I was even more stunned and confused by who else I saw. "Timothy!?" I said.

He stared blankly and then went back to preparing the boat.

"Aren't you going to help me?" I asked, at first relieved to see a familiar face but quickly realizing that maybe he wasn't there to help.

"I never liked you," Timothy sneered.

"Well, it's mutual," I simmered. And I realized how little we really know about people.

"Does Loretta know?" I asked.

Timothy didn't answer.

"Don't worry, boys. He won't shoot. He's one of *those* Amish, he won't fight. Put her on the boat. She's all mine now," Amos said.

And perhaps he was right.

 I felt sickened at the thought of firing a weapon in anger, of even holding something that was designed specifically to kill. It ran against all the teachings and lessons I had learned growing up.

Paige's eyes were pleading with me. *Shoot him!*

My fingers trembled on the trigger.

But as much as I question and struggle with my religion's rules, its values, morals, and culture make up who I am. I'm not sure a true pacifist can flip to being a killer any more than a camel can become a giraffe. But isn't it human nature also to protect a loved one?

Shoot him! her eyes pled.

Everything seemed in super slow-motion, like Amos's pitch that one summer evening that just sort of seemed to hang over the plate.

 I knew if Jonas successfully loaded Paige onto the boat, I might not ever see her again. Still, if I fired the gun, I would lose myself forever. A part of me had already disappeared when I had stolen Mr.

Doty's identity. The rest of what I knew about myself would vanish in a bullet blast. By pulling the trigger, I would join the ranks of killers. I had already been a thief; did I also want to be a killer? But if I didn't pull the trigger, I would be joining the ranks of those who could've done something, but didn't. I had come all this way to avoid this outcome, and here I was about to let it happen. I thought just pointing the gun at them might be enough, but in the end I think Amos *wanted* me to have to fire it.

"Go, ahead, Jonas, put her on the boat. Get the engine started. He won't hurt us," Amos said. "He can't hurt us."

Amos looked at Paige and licked his lips.

"You know I always wanted Rachel but I never had the chance. But you picked an even better one. Paige is hot. You have good taste, Abe. She has lousy taste, but you have good taste."

"You turned away," I shouted to Amos.

"So did you!" Amos said, motioning to Paige. "And I don't think Ralph Doty would think you're some holier-than-thou good person."

I felt myself exploding inside.

"Feelings of the heart are not a violation of the *ordnung*," I said sternly.

"But swiping someone's identity is. And leaving is!" Amos shouted back.

"I haven't left and I don't plan to, and I'm redeeming myself now," I said.

Amos sneered.

So it came down to this: preserving Paige's life or preserving my values. My fingers started to squeeze the trigger. I aimed directly at Jonas, who, momentarily frozen, had now begun to load Paige onto the boat.

"You won't do it," Amos said. "You can't. You're too wedded to your ways. You could never shoot. You're a weak, spineless, pacifist."

"But *I'm* not," Tony said, training a gun directly at Amos.

I looked at Tony in stunned awe.

"But I thought…" I said.

"I kept trying to tell you not to grab that gun. It's not real. It's a toy.

I keep the real one under the seat."

Amos, Timothy, and Jonas were frozen, cornered.

"Now let the girl go," Tony said. He turned to me and whispered, "I've always wanted to say that."

CHAPTER 25
ABRAHAM

The sickening sound of shots rang out, and Jonas and Timothy both crumpled to the ground. Amos Raber stood frozen like an ice sculpture. Once Tony trained the gun on him, he put his hands up.

Tony was far nicer than Amos and his boys would have been. They intended to kill Paige, but Tony just shot them in the legs.

Once freed, Paige ran to me and practically leapt into my arms. Of course, we didn't get to embrace long. The shots had summoned the police, who then had to debrief her--and me--and it was a while before we were on our way back to Paige's brownstone. Paige had called her father, and soon there were representatives from the SEC on the scene interviewing Amos Raber. Timothy and Jonas were taken away in an ambulance. SEC investigators were also descending on Berne at that very moment.

It was a long night, that's for sure.

"I had wanted to show you 'Bank on It' and Lake Michigan, but this wasn't exactly the way I envisioned," Paige said on the way back to her apartment. Oh, and when we arrived back at her place, I had to explain Spooky. She was able to drive me back to the hitching post where I borrowed him. The driver was still on his shift and said it was the easiest money he ever made, so we drove him back to Wrigleyville to retrieve Spooky and his carriage.

*   *

*

I lingered in Chicago for a couple of days after Amos's capture. One reason was so the police could further interrogate me and clear me of any charges. Often in the fog of battle, it's difficult for authorities to sort out who was responsible for what. But I also wanted to be there for Paige. We were thrown together by fate, and now needed one another to untangle everything.

"I'd like to have better memories of *Bank on It* than what happened the other day, so how about that sailboat ride?" Paige had suggested to me, and I'd eagerly agreed. The city was becoming stifling, so being out on the open lake was appealing and refreshing.

"But let me pack the picnic lunch this time," Paige offered.

Paige packed a delicious lunch of homemade coleslaw, sandwiches, and honey bars.

"Did you make all of this yourself?" I asked.

"I learned from the best."

We spent the afternoon exploring, watching the shimmering Chicago skyline from afar. We talked a lot and I was able to observe species of seabirds that I had never seen before. Paige wore the same diminutive bikini that was in the photo on her computer.

"If only Tony could see me now, I don't think he'd get over it," I commented.

"Huh?"

"Oh, just making a comment about a friend of mine," I said.

"Well, I think Ashleigh would want to trade places with me," Paige said staring at me as I sunned myself on the boat.

"We need to make sure you don't get burned," Paige said. Her soft hands kneaded cool lotion into my shoulders, chest, and back, and I returned the favor for her. Alone on the open lake, we were soon a sensual tangle as the cooling breezes of Lake Michigan blew over us. We held one another as the lake held *Bank on It*. For the magic of those moments, under the non-judgmental eyes of the lake, we were one. We were not an Amish and a non-Amish, we were just two passionate people who felt a connection.

But I also knew I needed to get back. Dad needed me at the shop, and this was turning into a far longer, more expensive journey than I had ever imagined. There was also the Neuenschwanders' final day in their home, which was coming up. And there was some unfinished business.

*   *   *

"I'm going to go stay at a friend's house in Indiana for a while," Paige told her parents a couple of days after her traumatic kidnapping.

"It's okay. You've been through quite an ordeal. I don't blame you if you need to clear your head a bit," Richard Roberts said, sipping a glass of white wine.

"Who are you staying with?" Rita asked.

"Oh…my Amish friends…would love for you to meet them sometime," Paige said.

"You've been talking a lot about this Abe lately…he's how you got tangled up in this whole mess in the first place, right? I thought you had learned your lesson about the kind of men you are attracted to," Rita said, a veiled reference to her daughter's troubled past.

"Oh, Mom, you have got to be kidding. Abe is hardly going around setting buildings on fire. Truly, he's one of the most intelligent, well-rounded men I have ever met," Paige gushed.

"Well, I didn't spend $250,000 to send you to the best law school so you could end up shacking up with some eighth-grade-educated buggy maker," Paige's mom said tartly.

"That's it. Bye," Paige huffed, leaving her parent's suburban house.

ABRAHAM

Her Dad stood silently, a stern look on his face, but I knew he was my best hope. So, while Paige was at her office the next day tying up some loose ends, I had a meeting with Richard Roberts. He was my best chance at redemption.

*   *

*

PAIGE

"So you're the amazing Abe?" Ashleigh asked.

I blushed. I still wasn't used to, nor did I crave, the attention. The Chicago newspapers did cover this event. There was no way not to, but I managed to keep the focus on Amos, not me. The few times I saw newspaper photographers around, I slinked into the shadows. I remembered Loretta's earlier admonitions. I got lucky because on the same day this happened to us, a Chicago alderman was ensnared in a sex scandal that ended up diverting what probably would have been a far more intense media spotlight.

"I'll be back," Paige said to Ashleigh. "I'm taking some time to think, spend some time with Abe, but I'll be back."

"Okay, so you want me to water the plants, feed the fish, get your mail. I'll take care of it all, and..." Ashleigh said, her voice lowering to a whisper. "You are right, he is a cutie. If he has any brothers out there or hot-looking friends, let me know...I just might join you."

Paige put in a request for a leave of absence from the firm, ostensibly to return in three weeks, although she doubted she'd work there again. She wasn't sure what she wanted to do. There was an attraction to me and a definite appreciation for the Amish way. I don't think she ever was contemplating "becoming Amish." It's tempting for me to say that it's impossible for someone to truly "become Amish", but I've actually met people who have made the journey.

*   *

*

In a gray cinderblock courtroom in Indiana, the Neuenschwanders' home was up for auction. The weekly auctions were part of a streamlined "fast foreclosure" process adopted by the state to try to clear the dockets of a massive glut of foreclosures gumming up the system. But nothing happening with Plain Investments' imminent implosion would be enough to stop the Neuenschwanders' foreclosure. It was too late for any appeals or last-minute legal maneuvers. The machinery of the judicial system ground decrepitly and sluggishly, as if it had a life of its own. Once started, there really was no way to quickly apply the brakes. A judge would call out the names of the parcels, packets would be passed around with photos and attorneys, speculators or buyers would ask other questions, bids would be made, and the properties unloaded or deeded back to the bank. It was all a rather dull, dry procedure.

Parcel #101: Lovely lakefront home in northern Indiana, 4 bedrooms, 3 1/2 baths.

A few ooohs, and ahhhs rippled through the chambers as packets were passed around. Ultimately, though, there were no buyers, and the bank was left holding someone's vacation cottage.

While the SEC and FBI were taking care of business elsewhere, a dapper Richard Roberts strode into the county courthouse in Decatur, Indiana.

"Property at 23879 South County Road 1500 -- how do you pronounce this name? NEW-IN-SCHWANDER -- will start at $85,000."

"I'll take it," Richard said.

The judge raised his eyebrows.

"Sight unseen?"

"Yes."

*   *

*

Forty buggies were parked outside of the Neuenschwanders' as people packed plastic totes full of belongings. Boxes were taped shut and rooms emptied. Women made sandwiches on a picnic table outside and handed them to the young men who were doing the heavy lifting.

"They got Amos, but Melvin Beachy slipped away. Dorcas was our hero here. She kept him cornered in the hay mow most of the night, wanted to make out with him...." Roman said.

"Whoa..." I said at the next sight.

It was my kid brother Daniel walking hand in hand with...Katie Burkholder.

"Well, you weren't exactly available for her," Daniel said with a blush.

Katie giggled.

The young couple joined other teenagers who were helping the Neuenschwanders move. Paige and I had come back to Indiana the previous day. One of my friends owned a guest cottage nearby and was eager to find a renter. Paige decided to move in there for a while so she and I could spend some time together and she could think. While we felt connected, Paige and I still kept our blossoming romance low key. This was a somber occasion for everyone here as we packed up the Neuenschwander's belongings.

I was nervous when I first arrived at the Neuenschwanders because Monroe Hochstetler was also there.

"I need to speak with you," he said to me sternly, patting his pocket. I heard the crumple of an envelope. He didn't look amused. I figured this was probably the end of my time in the church. Sometimes a church member gets a letter of dismissal from the bishop as a formality, spelling out the offense and the consequence. In my case, it would be shunning. I knew it, he knew it.

But we were all interrupted by a navy blue Mercedes that thumped down the rutted driveway of the Neuenschwanders, a cloud of dust coating the car.

"Are you from the bank?" a young man asked the driver.

"As a matter of fact, I am. And I'm looking for Mr. Mose Neuenschwander," Richard said.

"Over there," the boy pointed.

"Thank you," Richard said, tipping his hat politely. Paige's dad could cut a dashing figure with his retro bow-tie, jacket, and bowler hat.

Mose and Lizzie were packing the last of the kerosene lamps from their house, which was now completely empty.

"Richard Roberts, Sterling Bank," Richard said, flicking a business card at Mose.

"No, sir, a bank is what got us in trouble in the first place. No sir, no way. No disrespect meant, but we don't have time."

"Ma'am?" Richard said, turning to Lizzie, whose face looked ashen.

She shook her head. "We've been down that road before. Why don't you peddle your product elsewhere?"

"I have some papers for you to sign and I'll be on my way," Richard said.

"What? No, not signing anything…" a weary Mose said.

"*Daddy?*"

"You know one another?" Lizzie asked.

"He's my father," Paige said, giving him a hug.

"My daughter told me you wouldn't fight the foreclosure, which, frankly, I found a little puzzling, but fine. No disrespect meant. You lost your money illegally, so your lack of fight was without merit…silly, frankly, no disrespect meant. Here's your house. Bought it for you this morning, and I am deeding it back to you."

Mose's eyes widened.

"But I didn't want to fight…"

"Sure, fine. Here's your home back. Sign here."

Mose signed on the dotted line.

"Good day, Mr. and Mrs. Neuenschwander," Richard said with a smile and tip of his hat, heading out the door onto the Neuenschwander's spacious lawn.

Paige hugged her father long and hard.

"Daddy, I can't believe this. You're amazing."

"May I?" I said, motioning to Paige that I wanted to speak to Richard. I drew him aside and whispered the additional information he needed. We compared notes. He nodded.

"I'd also like to speak to Milo Keim, Pete Stutzman, and Joseph Coblentz," Richard announced to the growing crowd.

A murmur rippled through the assemblage and one by one the people called walked forward. They huddled around Richard Roberts. "My bank has purchased your homes from your bank. Here are your new payment books. The payments will be lower and you should own your homes free and clear within five years," he said, handing out payment books. "If you ever run into problems, all you have to do is call."

"Sir?" Milo Keim made a phone-type motion with his hand, shaking his head.

"Right…you don't have phones…okay, all you have to do is write," Richard said.

Everyone laughed.

"Mr. Roberts...I don't know what to say," a stunned Mr. Keim finally said.

"Don't thank me, thank Abraham. He made this all happen," Richard said. "Now, I have one more person I need to see. Good day, everyone."

Monroe Hochstetler watched it all unfold. His jaw could be seen dropping slightly underneath his white beard. Jacob Eicher and LeRoy Miller, who were standing nearby, glanced at one another. There were whispers.

Word began to spread through the crowd about what had just happened. Suddenly more people began arriving at the Neuenschwanders' on foot and by buggy. Cookies and casseroles appeared from all directions.

A sawdust-covered Amish man came up and gave Richard a hug.

"Uh, thanks…" Richard said, quickly brushing off his finely-tailored suit.

Rita, who had remained morosely in the car, dressed impeccably in a black pants suit and pearls, got out and tentatively tiptoed down the driveway, past some horse gifts and over to the table where refreshments were being served. She winced at the sandwiches, thick casseroles, Oreo pudding desserts, and peanut butter cookies. It definitely wasn't the elegant spread she was accustomed to. She glared across the table at her daughter and didn't say a word. A carnival-like sense of elation had rippled across the crowd of people. Rita Roberts was the only one unhappy.

"Well, you must be…very…proud…of your daughter," Monroe Hochstetler said haltingly.

"I'm no longer speaking to my daughter. I want nothing to do with her," Rita said icily.

"Wait a minute, you are shunning? You can't do that, that's what WE do!" Monroe Hochstetler said in disbelief.

"I beg your pardon?" Rita asked-.

"The *bann*….shunning, it's what we practice on a church member who has gone wayward, but I've never run into it reverse before…never heard of an English shunning," Bishop Hochstetler said.

"Oh, for Heaven's sake…" Rita said dismissively, heading back for her car.

The action may not be pretty, but the reason behind it is pure love. We truly believe in our church and way of life, and sometimes a good shunning makes the offender take a step back and examine his or her actions.

And speaking of shunning, if Bishop Hochstetler had a punishment to mete out, I wanted to take my medicine and get it over with. I'd figure out what to do later. Monroe Hochstetler was standing by an open fire. Someone had anchored a massive black kettle ~~anchored~~ over the fire where a meaty venison stew was simmering.

I snatched a snickerdoodle off a plate and took a bite. Even when I was about to be shunned, I couldn't resist a good cookie.

"What do you think of my snickerdoodles?" Sarah Yoder asked me.

"They're a bit dry," I replied.

Sarah seemed taken aback by the candor. Then Elmo Gingerich stopped me. "I'd like to talk to you about maybe teaming up with your shop. There might be areas where we can cooperate in and make some more money."

"I don't think so, really. I've never completely trusted you. Talk to you later," I said. Candor can be cruel. But I was tired of lies and deception. I just wanted to say what was on my mind.

"Whoa...is this a new Mr. Lincoln we're seeing?" Loretta asked after hearing the exchanges.

"Yes, call me Honest Abe...." I said.

And everyone laughed. But I wasn't joking. The truth was liberating.

"Bishop Hochstetler, you wished to speak with me?"

"Oh, yes...yes," he said, the breeze blowing his cotton-colored beard.

"I just...just...wanted to tell you that we're all very pleased you're home safe and sound." Monroe had a broad smile on his face as he took an envelope out of his pocket and tossed it into the fire where someone had put a big iron kettle full of homemade soup.

Rita turned away.

"Let's go, Richard." She headed to the car, narrowly missing some horse gifts along the way.

Loretta was standing under the shade of an apple tree in the Neuenschwanders' yard. At first, I think, she was hesitant to approach me. But she did.

"Abe, I'm so happy you're back and okay," Loretta said, giving me a big embrace.

Loretta gave Paige a big hug.

"I'm sorry for all of the things I said about you, Abe. You're a good, good man. Mom always told me not to be fooled by the shiniest, reddest apples in the store, that sometimes the best-tasting peaches and apples have a few bruises on them," Loretta said.

"Well, I must taste amazing," I said.

We all laughed.

"And, Paige...I'm happy to see you also. I'm sorry about what I said last time you were here. You're always welcome here."

Paige hugged her back. "And I'm sorry about Timothy. This must have been very difficult for you," she said.

"I had no idea...I just thought he was great at saving money. I guess

I should have questioned more," Loretta sighed meekly.

"Thank you, that means a lot. You've got an amazing brother. He saved me. I'm here because of him," Paige said, interlocking her fingers with mine as we stood under the tree away from the crowd. Loretta noticed our affection, and so did Paige's mother. She glared out the window as their car disappeared in the dust.

*   *   *

Richard Roberts had one more envelope in his possession, and despite his wife's objections he pressed ahead. He could deal with Rita later. His Mercedes bumped down the long driveway and pulled to a stop in front of Mr. Doty's two-story white clapboard house. "Ralph, it's been a long time," Richard Roberts would say. Richard had arranged for the refinancing of Mr. Doty's house.

All had come full circle.

EPILOGUE

ABRAHAM & PAIGE

The embers of true romance are rare and when experienced they should be nurtured, not extinguished. Paige and I realize our romance is unconventional, but it's not unprecedented. History is full of stories of cultural collisions that resulted in hijackings of the heart. Even among the Amish it's not unheard of. A minister in our church, when deciding what to do, cited the case of a couple in Ohio in which the husband was not Amish and the wife was. The local bishop saw the devotion and the noble, moral principles their lives were dedicated to, and decided to permit this "mixed marriage." Opposites make for obstacles, but they can be overcome in the end, whether one-half of a couple is Amish and the other English, whether one-half is wedded to rules and the other to spontaneity. We decided not to let something slip away because of religion and rules. We were determined to make it work.

Paige and I were going to go for a long walk in the back prairie after lunch to talk about our futures. I wasn't going to leave the Amish. But maybe she was a Seeker?
But as we approached the pond I saw someone. At first I didn't recognize her, but then I saw familiar locks of red hair visible beneath a black kapp. She was sitting on a rock by the pond. Paige seemed startled.

"Abe?" the red-head said.

It was Rachel Miller.

RECIPE APPENDIX

AMISH PAT-A-PAN PIE CRUST

1 1 /2 teaspoons sugar
1 /2 teaspoon salt
1 /2 cup vegetable oil
3 tablespoons cold milk

Place the flour, sugar, and salt in the pie pan and mix with fingertips until evenly blended. In a measuring cup, combine the oil and milk, and beat until creamy. Pour all at once over the flour mixture. Mix with a fork until the flour mixture is completely moistened. Pat the dough with your fingers, first at the sides of the plate and then across the bottom. Flute the edges. Shell is now ready to be filled. If you are preparing a shell to fill later or your recipe requires a pre-baked crust, preheat oven to 425. Prick the surface of the pastry with a fork and bake 15 minutes. Check often and prick more if needed.

SALOME'S RASPBERRY PUDDING PIE

1 cup water

1 tablespoon cornstarch

1 /4 cup water

1 3.5 ounce box of raspberry Jello

3 cups fresh raspberries

1 /2 cup granulated sugar

1 /8 teaspoon salt

Vanilla filling

1 /2 cup cornstarch

1 /8 teaspoon salt

3 egg yolks

3 cups milk, scalded

1 1/3 cups granulated sugar

1 teaspoon vanilla extract

1 cup milk

For the raspberry pudding: heat the water and sugar. Mix the cornstarch, salt, water and lemon. Add to water, sugar, mixture.Boil until mixture is clear.Add gelatin and stir to dissolve.Add raspberries and cool.for the VANILLA FILLING. place 3 cups of milk in pan. Heat to scalding.Mix cornstarch, sugar, salt, vanilla extract, egg yolks, and 1 cup of milk.Slowly blend into hot milk, stirring constantly until thick.Cool. Pour 2 cups of vanilla filling into each pie shell. Place 2 cups of Raspberry Pudding on top of Vanilla filling. Top with whipped cream.

SALOME'S OATMEAL PIE

1 pat-a-pan pie crust (see above)
2 large eggs
3 /4 cup dark brown sugar
1 /2 cup (1 stick) butter, softened
1 /4 cup dark corn syrup
1 cup quick-cooking rolled oats

Preheat oven to 325. In a large bowl, cream together the eggs, sugar, and butter. Add the corn syrup and oats, and mix well until the mixture is well-blended and brown in color. Pour into the unbaked pie shell. Bake until a toothpick inserted in the center comes out clean, about 1 hour.

MOSE'S BARBECUED HAMBURGERS

2 pounds ground beef

1/2 cup ketchup

6 tablespoons brown sugar

6 teaspoons Worcestershire sauce

Onion powder

1 cup tomato juice

6 tablespoons apple cider vinegar

6 teaspoons prepared mustard

Brown the ground beef sprinkled with onion powder. Add the remaining ingredients and simmer slowly for 45 minutes. Pile into hamburger buns/rolls to serve.

VELMA'S DOUBLE TREAT COOKIES

3 cups all-purpose flour

2 teaspoons baking soda

1/2 teaspoon salt

1 cup melted butter

1 cup peanut butter

1 cup M&M'S®

1 cup sugar

1 cup brown sugar, firmly packed

2 eggs

1 teaspoon vanilla extract

Mix the ingredients and drop by spoonfuls onto an ungreased cookie sheet. Bake at 350 degrees for 10 minutes.

EGG DUTCH

5 eggs

1 teaspoon salt

Pepper to taste

1 heaping tablespoon flour

1 cup milk

Put eggs, salt, pepper, flour, and milk into a medium bowl. Beat. Pour into a greased skillet and cover with a tight lid. Place over medium heat. Cut and turn when half done and finish baking. Serves 6

AMISH MACARONI SALAD

3 cups cooked macaroni

3 eggs, boiled and chopped

1 /2 cup carrots

3 /4 cup celery

1 cup salad dressing

1 /4 cup sugar

2 teaspoons mustard

Salt and pepper to taste

In a large bowl, mix all of the above. Stir and toss. Delicious

HOMEMADE HAYSTACK SUPPER

1 3/ 4 cups soda crackers, crushed

3 pounds hamburger, browned and 3 tablespoons taco seasoning added

4 cups lettuce, shredded

3 medium tomatoes, chopped

2 cups green peppers, chopped

1 large onion, chopped

Other vegetables as desired

Spaghetti, rice or both (cooked until soft), amount enough to suit

Put some of each on plate, one layer at a time. Top with shredded cheese or a homemade cheese sauce. Also good to add is salsa or ranch dressing if you want. This will serve a family of six, but amounts can be adjusted to suit your taste.

WASHDAY CASSEROLE

3 pounds hamburger

3 onions, chopped

3 cups potatoes, peeled and diced

3 cups celery, diced

3 cups cooked spaghetti

2 cans (10 3/4 ounces) cream of mushroom soup

9 slices bacon

32 ounces tomato juice

1 pound cheddar cheese, grated

Brown hamburger and onions in a pan. Drain and pour hamburger mix into a large casserole or deep 9 x 13-inch baking pan. Add potatoes, celery, and spaghetti to casserole and mix lightly with hamburger. Pour mushroom soup on top and spread evenly. Fry bacon and lay on top. Pour tomato juice over this. Add cheese over that. Bake 1 1 /2 hours at 350 degrees.

Serves 10 to 12

HOMEMADE ICE CREAM

10 cups milk

7 eggs

3 1/2 cups sugar

4 teaspoons vanilla

1 teaspoon salt

Beat eggs, then add remaining ingredients and mix. Pour into freezer bowl and freeze. Enjoy.

AMISH BREAKFAST CASSEROLE

6 slices white or wheat bread, crumbled

6 eggs

2 cups milk

1 onion, diced (optional)

1/2 teaspoon salt

1 pound crumbled bacon, fried and drained

1 pound grated Colby cheese

Preheat the oven to 325. Put the bread in the bottom of a greased 9 x 13-inch baking dish. In a separate bowl, beat the eggs, then add the milk, onion, salt, and bacon. Pour everything over the bread. Bake for 45 minutes, then top with cheese and bake an additional 10 to 15 minutes or until golden brown.

Serves 6 to 8

AMISH EGG-IN-NEST

1 egg

1 piece of bread

2 tablespoons of butter

Salt and pepper to taste

Cut or tear a 2-inch hole out of the center of a slice of bread. Melt butter in a frying pan over medium heat. Add the bread and crack an egg into the hole in the bread. Season with salt and pepper and cook until the bottom of the bread is golden brown.

Made in the USA
Charleston, SC
15 January 2017